Nicole Helm grew up with her nose in a book and the dream of one day becoming a writer. Luckily, after a few failed career choices, she gets to follow that dream—writing down-to-earth contemporary romance and romantic suspense. From farmers to cowboys, Midwest to *the* West, Nicole writes stories about people finding themselves and finding love in the process. She lives in Missouri with her husband and two sons, and dreams of someday owning a barn.

Cindi Myers is the author of more than seventy-five novels. When she's not plotting new romance storylines, she enjoys skiing, gardening, cooking, crafting and daydreaming. A lover of small-town life, she lives with her husband and two spoiled dogs in the Colorado mountains.

Discover more at millsandboon.co.uk

COLD CASE PROTECTION

NICOLE HELM

TWIN JEOPARDY

CINDI MYERS

MILLS & BOON

First Published in Great Britain 2024
by Mills & Boon, an imprint of HarperCollins*Publishers* Ltd
1 London Bridge Street, London, SE1 9GF

www.harpercollins.co.uk

HarperCollins*Publishers*
Macken House, 39/40 Mayor Street Upper,
Dublin 1, D01 C9W8, Ireland

Cold Case Protection © 2024 Nicole Helm
Twin Jeopardy © 2024 Cynthia Myers

ISBN: 978-0-263-32257-6

1224

MIX
Paper | Supporting
responsible forestry
FSC™ C007454

This book contains FSC™ certified paper and other controlled sources to ensure responsible forest management.

For more information visit: www.harpercollins.co.uk/green

Printed and Bound in the UK using 100% Renewable Electricity at CPI Group (UK) Ltd, Croydon, CR0 4YY

COLD CASE PROTECTION

NICOLE HELM

For the dogs we miss.

Chapter One

Carlyle Daniels had grown up in a tight-knit family. Dysfunctional, trauma-bonded—no doubt—but close. She supposed that's why she loved being absorbed into the Hudson clan. Their tight-knit was familiar, but bigger—because there were so many more of them.

So, yeah, a few more overprotective males in the mix, but she had *sisters* now—both honorary and in-law, because her oldest brother, Walker, had married Mary Hudson last fall.

Carlyle liked to talk a big game. She *really* liked to tease her oldest brother about how lame it was he'd gotten old and settled down, but deep down she could not have been happier for him. After spending most of his adult life trying to keep *her* safe while they tried to figure out who killed their mother, he now got to settle into just...normal. He worked as a cold case investigator for Hudson Sibling Solutions and helped out on the Hudson Ranch and was going to be a *dad* in a few months.

Her heart nearly burst from all the happy. Not that she admitted that to anyone.

She'd been working as Cash Hudson's assistant at his dog-training business on the ranch for almost a year now. She'd settled into life on the Hudson Ranch and in Sunrise, Wyoming. It was still weird to stay put, to not always have to look over her shoulder, to know she just got to…make a life, but she was handling it.

What she was not handling so well was a very inappropriate crush on her boss—who was also her sister-in-law's brother, which meant she probably *shouldn't* ever fantasize about kissing him.

But she did. Far too often. And normally she was an act-first-and-think-later type of woman, but there were two problems with that. First, she no longer got to bail if she didn't like her circumstances. She was building a life and all that, and bailing would bum Walker out which just felt mean and ungrateful.

Second, Cash had a daughter, who Carlyle adored. Izzy Hudson was twelve, smart as a whip, sweet and funny. She also had a little flash of something Carlyle recognized. Carlyle didn't know how to explain it, but she knew Cash didn't see it. She didn't think any of Izzy's family saw it, because the girl didn't *want* them to see it.

Carlyle saw through Izzy's masks all too well. She'd been the same all those years ago, keeping secrets so big and so well, her brothers hadn't found out until last year. So, she felt honor bound to keep an eye on the girl, because no doubt one of these days she was going to run headfirst into trouble.

Carlyle knew the lifelong bruises that could come from that, so she wanted to be…well, if not the thing that stopped the girl, the cushion to any catastrophic falls. She considered herself something of a been-there-done-that guardian angel.

Carlyle looked up from the obstacle course she'd been setting up for the level-one dogs and surveyed her work. She was satisfied and knew Cash would be too. He hadn't been super excited about hiring her. The fact he'd even done it had been because Mary had insisted or persuaded him to—but

Carlyle knew that was more about him being a control freak than anything *against* her.

She liked to think she'd proved herself the past year—as a hard worker, as someone he could trust. She glanced over at the cabin that was Cash and Izzy's residence, while everyone else lived up in the main house. Palmer and Louisa were just a few weeks out from a wedding and finishing up their house on the other end of the property, but everyone else seemed content to stay in the main house. It was certainly big enough.

Carlyle sometimes felt like the odd man out. She wanted to be like Zeke, her other brother, and have her own place in town, but staying on the property made a lot more sense for what her work schedule was like.

And for keeping an eye on Izzy.

Who, speak of the devil, stepped out of the front door of her cabin, followed by her father and then Copper, one of the dogs retired from cold case and search and rescue work.

Carlyle sighed, in spite of herself. There was something *really* detrimental to a woman's sense when watching a man be good with animals and a really good dad whose top priority, always, was his daughter's safety.

Or maybe that was just her daddy issues. Considering her fathers—both the one she'd thought was hers, and the one who'd actually been hers—had tried to kill her. More than once.

But Don, the fake dad, was dead. Connor, the real dad, was in jail for the rest of his life. So, no dads. Just brothers who'd acted *like* fathers.

And now, for the first time in her life, safety. A place to stay. A place to put down roots. She had not just her brothers, but a whole network of people to belong to.

Copper pranced up to her and she crouched to pet his soft, silky face. "There's a boy," she murmured.

She glanced up as Cash and Izzy approached. Cash was a tall, dark mountain of a guy. All broad shoulders and cowboy swagger—down to the cowboy hat on his head and the boots on his feet. His dark eyes studied her in a way she had yet to figure out. Not assessing, exactly, but certainly not with the ease or warmth with which he looked at his family.

And still, it made silly little butterflies camp out in her stomach. She felt the heat of a blush warming her cheeks like she was some giggly, virginal teenager when she decidedly was *not*.

She was a hard-hearted, whirling dervish of a woman who'd grown up fast and hard and had somehow survived. Survival had led her here.

Things were good. She was happy. She wouldn't ruin that by throwing herself at Cash, and she wouldn't ruin it by failing at this job or messing up being part of this family network.

No, for the first time in her life, Carlyle was going to do things right.

CARLYLE DANIELS WAS a problem. Worse, Cash Hudson couldn't even admit that to *anyone* in his life. She was a good worker, Izzy *loved* her, the animals *loved* her and she was an even better assistant than he'd imagined she'd be.

But he found himself thinking about her way too much, long before he'd stepped out of the cabin this morning to see her across the yard getting work for the day set up.

He too often found himself trying to make her laugh, because she didn't do it often enough and the sound made him smile…which he also knew *he* didn't do enough. As his siblings and daughter routinely told him so.

But if anyone had *any* clue he smiled more around Carlyle than he did around anyone other than Izzy, he'd be flayed alive.

He was too old for her—in years and experience. He was a father, and he had one disastrous marriage under his belt. He could look back and give himself a break—he'd been sixteen, reckless enough to get his high school girlfriend pregnant, and foolish enough to think marriage would make everything okay.

Maybe he was older, wiser, more mature these days, but that didn't mean he could ever be *good* for anyone. Didn't mean he'd ever risk Izzy's feelings again when she already had oceans of hurt over the mother she hadn't gotten to choose.

He wasn't even interested in Carlyle. He just thought she was hot and all the settling down going on around the Hudson Ranch was getting to him. Grant and Mary were fine enough. They were calm, settle-down-type people. Mary might be younger than him, but he'd always figured her for the marriage-and-kids type—and even if he liked to play disapproving older brother, Walker Daniels was about as besotted with Mary as a brother could want for his sister.

Grant was older, far more serious, and he and Dahlia had taken what felt like forever to finally even get engaged, so that was all well and good. Cash could take all those little blows that reminded him time marched on.

But it was Palmer and Anna who *really* got to him. Younger than him. The reckless ones. The wild ones. He'd never have pinned Palmer for marriage, and he'd never thought anyone would want to put up with the tornado that was Anna.

But Palmer was getting married in a few weeks, and by all accounts Louisa was the answer to any wildness inside of him. Anna was a *mother* now, and a damn good one, and somehow she'd found a man who thought all her sharp edges were just the thing to shackle him down forever.

Someday, sooner than he'd ever want, Izzy would be an

adult. Making her own choices like his siblings were doing. Izzy would go off into that dangerous world and *then what*?

Cash pushed out an irritated breath. Well, there was always Jack. Single forever, likely, being that he was the oldest and Cash couldn't remember the last time he'd been on a date, or even gone out for a night of fun.

They could be two old men bemoaning the future and the world together.

And no one would ever know he had an uncomfortable *thing* for Carlyle. He blew out a breath before they finally approached the obstacle course. "Morning," he offered gruffly.

"Good morning," she said brightly, grinning at Izzy as she stood up from petting Copper.

"I'm going to walk Izzy over to the main house, then we'll get started."

"Dad," Izzy groaned, making the simple word about ten syllables long. "I can walk to the house by myself. It's *right there*." She pointed at the house in question. Yes, within his sight, but…

Too much had happened. Too much *could* happen. As long as his ex-wife was out there, Izzy wouldn't leave his side, unless she was with one of his family members.

"I'll be right back," he said to Carlyle.

Izzy didn't groan or grumble any more. He supposed she was too used to it. Or knew he wasn't going to bend. He wished he could. He wished he could give her everything she wanted, but there'd been too many close calls.

They climbed up the porch to the main house in silence and he opened the back door that led into a mudroom.

"I'm not a baby," Izzy grumbled. Probably since she knew he would follow her right into the house until he found someone to keep an eye on her.

He didn't say what he wanted to. *You're* my *baby*. "I know, and I'm sorry." They walked into the dining room, and Mary was already situated at the table with her big agenda book and a couple different colored pens.

She looked up as they entered and smiled at Izzy.

Cash would never not feel guilty that Izzy ended up with such a terrible mom, but Mary as an aunt was the next best thing, he knew.

"I'm craving cookies. What do you think? Should we make chocolate chip or peanut butter?"

Izzy didn't smile at her aunt, she just gave Cash a kind of killing look and then sighed. "What do you think the baby wants?" She went over and took the seat next to Mary at the table.

Mary slung an arm around Izzy's shoulders, and Izzy leaned in, putting a hand over Mary's little bump.

Izzy didn't want to be treated like a baby, she didn't want him being so overprotective, but she also loved her family. She was excited about cousins after being the only kid on the ranch for so long, and she *liked* spending time with her aunts and uncles.

So this wasn't a punishment. He tried to remind himself of that as he retraced his steps back to where Carlyle was waiting. She'd brought out the level-one dogs, and they were lined up waiting for their orders.

Because they were level one, there was still some tail wagging, some whining, some irregular lining up, but they were good dogs getting close to moving to level two. They all kept their gazes trained on Carlyle, and she stood there looking like some kind of queen of dogs. Her long, dark ponytail dancing in the wind, chin slightly raised, gray-blue eyes surveying her kingdom of furry subjects.

He came to stand next to her and didn't say anything at first. Ignored the way his chest got a little tight when she glanced his way, like he was part of that array of subjects she ruled.

She could, he had no doubt. If he was someone else in a totally different situation, she no doubt would.

"She's tough," Carlyle said, not bothering to explain she was talking about Izzy.

As if he didn't know that about his daughter. As if he hadn't raised her to be tough. As if life hadn't forced her to be. "Yeah, and the world is mean."

"Take it from someone who's been there and done that, it doesn't matter how well-intentioned the protection is, at a certain point, it just chafes."

Cash knew she wasn't wrong, but it didn't matter. "I'd rather a little chafing than any of the other alternatives."

Carlyle sighed, but she didn't argue with him. She surveyed the lineup of dogs. "Well, you want to start or should I?"

Carlyle was good at this. A natural. "Take them through the whole thing."

She raised an eyebrow. He hadn't let her do that before all on her own, but…it was time. He couldn't give his daughter the space she needed to *breathe*, so he might as well unclench here where it didn't matter so much. "You can do it."

She grinned at him, eyes dancing with a mischief that was far too inviting, and completely not allowed in his life.

"I know," she said, then turned to the dogs and took them through the training course. Perfectly. A natural.

A problem.

Chapter Two

Carlyle had never been a good sleeper in the best of times. She wouldn't admit it to anybody, but she preferred to sleep with the lights on. The dark freaked her out when she was alone. Too many shadows. Too many unknowns.

But she'd learned that first night at the Hudson house that living with too many people meant they noticed. A light under the door at all hours, or when they woke up before her and walked by her window outside, off to do their chores. Then there were questions.

So, she dealt with the dark the best she could. She focused on how safe the Hudson ranch was. Due to the nature of solving cold cases, and the danger they'd seen over the past year, they had all kinds of security systems and surveillance.

Besides, the man who wanted her dead was safe behind maximum security prison-bars. But a lifetime's worth of running—because even before her mother had been murdered they'd been on the run—meant she had a hard time shaking fear loose.

Tonight was no different. Lately, she'd been sort of letting fantasies of Cash lull her off to sleep, but she was beginning to think that wasn't very healthy. She'd gone to the Lariat last night—the local bar—with Chloe Brink, one of Jack's deputies at Sunrise Sheriff's Department, and three different men had hit on her.

She hadn't been the slightest bit interested. Worse than all that, Chloe had called her out on it.

Uh oh. You've got the look.

What's the look?

The look of a woman hung up on a Hudson who is perennially in the dark.

Carlyle wasn't sure she'd felt that embarrassed since Walker had tried to give her a sex talk when she'd been fourteen.

So, which one is it? Chloe had asked, like it was just a foregone conclusion she was hung up on a Hudson. *A single one, I hope.*

Oh my God, yes. Which was an admission, and she couldn't believe she'd been stupid enough to fall for such an easy ploy.

Chloe had grinned. *Doesn't leave too many of them these days. Cash is more age appropriate.*

Does that make Jack more age appropriate for you? Carlyle had retorted. Getting too bent out of shape about the truth, but not being able to stop herself.

Chloe had looked at her bottle with a hard kind of unreadable stare. *Jack is my boss.*

Cash is my *boss.*

Chloe had finished off her one and only beer, because she was driving. *Maybe we've both got issues.* Which had made Carlyle snort out a laugh.

Then Chloe had driven her back to the ranch and idled outside the big house, staring at it with an opaque expression. She'd sighed, a world's worth of knowing in her voice. *They'll mess you up, Car. If I were you, I'd steer clear.*

Carlyle hadn't known what to say to that. Chloe was the first friend she'd made outside of the Hudson ranch, and she didn't want to be a jerk. She liked the feeling of having someone to go to who didn't revolve around *family*. Like she was a normal, functioning adult who had not just a strong family life, but friends. Interests. Things outside this sprawling ranch.

Maybe a boyfriend who was *not* her boss.

She decided then and there she was not going to fantasize about Cash to fall asleep anymore. She would think about the dogs. About work. About Izzy.

But all those things just circled back to Cash.

Eventually, she got irritated enough with herself that she slid out of bed. She went over to the armchair next to the window. She sat down on it and rested her arms on the windowsill and looked out at the great, vast night around Hudson Ranch.

The stars sparkled above. This place was so beautiful. She'd grown up jumping from city to city, but she was certain— deep in her bones—she'd been made for *this*. Mountains and sky and fresh air.

She knew her brother Zeke didn't feel comfortable taking too much from the Hudsons, but Carlyle liked to think they'd earned it with the way they'd grown up. Why not enjoy the generosity of people who could spare it?

Not that the Hudsons had seen only sunshine and roses. Their parents had disappeared when they'd been kids, and only the determined, taciturn dedication of their oldest brother, Jack, had kept the family together.

But they'd had this ranch, they'd had money and the community of Sunrise. They'd even built their own cold case investigation company. All Carlyle had ever had since her mother had been murdered was Walker and Zeke.

She'd damn well enjoy a nice house and pretty surroundings now no matter how they came along.

Except just as she was thinking it, like some kind of grand cosmic joke, the security light kept on at all hours—since the trouble last year—went out. Just one moment it was on, the next it wasn't.

She frowned. It was supposed to stay on all night. Still, the landscape was well lit by the moon and stars and... Was that a shadow over by Cash's cabin?

"You're being ridiculous," she whispered to herself. "Paranoid." But she pressed closer to the window, squinting in the dark. It was probably a dog. Or a bear.

But it looked damn human. And the security light had gone off.

"Don't overreact," she whispered to herself again. She went back to her bed and reached for the lamp. She'd spend the next hour or so reading or something. She turned the switch.

Nothing happened.

She sucked in a shaky breath, let it out. *Coincidence.* The bulb had just burned out at an inopportune time. Something normal. Boring. If she went around waking everyone up and screaming, she would look panic-addled. They'd all start treating her with kid gloves, like she was some kind of victim.

When she was a *survivor.* She swallowed and moved over to the switch by the door. She flipped the switch.

Once again, nothing happened.

She flipped it again. Once, twice. Three times.

The lights wouldn't go on. Terror swept through her. Not an accident. Not a figment of her overactive imagination. But it could be a perfectly innocent loss of power, she tried to remind herself over the panic. Even though it wasn't storming. Even though this had never happened the whole time she'd been living here.

She rushed back over to the window, hoping she'd look out into the night and not see a thing.

But *something* was moving around Cash's cabin in the

moonlight. No power shouldn't matter when it came to the security systems. They should have a backup, but…

Maybe it was nothing. Maybe the security system would catch it. So many maybes.

She couldn't just stay here and do nothing. She thought about texting Cash, but again… If it was nothing, she couldn't stand looking like she didn't have a handle on everything she'd been through.

She strode over to her closet and keyed in the code for the gun safe she kept on the top shelf. She pulled out her gun and then left her room. She considered knocking on Jack's bedroom door since it was the only other bedroom on the main floor, but no. It would be too embarrassing to be wrong with any of these people.

Besides, she had a gun. She knew how to use it. She knew how to handle danger. So, she'd handle this on her own because it was *nothing*, and no one would have to know she'd overreacted.

It was fine. She'd check it out, make *sure* it was fine, then wake someone up about the power outage. Once she was sure there was no other danger.

She unlocked the side door and slid out without making a sound. She looked up to where she knew a camera was situated. They were motion activated and should have moved with her. Even in the dark.

They didn't.

Power outage. Backup outage. It was…fine. It had to be.

She moved off the porch and toward Cash's cabin, led by moonlight and a spiraling fear that made it hard to breathe evenly. But the closer she got, the more she could see the outline of a shadow. At the side of the house. The side she knew Izzy's room was on. She wanted it to be a dog, but when no growls or barks broke out, she knew it couldn't be true.

Carlyle crept closer. Her heart was thundering in her chest, but she'd been in positions like this before. Once she was close enough, she cocked her gun.

"Freeze," she ordered sharply.

The shadow stopped. It turned toward her. He or she was standing right next to the window to Izzy's room. The window was open a crack, a little light shining on the other side of that curtain. Izzy's night-light no doubt.

Oh God. Carlyle should have called someone. Said something. She should have trusted her gut. When had she stopped doing that?

"If you don't tell me who you are in two seconds, I'm going to shoot," Carlyle said. Luckily, a life of danger meant that even though her insides shook and terror had taken hold, she sounded cool and in charge.

But the figure didn't speak. Carlyle heard the soft sound of a growl from inside. No doubt Copper. Hopefully alerting Cash or Izzy that there was trouble.

Still the figure didn't speak.

Carlyle raised her voice, held the gun steady. "Okay then. One—"

A high, piercing scream tore through the world around them. Then raucous barking followed.

Izzy. Copper. Cash.

But they were inside. Was someone in there with them? Was someone hurting Izzy in the cabin? What would have happened to Cash if that was the case?

So focused on thoughts of Izzy and Cash, Carlyle forgot about the present danger and turned toward the cabin.

The blow was so hard, it seemed to rattle her bones and she lost her footing, her balance. She fell onto the hard, cold ground, the blow now burning. Like she'd been…stabbed in the process?

But the hard sound of footsteps retreating meant whoever had been there was running away. They'd never spoken.

But...the scream. Someone was inside with Izzy. Carlyle had to get... She tried to get up, but the pain about took her out. She rolled over onto her stomach, tried to get to her hands and knees. She managed, but only just barely. She had to grit her teeth against the pain, and the fuzzy lightheadedness that wanted to take over.

She heard the slam of a door, footsteps. Copper ran up to her first and licked her face, whimpering. "Thanks, bud," she muttered. She looked beyond the dog to the other footsteps.

Cash. Barefoot, hair haphazard, gun in one hand and flashlight in the other. But he was standing and whole.

"Carlyle," he said, clearly with nothing but confusion.

"They got away." Had she lost consciousness? "Izzy?"

"I'm okay," came the girl's wavering voice. She was huddled behind Cash, holding on to him for dear life.

"Cops are on their way," Cash said as he approached. "What the hell happened?" He swept the flashlight over her head, then down her shoulders.

"I saw someone outside Izzy's window. I..."

"Daddy, she's bleeding."

Cash swore, immediately kneeling at Carlyle's side. "Come on." Then he lifted her up into his arms.

IT WAS TOO dark to walk her across the yard to the main house safely. Someone had been out here and gotten away, so he couldn't risk Izzy out in the open.

"Hold the door open for me, Iz."

She scrambled to do just that as Cash carried Carlyle to the cabin porch. "You still with me?" he asked through gritted teeth as he maneuvered her into the dark entryway.

"I'm okay. Really. They just knocked into me. I think I hit my head."

That would explain the blood, hopefully. Head wounds usually bled more than was necessary. It needed to be...something like that. He needed to get a good look at her though, see for himself. He laid her down on the couch in the living room as Izzy flipped on the lights. He didn't need to tell Izzy to lock all the doors or stay close. She was too used to this.

He wanted to swear again, but he kept it inside his head. He studied Carlyle's face, saw no traces of blood. "Where'd you hit your head?"

"Uh..." She reached up, patted around. "I guess I didn't. I'm okay."

But there'd been blood. He frowned at her. What the hell was she... His thoughts trailed off as his gaze tracked down her shirt. There on her side, her shirt was all bloody...and the blood was soaking into his couch.

This time he did swear, and Izzy didn't even scold him. "Why didn't you tell me?" he demanded, reaching forward to lift her shirt.

Carlyle's eyes darted behind him as she grabbed his wrist to stop him from lifting up her shirt.

She was looking worriedly at Izzy. She was trying to protect Izzy. "It's okay. Really. Got any Band-Aids?" She tried to laugh, but it clearly hurt because she squeezed her eyes shut.

She was going to need *stitches*, not a Band-Aid, with that amount of blood. Cash didn't know how to sort through every terrible emotion battering him. She was injured, Izzy was terrified. Hell, *he* was terrified, but he wanted Izzy out of earshot before he asked Carlyle what happened.

A knock sounded at the door, and even though Cash knew bad guys didn't *knock*, he grabbed onto Izzy before she could rush to answer.

"Who is it?" he called out.

"Jack."

Since he recognized his brother's voice, he let Izzy go. "Go ahead."

Izzy scrambled for the front door and let Jack in. Jack locked the door behind him and then strode forward.

"Grant, Hawk and Palmer are checking the perimeter. Anna's trying to figure out what happened to the security system. Fill me in," he demanded, all sheriff even though he was in pajamas. He held his gun in one hand, cell in the other.

Cash looked at Carlyle. Her worried gaze was on Izzy. Something twisted in his gut, sharp and complicated, but he pushed it away. Had to focus on the task at hand.

"Iz?" he forced himself to say. "Can you go grab a washcloth and some bandages? Some of the antibiotic ointment. We'll get Carlyle all fixed up." Which was a lie, but it would get Izzy out of earshot for a minute or two.

She nodded and ran for the hallway.

Cash looked at Jack, kept his voice low. "Carlyle needs to go to the hospital."

"The 911 call should pull in an ambulance. If not, one of my deputies will run her there on code. Let's try to sort out what happened so she can go straight there."

"I couldn't sleep," Carlyle said. And she *sounded* alert and with it. Maybe the bleeding wasn't so bad.

"I was just sitting in my room, looking at the stars out the window, and the security light went off." She swallowed. "At first, I thought…it was just nothing. Then the lights didn't work. I thought I saw a shadow so I…came to check it out."

"Without telling anyone?"

"Yeah, without telling anyone," she replied, not bitterly exactly, but certainly with some acid in her tone. "That shadow could have been anything, including a figment of my imagination."

"But it wasn't," Cash said. Because Izzy had screamed. He'd rushed to her bedroom to find Copper growling at the window and Izzy cowering in the corner.

"I don't have any great details," Carlyle continued. "It was all shadows. There was someone by Izzy's window. I had my gun, so I told them to stop. Tell me who they were. But then Izzy screamed, and Copper went nuts inside and I... I got distracted. So the person rushed me." She looked down at the bloody shirt. "I guess stabbed me too."

Jack nodded, no doubt filing away all the information. And his brothers and brother-in-law checking the perimeter would look for prints. Any evidence of whoever had been here.

But someone had been right outside his daughter's window, and he hadn't even *known*. He'd come to rely on those security cameras and look where it had led him.

Izzy rushed back in with the first aid kit and a dripping washcloth. Cash took them from her and then maneuvered her so she was facing Jack, not Carlyle and her bloody shirt.

Jack knelt in front of Izzy, put his hand on her shoulder. "What made you scream?"

She swallowed and Cash was overwhelmed with the guilt of how little he'd been able to protect her from danger. She was only twelve and she'd already seen far too much for a grown woman, let alone a middle schooler. He'd tried to shelter her from so much and failed. Every single time.

Cash lifted up Carlyle's shirt. The bloody gash on her side, just above her hip—where an intricate and colorful tattoo wound around pale skin—would definitely need stitches, and that was probably his fault too. He pressed the washcloth to it, then put her shirt back down. He took her hand and pressed it on the shirt over the lump of washcloth. "Can you hold it?"

She nodded as Izzy began to answer Jack's question.

"Copper was growling," she said. "It woke me up. I was getting out of bed to get you, Dad. But then... I heard a weird noise. It took me a minute to figure out it was someone opening my window. Then I heard voices and I just...screamed."

"What kind of voices, honey?" Jack asked, rubbing a hand up and down her arm.

"I heard someone say *stop*." She looked over her shoulder at Carlyle. "You, right?"

Carlyle nodded.

"Then I heard this kind of...creepy breathing. Right by my window. Copper was really growling now and I... I didn't know what else to do."

"You did good," Carlyle said firmly.

Izzy's bottom lip wobbled before she steadied it. "You're hurt."

Carlyle shrugged. "I'm fine."

A pounding started at the door. Not police yet, from the sounds of it. Carlyle's expression went grim. "You better let him in before he tears the door down with his bare hands."

Jack sighed and got up, unlocked the door and opened it for one of Carlyle's brothers.

Walker was barefoot. Hair wild. Eyes hot and angry. Yeah, Cash couldn't blame him. He'd be looking the same if situations were reversed.

"What the hell is going..." His gaze landed on Carlyle on the couch, and even though she was holding pressure on the wound, the blood was visible on her shirt and the couch. Walker started to swear as he crossed the room to her.

"Come on, Walker," she said firmly, even though she was too pale and this was taking too damn long. "Not in front of the kid."

Walker came up short as if finally realizing there were

other people in the room, one of them a twelve-year-old girl. He blinked once at Izzy, then his expression went blank. "Someone explain to me what's happening."

"No big deal. Just got a little knocked around when I found someone outside Izzy's window. Cops are on the way."

"An ambulance too, I hope."

"It's okay. She's going to be okay. She said so," Izzy said, sounding very close to tears.

Cash pulled her into him, gave her a squeeze. "She's going to be just fine, but we'll have a doctor check her out just in case."

"Hopefully he'll be cute," Carlyle said, making Walker groan.

But it also did what it was supposed to do, Cash supposed. Izzy didn't look *quite* so distraught. Walker didn't look *quite* so murderous. She'd lightened the tone, made them think that because she could crack a joke all was well.

The door opened behind Walker, this time Hawk. "Didn't find anything," he said, his expression cool and blank. "Cops are coming up the drive. Why don't we move up to the main house for questioning. They're going to want to search around the cabin anyway."

"I'm going to take Carlyle to the damn hospital myself," Walker said.

"Barefoot?" Carlyle replied with a raised eyebrow. "Going to toss me in your truck too?"

Her brother scowled deeply, but by that time a police cruiser had parked outside the cabin. Then it became the usual. The far too usual. Cops and an EMT and moving to the main house while Carlyle and Walker went to the hospital.

There were questions, so many questions, and an exhausted Izzy curled up on his lap because she was afraid. Terrified. So terrified that he didn't even bother to bundle her up into one of the guest rooms upstairs. He just sat on the couch and let her sleep in his lap long after everyone had gone or retreated back to bed.

Like she was a baby again. He brushed a hand over her tangled hair. "I'm sorry I haven't done a better job, baby," he muttered. Like he had so many times over the years. No matter how hard he tried, he couldn't seem to give her the life she deserved.

The police had no answers, but Jack was down at the sheriff's department to find out what he could. They'd all work together to figure it out, to get answers, to protect Izzy. But Cash was so tired of this…constant battle. Every time he eased into some new season of his life, something like this happened.

Sometime before dawn, he heard light footsteps and looked up to see Anna enter the room, carrying a fussy Caroline. Anna sank into the rocking chair across from the couch where he sat, Izzy asleep across his lap.

Cash had a very vivid memory of being sick one winter not long after Anna had been born, sleeping on this couch, and waking up to his mother in the same position with baby Anna.

Now Anna was the mother, and he hadn't seen his own for half his life. Time just kept inching on.

"The obvious answer is Chessa," Anna whispered, her expression hot and mean even as she snuggled Caroline to her chest. Anna and Chessa hadn't gotten along even when Cash had still been married to Izzy's mother.

"Maybe," Cash said. He knew she was talking about who was outside Izzy's window overnight, but it didn't sit right. Chessa was tiny. Granted, when she was high she could inflict some damage, but it was hard to believe she could do the damage done to Carlyle.

An even bigger stretch was Chessa having the know-how to cut the electricity. She might know the ranch well enough, but she wouldn't know how to tamper with the generator and make sure all the security system batteries were dead *along* with cutting the electricity.

"Not on her own. No, but who else would be after Izzy?" Anna demanded.

"I don't know," Cash muttered, looking down at his sleeping daughter. But they needed an answer this time.

A final one.

Chapter Three

Carlyle was bitter about the stitches. She hated needles and hospitals and know-it-all doctors even when they *were* cute.

She was bitter about Walker hulking about like some kind of overprotective dad when she was *fine*. "Go home to your wife."

"I'm going to have the doctor check you for brain damage."

She rolled her eyes. This lousy hospital bed was uncomfortable, and the IV in her arm was making her want to crawl out of her skin. Made worse when Walker finally stopped *pacing* and sat down on the hospital bed next to her.

"What were you doing out there, Car?"

"Checking out a threat."

"Why didn't you come get me?"

"I'm not a kid. You gotta get that through your head. I wasn't going to wake you and your pregnant wife up when I wasn't even sure it *was* a threat."

"You should have. Or called Cash. Or grabbed Jack. Literally an entire ranch full of people who would have helped at your fingertips, and you walk out into the dark alone. Everything could have gone so much worse."

Carlyle looked hard out the window. Day had risen. Cars came and went from the parking lot. She had to blink back tears. It could have been so much worse, but this was bad enough because if she'd had backup, maybe whoever it was wouldn't have gotten away.

"I feel guilty enough, thanks."

He sighed and patted her IV-less arm. "I'm not trying to make you feel guilty."

"Doing a hell of a job anyway."

"Whether or not they track down who it was, you stopped something from happening to that little girl, Carlyle."

"The police don't have anything, do they?"

"Not yet. Mary's updating me as she hears, but we won't know what Jack's found until he's done."

"It just means she's going to keep being in danger."

"And she's got an army of people protecting her, Car. It's not the same. All you had was us."

She hated that he could see through her so easily, that he might be feeling his own guilt. "You two were pretty top notch."

"Not like the Hudsons."

No, they hadn't had a ranch or a community or much of anything the Hudsons offered Izzy. A sheriff as an uncle among them.

"We did the best with what we had. Not exactly your fault."

"Nah." He squeezed her hand. "But the things we blame ourselves for don't have to be our actual fault to feel like we should have made a different choice. But there's no different choice. There's only the one you make in the moment, and then how you learn from it. Don't go it alone, Car. Not anymore. None of us needs to."

"This feels like a pep talk for our brother."

"Yeah, but he's not chained to a hospital bed, so he just leaves when I try."

"I know it's not my fault," she said, both because it was true and because he needed to hear her say it. "I know it worked out that I happened to look out there when someone was sneaking around." Or maybe if she didn't *know* it, she tried to convince herself of it. "It had to be her mom, right?"

"That's what most of them think."

"Most?"

"According to Mary, Cash isn't totally sold, at least on it just being her. Doesn't think the mom has it in her to orchestrate that kind of attack on her own."

Carlyle frowned at that. It *was* pretty orchestrated. It was a lot for one person to handle, because it wasn't just cutting the security light and the electricity, it was debilitating all the security backups and getting to Izzy all in a short period of time. But *why*?

"We'll get to the bottom of it," Walker said. "And more, we'll all protect Izzy. She's lucky she's got so many people who've got her back."

But it wasn't luck to be a little girl who felt like a target. Carlyle should know. Luckily, the doctor came in, because she didn't know how to convince Walker she was fine, or that she didn't feel guilt, or that she was going to magically not worry about Izzy no matter how many people were looking after her.

It took another couple hours, mostly of waiting until she wanted to scream, before they finally released her and Walker drove her back to Hudson Ranch. Walker walked her right to her room—no detours allowed. Mary was waiting there for her, and it was clear she'd tidied up Carlyle's room, changed the sheets, had a tray of snacks waiting.

"I don't want to be fussed over," Carlyle grumbled as she got into her bed, hating that it was a lie. She absolutely wanted pillows fluffed and snacks delivered and Mary's soft, easy presence. She was so perfect, and Carlyle might have hated her for it if Mary didn't love Walker so much, if she wasn't going to make the best mom to Carlyle's future niece or nephew.

"Oh, dear," Mary said, sounding truly perplexed. "You sure got messed up with the wrong family, then." She arranged the tray on the nightstand and shot Carlyle a grin.

Carlyle wanted to keep pouting, but it was too hard. Mary really did embody that old saying about glowing while pregnant. And Walker sliding his arm around her waist and looking down at her like she hung the moon only added to it.

It was everything she wanted for her brother, but if she thought too much about it, the lack of sleep and pain medicine would likely make her cry and she didn't want to indulge in that just yet.

"You know, a girl who's been stabbed deserves to know the gender of her first niece or nephew."

Mary looked up at Walker, who gave a nod. "It's a boy," Mary said, her smile soft and wide.

Carlyle hadn't expected Mary to actually answer. She really hadn't. It made her want to cry all over again.

Luckily, Izzy popped her head in the doorway. Mary moved out of the way to let Izzy in. "Can you keep an eye on her for me, Izzy? I've got some brownies in the oven I need to check on and Walker has some work to do."

Izzy nodded solemnly, and when they left the room Izzy produced a little clutch of wildflowers she'd clearly picked and tied together with a pretty little ribbon. She walked over to where Carlyle sat on the bed and held them out.

"Do you like them?"

"I *love* them." Carlyle took the outstretched flowers and a took a deep sniff of the blooms, then patted the space on the bed next to her. "Hop up. I'm not fragile."

Izzy was studying her with big, worried eyes, but eventually she crawled up onto the other side of the bed. Carlyle lifted her shirt high enough so Izzy could see the small bandage over her stitches.

"See? It's nothing."

Izzy reached out and touched the edge of the bandage, then Carlyle's tattoo, her mouth all pursed together in a frown. "My friend's aunt got shot in the leg. It was a long time ago, but it still hurts her sometimes."

"My God, what's in the water around here?"

That *almost* made Izzy smile. She cocked her head. "What's your tattoo of?"

Carlyle dropped her shirt. She didn't think Cash seemed like the type of person who'd be thrilled with his daughter getting a tour of Carlyle's tattoos. She had a few, all easily hidden by normal clothes.

Izzy sighed at Carlyle's lack of response, but she didn't push it. "I know this has something to do with my mother. I don't know why she... I don't know. But I'm sorry that—"

Carlyle pulled her as close as she could without causing too much physical pain under the weird numbness of pain meds. "Listen." *Life's a bitch and then you die* was on the tip of her tongue, but Cash probably wouldn't like that one piece of advice, even if it was borderline suitable for a twelve-year-old. "I don't do sorrys. Because I don't do anything I don't want. So no one's gotta be sorry when I wade in, because I did it because I wanted to."

"But—"

"No buts. Them's the breaks, kid. Now, I went through some scary stuff when I was your age too. And it's not that different. My mom was okay, and I had some pretty good older brothers, but my dad sucked. Hard. The kind that put us all in danger. So, I know how it feels. I do."

Izzy didn't say anything, just looked down at her hands in her lap. But slowly, ever so slowly, she leaned her head on Carlyle's shoulder.

Carlyle might have lost it right there, but she knew she had to be strong for Izzy. "It makes you feel helpless, but… It's a good lesson. You can't control anyone but yourself. So you focus on being the best version of yourself you can be. And sometimes you go through hard stuff that makes you wonder *why*, but then…there's all this."

Carlyle pointed out the window. Izzy's eyebrows drew together as if she didn't understand what Carlyle meant.

"I've been holding my own for the past two years because I wanted some space from my brothers. I was alone, and I was lonely. And scared. It was hard to get through that, but now I get to be here. Horses. Dogs. I'm going to be an aunt. And you're going to be a cousin. That's pretty cool."

Izzy nodded after a while. "I like babies. Caroline cries a lot, but she's so cute."

"Yeah. I'm not saying you don't get to be scared or unhappy because you've got an awesome family and place to live, but what I want you to understand, accept, *know* is that everyone in this place will do whatever they can to keep you safe, and that's nothing to be sorry about. Even though sometimes it doesn't feel like it, that's a gift. We'll all keep you safe. That doesn't mean you're weak, or a burden. Because you've got some responsibility too. You were going to get your dad. You screamed. You did the right things."

"Maybe," Izzy said, but she was clearly not fully buying it. "Can I ask you a favor?"

"Anything."

She lifted her head, turned those big blue eyes on Carlyle. "I want to learn how to shoot a gun, Carlyle. And you're the only one who'll teach me."

Ahh… Hell.

LITERALLY LESS THAN forty-eight hours after she'd been *stabbed*, Carlyle was in the dog pens, being a pain in his ass.

"You aren't working," Cash said. Ordered. "Go back to the house."

"If I don't have something to do, I'm going to lose my mind."

"Take up knitting."

"I'd rather bleed out, thanks."

He laughed in spite of himself. Which was bad because she grinned at him and wouldn't take him seriously now.

"The doctor said no heavy lifting," she continued. "But the nurse said I should keep mobile. I don't want to get all stiff and weak over a few stitches. Besides, I needed to talk to you about something away from Izzy. Work seemed about the only option."

Cash frowned. He didn't like the sound of that. At all. Particularly when Carlyle looked...nervous.

"How do you feel about Izzy and... Look. She came and talked to me yesterday... The thing is..."

"Spit it out, Carlyle," he snapped, because he couldn't begin to fathom what this was that would have Carlyle, of all people, stumbling over her words. About *his* daughter.

"She wants me to teach her how to shoot a gun."

Cash barked out a laugh, and not a nice one. "She knows that's not happening. I've told her she has to wait until she's sixteen. And I don't appreciate her trying to talk you into going against that very clear rule. I'm going to go over there right now and—"

Carlyle grabbed him, held him in place. "You can't tell her I told you. She'll never tell me anything again."

"Good! She shouldn't be telling *you* anything anyway."

Her head drew back like he'd slapped her, and it took him a second, but he got it. Too late, but he got it.

"I didn't mean it like that."

She stepped away from him and crossed her arms over her

chest, her expression cool and detached. Trying to hide the hurt. "Oh, yeah? How did you mean it?"

He blew out a long breath. *This* was why he'd kept their lives somewhat isolated. *This* was why he hadn't wanted an assistant. Why he and Izzy lived in their own space.

He was in charge of his daughter, and he didn't do well with anyone butting in telling him how to do that.

Now he had to somehow apologize to Carlyle for something he *hadn't* meant, while making it clear she could in no way get involved in this decision regarding his daughter.

"You don't understand." He shoved a hand through his hair, trying to find the words. "How hard this…" He blew out a breath. Maybe he didn't have the right words, but he had a very clear truth. "My daughter *loves* you, straight through."

Carlyle looked at him with that expression she very rarely showed. It was a little too vulnerable for her usual badass bravado. And it weakened his defenses against her, because he knew better than most that soft spots and hurts lived under a tough exterior.

"I love her too," Carlyle said, very quietly. Seriously.

"Yeah. I know. I do…know that. Hell, Car, you've got a stab wound to prove it. But she came to you on this because she knows I'll say no. She wants it to be a secret. I can't accept that. I won't, not with all this going on. Secrets between us aren't safe, and I know she hates it, but sometimes you hate the things people do to protect you."

Carlyle swallowed visibly. But she nodded. "I'm not going to do it against your wishes. If I was going to do that, I wouldn't have told you in the first place. Just let me… Let me try to make it her idea to tell you, okay? I'll try to convince her to tell you before we do anything, but you can't go storming in there yelling at her that she can't. She's *scared*, Cash. And she has every right to want to do something about it."

"Nothing is happening to her."

"No, nothing is. I know you're scared too. We *all* are. But she's a kid who feels like everything is happening *to* her. Why wait four years? What's that going to change? I know you have to be the worried, careful dad. I get that, I really do. But you don't get how it feels to be that kid. You're an adult who gets to feel like you have some kind of control."

"You think I feel like I have *any* kind of control?" he shot back. He hadn't felt in control of a damn thing since his parents disappeared when he was fourteen.

Carlyle crossed over to him, put her hand on his arm. "But when we're adults, we get to *do* stuff about that feeling. You can't expect her to just sit there and be protected. Trust me, Cash. I know your family has been through some bad stuff, and no doubt Jack did annoying things to try to protect you, but it's got nothing on being the youngest kid in a group full of people who think they know what's best."

He tried to take that on board because it was true. Carlyle had been more in Izzy's shoes than he ever had been. Maybe he'd felt like his entire adult life had been about rolling with a hundred different punches, but he supposed Carlyle was right. He could punch back whenever he wanted, and he was always telling Izzy to let him handle it.

"I don't like the idea of her dealing with guns. Not at this age. Maybe I'm wrong, but that was always the family rule. Unless you wanted to go hunting, no guns until sixteen."

"Can't you make a compromise for special life circumstances? Can't you at least teach her how to *shoot* one, even if you don't want her to have access to a firearm?"

"What'd be the point of that?"

"Knowledge, Cash. Knowing how to do stuff makes you feel like you can…handle things. I don't know how else to explain it. Knowledge is power."

Cash didn't know how to take that fully on board. It wasn't that he thought she was wrong. Worse, it felt like she was right. And all the ways he'd tried to protect Izzy from things—from her knowing bad things, understanding awful things—might have been the wrong choice.

"She's the most important person in the world to me. I just want to protect her."

"I know." Carlyle swallowed, like this was hard for *her*. "I think I know better than most. And while I can't know how you are feeling as a parent, I have been in her situation. I know what she needs, Cash. I know what it's like to know someone out there is after you, and it doesn't matter. I had the two best brothers in the world protecting me, but it didn't *matter*. I kept secrets I shouldn't have, secrets that got my brother shot, and put all of us, including you guys, in danger. I just... If I can help her and you not go through that, I will stick my nose where it doesn't belong. Sorry."

Her hand was still on his arm, and he understood that she was trying to *help*. He had so much help, so much support in his family, but Carlyle really was the only one who had a kind of insight into what it felt like to be in Izzy's position. Cash had never really thought of that before.

He patted her hand. "I appreciate it, even when I don't."

She laughed at that, her mouth curving and her blue-gray eyes taking on that little sparkle of mischief that was so much *her*. "I guess it helps I don't mind ticking people off."

"You?" he replied, with mock surprise, which made her laugh again.

There was something about the sound of it. Like a magnet. He always found himself moving closer. Getting a little lost in that dimple in her cheek.

Someone behind him cleared their throat and Carlyle jumped while Cash dropped his hand from over hers, like they'd been caught doing something other than *talking about his daughter.*

"Sorry to interrupt," Jack said as Cash turned to face him.

"Not interrupting," Cash muttered, shoving his hands into his pockets. He would have felt embarrassed, or worried what Jack thought, if he hadn't recognized that blank, cop look on his brother's face. Bad news. Cash moved forward. "What is it? Iz—"

"It isn't about Izzy," Jack said, quick and concise. "She's at the house and is fine."

"Then what is it?"

"Bent County found Chessa."

"Good." Cash knew it wouldn't be that simple, but it was a start. "Are you going to go question her or are they? I'd like you to be there. I'd…"

Jack let out a breath. Stepped forward. Bad news, all around, Cash could feel it. Like Mom and Dad all over again. Jack reached out, put a hand on his shoulder. "She's dead, Cash."

Cash had no idea how to absorb that. But that wasn't all.

"It's looking like murder."

Chapter Four

Carlyle knew she couldn't possibly feel as shocked as Cash, but it was close. Dead. Murder. A kidnapping attempt that now made even less sense.

And the two Hudson brothers, standing there *so* still. Jack's hand on Cash's shoulder and Cash barely even taking a breath.

"I don't understand," he finally said, his voice little more than a scrape. "She...she was murdered?"

"That's the premise they're operating under. I'm still working on getting more details out of Bent County. It's an ongoing investigation and they know I've got personal ties, so I'm getting shut out. I sent Chloe over to the coroner's office to see if she could get something for us to go on. But I have a bad feeling this will work its way through the town grapevine, so I wanted to tell you before you got exaggerated word of it from someone else."

Carlyle had an uncomfortable, vivid flashback of Walker telling her what had happened when she'd been at school that she...she had to look away, take a few steps back.

This wasn't about her. This wasn't...the past. Not her mother murdered all because Carlyle had been tired of moving around, had thrown a fit because she wanted to stay in one place.

It was just the horrible roll of the dice that scattered similar tragedies around the world. And how her mother had dealt with the man who'd wanted her dead was hardly Carlyle's fault, no matter how often she felt like it was.

"I have to tell Izzy," Cash said, his voice still that awful, pained gasp of a man drowning.

"You could wait," Jack said. "Give us some time to find more answers. She's not leaving the ranch, so it's not like she'll have contact with anyone running their mouth. Let's take some time to get all the information."

"She'll know." Carlyle knew she should have kept her mouth shut, this wasn't her family, her business. But she... Even more so now, she had been in Izzy's shoes. Her mother had been murdered when she'd been a kid. And Carlyle had *loved* her mother, depended on her for everything, blamed herself for her death, so it was different. It was so different.

But right now, it felt the same. It was too many commonalities, and too much understanding Izzy's position to keep her mouth shut. She retraced her steps to stand next to Cash again, to face off against Jack.

"She won't know if no one tells her," Jack said, a clear warning in his hard tone.

Carlyle should nod and agree because this wasn't her family or her business, and it'd be smart to heed Jack's warning. But... She turned to Cash. "It doesn't matter how careful you all are. If *you* know something *she* doesn't, that's this big and this important, she'll feel it. And she'll worry it's about what happened at the cabin. She'll make it into something else, she will feel...like an outsider. Trust me, when you feel like that, you make bad choices."

Cash turned to look at her, but every move seemed weighed down. Like he was swimming through molasses. In his head, it probably felt like it.

"What do you mean, Carlyle?" he asked, with the weight of the world on his shoulders.

She wished she could heft some of the load. "I just mean..." She looked from Cash to Jack then back again because Cash was clearly the only receptive audience. "My mother was murdered too, you know. When I was Izzy's age. Walker and Zeke... They tried to shelter me, keep the sordid details from me, but the thing was, I already was too deep in. I knew secrets, but they tried to keep me separate. I know it was to protect me. I know they were trying to do the right thing, the *good* thing, but it put us at cross purposes. We spent too many years..." She trailed off. She didn't need to go down the full tangent of her life. "I know this isn't the same situation. You aren't Walker and I'm not Izzy, but I just know what it's like to be in her position. You feel powerless, and you'll do some pretty reckless things to find some power. Especially if everyone you love is keeping something from you."

"*You* felt that way," Jack pointed out.

Carlyle tried not to scowl at him, but hiding her frustration with him was a hard-won thing. She managed not to scowl, but her tone was snappish when she spoke. "Yeah. You got a lot of experience being a twelve-year-old girl whose mother was murdered?"

Jack, predictably, said nothing in response. That was the problem with all this childhood trauma bred into the very fabric of this ranch. They thought because they'd had it rough, they understood all the layers of what was rough for anyone else.

But Carlyle could see, very clearly, there was something very different about losing your parents suddenly and without knowing what really happened, and knowing that someone had *killed* one of them, on purpose, for you to find.

The Hudsons looked at Izzy and saw their own problems,

but even Carlyle couldn't begin to guess what the little girl felt about the terrible mother she'd barely known—by all accounts—being murdered.

What Carlyle *did* understand was being the little girl left out of the discussion, someone not *part* of what was going on.

"I know you guys had stuff too," Carlyle said, her focus on Cash because he's who she had to convince. He had the final say in his daughter's life. "I can't imagine what it's like to have your parents disappear into thin air, but it's not the same." Of course, Carlyle couldn't resist a *little* dig. "You were in charge, Jack. She's not. And she knows it."

Jack's scowl was epic. He crossed his impressive arms over his chest, all tall and glowering and intimidating.

Too bad Carlyle had grown up at the feet of intimidating. She didn't so much as *blink* at him.

"You know I'm right," she said to Cash. "I think you have to know I'm right."

Cash didn't look at her. He looked at some spot on the ground. Making Carlyle realize this wasn't *just* about Izzy. Maybe this Chessa was his *ex*-wife, maybe he didn't love her anymore, but he'd married her once. Had a kid.

He'd lost something too.

Sympathy swept through her, and she reached out to touch his arm or something, but he chose that moment to move forward. "I'm going to go tell her," Cash muttered, pushing past Jack.

Leaving Carlyle to face off against a clearly very disapproving Jack. Which she should have left alone, but disapproving authority had never sat well with her, no matter how well-meaning.

"You don't have to agree with him or me, Jack. She's not my kid and she's not your kid."

"They're all mine," he muttered, but he didn't argue anymore, just turned and strode away as Cash had.

Leaving Carlyle alone with the dogs. Her side throbbing, her heart aching and far too many memories making it all too easy to worry about what Izzy might do next.

But the one thing she was reminded of quite plainly by Jack's parting words hurt just as much.

None of them were *hers*.

CASH WENT FOR whiskey that night. He rarely drank anymore. At most, a beer here or there. Never hard liquor. Never with Izzy under the same roof. It tended to remind him a little too much of the hell he'd raised when he was far too young.

It was hard to remember that kid. He was nothing like the boy who'd lost his parents—angry and confused and scared, but too much of a fourteen-year-old to admit it. So he'd caused trouble, fought with Jack, drank, ran with the wrong crowd.

Everything had changed at seventeen when Izzy had been born. So tiny. So *his*. A responsibility he owed to everyone in his life to see through. To take more seriously than any other responsibility he'd ever been gifted. He'd given up everything wild in that moment.

Chessa had never felt that. At the core of all their marital issues, that was number one. Everything in Cash's life had changed when Izzy had taken her first breath, and Chessa had wanted nothing to change. Cash hadn't struggled to give up their wild, reckless ways. Chessa had always been desperate for one more hit.

Now Chessa was dead. He'd always known she was heading in that direction. Too much drinking. Drugs. Getting mixed up with dangerous people all for a hit. He'd felt at turns guilty about it, and at turns—which made the guilt nearly swamp him now—wished she'd just get it over with so he wouldn't have to worry about her hurting Izzy anymore.

She'd lost the ability to hurt him a long time ago, if she'd ever had it to begin with.

A sad state of affairs, through and through.

Now he'd had to tell his daughter her mother was dead. At someone else's hand. He'd planned on just telling her Chessa had died, leave the details out of it, but Carlyle's words had haunted him.

So he'd told Izzy the truth. A slightly sanitized version of what little he knew, but definitely the important parts.

Izzy hadn't cried. She'd been upset, he knew. She hadn't tried to hide the hurt. But it was more fear and confusion.

And definitely hiding something. He wouldn't have seen it if Carlyle hadn't brought up her own experiences, but she was right. Trying to protect Izzy had only led him to this place where his little girl didn't trust him with everything.

He let out a long breath. Why not get really drunk? There were a hundred people in this house to take care of things, and as long as no one fully knew what had happened with Chessa, and the kidnapping attempt, Izzy would be sleeping at the big house. More eyes, more bodies, more protection.

But not more answers.

The storm door squeaked open and Carlyle slid out into the dark, one of his dogs trailing after her. Copper would be up in Izzy's room, but Swiftie—who should be sleeping out at the dog barn—had clearly latched on to Carlyle.

Both woman and dog surveyed him, then Carlyle jutted her chin at the porch chair. "Mind if I join you?"

"Would it matter if I did mind?"

Her mouth curved at that, and she went over and settled herself next to him on the porch swing rather than the open chair. Swiftie settled under her feet.

He didn't scowl, but he wanted to.

"I don't want to butt in," she began.

He snorted. "Don't you?"

She sighed, then grabbed his drink—right out of his hand—and took a deep swig like it was a shot. *Hers* for the taking.

"Are you even old enough to drink?" Because he liked to remind himself—when he was feeling a little too bruised and bloody and tempted to lean on her—that she was over five years younger than him, and he had no business wanting her company.

She gave him a killing look. "It wouldn't matter to me if I was, but I'm not *that* young, Cash. In fact, I'll be twenty-four next month." She handed the glass back to him.

He grunted. "I had a seven-year-old by the time I was twenty-four."

"And I had put a famous and powerful senator in jail by the time I was twenty-three. Want to keep playing this game?"

She really was something else. Everything inside him felt too heavy to allow a laugh to escape, but she made him *almost* want to.

"I'm too tired, and not drunk enough, to play any games."

"Well, if I were you, I wouldn't go down the drunk route. I know how this goes. I can't tell if Jack knows and is sparing you, or if he's in denial because you're all upstanding Hudsons. They're going to look at you first."

"Who?"

She turned to him then, her gray-blue eyes as serious as her expression in the dim light of the repaired security pole. *Some security.*

"The cops. When someone is murdered, the significant other is the first person they start digging into."

"I haven't been Chessa's significant other for a decade. I haven't even had contact with her in close to five years. The few times she's come sniffing around, someone else dealt with her."

"Doesn't matter. The *ex* with custody of their kid? Especially a kid who's been a target? Primo suspect."

"No one who knows me is going to think I killed my own daughter's mother. No one with any sense is going to think I waited all these years to do it, either. Why now? I *do* have custody. I have everything. Chessa was the one with nothing." Because of her own choices, he had to remind himself.

"Jack isn't investigating. Bent County is. And even if he was, even if someone who 'knows you' was, they shouldn't."

"Why the hell not?"

"Because he's your *brother*. Because personal connection is a red flag, Cash. You want people thinking you did it? You want to be a true crime podcast in ten years so people can look at Izzy and wonder? You can list all the reasons people shouldn't suspect you, but all anyone is going to see is that you're the ex-husband."

If he sat with what she was saying, he understood. If he could detach himself from the situation, he'd probably agree with her.

But they were talking about *him*. And Izzy. And Chessa. And murder.

"I didn't kill anyone."

"Well, I know that. But do you have a good enough alibi? Was that weird kidnapping attempt some kind of…decoy? You gotta start thinking with that investigator brain of yours, because the cops are slow and wrong half the time."

"I'm not an investigator anymore."

"You try to stay out of it for Izzy. I get that and I haven't been around that long. But I also see how much you *want* to be involved. You've got the skills. If not by use, by osmosis. And lucky for you, I've got the knowledge of how this goes down. You're on their list of suspects, and once they have a time of death, they're going to want to know where you were."

Sometimes, she made no sense and yet he felt like she saw right through him all at the same time.

"I happen to trust the cops, Carlyle."

"You shouldn't. They're not gods, Cash. Not saying they're bad or evil. They're just people. Human, capable of error and getting drowned in too much red tape. And if I'm trusting just people, it's going to be the people I know and love who don't have to worry about paperwork. We need to look into it ourselves, and *you* need an ironclad alibi."

He wanted to beat his head against a wall, but that wouldn't change anything. If there was one thing he understood in this life, it was that the blows never stopped coming, no matter how many you'd already had.

"Look, I appreciate the advice. Maybe you're not even wrong. I don't know. But I know I didn't do it. There can't be any proof I did, because I didn't. I'm just going to keep my head down and make sure Izzy's okay. No investigating around the cops, no worrying about alibis. Just her well-being."

Carlyle paused for a very long time, abnormally still and looking out at the twinkling night with a serious expression on her face when she was usually a whirl of excess energy and movement.

When she finally spoke, it was quietly and seriously. "She's never going to thank you for martyring yourself for her. She's going to wonder why her dad didn't have a life." She took another long sip of his drink. "And then probably blame herself for it."

She looked a little miserable, which was unfair since she was telling him *he* was about to be a prime suspect for murder. "Speaking from experience again?"

"Yeah. I had to kick Walker out of my life so he'd go live his." She turned, flashed that smile that always looked a little dangerous, but in this light he saw it for what it was. Deflection. "Look at him now. Married. About to be a dad. I did that, and has he thanked me?"

Cash could see the similarities between him and Walker whether he wanted to or not. Between Carlyle and Izzy. But... "I get it. You lived this weird version of what she's going through, but you're not the same." He took the glass from her, finished off the drink. Not enough to get drunk, but she was probably right about that being a bad idea.

"No. No two people are the same. Maybe it's different when it's your dad giving up everything he enjoys for you. But you've walked a little in our shoes too, Cash. Don't you ever worry about Jack and all he's given up to keep you guys going?"

He wanted to swear, because of course he worried about that. Because it was true. Jack had sacrificed a million times over, to keep them together, to keep the ranch going, to start Hudson Sibling Solutions. And on and on it went.

Cash looked at the empty glass in his hands. He knew he shouldn't say any more. Shouldn't prolong whatever this was. A pep talk or advice or whatever. But he felt like the words... had to be said. She was the only safe place to say them.

It was the strangest realization, in this already strange moment, that he didn't really *have* much of a safe place. Not when he was so busy trying to protect his daughter, his siblings, himself.

He didn't need to do that with Carlyle. "I used to wish she was dead. I just thought it'd be easier."

She was quiet, but only for a second or two. Then she put her hand on his shoulder, much like Jack had earlier today when he'd delivered the news.

But Carlyle's slim hand felt different than his brother's. Like comfort without the strings of who they were. Because she was right about too many things. And she understood these…strange, twisted, tenuous trauma-laden relationships.

"I don't blame you, Cash. I doubt you're the only person in your family to feel the same. Izzy included. But don't tell it to the cops. My bet? They'll be sniffing around first thing in the morning. Have an alibi. Even if you have to lie."

"Why would I lie?"

"Because if the murder happened some night you and Izzy were sleeping in the cabin out there, that's not enough of an alibi. They'll ask you to prove you didn't sneak out and do it and sneak back."

"With Izzy sleeping *alone*?"

Carlyle shrugged. "She's twelve, Cash. Not an infant. And *I* know you wouldn't leave her alone. Anyone here knows you wouldn't, but that doesn't mean much to cops looking for someone to lay the blame on. You have to be smart about this. Izzy needs you to be smart about this. Sometimes being smart means bending the truth a bit. You've got this big mess of a family behind you, and you're innocent, so that helps, but you can't let it make you complacent."

He studied her. So serious and earnest, which was not her usual MO. "Which one of them sent you out to pep talk me?"

She frowned quizzically, as if she didn't understand what he meant at first. Then she looked at the house, and something in her expression changed again. But he couldn't read it.

But he got the feeling it meant *no one* had sent her out. She had come out all on her own. Wanting to offer him advice to protect himself.

He didn't know what to do with that.

She got up off the swing. "I'm your guardian angel, obviously." She flashed that mischievous grin, but it didn't land. She was making a joke out of it because she was uncomfortable.

And since she was, he played a long. "Angel? Hardly."

"I am *reformed*."

He snorted, but he got to his feet too. She moved for the door, but he reached out, got ahold of her hand to stop her. He gave it a squeeze.

"Thanks. I do appreciate the butting in, even when I don't like it. Because Izzy is the most important thing. I'll listen to anyone if I think it'll keep her safe. So butt in, be annoying. If it's for her benefit, I'll deal."

She looked down at their hands, but she didn't pull away or act like she was uncomfortable. He couldn't see her expression, but they just stood there on his family's porch holding hands.

Which suddenly made *him* feel uncomfortable, because it felt like all those intimate connections he'd spent years avoiding. Shrank his world down to not feel anything that didn't involve his family. Because shrinking down was *safe*, and he had to be safe. For Izzy. No matter what Carlyle said.

He dropped her hand, and she looked up. But she didn't quite meet his gaze.

"Any time," she said breezily, grabbing the storm door and opening it. Swiftie trailed behind her as she stepped inside and away from him.

He watched them disappear inside and wondered why it felt like a mistake.

Chapter Five

Carlyle shook out her hand as she walked back to her room. Not the time or place to get all…*whatever* over a little hand-holding. Over actually helping someone, instead of always being the one who had to be helped.

Cash thought she was young, and wrong.

But he'd listened to her. Thanked her. Squeezed her hand like what she had offered meant something. It did a hell of a number on that pointless soft heart of hers she was always trying to bury.

She opened her bedroom door. "You, Carlyle Daniels, are a grade A—" Before she could finish insulting herself, she stopped short. Froze.

Izzy was sitting in the middle of Carlyle's bed. Crying.

What Carlyle wanted to do was cross the room and gather Izzy up in her arms and tell the little girl she would literally fight every last demon to the death if she stopped crying.

But that was what no one—men in particular—ever understood. Sometimes, it wasn't about someone fighting the battles *for* you. Sometimes, it was about feeling you had the power to fight them yourself.

So Carlyle did her best to take her time, to tack on a smile. To give Izzy a little space at first.

"Hey. What are you doing in here? Pretty sure your dad will

have a meltdown if he goes to check in on you and you're not in bed." Carlyle moved to the bed and took a seat on the edge.

Izzy sniffled, wiping her nose with her sleeve of her pajamas. "I've got ten more minutes. He's like clockwork."

Oof. How well she knew these little games. The way some kids observed too much, filed far too much away. All to hopefully never be caught off guard again.

But the off guard always came.

Carlyle gently laid her hand on Izzy's shoulder. Much like she had with Cash outside. Two hurting people, so determined to hurt *away* from each other, rather than show each other their vulnerable underbellies.

Oof times a million.

"I know you're scared. You've got every right to be right now. And you're probably tired of hearing it, but it's true. No one's going to hurt you, Izzy. You are the most protected girl in Wyoming. I'm working on convincing your dad to let you learn how to shoot. Because you should feel like you can protect yourself too, but he's gotta be on board with it. You've both got to be honest with each other."

But Izzy was shaking her head before Carlyle even finished. "I'm not worried about protecting *me*," Izzy said, like Carlyle was crazy. "I don't want anyone to hurt my dad."

Carlyle felt a bit like she'd been stabbed all over again. But she tried not to let it show. "Why would anyone hurt your dad? Look, I realize I'm relatively new to the situation, but it sounds like Chessa was mixed up in some dangerous stuff. Stuff your dad wouldn't touch with a million-foot pole."

Izzy's expression was stubborn. Her eyes were shiny and puffy, but she'd stopped actively crying. "I don't think someone tries to get me one night, and Chessa shows up two days later dead, and it doesn't connect. It *has* to connect. I'm worried it connects to my dad, not me."

She sounded so adult. So like her father. But she brought up an interesting and terrifying point. With Chessa out of the way, what did anyone want with Izzy? What had Chessa even wanted with Izzy if, by all accounts, she hadn't wanted to be a mother?

Didn't that mean Cash might be the *actual* target? What better way to get to him than through the daughter he cherished and protected above all else?

Carlyle studied the girl, trying to find a good place for her whirling thoughts to land. There were still tears in Izzy's eyes, but underneath was a quick mind that caught on. That understood.

No matter how little her family wanted her to.

"The two things might not connect," Carlyle offered, even though she didn't know how that would possibly be true. "Maybe it's just bad timing Chessa was murdered."

"Maybe," Izzy agreed, still reminding Carlyle a bit too much of Cash right then. The careful, measured way she didn't *argue* with what Carlyle had said, but was clearly internally working through all the ways she didn't agree.

And she was going to keep those thoughts bottled up and to herself, because she didn't think the adults listened. Carlyle squeezed her shoulder. "So, how *could* it connect? What do you think?"

Izzy blinked. Once. Then looked down at her hands. "No one cares what I think," she muttered.

"First of all, I know that isn't true. You all care about each other more than just about anybody. But I think all that care, mixed up with danger, tends to a lot of…isolating yourselves and keeping secrets. You're here, in my room, crying, because you don't want your dad to see you're upset, right?"

"I know it hurts his feelings when I cry. I know… He's like the *best* dad. I do know that. I don't think he does."

Stab me in the heart, kid. "I mean, maybe you could tell him. Or not keep secrets from him."

She watched the mutinous expression begin to storm across Izzy's face and quickly changed tactics.

"Tell me how you think it connects, Izzy. Let's see what we can figure out."

The girl frowned. "Well, it's not the first time my mom tried to take me, right? If it *was* my mom who hurt you."

Carlyle hadn't heard the whole story of that, but there'd been rumblings from the Hudson contingent about an incident a while back.

"Last year," Izzy continued. "She helped that guy who tried to hurt Aunt Anna and shot Uncle Hawk? She told Uncle Hawk that she…" Izzy curled her hand into the bedspread. "She wanted to sell me or something. I don't really get that, but everyone was pretty upset about it."

Carlyle felt like she couldn't *breathe*. Sell… What an absolutely awful thing. Surely…

"No one told you about it?" Izzy asked, clearly reading Carlyle's shock.

Carlyle shook her head, unable to find her voice. Sell your own kid? Hell, her biological father had tried to have her killed, so she shouldn't be surprised at how terrible parents could be, but…

"They didn't tell me either, but I heard them talking. I always hear them talking, no matter how sneaky they think they're being." She picked at the bedspread. "But Aunt Anna and Uncle Hawk and Dad and everybody stopped that whole thing. They outsmarted the guy. Well, mostly. He shot Uncle Hawk."

Carlyle was struggling to come up with words. She'd always thought she had it pretty rough, but this girl had seen her damn share.

Izzy looked up at Carlyle earnestly. "That guy was mad because Hudson Sibling Solutions hadn't found his son alive. He wanted like revenge or something. So, what if all this is like…revenge? My mother didn't like Dad or our family. Maybe someone else didn't either. Maybe someone doesn't want to hurt *me*. They want to hurt my dad. Take me. Murder my mother. I don't know how *that* would hurt him, but maybe someone thought it would because she was my mother."

Carlyle could think of a reason someone would murder Chessa to hurt Cash. If they were going to have him take the fall.

But as much as she was all about the truth and not keeping secrets, Izzy didn't need to know that. Not yet.

"That's possible," she agreed, though it killed her to put that look of worry in the girl's eyes. "But right now, it's just as possible as anything else. Do you…know anyone who'd want to hurt your dad?"

"I know my mother hated him. Hated all of us. So maybe someone who knew her?"

"Not a bad thread to tug." But someone who had a relationship with Chessa probably hadn't killed her. Probably. But if the Hudsons had enemies… "I'll look into it."

"Really?"

"Really. And if you think of anyone, or anything that seems fishy—not just lately but even years ago—you tell me. We'll see if we can put it all together."

"We?" Izzy asked suspiciously.

"Look, I'm not going to go behind your dad's back. I'm not going to lie to him. The way I see it, you all need to do better at working together. Not separately."

"He won't listen. He'll just keep hiding me away. Telling me to stay safe and stay out of it."

"Maybe," Carlyle agreed equitably. "But he'll be wrong to

do it, and I'll tell him so. We're going to work together on this one. All of us. I'll see to it." Because Izzy's thought process was a good one, and maybe they didn't need to terrify her with all the possibilities, but she had to feel like she wasn't just someone to be hidden away.

Izzy studied her with big, serious blue eyes. Carlyle didn't know what to do with the intense gaze, so she just…took it.

"I don't want anything to happen to him, Carlyle," Izzy said, her voice little more than a whisper. "Even when I'm mad, I…"

"Listen…" She figured if it worked for the father, why not for the daughter? "You don't have to worry about your dad. I'm going to look after him. I'm going to be his guardian angel." Then she couldn't resist it anymore. She pulled Izzy into a tight hug. "I swear, Iz. I'll keep him safe." *Both of you.* "Whatever I have to do."

She'd keep that promise, no matter what it took.

CARLYLE HAD BEEN RIGHT. First thing in the morning, two Bent County detectives were waiting in the living room before Cash had even gotten his coffee. He sidestepped them and took the back way into the kitchen before they saw him.

He needed to prepare himself.

Mary was already looking fresh and neat per usual, had coffee mercifully brewing, and a whole breakfast spread on its way.

"Don't you ever have morning sickness?"

"Why do you think I'm up this early? Wakes me up before the sun, but then when the sun comes up, I'm *starving.*" She nodded toward the front of the house. "They want to talk to all of us, but you first. I told them to wait," Mary said, frowning over the tray of breakfast foods she was putting together. "And suggested that the next time they wanted to do some questioning they should maybe call first. Or appear at a decent hour."

"Did they point out they're trying to solve a murder?"

Mary puffed out a breath. "Regardless. That's no excuse for bad manners."

"It probably is exactly the excuse for that."

Mary clearly did not agree, but she was not an arguer. "Take your time. Drink your coffee in here. I'll keep them busy until you're ready."

"I'll never be ready," Cash muttered. How did a person answer questions about their ex-wife's murder? His daughter's awful mother? He studied Mary, Carlyle's words from last night haunting him now that she'd been right about the cops' appearance.

"Carlyle's worried about my alibi."

Mary stopped what she was doing, looked at him, a slightly arrested expression on her face. "Walker said the same thing."

"Did you tell him the police know what they're doing, and I'm innocent so he's overreacting?"

Mary blinked. "Well. Yes."

"Yeah. I'm starting to wonder if we're *underreacting*."

"We have security footage," Mary said, her umbrage fully in place. "That will prove that you were here and—"

"Yeah, about that?" Palmer said, also coming into the kitchen through the back way. No doubt avoiding the cops too. "We don't have security footage."

"What?" Mary and Cash demanded in unison.

"I was up all night dealing with the security network. I figured the cops would want proof of where we all were, and that's easy enough, right?" Palmer poured himself a big mug of coffee. "It's all been wiped. Everything before the kidnapping attempt. It looks like some kind of...reset put in motion by the backup batteries failing, and maybe it is, but the timing is suspect."

Cash set his coffee down. This was...bad. Really, really bad.

"If Chessa was killed *after* the night Carlyle got stabbed, we've got all the footage we need. But..."

"It's going to be before," Cash finished for him.

"You don't know that," Mary insisted.

But he did. In his bones. Coincidences didn't just *happen*. Not like this.

"Just tell the truth," Mary said, even with worry etched into every inch of her expression. "You don't have anything to hide."

"Yeah," Cash agreed. He didn't have anything to hide, but he couldn't help but wonder if Carlyle would be right yet again. He took the mug of coffee. "Might as well get this over with," he grumbled, then he pushed off the counter and headed for the living room.

He knew the male detective. Thomas Hart was with Bent County and had worked on a few of their cases last year. He didn't know the blonde woman.

"Hart," he greeted. "Mary said you have some questions for me?"

They both stood up, and Thomas gestured toward the woman. "My partner, Detective Delaney-Carson."

"Ma'am."

She nodded and shook his hand, then they sat.

The woman took the lead. "A lot of this is just procedure. Outlining the players. Trying to get a sense of who might have seen Ms. Scott alive last."

Cash nodded. "I can guarantee you it wasn't me. I haven't actually seen her in years."

"There was a report from last year and the year before that she was on your property."

"The first time, she dealt with Anna and only Anna as far as I know. Second time, she was involved in the kidnapping and attempted murder, if I recall correctly, of Hawk Steele. All dealt with by other members of my family and the Sunrise Sheriff's Department."

"Where your brother is sheriff?" she asked lightly.

But it wasn't a question.

The detective made some notes on a pad of paper. Then continued to ask the usual inquiries. What was their relationship like? Non-existent. How did he feel about Chessa's lack of mothering? Ticked off but philosophical considering he didn't want Izzy around her when she was high. What did he know about Chessa's drug use and on and on.

But Cash *was* too much of an investigator at heart, even if he tried not to be. They were asking a lot of roundabout questions, but they were working up to something specific.

He waited them out, refusing to let his impatience show. They wouldn't hear anger or frustration when they listened to the interview tape back. They'd hear boredom and compliance.

"So, where were you the night of June first?"

And there it was. They had a time of death—some time the evening of June first. The day *before* the kidnap attempt. Now, they wanted his alibi. Cash blew out a breath. Trying to think of both the truth and how the hell he was going to get out of this. "Monday, right? Izzy's on summer break so our schedule is a little looser than normal, but I spend every night in the same place. In my cabin, on this property, with my daughter."

"Can you take us through that particular night?"

"I don't remember anything specific. But the usual pattern is eating dinner around six. Sometimes here at the main house, but if I remember correctly, we had spaghetti night at the cabin. Then we go play with the dogs until sunset. We go inside, Izzy takes a shower while I clean up the dinner mess. She goes to bed, then I watch TV, or do some reading, and then go to sleep."

"Alone, presumably?"

Cash wanted to scowl. Wanted to yell. Carlyle had been right. They didn't see it as enough of an alibi.

"It's okay. You can tell them."

Cash jerked at the new voice, looked over his shoulder at where Carlyle stood in the entrance to the room. She looked tired, but she was dressed for a morning of dog training. Swiftie sat at her feet, tail softly swishing back and forth.

"Tell them what?" he asked, wholly and utterly confused at what she thought she was doing.

"We've been keeping it on the down-low, but he wasn't alone. We were together."

What the hell was she doing? *Lying* to the cops? He stood and turned to face her, to try to get it through to her whatever she was doing was *not* the way to handle this, without giving anything away to the cops. "Carlyle."

But her gaze was steady on the detectives, her expression stubborn. "It's kind of a secret, but I'd rather tell the truth than have you guys looking in the wrong direction. I was with him. In his cabin. In his bedroom. For most of the night that night."

Chapter Six

"Can anyone corroborate that story?" the detective asked, keeping any thoughts she had on the subject closed behind an easygoing expression.

But Carlyle knew how to lie to cops. She knew how to make them believe it. She *knew*, and she'd made a promise to Izzy. "Like I said, it's a bit of a secret. We've been sneaking around. You know, family can be complicated, and we wanted to see where it went before Izzy got involved. Not to mention my brothers."

Carlyle watched as the two detectives exchanged a look. It wasn't disbelief exactly, but they certainly weren't falling for it hook, line and sinker. The woman wrote down a few lines in her notebook.

Carlyle moved farther into the room. She didn't dare look at Cash's expression. He was probably blowing the whole thing, so she had to focus on the cops. Focus on saving him from his noble self.

"I bet if you asked anyone around here, they'd say the same thing. Maybe they didn't *see* me at Cash's cabin, or know anything was going on, but they've wondered. Noticed little things. Maybe someone will remember something from that night, even."

"So, you're saying you were in Cash Hudson's cabin—"

"*Bedroom*," Carlyle corrected the male cop, hoping to God her cheeks weren't turning red. She could not actually *think* about being in Cash's bedroom, even as she convinced these cops that was just the usual.

"I saw Carlyle sneak into the main house very early that morning. Coming from the direction of Cash's cabin."

Everyone turned to Mary, who was pushing a little cart with a tray of food on top. She stopped the cart in front of the detectives. "Please, help yourselves. But Carlyle is right. I did see something, and I didn't say anything to anyone about it."

"Why not?"

"My husband is her very protective older brother, and Cash is *my* brother. I thought I'd just keep it to myself until they were ready to be open about it. It wasn't really any of my business what my adult brother and adult sister-in-law were getting up to in the middle of the night."

Carlyle wanted to cheer. Mary was lying. *Mary.* Carlyle might have expected the quick thinking and subterfuge of Anna, but Mary was so proper, so upstanding. But she was also always surprising people.

"What time was this?" the female detective asked, pen poised on the pad of paper.

"I don't know exactly. I'm up and down with morning sickness all night half the time. After midnight, definitely. So morning, but very early. Before the sun was up."

She was so smooth, and not too specific. *Just* specific enough to corroborate Carlyle's story and give a large window of an alibi to Cash. It was a *revelation*.

Carlyle had to look back at the detectives to keep from grinning. She couldn't look at Cash. It would ruin her act, she knew.

"Thank you for your cooperation. We'd like to speak to

Anna Hudson-Steele next. She had a run-in with Chessa Scott a while back?"

"She did," Mary said primly. "Help yourselves to food, detectives. My sister will be down once she's done *feeding* her baby." And with that, Mary sailed back into the kitchen.

"What about Hawk Steele? Can he be bothered this morning?" the man asked, with only a *hint* of sarcasm in his tone.

"Yeah, we'll go get him," Cash said. He took Carlyle by the elbow, and she realized she was the *we* in this situation. He pulled her out of the room, down the hallway, and didn't say a word.

When she finally worked up the nerve to look at his expression, it was a cold kind of fury she'd only ever seen on his face that night of the would-be kidnapping.

"If you're going to yell at me, you should probably wait until they're gone," Carlyle muttered under her breath. He didn't drop her arm even though they were out of earshot. He just dragged her along and up the stairs.

"I'm not going to yell at you," he muttered. He knocked softly on Anna and Hawk's door.

Hawk opened it, scowling already. But he was dressed, and Anna was rocking baby Caroline in the corner in her pajamas.

"I take it the cops want to talk to me."

"News travels fast. They asked for Anna first, though."

Hawk's scowl deepened. "I'll handle it."

"Oh, I don't mind talking to them once Caroline's done," Anna said. "Considering how often I have to feed this ravenous barnacle, it's going to be very hard to pin this one on me. They ask you for an alibi?" Anna asked Cash.

"Yeah," Cash said. He kept his expression carefully neutral. "For the night of June first. Carlyle supplied one."

"How did Carlyle supply an alibi for the whole night..."

Anna trailed off. "Oh." Her gaze was sharp—from Cash to Carlyle then back again. "Well."

Carlyle had to fight off another wave of embarrassment as Cash didn't explain it away. He let Hawk and Anna just... believe it was true. And she'd never been one for embarrassment, but this was just...weird.

"I'll go talk to them until you're ready," Hawk said darkly. He bent over and brushed a kiss across Anna's cheek, then Caroline's. "And when you come down, do not be yourself."

Anna grinned up at him. "I could not possibly fathom what you mean, darling."

He grunted, but turned and left the room. He closed the door behind him so Cash, Hawk and Carlyle all stood in the hall.

Hawk paused. "If they get too hung up looking at any of us, whoever actually did it is going to disappear."

Cash nodded grimly, but Carlyle didn't need to nod because hadn't that been her whole point with the fake alibi? This needed to be a concerted effort to not just rely on the cops who had to follow procedures and every viable option.

Hawk strode down the hallway toward the stairs. Carlyle moved to follow, but Cash took her by the arm again and pulled her down the hallway to a room at the end of it. She assumed it was the room he slept in when he stayed at the main house.

He closed the door behind them, and Carlyle tried not to feel nervous. She didn't do nervous. She'd done what was right, what would help. He could be mad at her all he wanted, but she was *right*.

And still, her stomach jittered with worry.

"You were right." He blew out a long breath. "They'll look into Anna because she had a fight with Chessa a long time ago. They'll look into Hawk because Chessa was involved in hurting him, but mostly they think I'm the prime suspect."

"So are you going to thank me for my quick thinking?" she asked, trying for her usual flippant tone.

He glared at her. "I don't like this. Lies come back to bite. Why do you think I let Anna think..." He shook his head. "It's best that only you, me and Mary know the alibi is a lie. I need you to agree to that."

"What about Walker? I don't mind lying to him, but you're going to have to make sure Mary is okay with it."

"Hell, I don't know. I guess that's up to Mary."

"What about Izzy? They're going to want to question her."

"They can go to hell."

"Cash—"

"Don't. Don't start on the she needs to have some choice or power or whatever."

He sounded so...at the end of his rope. Just barely hanging on by a thread. She wanted to soothe him somehow. But now wasn't the time. They had to act. He had to get over this hang-up. "Okay. I won't start on that, but... Izzy has some theories."

"Theories?"

"About how the events might connect. About who the actual target might be. She's smart. She's—"

"Twelve."

"Yeah, Cash. *Twelve*. Not two. She's looking for patterns, links, and she's worried about you. Scared to death *you'll* get hurt in all this. We have to work together. All of us. Maybe the cops will beat us to answers, but maybe they won't. So, let's *all* work together. On the same page. *With* Izzy. If you let her in on this, at least a little, she's not going to be crying in my room worrying that you're going to end up like Chessa."

She hadn't *meant* to let the crying part spill, but she didn't know how to get through his thick skull.

He closed his eyes, clearly in pain—emotional pain. And she couldn't stop herself anymore. She crossed the room to him, put her hand over his heart.

"You're both trying so hard to protect each other that you are shutting each other out, and I don't think that's what either of you want, Cash."

He opened his eyes and looked down at her. A million things swam in the dark depths, mostly bad things. Hurt and worry and she just wanted to *fix* it for him. Her free hand came up and touched his cheek.

"I promise, letting her in isn't going to ruin her life. Giving her some agency isn't going to fling her into danger. She's already *in* danger. Let's give her the tools to find some power. And protect the hell out of her while we do. All of us. Your siblings. Mine. And your amazing daughter. I have faith in the Hudson-Daniels machine, Cash. Do you?"

He inhaled slowly and she knew she should take her hand off his face. She knew she should step away.

But she didn't. As the moment stretched out, she just stood there, while he slowly let out his breath and didn't move away.

But when he inhaled again, he patted her hand, as if she was a child, and then stepped back. "Thanks, Carlyle," he said, though his voice was rough. "You're right. Let's get everyone together and go from there."

Then he left her in that room, heart feeling bruised and wrung out, tears she didn't understand in her eyes. But she'd gotten her point across.

Everyone together.

She had to believe that would matter.

CASH TENDED TO avoid big family meetings. He didn't like Izzy getting too involved in whatever was going on, particularly ever since Izzy had witnessed a gun to Anna's head last year. But Carlyle had been insistent and… He wanted her to be wrong about it, but no matter how he looked at it, he couldn't convince himself she was.

She understood Izzy's position too well. And she was right, the Hudson-Daniels machine was better than any police department in the world.

She just kept being right. He rubbed at his chest, where she'd put her hand. Like she could impress upon him all these truths he'd been avoiding for years. Like she could just crumble all those walls he'd built to keep his daughter safe.

And failed, time and time again.

He could admit failure. You couldn't be a parent for twelve years, particularly under the circumstances in which he'd been a parent, and think you couldn't fail, but gathering up all his siblings to discuss that failure felt a bit *much*.

But they all gathered, in the big living room with his siblings where they'd once crushed together on the couch to watch movies. Their parents would always make a huge batch of popcorn and then curl up on the love seat that he now had at his cabin.

He'd always thought those first few years without them would be the hardest. Being a teenager, not knowing what happened to them. But it was now. With Izzy nearing the age he'd been when he lost them. With his memories of them getting fuzzier and fuzzier.

When he was so tired, so exhausted and wrung out he wanted to lay the weight of all this awfulness on someone else's lap. Just for a minute or two.

He supposed, if he let himself get over the whole *failure* part, this was as close to that as he was going to get. Anna in Hawk's lap on the armchair, Caroline's baby monitor on the little table next to them. Palmer and Louisa and Grant and Dahlia shoved together on the couch, in the almost exact same position—his brother's arm around his fiancée. Walker and Mary on the window seat. Zeke, Walker and Carlyle's brother who lived in Sunrise and kept somewhat more separate from everyone else, stood next to them, arms crossed over his chest.

He almost perfectly mirrored Jack, who stood on the other side of the room, looking grim, while Izzy and Carlyle lay on the floor with the dogs.

Cash never ran these meetings. He'd been as separate as he could be. Now, this was his problem and he had to take charge.

"So, we all know what happened. Chessa was murdered on June first. Sometime at night. The police have now questioned me, Hawk, Anna and Jack. What's next?" Cash looked at Jack. Since he was the sheriff, had even worked for Bent County for the first few years of his police career, he'd have an idea of their investigative tactics.

"Now that they have a time of death, likely, they'll start looking into her movements that night. If they can narrow down the location of the last place she was seen alive, they'll try to find people who saw her, get their impressions."

"Any idea where she was found?"

"They're being really careful because they don't want me to know too much and pass it on to you. But Chloe talked to the coroner. Didn't get much, but she thinks she was found *in* Bent."

"My money is on Rightful Claim. The saloon there? If Chessa was in Bent, she didn't pass up going to a bar." Anna turned to her husband. "We could go have a night on the town. Ask some questions."

Hawk shook his head. "The guy who owns that saloon is married to Detective Delaney-Carson," Hawk said, referring to the female detective. "I don't think going there and questioning anyone is a good idea if it might get back to the detective. We need Bent County to think we're just waiting for them to solve it."

"I could do it," Zeke said. "I know how to be stealthy, and I don't have as known of a connection to you guys. At least in Bent." He turned his gaze from Anna and Hawk to Cash.

Because, apparently, this was somehow *his* deal, when he'd avoided making these kinds of decisions for twelve years.

Cash gave him a nod. "That'll work. Palmer, any fixes for the missing security footage?"

Palmer shook his head. "It's been wiped, that's for sure. I've got a friend over in Wilde seeing if he can't do better than me, but it's not looking good. But to that point, Chessa wasn't acting alone. Clearly. She didn't have that kind of skill or background. By my way of thinking, whoever killed her worked with her on that kidnapping attempt."

"It wasn't Chessa at my window the other night," Izzy said. She'd moved so she was pressed against Carlyle, like she was looking for some comfort. Cash waited to feel some kind of… discomfort or jealousy, but he could only feel gratitude that Izzy had different people to lean on, gain confidence from.

God knew Carlyle had more than her share.

"How do you know that?" Jack asked gently.

"I don't know. It just…wasn't. She…she's like…" Izzy threw her hands in the air, clearly struggling to find the words she wanted to. "She's just not careful. She would have just… like bashed in the window or something. Aunt Anna, when she came here that one Christmas, you said she was a bull in a china shop. Always had been."

Anna nodded. "Yeah, *careful* isn't Chessa's usual style, but… She knew how much trouble she could get into. Maybe she figured out how to be stealthy."

Izzy shook her head and so did Carlyle.

"Whoever ran into me was pretty…solid," Carlyle said.

"From everything you guys have told me, Chessa was shorter, less substantial. Whoever knocked me to the ground was taller than me. Wider. If Chessa was involved, it wasn't her at the window, and it wasn't her doing the security stuff. Maybe we need to consider the fact she wasn't involved at all?"

Cash looked at her. *Knocked me to the ground* when she'd been stabbed. Because there was the whole truth and then there was being careful about not overwhelming Izzy with it. He had to appreciate the fact Carlyle saw some nuance and balance to the situation.

Carlyle dipped her head, whispered something into Izzy's ear. Izzy frowned, but then she nodded. "I don't think the kidnapping thing was about me. Or Chessa, really. I know she told Uncle Hawk she wanted to sell me or whatever, but that was just about getting money."

Cash felt like he'd been stabbed. She'd *heard* that? When he'd worked so hard to keep her in the dark about the worst things Chessa could be.

"Go on. Say the rest," Carlyle encouraged, while Cash reeled. But Izzy wasn't done dropping bombs.

Izzy took a deep breath. "I think someone wants to hurt *you*, Dad. Or maybe the whole family. But mostly you."

And Cash was left utterly speechless.

Chapter Seven

Carlyle watched as the color simply leached out of Cash's face. It made Carlyle feel awful for him, but at the same time, she thought that reaction was good. He wasn't denying it out of hand.

He knew it wasn't just possible, it was a *reasonable* theory. Which meant they could act on it, instead of wasting time trying to convince him it was possible.

It had taken Izzy a lot of courage to say it to a room full of adults, and no one was arguing with her or discounting her. It warmed Carlyle's heart, because her brothers had *always* meant well, but they'd been young men saddled with the responsibility of a little sister. They'd discounted her, scoffed at her, and often made her feel foolish without *meaning* to.

But the Hudsons knew better. They were mature, and had the experiences and enough of a framework to all instinctively give Izzy the feeling she'd helped.

"If someone was targeting Cash, Chessa would be at the top of the list," Jack said, not as a counterpoint, but more thoughtfully. Like thinking Izzy's point through. "Izzy is on to something, but I don't think we can fully discount Chessa's involvement."

"Absolutely. Chessa could very well be involved," Carlyle offered. "But she's not the *point*. She's…"

"A pawn," Anna finished for Carlyle. "She was a pawn last year. Darrin Monroe used her because she hated us. But his goal wasn't her goal. She wasn't…with it enough to have a clear goal. It was about feeding the addiction. Not about like…actual plots and plans."

"She could have gotten mixed up with someone who had the plots and plans, and she was the one who chose the target," Cash said grimly, and with a careful look at his daughter.

Because even though by all accounts Chessa was a bit of a monster, wanting to sell her own child, Cash cared about how that affected his daughter.

"I think we should go back and look through what happened with the guy who wanted revenge on you guys. Who was involved, beyond him and Chessa. Let me look at the file or report or whatever. Yours or Sunrise's. Maybe I'll see something you guys didn't since you know all the players." Carlyle looked around the room. She couldn't make out what everyone's expressions meant, but there was really only one person who mattered.

She glanced at Cash.

But it was Jack who spoke. "He just had a personal vendetta against us. Darrin is in a high-security psychiatric hospital, so I just don't see how it could connect."

"I don't either. Not yet. And maybe it doesn't. But isn't that what we do?" Mary asked. "Pull threads until something unravels. This is another thread to pull, and it's less likely to draw the attention of Bent County. Zeke sees if he can gather anything in Bent. Carlyle goes over that case. Chloe keeps trying to see what other information she can get out of Bent County to pass along to Jack."

The conversation from then on was more logistics than anything else, and Izzy practically climbed into Carlyle's lap. Carlyle held the girl close, hoping Cash didn't see this as a failure. That just because Izzy was upset didn't mean she shouldn't be here. Upset was just part of the deal when your mother was murdered, whether you loved her or not.

When they finally started to scatter, Cash reached down and helped Izzy to her feet. "Come on. Time for bed." Copper got up too, so Carlyle got to her feet. Before Cash led Izzy away, Izzy turned and threw her arms around Carlyle.

She hugged the girl back, reluctant to let go. There was no way to convince Izzy she was safe. Carlyle knew that better than anyone, but she was understanding more and more the lengths her brothers had gone to try. The lengths Cash and his family went to try.

When Izzy finally released her from the hug, she grabbed her hand. "Come with," she said.

Carlyle didn't know where she was coming with to, but she wasn't about to argue with the girl. She let Izzy lead her, side by side with Cash, deeper into the house and up the stairs, Copper and Swiftie following along.

They stopped at a door and Izzy turned to Carlyle and wrapped her arms around her one more time. "Thank you," she whispered, and squeezed tight.

Carlyle hugged her back, running a hand over her braid. "No thanks necessary, Iz. Friends help each other out."

Izzy's mouth curved, the first smile Carlyle had seen on her face all day. Cash opened the door and silently led Izzy inside with Copper. She was sharing Caroline's nursery, because it was in the center of the house, and because there was a video baby monitor in there.

Caroline was already asleep in her crib, so Izzy had to sneak in quietly. Cash moved behind her, tucked her in. They whispered something to each other, and Carlyle knew she shouldn't stand there and *watch*, but she couldn't help herself.

He loved his daughter *so* much. There was no doubt he'd

do anything and everything to keep her safe, and the fact he wasn't perfect at it only made the whole thing…that much more poignant. That you could love someone so hard, and fail again and again, and just keep trying.

It put a weird lump in her throat, and a longing in her heart she didn't understand.

When Cash exited the room, pulling the door carefully closed behind him, he gestured for her to follow him. She didn't know what else to do. All worked up internally, she really wanted to go hide in her room and work on some kind of…protection against all this *feeling*.

Instead, she followed him into the bedroom from yesterday.

The bedroom he was staying in.

He closed the door behind them, leaving the dog on the other side.

It was nothing, Carlyle *knew* it was nothing and yet she could also feel the heat climbing into her cheeks. Her stomach fluttered at the mere…thought.

Get it together.

"That was productive," she offered, trying to sound her usual irreverent self…and fearing it came out more like the squeaky words of a coward. "The Hudson-Daniels show is on a roll."

"Between Zeke going to Bent and you going over an old case, it's sounding more like the Daniels show."

"Does it matter who's doing it if it gets done?" she countered, feeling defensive and sympathetic all at the same time.

"No, it doesn't," he said, with a kind of firmness that brooked no argument. Or the kind of firmness someone used when they were trying to convince themselves of something.

He said nothing else, made no effort to break the silence or explain to her why she was here.

"So…" She had no idea why he'd brought her in here, and

the longer they stood, in his room, alone, on opposite sides of a messily made *bed*, the more she wanted to jump out of her own skin.

"Look, there needs to be some effort to…" He trailed off, never finishing his sentence.

"To what?" she asked, since she sincerely had no idea what he was talking about.

He opened his mouth, closed it, then a knock interrupted whatever he was going to come up with. He sighed heavily, then gave her a sharp look.

"Look rumpled."

"What?"

"You came up with this alibi. Now you gotta play along with it." Then he stalked over to the door, clearly unhappy with the whole situation. Cash opened the door, and her brother stood at the threshold.

When Walker saw *her*, looking rumpled as ordered, sitting on the edge of the bed, his eyes hardened.

So, she grinned at him. "Heya, Walk."

CASH WISHED IT WAS…literally anyone else. Except maybe Zeke. He did not want to deal with either of Carlyle's brothers over something that wasn't even true.

No matter how she'd blushed when he'd closed the door behind them. Which was not something he could think about. Certainly not his body's response to it. Not now. Not ever.

He wasn't thrilled about this turn of events, but he had to see it through. And if Walker was standing there looking like he might actually take a piece out of him, it meant Mary hadn't spilled the beans about this all being fake.

Which was something. Not that Cash particularly wanted to play along with this fiction, but he felt like he didn't have a choice. They'd used it with the cops, now it just had to be…

"What the hell are you two doing?" Walker demanded.

Carlyle's eyes got real wide, comically wide. Clearly, she was needling her brother. "Talking, Walker. Whatever else could we be up to?" She walked over and stood next to Cash. Too close, judging by the way Walker's gaze got even harder. Cash wouldn't know because he was keeping his gaze resolutely anywhere but on her.

"Laying it on a little thick, Car," Cash muttered, torn between a dark kind of amusement, because it *was* funny, and just...wishing he was not in the middle of any part of this situation.

Carlyle moved to face him, so he *had* to look at her, and she trailed her finger down his chest—*Jesus*—and smirked. "That's what I do, babe."

Then she flounced out of the room, over Walker's sputtering. Swiftie got up and followed her down the hallway.

Cash regretted every decision that had led him here.

Particularly when Walker's rather large hands clenched into fists. "I want to know what's going on between you and Carlyle. What you think you're doing with my baby sister, who's a good seven years younger than you."

Cash might have felt some sympathy for Walker, what with having two younger sisters of his own. He understood the need to be protective, to maybe warn a guy off. But one of those sisters was Walker's wife, so... "What's the age difference between you and Mary again?"

"Less than seven," Walker said darkly.

"Yeah, by like a *month*," Cash replied with as much sarcasm as he could muster. "You don't have much of a leg to stand on, you know. My sister got kidnapped because of you. I don't recall getting involved." Because he never did, did he? And it hadn't helped him at all. "So far, I've given your sister a job and—"

"Yeah, *and*. The *and* is what I'm ticked about."

Cash scrubbed his hands over his face. "Isn't my current circumstance enough of a disaster without whatever this is?"

"Yeah, and you've got my sister involved in it."

"She got herself involved. I tried to stop her. A million, trillion people could try to stop her. She doesn't *stop*. Don't pretend you don't know that."

"She's got a bad habit of wanting to help a lost cause."

Cash laughed, a little bitterly, because boy was he a damn lost cause. "What do you want me to say, Walker? To do? Because unless it involves mind control, we both know *she* is going to do whatever the hell she wants."

"You just steer clear. She doesn't need to get messed up in this. She shouldn't be at those meetings, or in your room, or getting *stabbed*, Cash." Then he turned around, like he'd given a directive he expected to be followed wholesale, no argument.

Which was right. Cash shouldn't be able to argue with it, because it was all things he'd said about his daughter, and if he didn't have a daughter, things he'd likely be saying about his sisters.

But…maybe Carlyle had gotten to him because he could see this too easily from *her* point of view. Not Walker's or his.

"Maybe you don't give her enough credit, Walker."

Walker stopped at the doorway. Turned, slowly. Cash was sure it was meant to be intimidating, but he was too tired and Walker wasn't any older or stronger or different than him.

If anything, they were too damn much alike.

"Excuse me?" he asked, very slowly.

"So far, your sister has proven my instincts wrong at just about every turn. You think I was going to let my daughter sit in the middle of that meeting, talking about her mother's murder? Hell no. That was all Carlyle. Because as she likes to keep telling me, she's been in Izzy's shoes."

There was a flicker of something in Walker's expression that Cash recognized all too well. Guilt. Because boy had they walked damn similar paths.

"I get it. Better than anyone, probably. The way you feel. The things you do to protect someone you love who you see as more vulnerable. But Carlyle's not. No more vulnerable than you. Than me. She's smart and she's strong. Not invincible, though she might think it, but the thing she seems most adamant about is that she doesn't need someone to swoop in and save her or hide her away from the bad things. And I realize I'm not a great catch, but I'm hardly a bad thing you need to save her from."

"Maybe. I know she can't see it that way, but for *me*, I have been Carlyle's dad from the time she was Izzy's age, whether any of us liked it or not. So it doesn't matter how old, how not-vulnerable, how whatever she gets, I'm always going to do what I can to protect her. It's what fathers do, and I know you know that."

"Yeah, I do know that. Understand it. But recall, we've got our own orphan situation over here. There's a reason no one bashed your face in when you started up with Mary. Because we could all see you were so head over heels in love with her, you'd destroy yourself before you hurt her on purpose. It isn't always about…protecting them from every difficulty."

"You saying you're in love with my sister?" Walker asked, a little *too* casually.

Damn. "I'm saying, do you really think I'm going to do anything to mess her up? Do you, knowing my family, knowing me, really think she needs you to butt in? Bud, she'll kick my ass from here to Kentucky if she sees fit. And I can't go anywhere, so I'll just have to suck it up and have my ass kicked."

"Maybe if you didn't have the kid, but she's got a soft spot for Izzy. She won't hurt you if it'd hurt your daughter."

Cash wondered if the blows would ever just stop, give him a chance to breathe, adjust, move on and heal one bruise before another came. "Fine, I give you permission to kick my ass if it comes to it. Happy?"

Walker studied him. "I'll send Zeke to do it. He's meaner." But he grinned, a bit too much like Carlyle for comfort. Then he sobered up. "I know you're a good guy, Cash. That's not the issue. The issue is you got a kid to put first, and at some point... Carlyle deserves a life where she gets to come in first."

"I'm sure she does," Cash agreed, surprised to find that it...hurt more than it should that he agreed with Walker. Because this was all pretend. Not real. So it didn't matter what he couldn't give her.

And never would.

Chapter Eight

With extra people in the main house, Carlyle felt even less like she could sleep with the lights on. Which meant sleeping was a bit of a bust, and now that she'd been traumatized and stabbed from something as simple as looking out the window on a starry night, that was hardly the relaxing pastime it had once been.

Maybe she just needed a snack. Something heavy and fatty that would make her nice and sleepy. She left her room, ready to sneak over to the kitchen, but something...creaked above.

Someone was moving around upstairs. And considering there were what felt like a hundred people in this house, it could be anyone. Hell, it could be the house settling.

But her gut had been right last time. Someone bad *had* been outside. Maybe it was unlikely anyone *bad* had gotten upstairs, but it wasn't *impossible*.

She looked at Swiftie. The dog would make too much noise if she followed. Carlyle crouched, looked the dog in the eye. "Stay," she whispered firmly.

Heart pounding, nerves humming, she snuck her way up the stairs, being careful to try and avoid the ones that squeaked. She'd learned long ago to make sure she knew how to move around anywhere she was living without making a noise.

But when she carefully crested the stairs, the hallway was

illuminated by a night-light plugged into the wall. There was no lurking shadow or stranger.

Just Cash.

Not walking up and down the hallway, not going from one room to another. Just sitting on the hallway floor, his back to the wall right next to Izzy's door. Carlyle figured she should probably turn around, sneak back downstairs and...leave it. Leave this.

But he looked so *alone*, and she just couldn't stand it. She purposefully made some noise before stepping into his line of vision.

His head snapped up, but once he recognized her, some of the tenseness in his shoulders released. "What are you doing up?" he asked in a whisper when she got close enough.

"Can't sleep." She didn't need to ask him what he was doing. It was pretty obvious. She went ahead and moved into a sitting position on the floor next to him. "Going to sit out here all night?"

"No." He had his legs out in front of him, his head resting back against the wall. Kind of the picture of defeat, but she knew he wasn't defeated. Because he'd never give up while his daughter might be in danger. That was just the kind of guy he was. Why else would she be halfway to messed up over him?

"I know she's okay," he said, like Carlyle had demanded an explanation when she hadn't. "But sometimes..."

"I think you've got all the fairest reasons to be a little paranoid. But you know what I do when I can't sleep?"

He looked over at her, one eyebrow raised. "Roam the house? Sneak around in the dark getting stabbed?"

She kept her laugh quiet. "Yeah, that. And find something productive to do. Let's go unearth that case file you guys were talking about tonight. We can go over it together until we're too sleepy to fight it."

"I wasn't involved in that case. I don't get involved in cases." He said it so firmly.

She understood this wasn't stubbornness for the sake of being stubborn, but something he needed to believe. That by keeping his nose out of things, he wasn't just protecting Izzy *now*, but always had been. That the choice, the sacrifice had been the *right* one.

But Carlyle knew all too well sometimes there was no *right* choice, there was only what you did to survive. Physically. Emotionally.

Sometimes it felt like she understood him better than she understood herself. Because she understood what he felt, but not why she was being all soft and gooey over this mess of a man in the privacy of her own head.

But here she was. "Involved or not, you were there. And so was Izzy." *And so was Chessa*, but she didn't say that out loud because she didn't think it needed to be said. She got back to her feet, held out a hand. "Come on. Better than sitting here like a sad weirdo."

He snorted, and it took him a second or two, but he finally took her offered hand and let her help him up. She wanted to keep holding onto his hand, but she dropped it. She might be gooey, but she was no fool.

"She wouldn't be happy to find you out here," Carlyle said. Not an admonition, just a reminder.

He shook his head. "I know."

Carlyle nodded, then turned away from him and the urge to put her arms around him and *comfort* him. She headed back downstairs, where they'd be able to talk at a more reasonable level and Carlyle knew there was a room full of files.

And they could focus on *that*, not this feeling inside of her.

Swiftie was waiting at the bottom of the stairs, then followed as they made their way to the office.

"Wait here, I'll get the keys," Cash said.

So she waited by the door to the office. She reminded herself she was just…helping him out. Giving him something to do. Giving herself something to do. It was better than going stir-crazy in that little bedroom, desperately trying *not* to think about him.

And his bed.

She nearly jumped a foot high when he returned, because she'd been too busy trying to push that thought away that she hadn't even been listening. He unlocked the door and pushed it open, moving inside first. He went right for a file cabinet, shuffled through some folders, then pulled one out.

He turned to face her, but the room was so crowded with stuff—filing cabinets and security equipment and an array of computers and printers—there wasn't much space at all.

Just them facing each other in a small, dim room. Even the dog had stayed outside the doorway.

It was too small. They were too close. It was too…

"Let's go out into the living room," he suggested.

Carlyle nodded and followed him out to the spacious living room. She sat down on the couch, but then he sat right next to her.

So much for distance.

He opened the file and spread out the contents on the coffee table as Swiftie settled herself under the table. "Jack double-checked earlier. Darrin is still in the state hospital under maximum guard. Jack should have a list of anyone who's visited him by tomorrow, the next day at the latest. So, we'll look into it, but it just feels like a dead end."

Carlyle picked up a few pieces of paper stapled together. It outlined everything that had happened. "Who wrote this account?"

"Everyone. Anna started it with everything she knew, then we each went over it and added things."

Carlyle read the entire document, then went through it line by line to try to work out any players the Hudsons might have overlooked. Chessa had been arrested before Darrin had made an appearance. She'd worked with him to take Hawk against his will, but Chessa was the one who got caught and arrested.

But then she'd been let go. Her bail posted by one of the Hudson ranch hands. A traitor, basically.

"What about this cop who let Chessa go?" she asked, pointing at the name *Bryan Ferguson*.

"What about him? He just followed procedure. Tripp Anthony, on the order of Darrin Monroe, is the one who paid her bail and got her out because Darrin was paying him too. There was nothing out of the ordinary on the cop's side. Just a mistake."

"But wouldn't he know that Chessa wasn't your average jailbird? Wouldn't he know Jack was involved and give him some warning? It seems like an epic screwup to let her go and two hours pass before Jack finds out."

"Jack chewed him a new one, I'm pretty sure. It was all on the up and up, procedure wise. I don't know that it's some great conspiracy when it had been an honest mistake. Jack trusts his team."

She was about to argue with that, but he held up a hand. "*But* we can see what Jack has to say in the morning. Mary's right, it's all just pulling at threads. We pull at them all, no matter how seemingly pointless or wrong, until we have answers."

Carlyle nodded. But she looked at the name. Honest mistakes happened all the time, but a cop should know better.

Cash yawned. "And I think I've hit the wall of exhaustion that *might* let me get a few hours before chores. We should try to get some sleep."

Carlyle nodded and knew she should just…agree. Not chase

the desperate desire to keep him right here. "You know, I could hang out in your room. Emerge in the morning. Really let everyone talk. I could sleep in a chair or on the floor or something. Not suggesting we share a bed or anything."

He paused—midstretch—like she'd done something really shocking. But then he dropped his arms, and expressly did *not* look her in the eye.

"Not a terrible idea, but Izzy might see, and I wouldn't want Izzy to get the wrong idea. I'm not sure how she'd feel. I know she loves you, but she's never seen me with anyone before."

Carlyle knew Cash leaned toward *monk*, but she thought it was more a recent phenomenon. He'd been like seventeen when Izzy was born, probably not even twenty when he'd gotten divorced. Surely in his younger years he'd... "Never?"

Cash shrugged. "Weirdly, the disastrous end of my marriage made me a little leery of trying to start something up with someone and a toddler at home makes it a little hard to take a night off and...have fun."

"I call baloney. You've always had like five built-in babysitters."

"Not *always*. Between Jack's work schedule, and Grant being deployed for a while, Anna and Palmer doing the rodeo, Mary going to college. It's not like now. Everyone scattered."

Except him. He'd always been right here. Because of Izzy. "So you just..." She shook her head. She just couldn't believe it. She'd found time to have a little *fun* when she'd been the target of a murderer, so... She narrowed her eyes at him. "You just didn't want anyone to *know* you were off to get laid."

He made a choking noise, which of course was why she'd put it like that.

"Regardless of *why*, I wasn't. I..." He shook his head. "Why are we having this discussion?"

"You're not saying… Like, *all* this what? Decade? Since you've been divorced you haven't once—"

"Please don't say *get laid* again. Carlyle, this is not…" But he clearly couldn't find the words. She didn't know if it was embarrassment or what. She did know she should let it go.

But she couldn't.

"That's a long, long time not to…have *fun*."

"Good night, Carlyle," he said firmly, and stalked off. She heard the stairs squeak under his weight, could track his progress to his room down the hallway.

She sighed. *Ten years.* All because he had a kid at home? No, it had to be more complicated than that. It had to be something about his marriage, about Chessa.

Who was dead. Murdered. And the real thing she needed to focus on. She stayed in the living room, forced herself to go over the report, and not consider any *fun* she could have with Cash Hudson.

CASH WOKE UP in a foul mood. He could blame it on murder and being a suspect and not being able to sleep in his own damn house, but mostly it was the fact that Carlyle asking him about *fun* had really messed with his mind.

Because it was far too easy to imagine having fun with *her*, and considering his ex-wife was dead and he was suspect number one, that was really not the place his mind should be drifting.

Ever. But especially now.

He had long ago convinced himself that sex was unnecessary. That the enjoyment of it—just like booze and carelessness—was for the young and unencumbered. While Palmer had been sleeping his way through half of Sunrise, Cash had considered himself *better*. Or tried to.

Now…

He threw the covers off, trying not to groan out loud. It was early yet, but an early breakfast, a gallon of coffee and some work with the dogs could maybe take his mind off all the annoying caveats it seemed bound and determined to wander down.

Once downstairs, the smell of breakfast filled the air like it usually did. Mary had already been up and about, whipping up her normal spread. They'd really be in for it once she had the baby and had to take some time off from being the organizer and cook and keeping them all in line.

Mary wasn't in the kitchen, but he helped himself to the food out on warmers. When Cash got to the dining room, there was no one to be found except Jack. He was dressed in his sheriff uniform—khaki pants and a perfectly pressed Sunrise polo. He had his phone in one hand and a fork in the other.

"Morning," Cash offered.

"Morning," Jack replied, setting down his phone. "Sleep okay?"

Cash chuckled, only a little bitterly. "Sure. Nothing like a little possible murder charge to really help a guy sleep."

Jack's return smile was wry.

"Carlyle and I went over the file last night. Couldn't sleep. She wants us to look deeper into Deputy Ferguson."

Jack's expression darkened. "I haven't let him forget what a colossal mistake that was. But the kid is ineffectual at best. Not a cold-blooded killer."

"I know. But what have we got to lose to let her poke into him? Maybe it unties some other knot."

Jack nodded. Not because he thought he was wrong about Ferguson, but because this was how you investigated. And maybe their expertise was cold cases, but it was the same. The way he saw it, they were trying to avoid a cold case.

Just as much as they were trying to avoid him going to jail.

And as much as he should focus on Ferguson, avoiding jail, etcetera, all he could think about was Carlyle. What she'd said last night, and why she'd made him question if he'd been doing the right thing all these years by avoiding *fun*.

In front of him sat his role model, so to speak. "You've been single forever."

Jack paused with the fork full of egg halfway up to his mouth, then set it down on the plate. "I'm sorry. What?"

"If you have a night out on the town, you certainly keep it on the down-low. I've never once met a woman you were dating. At least, not since *you* were in high school, which I'll be kind and point out was a very long time ago."

Jack blinked. Once. His face had gotten very carefully blank. "I'll repeat myself. *What?*"

"I'm just trying to work out why you've kept yourself living like a monk all these years. I know why *I* do. It made sense for a while, but it doesn't anymore."

Jack's voice took on that holier-than-thou, I'm-in-charge iciness. "I don't see what business it is of yours, Cash. I don't see why we're having this conversation."

"I spent ten years quite convinced I was making the best, most right choice for Izzy by staying away from even a hint of…fun. I assumed you were making the same choice for us. But here we are, all adults. Most of your little chicks married. Why still live like a monk?"

"If this is because you decided to hook up with Carlyle and think I need some kind of…encouragement to go have *fun*, I feel like I should remind you of something far more important. You are the main suspect in the murder investigation of your ex-wife and your daughter's mother. Don't concern yourself with my personal life."

"Or lack thereof?"

"Sure. Right. Just… Can we focus on Ferguson?"

Cash had the totally foundation-crumbling realization that his brother was lying. He *did* have a personal life, or thought he did. Hidden somewhere.

But now was not the time to dig into it.

Probably.

He heard someone in the kitchen, and since Swiftie pranced in and took a seat under the table, Cash figured it was Carlyle.

Then Carlyle appeared, plate piled high. "Morning, boys," she said, sliding into the seat next to Cash. She gave the first bite of food to Swiftie, which Cash should scold her for.

But he didn't.

"Sounded a bit tense. Are we bickering in here?" She made a little tsk-tsking sound.

And Cash had the fully out-of-body, out-of-character impulse to follow Carlyle's example. Irreverent. Never afraid to say the wrong thing, the shocking thing.

"I was just talking to Jack about relationships."

"Juicy."

"I'm beginning to think he has a secret one."

Carlyle's eyes widened. Jack's glare was *glacial*. Cash couldn't help but grin.

"You've really rubbed off on him, Carlyle," Jack said, standing. "Enjoy each other's company while it lasts, I suppose. Because if we don't figure out the *true* concerns of the day, Cash might be spending his mornings talking with the other inmates in Bent County Jail."

And with that, he left.

Carlyle let out a low whistle. "I've never seen him react that way, even to Anna. Why are you picking on your poor brother?"

"Misery loves company?"

She laughed. "What did he say about Bryan Ferguson?"

"He stuck with his initial assessment but gave you free rein to poke into him as you see fit. If you find a lead, he'll follow it." She shoveled some eggs into her mouth and nodded along.

"Excellent," she said.

And he found he couldn't quite stop looking at her. She wasn't fear*less*, but she did a hell of a job acting it. She wasn't reckless with things that were important, but she clearly only counted *people* as important, and his daughter was one of those people. She had a whole different outlook on the world, but at its core the things she valued were the same as the things he valued.

A strange, twisting and oddly weight-lifting realization to have.

She must have noticed his staring. She turned to him, those expressive blue-gray eyes confused as she wiped at her face. "What? Egg on my face?"

"No. Nothing," he replied, because he didn't have the words for *what*, but he was starting to think he needed to figure them out.

Chapter Nine

Carlyle used her beat-up old laptop to do a rudimentary search on Bryan Ferguson. While she was at it, she started looking into the ranch hand who'd facilitated the payment of the bail. He'd died, but that didn't mean there weren't connections somewhere.

Her entire life had been about following the strange, twisting turns of connection. And then avoiding them when she could.

When she thought her eyes would cross, she went outside and over to the dog barn. It was technically her day off, but she would needle Cash into giving her some work to do. She had to work out her body so her mind—which was going in circles—didn't drive her over the edge.

She'd have liked to have been the one teaching Izzy how to shoot, but in the end that job had gone to Grant, who had the most patience out of anyone. Besides, with the stitches, no one wanted her repeatedly shooting a weapon, no matter how well she could handle it.

So, she went to the dog barn instead. Cash had all kinds of dogs. So there was always all kinds of work to do. She tended to avoid the paperwork if she could. She much preferred the training and being outside.

Swiftie followed her over to where Cash had three of his

younger dogs. He had Izzy up on a horse, and Carlyle quickly realized this was less about training the dogs themselves, and more about giving Izzy the opportunity to train.

He stood, elbows resting on the top of the fence while Izzy took the horse through a walk then a gallop, and shouted different commands to the dogs. Carlyle came to stand beside Cash.

"It's your day off," he said by way of greeting.

"I knew you were going to throw that in my face. I needed a break from my computer. Consider today volunteer work."

He rolled his eyes, but they both stood and watched as Izzy expertly put the dogs and horse through their paces. Carlyle grinned. "Damn, she's a natural, isn't she?"

"It comes with growing up on a ranch surrounded by animals, but she's got a special touch with them, that's for sure." All proud dad. She wanted to lean her head against his shoulder and just enjoy the moment.

If she said that to anyone, they'd think it out of character. She was loud. She was wild. Not traditional, not *soft*.

But sometimes, that armor she'd spent so long building started to feel heavy, like it needed to be taken off.

She sighed and watched Izzy maneuver the horse and command the dogs, all the while keeping a respectable space between her and Cash. Little glimpses of the woman Izzy would grow up to be someday flashed through her mind.

Carlyle watched, but no matter how much she wanted a distraction, her mind kept going back to the problem at hand. Izzy as a kid. Izzy as a woman. It got her thinking. Did she need to look back *further* into the cop's and the former ranch hand's lives? Not just rap sheets—Tripp a small, petty one up to his involvement last year, Ferguson nothing—but maybe earlier in their lives to try and find a connection to each other.

Izzy gave a sharp command to the dogs, and two of the

three immediately obeyed. Carlyle tapped her fingers on the fence, watching, thinking.

Cash put his hand over her tapping fingers, stilling them. "Worrying?"

"Thinking," she replied.

He did *not* withdraw his hand, and she held herself very still, trying not to react. Trying not to think anything of it. Friendly gesture. Simple gesture. Clearly just annoyed with her tapping.

"I feel like that should be concerning to me."

She grinned at him. "Me thinking *is* very concerning. This Ferguson guy. What are the chances I can sweet-talk him into saying something he shouldn't?"

Cash's expression was very...odd. She kind of expected him to laugh or lecture her about not getting too involved. But this was neither of those things, and she didn't know what to do with it.

"Probably not the right tactic. Ferguson says to anyone you were...whatever, that's going to poke a hole in that alibi you just had to give me. *We're* supposed to be secretly engaging in sleepovers, remember?"

She glanced over at him, meeting that dark gaze. And there *was* something different in it. Or her brain was a little fuzzy because his very *large*, calloused hand was still resting over hers. "Yeah, I remember," she said.

Breathlessly. Like some kind of *fool*.

"If you've got some questions for Ferguson, let's bring them to Jack. See if he can ask them."

"Is Jack talking to you right now?"

Cash laughed, the corners of his eyes crinkling. He adjusted his cowboy hat, finally took his hand back. "Ah, he's just a bit prickly in the mornings."

"And every other time I've interacted with him. Well, un-

less Izzy is around. He does have a soft spot for her." Carlyle
kept her gaze on the little girl, the whole thing…overwhelm-
ing for reasons she couldn't quite articulate.

She just knew that she'd been hard on Cash when it came
to how he treated Izzy. She'd been telling him what he'd done
wrong. So maybe he deserved to know what he'd done right
too. "For anything you think you didn't give her, family mat-
ters. My brothers were everything, even when I was trying to
get them to give me some space. They were my foundation.
She doesn't just have you, she has all of them, and all of this."

"Kinda luck of the draw."

"Maybe. But you could have moved somewhere else. Gotten farther away from cold cases and danger. They don't need
you to run the ranch and you don't need them to run your dog
business. You stayed for yourself, but you stayed for her too."

"And how are you so sure about that?"

When she looked over at him, her heart hammered against
her chest. His expression was…different. Not that *woe is me*
or determined, protective dad mode. Something more open.
Something more…

She didn't know. So she put her armor back in place, flashed
that grin. "I am a keen observer of human nature." But she
couldn't keep up the act. "You're not so hard to figure out."

"You are," he replied, so seriously.

She scoffed, or tried to, but her throat was a little tight. "I
don't see how."

"You're an excellent mask wearer. I should know. But, per
usual, Izzy gets under it. No one can resist Izzy."

"She's the best."

"Yeah. And there's a softy under all the *Carlyle* of it all."

Carlyle gave a fake injured sniff. "I do not know what
you're referring to."

He laughed. *Again.* He was smiling. *At her.* And there was something warm and wonderful and *awful* blooming in her chest. She should look away, walk away, lock herself up with the computer and find him some answers.

But her phone rang, and she jumped at the loud, surprising jangle. Less than steady, she pulled her phone out of her pocket. She had to clear her throat to talk.

"It's Zeke. I'll, uh, be right back." She swiped her finger across the screen, turned her back on Cash and took a few steps away. "What?" she demanded.

"Hi to you too."

"I'm working."

"Today's your day off."

"Yeah, but I'm working on case stuff."

"Yeah, me too. I was just calling to see if you'd come up with anything I should be on the lookout for tonight in Bent. Any people I should ask around about being seen with Chessa, that kind of thing."

Not a bad idea. "Bryan Ferguson and Tripp Anthony. Don't necessarily bring up Chessa connecting to them. Just see if you get any kind of reaction from it, some idea of if anyone knew them or what they think about them."

"And if I do get some information?"

"Just file it away. Come out to the ranch for breakfast tomorrow and we'll go over what you find."

"You getting too deep in this, Car?"

"Probably. Why?"

Zeke sighed. "You should be out having some fun or something. Not getting dragged into more investigations and danger and running. Haven't you had enough of that?"

"Maybe I *like* danger. I'd think *you'd* understand that, mister spy operative."

"Former. I'm enjoying the quiet life."

"My butt," she muttered, turning to look back at Cash and

Izzy. Izzy had gotten off the horse and she and Cash were standing next to it, watching the dogs run and tumble over each other.

In the middle of all this, they were laughing.

Carlyle didn't care what kind of fool it made her, she wanted to be part of it.

CASH KNEW SHE'D walked away to talk to her brother in private because they were discussing the murder case and what *they* were doing about it. Which made him uneasy, because he didn't like the idea of them planning something on their own.

And it had nothing to do with her suggesting sweet-talking anybody. Or mostly not about that.

Izzy was chattering on about music and concerts and her usual twelve-year-old stuff and it made him want to believe everything was going to be okay. If she could be worried about cute drummers and the importance of musical *eras*, then maybe he could...do that too.

Maybe not worry about cute drummers but allow himself the bandwidth to focus on more than danger and protection. He wasn't sure he knew how to do that anymore. It had become such a habit, such a comfort zone. Shrank his world down until it was just him, Izzy and dogs.

But it hadn't saved her from trauma, from danger. Maybe he needed to...open up again. Maybe the real lesson in all of this was that he couldn't control the world or the people around him, but he could control the hours and minutes here, and how he thought about them.

He went through the rest of the day making a conscious effort to do just that. To engage in frivolous conversations with Izzy, even when he was walking her to and from the stables to the house in a nod toward keeping her safe. To take a fussy Caroline from a very frustrated and frazzled Anna.

"She's a demon bent on world destruction," Anna said darkly, collapsing onto the couch.

"Like mother, like daughter," Cash replied, making Anna laugh. He walked Caroline in the same relentless circle he used to walk Izzy in when it was the only thing that would put her to sleep. Once Caroline was asleep, and so was Anna, Cash put Caroline in her crib in her room, put the baby monitor speaker next to a sleeping Anna, then checked in on Mary and Izzy. They had their heads together, cooking up something for dinner. He did his routine chores, and he didn't let the darkness of Chessa's murder invalidate all the light in his life.

Carlyle had been right. He could have left. He could have secreted Izzy away any of the times danger came knocking at their door. And he had, in a way, by keeping her cooped up in that cabin. But he'd never been able to dream of raising her without his family, without the legacy of this ranch. Even when trauma and tragedy followed, this was home.

So when the house was dark and quiet, and Izzy was tucked safely into bed, he went down to Carlyle's room.

Because she was a different kind of light he'd *never* allowed himself to have, and maybe it was time to change that.

When she opened her door, she didn't *startle* exactly, but she definitely hadn't been expecting him. Maybe she hadn't really been expecting anyone.

"Hey. What's up?" Swiftie's tail thumped over in the corner. Cash gave her a little hand signal that had the dog trotting out of the room.

"Nothing in particular. Just thought I'd see if you'd found anything new about Ferguson or Tripp." Starting with murder cases. Lame, even for someone as rusty as him.

She was frowning at Swiftie's retreating tail, but then shook her head and turned and walked toward her bed, where a laptop and a notebook and papers were strewn about. She gestured toward them with some frustration. "Not really. There has to be a connection between these two. Why these two guys, you know? How did that Darrin guy get them to help him? But I'm coming up damn empty and it's irritating the hell out of me."

He should use that as a segue to discuss other things, but he couldn't seem to make himself. "Ferguson wasn't a target. He just happened to be the one handling bonds that night."

Carlyle shook her head. "I don't buy that. If it had been Jack or Chloe, would Darrin have sent Tripp to pay her bail? Hell no. It was more careful, more targeted. Too many people would have had to know Tripp was a ranch hand here."

"So they waited till the least likely person was handling it."

"Maybe." Probably, in fact. He didn't want to tell her that if there was a connection, surely someone would have found it by now, when it seemed so important to her to find one. So, he changed the subject.

"Any word from Zeke?"

"No. I told him to come over in the morning and give us an account of what he found, if anything. He'll probably hang out at the bar until at least around it closes. I don't think a lot of baddies are out at—" she glanced over at the clock on her nightstand "—ten fifteen."

"You never know."

She shrugged, and a silence stretched out. This wasn't that unusual. They worked together. Sometimes they dealt in silences. But this one wasn't easy, companionable, or all that comfortable.

So stop beating around the bush, dumbass. "Remember when we were talking about me not...having any fun?"

"Uh, yeah. Sure." She seemed...really uncertain with his change of topic, and maybe that shouldn't amuse him, but managing to set Carlyle a little off-balance—when that was usually her expertise—was kind of nice. "Gonna start hitting the bar scene?"

An attempt to put him off-balance, but not a good one. He only smiled. "No. I don't think so."

"Ah, so…" She cleared her throat, looked at the computer, then at him. No, not at him. Some spot on the wall behind him. "What about it?"

"I thought about it. All day. How I'd pretty much put *fun* out of my head the past twelve years, best I could. But then I got to thinking… In six years, Izzy is going to want to go off to college, I have no doubt, and I'll have to let her. I'll have to let her just…walk away." Which he just…couldn't think about right now. He still had six years. No use mourning something that wasn't here *yet*, even if he had to accept it would be here *someday*.

"Right. So, what, you're going to wait six more years to… have fun?"

He shook his head. "No, you were right. She's not going to thank me for making my entire life her protection. She's going to sit at this dinner table someday, like I did this morning with Jack, and wonder what the hell he's been doing with his life."

"You know, I do have a theory about what Jack's been doing. Or who."

Cash closed his eyes, shook his head. "I don't want to talk about Jack and theories."

"I'm just saying, I went to…"

She trailed off as he stepped closer. Close enough to see the way her dark hair had little glints of red. The way her eyes were too gray to be blue and too blue to be gray. The way her breath kind of caught and then she let it slowly out, watching him not warily, exactly.

Because she was fierce and strong and confident, but she

wasn't made of impenetrable armor. He affected her in *some* way, and that was enough to reach out, touch her cheek.

"I like you, Carlyle. You've untied something inside of me that was tied so tight I didn't even know it was there. It was just a weight, holding me down. And you lifted it."

She made an odd kind of sound he didn't know how to characterize, except maybe as a little surprised. Her eyes went bright, and she cleared her throat.

"Just to be clear," she said, and he saw the effort it took her to sound a little cavalier. To not outwardly react to his hand on her cheek. "I had plenty of...*fun* before coming here."

"Hell, Carlyle." She really did have a way. He didn't know why it amused the hell out of him when it really shouldn't have.

"But it wasn't the kind that ever meant anything. Not serious. Not thinking I'd ever be in one place, put down roots, stick. So, I don't exactly know how to do that part."

"Yeah, I've kind of avoided it like the plague after one disastrous marriage."

"Well, look at us, two dysfunctional peas in a pod."

He put his other hand on her other cheek, cupping her face gently, drawing her just a hair closer. It had been so long since he'd felt this—allowed himself to feel it. The heavy thud of his heart, the warmth in his blood. A want he'd closed off a long time ago.

"You know, maybe we should give ourselves a break. Is it dysfunction if we've built fairly good, functioning lives with jobs and family relationships and a lack of jail time?"

Carlyle shrugged, but her mouth curved. "Define *jail time*."

He shook his head, because it didn't matter *why* the things she said amused him, it only mattered that they did. That she lifted those weights away. That something here, between them, worked—no matter how little that made sense.

He lowered his mouth to hers. He paused, just a whisper from contact. Waited until her eyes lifted from his mouth to his gaze. Maybe that's what had first snuck under all his very impenetrable defenses. The unique color, the way—if he looked hard enough—that was the one place he could see that hint of vulnerability.

Then he kissed her, watching the way her eyes fluttered closed, feeling the way she softened into him like melted wax. Like she fit right here, in his arms.

That weight he'd been carrying so long lifted just enough to see the possibility of lifting more. Surviving the weights he couldn't lift. Expanding beyond the tight, hammered-down knot he'd pulled himself into for some bid at control and protection.

But life was in the opening up, not the closing down. So he opened up.

And Carlyle did too.

Chapter Ten

Carlyle woke up to the very odd sensation of her bed moving without *her* moving. And the realization she was very much *not* dressed.

But the *man* getting out of *her* bed was…or in the process of anyway. He reached for a sweatshirt, and she watched the play of muscles across his back. She couldn't imagine when he had time to work out, but as she'd had her hands all *over* those muscles last night, she knew they weren't just for show.

She allowed herself a little dreamy smile because he *was* dreamy. And last night had been…special. Which made a little wriggle of anxiety move through her. Since when did she get special?

He pulled on the sweatshirt and got up. When he looked over his shoulder and met her gaze, he smiled. He bent over the bed.

"You've got time to sleep yet. I've got chores." He brushed a kiss across her forehead, like that was the most natural thing in the world. Like he hadn't been dad-celibate for something like *twelve* years and knew what to do with…this.

She definitely did not know. Because he'd said all that about liking her and thinking she'd lifted some weight and what the hell was a woman supposed to do with *that*?

Particularly if he just...left. Like that was that. Off to do chores.

Was that that? Was this just some kind of...*fun*? Then what was she supposed to do with the whole *I like you* thing, and his daughter, and him? And her whole rooted life that had clearly been a really bad decision?

She could not stand the thought of going through the day not knowing what kind of punch this was so she could roll with it. "This is like...a thing, right?" she asked, before he opened the door to leave. "Not like a...random fun night to blow off a little steam? Because I can do either, but—"

He turned, then cocked his head and studied her from where he stood by the door. When he spoke, it was like he was choosing his words very carefully and she tried to brace herself for the disappointment.

"I don't have a life that allows for blowing off steam, Car."

"You could," she managed to say, though not quite as flippantly and *I-don't-care-what-you-do* as she might have liked. "If you needed to."

He didn't even hesitate. "I don't."

"Okay."

"Do *you* need to?"

She blinked. When she'd said all that stuff about roots? When he kissed her like the entire world had stopped existing? "No, I don't need to."

He smiled. "Good. I'll see you at breakfast."

She couldn't quite manage a smile back, even as he left. She felt a little too...raw and...and...*uncomfortable*.

She sat up in bed, ran her fingers through her tousled hair. *Sex*-tousled hair. Because she had had *sex* with Cash last night.

Multiple times.

Not just blowing off steam. Not *fun*. A physical reaction to the past year. Being friends and attracted to each other was probably always going to lead here. She'd have preferred less *murder* involved, but her life pretty much had always revolved around murder. Why should this be different?

And she was okay with that. She wouldn't be here if she wasn't, but there was something about going from what happened in *just* this room, and *just* between them, to out into the larger Hudson world.

Part of her wanted to crawl under the covers and just hide, and she didn't know why. Because she had never been afraid of anything—or at least hadn't *let* herself dwell in fear. She *acted*.

But this was… It wasn't about danger or fear or any of those things you could *fight*, it was just…her heart. It was easy, in a way, to brazen her way through life when it was all danger and protection and *threats*. Quite the opposite to Cash, she hadn't gone internal, shrunk her world with all the danger. She'd expanded it. Her whole life. It was the only way to survive in her circumstances, to fight out, to ignore fear, to be loud and present and *demanding*.

But both were extremes, and now it seemed they both had to find some middle ground. Maybe that made them good for each other. Maybe that made this all…positive.

But she still didn't know how to deal with his siblings, or hers, or—dear God—Izzy, knowing Cash Hudson had been *inside* her.

She allowed herself a groan then flung herself out of bed. Some old habits still helped a woman get through the day. Flinging her way into the thick of it was the only way she knew how to do this.

She got dressed, brushed out her *very* tousled hair. "You're not a coward. You've never been a coward," she lectured herself. Out loud. Then she opened the door, shook her hair back, squared her shoulders, ready to face whoever and—

Nearly jumped a foot.

Izzy was standing there. Swiftie and Copper on either side of her, like two little dog sentries.

"Jeez." Carlyle slammed a hand to her heart.

Izzy blinked. "I was just coming to get you for breakfast."

"Oh. Yeah, I'm coming." Carlyle tried to smile as she stepped out into the hallway, but she knew it stretched all wrong across her face. She was...uncomfortable. Because at the end of the day, everything that happened with Cash— and all his talk about living for himself—didn't matter if Izzy didn't like the idea.

Izzy came first, and she should. She'd spent her entire life with her dad apparently never even looking twice at a woman, and then Carlyle had come along and...

This was why people avoided roots. *This* was why Zeke had said no way to getting even deeper in the Hudson machine. It wasn't the kind of complicated someone could just shoot their way out of. She had to deal with untying all these awful, heavy knots weighted in her stomach.

"Is something wrong?" Izzy asked as they walked toward the dining room.

"No, of course not," Carlyle replied.

But Izzy stopped, blocking Carlyle's forward movement out of the hallway.

"You'd tell me, right?" she asked, eyebrows furrowed together as she frowned. A little suspiciously.

Which made Carlyle feel terrible. She bent over a little so she was eye level with Izzy, put her hand on the girl's shoulder.

"I promise. Nothing is *wrong*. I'm having a weird personal mental argument with myself about weird personal things. I promise."

Izzy smiled a little, but she studied Carlyle's face. "Is it because you like my dad?"

Carlyle had been calm in the face of so many crises, but none of that had prepared her for *this*. Her eyes widened, her mouth dropped open, and no slick words to talk herself out of this came out.

"So, that's a yes," Izzy said, a bit like… Carlyle was dim. Carlyle found herself completely speechless.

"He doesn't really do that," Izzy said gently, patting Carlyle's shoulder. "But don't worry. You can be *my* friend. You don't need to be his."

"Uh…" This was…so much worse than she'd imagined. Because Carlyle had the distinct feeling she was…being warned off. When it was a bit too late for that.

"Come on. I'm starving." Then Izzy took her hand and practically dragged her into the dining room.

A lot of the Hudsons were already there. And Zeke was clearly just arriving. Carlyle tried to feel normal instead of like some kind of robot who had to learn to act like humans. Izzy was talking about how she'd helped make the muffins that were on the buffet laid out with food as they went down the line with their plates. Carlyle tried to engage, but she just kept looking at every new person who entered, both hoping it would be and hoping it wouldn't be Cash.

She was going to have to tell him about Izzy's reaction. She was going to have to…do something. But when he entered the room and smiled at her, she knew she shouldn't smile back. She should be…something. Aloof or…cool. But she smiled back because he was just so damn handsome and amazing and…

Really, what did she think she was doing?

He came right over, grabbed a plate, then greeted Izzy before putting some food on his plate. When they moved to sit down, she was standing right next to him, feeling like her heart was going to burst out of her chest. Because Izzy was *right there*, but so were very *visual* memories of last night, and the sweet thing he'd said about her lifting weights and…

Cash ran his hand down her spine before they sat. Casual, but not *friendly*. That was an intimacy, a little bit *more*. Carlyle didn't want to look at anyone, see if they caught that, but she couldn't quite stop herself from glancing at Izzy. Who was frowning at her.

Well, damn.

But she had to focus on Zeke. On the task at hand. Murder and framing and connections.

Not a little girl warning her off her dad.

"The bar was pretty busy. I made the rounds, dropped some crumbs. Lots of people remembered Chessa, but nothing specific about the night she was murdered. At Car's request, I mentioned the cop and the ranch hand. Nothing too obvious," Zeke said once everyone was settled at the table. "No one came out and said anything too direct, but I got the distinct impression that Bryan Ferguson and Tripp Anthony had, on occasion, before last year, not just been seen at Rightful Claim, but had been seen *together* there. And routinely."

"I knew there had to be a connection," Carlyle said, pointing her fork at Cash. Then, because she couldn't help herself even when she was a tangle of Izzy-nerves, at Jack.

"I'm not sure that proves anything," Jack said, but his expression was dark. Angry, clearly. "But we'll look deeper into it. It's a thread to pull." He was clearly mad that he hadn't been right about his employee. But then again, the whole family had been wrong about Tripp, so why should this be different?

Before anyone could say anything else, the doorbell echoed through the house. Everyone paused, but it was Mary as usual who got up to get it.

"Sit," Walker grumbled, standing up himself.

Mary raised an eyebrow at him. "Pardon me?"

He scowled. "With what's going on, you're not answering the door."

Mary's expression didn't change, but she remained very still. "I see."

"You're a brave man, Walker," Hawk muttered from his end of the table, where he held Caroline in one arm and ate with the other hand.

"With danger all around, I don't think it's wise for the—"

"Bud, you better watch every next word," Carlyle said under her breath. Honestly, the fact her brother could still be such a caveman sometimes was ridiculous.

But Mary didn't get all mad or bent out of shape. She didn't glare daggers at her husband—like Anna was currently doing.

The doorbell rang again.

"Go right ahead, Walker. Be a big strong man and answer the door." Mary settled her hands over her bump and gave her husband a bland smile.

Walker swore, clearly realizing he'd dug himself a hole he was going to have to grovel out of later. But whoever was at the door wouldn't wait, so he stalked out of the room.

"I would have punched him," Anna said.

"Some methods are more effective than punching," Mary replied, all pleasant and cool. She was going to rip him a new one.

Carlyle couldn't ignore the fact she wouldn't mind seeing it. She loved the way Mary handled Walker—and most people. Carlyle wished she could emulate it, but she was too much of a Daniels. Bull in a china shop.

Mary would know what to say to Izzy. Mary would know how to handle Cash. Carlyle had a bad feeling she was going to break a hell of a lot of china on this new road she found herself on.

Walker returned, leading the female detective from Bent

County into the dining room. Whatever amusement there'd been was sucked out of the room. Everyone went immediately silent and wary. This just…couldn't be good.

The detective's smile was pleasant, but her eyes were sharp. "Good morning," she offered cheerfully. "Sorry to interrupt your meal, but this was a first-thing-in-the-morning kind of deal. And I didn't catch you at your place soon enough." She looked at Zeke. "So, let's talk about what you were doing in Bent last night." Then she helped herself to a seat.

CASH CONSIDERED MAKING an excuse to take Izzy out of the room. He was already on edge about having her listen to what Zeke had found out, but add the detective and it was too much. What twelve-year-old girl would be or should be involved in discussions about her mother's murder? No matter how not part of her life that mother had been.

Cash looked down at her, sitting next to him. She didn't look upset. She didn't seem overwrought. If anything, her expression reminded him a bit of Mary. Cool. Completely collected. Maybe even a little curious. He opened his mouth to say something, to tell her to leave, but hesitated before he could find some gentle way of doing it.

But she turned then looked up at him, all cool and *adult*, and shook her head. As if she knew what he was going to say. She was smart and had been his kid for all these twelve years, so she probably did know.

She didn't want to leave. She wanted to see this through. He didn't like it, but maybe he didn't have to. Maybe sometimes parents had to let their kids see something through, even if it hurt.

"Can I offer you something to eat?" Mary asked the detective.

The detective waved Mary's polite—if a little chilly—offer

away. "No, thank you. And I don't want to interrupt your breakfast. I only want some answers as to why you were snooping around Rightful Claim last night, Mr. Daniels. And since you weren't at your apartment this morning, I had the sneaking suspicion you might be here."

"My family is here," Zeke replied.

The detective's smile didn't slip in the slightest. "But they weren't in Bent last night. You were."

"I was just enjoying a drink. I didn't realize your husband was on the Bent County PD payroll." Zeke's return smile was *not* polite. It was sharp and it was mean. Cash didn't know that it was the right tact to take, but God knew he wasn't in charge of Zeke.

The detective remained wholly unfazed by Zeke's demeanor. She'd likely dealt with worse. "My husband tends to notice when people are running a line of questioning in his bar. He *is* married to a detective. He also notices when someone goes poking around in the alley behind the bar. Particularly when it's been the site of a recent investigation."

Zeke had not shared that information with the class. Cash frowned at him.

But Zeke shrugged. "Detective, I talked to some people. I don't know what more you want to hear."

Her eyes flicked briefly to Izzy. Then to Cash. She smiled, and it seemed genuinely kind. "Maybe we should discuss this more privately," she said to Zeke, but it was easy to see that *private* just meant away from Izzy.

"You don't have to," Izzy said firmly, sounding like an adult. But she took Cash's hand under the table, held on hard. "I know my mother was murdered, and I know you're trying to figure out who did it. I want to be here."

Detective Delaney-Carson studied Izzy's face, then smiled.

"Okay. You're free to go whenever you need to though. You get to decide."

Cash wanted to hang on to his frustration and distrust of the woman who clearly had him on her list of suspects, but it was hard to do when she was thinking about Izzy at all, let alone giving her an out.

"Listen," she said, clearly to all of them. "I understand that you all have an investigative business. That you—" she pointed to Anna "—even have an independent private investigator license. I understand and, in fact, am not even opposed to the group of you investigating in whatever ways you can. Legally, and in a way that can actually be used in a court of law, and in a way that does *not* end in some sort of misguided attempt at vigilante justice. But you have to work *with* us."

"Are you going to work with *us*?" Cash demanded.

The detective sighed. "Look, my hands are tied to a certain extent. I have a police department to answer to and laws to follow. A code of conduct, standard operating procedure. I'm sure you're aware," she added, looking at Jack.

Who nodded. Icily.

"I want to hear what you all think Bryan Ferguson and the late Tripp Anthony have to do with Chessa Scott's murder. And next time you think to ask around about anyone, I don't want to hear it from my husband. I want you to come to me or Hart. It is not our goal to arrest the wrong man," she said, looking at Cash pointedly.

Zeke didn't say anything, but he looked over at Cash. Almost like he was asking permission. Which was…a nice thing to do, actually. Cash gave him a nod.

"Carlyle pointed out that it was strange, or at least something worth looking into, that Ferguson was the one who handled Chessa Scott bonding out with Tripp Anthony last year. She's been trying to find a connection between them.

And I did last night. Not much to go on, but enough to know they were friendly. Seen together at Rightful Claim more than once."

The detective nodded thoughtfully. "When was the last time they were seen together?"

"It was unclear. Definitely last year before Tripp died, but I couldn't get a time frame."

"Did you make a list of who you spoke to?"

Zeke crossed his arms over his chest. "I didn't ask names."

She waved that away, clearly seeing through Zeke. "I'll want names. Trust me, my husband can give me a list of everyone you spoke with, but it'd be easier if you narrowed it down to the ones who'd seen the two men together. You can email them to me."

Zeke scowled, but the detective didn't seem to notice. "We've looked some into Bryan Ferguson. Just another reason it'd be better if you all came to us. Since Anthony is dead, he wasn't on our list, but he'd been dating Ms. Scott, yes?"

"That was what Chessa said when he bailed her out, according to Ferguson," Jack replied.

The detective nodded. "Does Ferguson know your family has been looking into him?"

Jack shook his head. "I certainly haven't told him or anyone at the department."

"I'm assuming the exception there is..." She trailed off, looked through her notebook. "Deputy Chloe Brink? The one who was questioning the coroner?"

Jack's expression got very hard. "She's looked into some things regarding the murder, but no. She doesn't know we've been looking into Ferguson."

"All right." The detective stood. "I'll have more questions likely, but I'm just going to reiterate that all of this goes a lot smoother if you trust me with what you find. We want the truth as much as you do." She turned her gaze to Cash. "Can you walk me out, Mr. Hudson?"

Cash didn't like that, but he didn't see what choice he had. He squeezed Izzy's hand then released it and stood to follow the detective out.

She didn't say anything until they got to the front door. "You've worked with Bent County before. You and your search dogs?"

Cash nodded, not sure where this was going. "A few years back when there was a missing boy over in the state park."

She nodded. "I read the report. Your dogs found him."

"In the nick of time."

"You've also helped Quinn Peterson at Fool's Gold Investigation."

Cash wasn't sure exactly what the detective knew about that case, what he should be straight about. It felt dangerous to let someone in, someone who thought he was capable of murder.

But she'd given Izzy some consideration and he couldn't ignore that went a long way in his book.

"She was looking for some specific evidence on a case. Had a scent and an area she thought it might be in, so the dogs searched and found it."

"Yeah. I'd like to do that, Mr. Hudson. But it would be a conflict of interest to tell you why."

"Can't really have my dogs help out if I don't know for what."

"I know, but maybe you have an employee, someone you're not related to, a colleague somewhere else? Who your dogs would listen to?"

"Me."

They both turned to where Carlyle was. Not *hiding* per se, but she had definitely been stealthily following them and listening to that conversation.

The detective sighed. "You have a personal connection to—"

"To who? Your prime suspect?" Carlyle demanded, crossing her arms over her chest, just as Zeke had back there.

"Car."

She turned her slightly belligerent look on him. "Anyone who your dogs will follow, or is qualified to lead your dogs, is going to have a personal connection to you." She turned her attention back to the detective. "I don't think you're bad at your job, Detective, so I think you knew you wouldn't find some random person unconnected to all of this to help you out. And you don't have access to other search dogs, or you wouldn't be asking. So let's not waste time."

"Ms. Daniels—"

"I know how these things go. I can facilitate a search that doesn't discredit your investigation. You wouldn't be here, asking him about his dogs, if you didn't think it could be done."

"You said yourself you're involved with Mr. Hudson. You're, in fact, his alibi. If you know how this goes, Ms. Daniels, then surely you understand how it looks."

"So, find a way to make it look good," Cash said. Because Carlyle was right. The detective wouldn't be wasting her time with this if she didn't think it could be done. "Carlyle is perfectly capable of handling the search dogs. If I stay out of it, and if you're with her the whole time, and it gets you what you're looking for…isn't it worth the risk that this one little thing doesn't hold up in court?"

She was quiet for a long-drawn-out moment. "Fine. When can you do it?"

"How about now?" Cash and Carlyle asked in unison.

Chapter Eleven

They immediately took the detective down to the dog barn. Carlyle tried not to feel nervous. She'd never taken the dogs off property on her own. She'd never led a full-on, nontraining search on her own.

But they were very carefully not giving away how unqualified Carlyle was to do this while the detective was in earshot.

"So, Carlyle and I will get the dogs loaded up in our Hudson Dog Services truck. We can drive out to the site—"

"You're going to have to stay here, Mr. Hudson."

"I'll stay in the truck and—"

The detective was already shaking her head. "This is already a stretch as is. I can't have you anywhere near the search area. You're going to have to stay here, Mr. Hudson. It's the only way."

Cash didn't look at her, but his expression was clear. He didn't like it.

"Ms. Daniels, I'm going to drive out to the site. I'm going to get everything ready on my end. When you've got the dogs loaded up, text me. I'll text you an address. I'm going to ask you not share that address with anyone. Is this the truck you'll be driving?"

"Yeah."

She noted down the make, model and license plate. "You'll

be cleared to drive up to the site. I'll see you soon." Then she turned and walked back toward the front of the main house where her police cruiser was parked.

Carlyle watched her go with mixed emotions. Then she looked at Cash with even *more* mixed emotions.

His expression was...concerned, she supposed. But not frustrated or angry like she'd expected.

"I can do this," she said, not because she was confident, but because she wanted to assure him. There was just...so much at stake that was *outside* her control. Usually she was only ever risking herself when she was storming through a bad decision.

"I know you can," Cash said, but he was looking at her, still with that concern, like he could *see* the anxiety on her even as she tried to hide it. "The dogs know what they're doing. All you have to do is facilitate. Just like anything else you've done with them. They're the pros. You've been doing this for a year. You know the ropes."

Carlyle nodded, and she knew she was doing a terrible job of keeping the worry off her face because Cash took her by the shoulders, gave them a squeeze. "You can do this. I know you can."

"I know I can." But he saw through her, so why not be honest? Maybe he could temper his expectations if she was. "It's just...a lot of pressure. I don't want to mess it up."

"You can't. All you're doing is taking them out there. Giving them some direction. They're the ones doing the job. If they mess up, Hick just won't get a special treat tonight."

He was trying to make a joke—she knew him well enough he wouldn't deny a dog a treat. But she couldn't force herself to smile or laugh.

"Even if this is a dead end, I'll tell you guys where we do

the search. I don't care what she said. We'll investigate it ourselves later if we have to and—"

Cash shook his head. "It won't be the place. She's testing
you. She'll meet you there then take you to a second location."

She hadn't thought of that, but he was right. Of course he
was right. The detective wasn't about to make this *easy*.

"Just let the dogs do the work, okay?" Cash said, squeezing
her shoulders again. "They'll find what's there, *if* it's there."

Carlyle wasn't so sure about that. If she didn't lead the dogs
the right way, she could mess everything up. But this was what
had to be done, and she was a *doer*. "I better get going," she
said. Because she wanted to keep that worry to herself, not
end up blurting it out to him so *he* worried more.

"Be careful. And don't go pissing off the detective just because she's pissing you off."

Carlyle pouted, if only to add some levity to this whole
awful situation. "But that's my favorite pastime."

"Try to play this one by the book, Daniels." Then he leaned
down and kissed her. And lingered there, his mouth on hers.
Unfurling all that warmth and yearning inside of her. Not just
a physical yearning, but an ache for something she hadn't let
herself want before.

Something she was still too afraid to name, even in the privacy of her own mind. Especially when she was reminded of
her run-in with Izzy earlier. She had to warn him lest he walk
into that minefield without any preparation.

But part of her was worried he'd drop her like a hot poker.
And she wouldn't even be able to blame him. His daughter
came first. Should come first.

So, because she was her, she ripped off the bandage. She
pulled her mouth away, cleared her throat and tried her best
to appear unaffected. "Just FYI, I don't think Izzy is too keen
on this whole thing."

"What whole thing?"

"The…us thing. Not like she thinks something's going on. Just that I think she picked up on my feelings for you, and she made it clear I should steer myself elsewhere."

His eyebrows furrowed. "She loves you."

"Yeah, but… She loves you more. The best and most. Sharing you is a pretty new concept. She's not a fan."

"I'll talk to her."

Carlyle immediately shook her head. "Look, this isn't my business, I know that, but you can't go *talk* to her after she warns me off. Then she thinks I'm some whiny tattletale. And that doesn't help anyone." Least of all Carlyle herself. It would just kill her if Izzy suddenly stopped trusting her.

"I'm going to have to talk to her anyway, Car. I'm not sneaking around pretending this isn't happening."

Oh, how her traitorous, silly little heart fluttered at that. "Okay, fine, but don't mention me. Don't mention not liking it. And when she tells you she doesn't, you listen. You can kick me to the curb over it." She was talking too fast, saying too much, but she couldn't quite stop herself. "No hard feelings. Just be straight with me, okay? No…beating around the bush or trying to make it nice. Just straight out."

He looked so…concerned. She didn't know what to do with that reaction. She wanted to run in the opposite direction. She didn't want…concern. She was tough. She was brave. She was…

He reached out and cupped her face in his hands. She was *toast*.

"My daughter dictates a lot of parts of my life, and rightfully so, but not everything," he said, so very seriously. "I still have to…be able… She can't dictate everything without any discussion. Without getting to the heart of it. That isn't fair to me and it's not raising my daughter the right way to let her just…always gets what she wants."

"You're going to keep…whatever we're doing…even if she hates it? Hates me because of it? Hates you because of it?" Carlyle didn't want that. As much as she wanted *him*, she didn't want that.

"I'm going to talk to her, Carlyle. Because there's no reason for her to not like me having a relationship with you—which is what we're doing. It might be uncomfortable for her at first, for all of us. It's new, and I don't expect it to be easy. But she doesn't get to decide wholesale. It has to be a discussion."

"And if after you've discussed it, she's still against it?"

"Let's take it one step at a time, Car. Like, step one. Go find this evidence the detective wants."

Carlyle wrinkled her nose. "What if it hurts your case?"

Cash sighed, dropped his hands. He looked out at where the detective had gone. "Did you see her when she looked at Izzy?"

"Yeah, she wanted her gone, but then when Izzy spoke up for herself, she gave her an out. Treated her like…a whole person, not just a kid to be shunted off. It was good."

"I wanted to take against her for having me on her list, but she's doing her due diligence. She also didn't stop Zeke last night, when it's clear her husband gave her the opportunity to. She's not telling us to butt out. She's bringing us even more in. Maybe it'll bite me in the ass, but I think I trust her."

Carlyle blew out a breath. "Yeah, I do too. But I don't trust this *whole thing*. Something's off and I don't like it."

"Agreed. All we can do is take it one step at a time." He tucked a strand of hair behind her ear, waited until she met his gaze. "Be careful, Car," he said seriously.

She'd never spent much time being careful, but she figured now was a good time to start. So, she smiled. "I will be."

CASH HAD BEEN forced to have a lot of tough conversations with his daughter over the years. Between everything with Chessa, to the danger the Hudsons routinely dealt in, to Anna getting pregnant *before* she was married to Hawk and where *did* babies come from then, to—quite frankly, the worst— puberty.

He hadn't done a good job every time, but he'd tried. If there was anything he'd had to accept in being a parent, it was that the best you could do was *try*, and if your trying sucked, you just had to get better. Lean on his family a little bit.

So, as Cash—plagued by uncertainty—walked toward the dog barn with his daughter, knowing he had to have this potentially difficult conversation, he realized it was not anything new.

But it *was* a new subject. Him being involved with someone. Finding the right balance between including Izzy and not letting her think she got to make his decisions *for* him. They were a family, but some things were private. Someday, she'd want to date, and he doubted very much he'd have a say.

He wanted to go jump off the nearest mountain at the thought.

"Can we work with the horses again today?" Izzy asked, swinging her arms in the pretty morning like she didn't have a care in the world. He wished she could always feel that way, particularly after this morning's breakfast.

"Well, technically it's Crew Three's turn, and Carlyle had to take them with her to work with the detective this morning." They should take Crew Two out on the trail, but Cash wanted this whole murder thing solved before they went too far from home base. "What if we take the puppies through the obstacle course instead?"

"Pita too?"

"I'll text Hawk." He pulled out his phone and texted Hawk

to send his dog out. None of them were puppies anymore, but until they had a new batch, they'd be known as the puppies.

"Before you get the rest of them out, I want to talk to you about something."

All the ease and happiness leaked out of her quickly. Her arms slumped and she shaded her eyes to look up at him.

"Nothing bad happened. This is a good thing I want to talk to you about, I like to think." He crouched to make himself eye level, though it wasn't much of a crouch anymore. She was going to be a tall one, and that ache of too much joy and wistfulness wrapped around his heart like it always did.

But that frown did not leave Izzy's face. She watched him with deep, deep suspicion as he tried to come up with the words.

He knew he should start out quickly, so she didn't invent terrible scenarios in her head, but he was struggling to find the words to start. "Iz... You... You like Carlyle."

Her frown deepened. Which wasn't exactly expected, but maybe it should have been with what Carlyle had told him.

"So?" she said, a little belligerently.

"So. I...like her too."

"She works for you."

"Yes, and she's a...friend."

"Cool," Izzy said, trying to turn away from him, but he reached out for her arm, kept her in place. Because her *cool* sounded anything but.

"I like her a lot, actually," he said firmly. Because he could interrogate Izzy's feelings on the matter instead of be clear about his own, but that felt like a bit of a cop-out. He'd already initiated this relationship with Carlyle. He wasn't going back on it. No matter how she'd assured him he *could*.

She had heartbreak in her eyes like no one had ever chosen her over anything. And maybe they hadn't, and he couldn't *choose* her over Izzy, but this wasn't…so cut-and-dried. Life never was. It wasn't about *choosing* over anyone else.

It was just life.

"As more than a friend," he continued, while Izzy scowled at him. "I wanted to let you know that."

"What? That she's suddenly your girlfriend?" Izzy said, with the snotty kind of look that usually irritated him.

He was not an old man, but man, the word *girlfriend* made him feel old and out of place. Still, it was a word that made sense to Izzy. No matter how snottily she'd said it.

"Yeah. You seem to have a problem with that. Which I have to say, I don't understand because I know you love her."

"Yeah, I do." She jerked her arm away from him. "Because she's *my* friend," Izzy said, exploding. "She's on *my* side. Finally, there's someone who doesn't listen to *you*. She listened to *me*. She cared about *me*." Izzy spun around and pointed at him. "Now…she's yours. And she'll listen to *you*."

There was a well of anger there that he hadn't anticipated. That he didn't know what to do with. But beyond just not understanding, her words hit at just about every little insecurity he had. "Izzy… Do you really think I don't listen? I don't care?"

Her face got all crumpled looking, like right before she cried. But before he could reach out for her, she stomped away from him. Not far. Just to the entrance of the barn.

"I just…"

Cash didn't know if she didn't have the words, or just couldn't squeeze them out. So he found some of his own to give her.

"You are the most important thing in my world. You always will be. I know I'm not perfect, but I know if I've made anything clear to you, it's that. That doesn't mean I don't have other important things. I always have. We are very lucky to have a big family, getting bigger every year, who we love and loves us back. They're all important."

Izzy turned very slowly. If she'd let any tears fall, she'd wiped them away first. "You love her?" she asked, her voice wavery and those tears still visible in her eyes, even if they didn't fall.

What was with everyone asking him that question? "I don't...know."

"Shouldn't you?"

"It's just complicated. Adult relationships aren't so cut-and-dried. And there are...extenuating circumstances." And now he just wished he could reverse time and *not* do this here. Or anywhere. Ever.

Izzy swallowed. "Everything keeps changing."

And how. "I know, baby. I can't promise you that'll stop. Life is change. You're going to grow up on me. And you're going to make your own decisions, and I don't have to like them. Though I hope I will. But I can promise... Nothing comes in front of you for me, Iz. And if we talk about it, we can work through whatever comes."

She looked down at the ground, and he knew she was trying so hard not to cry. "I just... Aunt Mary is going to have a baby, and she won't have time for me like she used to. You'll spend time with Carlyle, just like all the aunts and uncles... Except Jack." She looked up at him, all those tears making her blue eyes bluer. "Where do I fit if you all get married and have babies?"

He pulled her into his chest, and she didn't push him away. "You fit right here, baby. Because you are my baby. You're our first baby here on this ranch. Nothing changes that. Not more kids, not more people. You'll *always* be ours. Long before everyone else."

She leaned her head on his shoulder, and he felt the telltale tears seeping through his shirt. He rubbed her back, tried to find the words to ease this change in the midst of all this danger.

"You'll help with Mary's baby. Just like you're doing with Caroline. And…just think. You're going to middle school in the fall. There will be sports and clubs and all sorts of things." Things he'd always been leery about letting her join, but he clearly needed to…let go. Find a way to give her a bigger life, not a smaller one.

"I know it's hard to feel like everything is changing around you, but it's just…life moving along. You add people, you lose people." He pulled her back, so she had to look at him. "But nothing ever changes that you're part of this." He pointed out at the ranch, at the main house—where Pita was racing across the yard toward them. "Love just expands, baby. It's not something that can get used up."

She took a deep, shaky breath. "Chessa… She stopped loving me. She used it all up and then there was nothing left."

Cash wished there was some way to heal that wound, but he'd had to accept that he couldn't. Only time and growing up and being there for her could. Or maybe he just hoped it could.

"Your mom never loved much beyond herself. There are probably some reasons why that was, but I could never get to the heart of them. I tried, but… Nothing that Chessa ever felt or didn't, did or didn't, is about you. Nothing. And I know it might be hard to believe that, and maybe you can't just yet. But I want you to look at *all* the people who are here and think about them and their place in your life. Not the one person who isn't."

Izzy swallowed. "I just…don't want things to change. I want Carlyle to be my friend and…"

"She will be. Whatever is going on between Carlyle and me at any time isn't ever going to be about how you guys feel about each other. And I think you know Carlyle well enough to know she's not afraid of making me mad. She loves you, independently of me. She sticks up for you when she thinks it's right, because she's been in very similar shoes. That doesn't change just because we…date," he finished lamely. "I promise."

She let out a long breath, then nodded. "Okay. I guess… I guess it's okay then."

Cash didn't point out he hadn't been asking for permission, because it was nice to have. Because having her blessing meant something. "I love you, Iz. Nothing ever in a million years changes that. Nothing."

She curled into him, holding on tight. "I love you too, Dad."

Pita arrived with delighted yips and barks, jumping in between them with enthusiasm. Izzy laughed and released Cash to throw her arms around Pita and wrestle with him a bit. And for a moment, Cash let himself forget about murder, and Carlyle out on a search job, and the hole Chessa had left in his daughter's heart.

And just enjoyed the moment.

Chapter Twelve

Carlyle pulled up to the address the detective had texted her. Like Cash had said, it clearly wasn't the end location. The detective was alone, standing next to her police cruiser, in a kind of abandoned parking lot outside of Bent.

The detective held up her hand in a wave. Her other hand held a cell phone to her ear. Carlyle went ahead and parked and got out of the van, then took a surreptitious look around.

This location wasn't in the boundaries of the town of Bent, but it was close. The saloon Zeke had cased the other night couldn't be more than a mile or two away from this spot.

"Did you look under the potty stool?" the detective was saying into her phone.

Carlyle raised an eyebrow. What the hell was a *potty stool*?

"That's where I found it last time. I have to go. Yeah. Love you too, bye." She hit a button on her phone and pocketed it, smiling at Carlyle. "Sorry. Family emergency."

"A lot of potty stool-related emergencies?"

The detective laughed. "I have three kids under the age of six. So, yes."

Carlyle blinked. It was hard to imagine this very professional and with-it detective with *three* little kids. Not to mention, Carlyle had been to Rightful Claim, the bar the detective's husband owned. She knew what he looked like. "You're really married to that hot, tattooed saloon guy?"

"Yep."

"That's really hard to believe." She remembered Cash's words to not irritate the detective a little too late.

But the detective didn't get offended. She didn't even frown. She grinned. "Oh, Ms. Daniels, you have *no* idea." Then she pointed to Carlyle's truck. "Am I okay to ride with you in the truck to the search site?"

"Allergic to dogs?"

"No."

"Then you're good to go." Carlyle thought about bringing up the fact this wasn't how the detective said it would go, but then she decided to just roll with it. Let the detective dictate how this would go and just observe.

A woman could glean a lot just from observing. If she could keep her big mouth shut. Well, she'd *try*.

"Once we're inside the truck, I'm going to turn my body cam on. That way, we've got everything documented should we need it for a trial. Once we get to the site, Hart and two other Bent County deputies will be there. We've got the search area blocked off."

"And something for the dogs to use to search off of, I assume?"

"When we get there. Everything is going to go on camera. The more transparent we can be, the better off we'll be come trial."

"You keep talking about a trial, but we don't even have a suspect yet." The detective said *nothing*. "I thought we were working together."

"We are, Ms. Daniels. Believe it or not, I don't want to arrest Mr. Hudson. Off the record? I don't think he did it, and it's a waste of time trying to pin it on him."

"On the record?" Carlyle asked, because she wasn't dumb enough to be swayed by a little good cop, even without the presence of a bad cop.

"We're exploring every possible and reasonable avenue," she said, sounding very formal and official.

Carlyle really didn't want to like her, but she was making it hard. "Well, let's go find something for the record then."

The detective nodded. "Just remember. We're recording *everything*." She patted the little attachment to her police vest.

Carlyle nodded, appreciating the clarity. No attempt to get her to say something dumb and incriminating on camera. They got in the truck, and the dogs whined a little bit at the newcomer, but they were well trained enough to stay put.

The detective gave directions as Carlyle drove. They passed Rightful Claim, rounded the corner and entered the back alley.

Where Zeke had been *poking around*, as the detective had called it this morning. Carlyle didn't say anything about it. With the camera running, she figured it best she said as little as possible.

The detective got out, so Carlyle did too. Detective Hart and two uniformed deputies were waiting, and there was an area of the alley and the building behind the saloon sectioned off with crime-scene tape.

"The area taped off is what we're searching," Detective Delaney-Carson explained as they walked over to the other officers.

"What do you have for the dogs to get a scent?"

Hart produced a plastic bag. Inside was a torn scrap of fabric. Carlyle figured the streak of brown on the gray-and-pink fabric was blood. Chessa's blood.

She set that thought away as best she could.

"We can go in this building through that open door, but

only the ground floor. They can also search around out here within the tape, but not beyond."

"I'll have to be the one who gives the scent to them," Carlyle said, which wasn't *exactly* true, but true enough. "They won't understand what they're supposed to do if it's any of you. You'll also want to stand out of the way and remain mostly still so they're not distracted by you. I've got six dogs. They'll take turns in teams of two. When they're out in the field, you want to just stay out of their way."

"What if they want to go beyond the borders of the search?" one of the officers asked.

"I'll stop them." Carlyle looked around the blocked off area. It seemed such an odd location to be cordoned off. Had Chessa been found here? She glanced around, looking for security cameras, but didn't see any. "What if they hit on something beyond the borders? Can't I just let them go for it?"

"We don't have a search warrant for any area beyond," Detective Delaney-Carson said. "The street is fine, but inside or around certain buildings is private property. But if they're pointing to that area, we can work on expanding our search warrant with that due cause. So, you'll just let us know and we'll go from there."

Carlyle didn't know what to think of that, but she supposed it was just something to file away. Maybe Jack would have an idea what it meant and why.

She moved to the truck and unleashed the first two dogs. She prepped them for the search, then took the bag of evidence from Hart and opened it. Then she let the dogs do their thing. She followed them, and Detective Delaney-Carson followed her. The other three stayed where they were in different corners, patrolling the area so no one happened upon them, Carlyle guessed.

Both dogs immediately went for the building. Carlyle

shared a look with Detective Delaney-Carson then followed the dogs. The detective kept right by Carlyle's side, then stopped her before she entered the building.

"We already gave it a sweep, but we can't go upstairs, so let me go first."

Carlyle nodded and the woman drew her gun and went in first. Carlyle followed her in. The dogs sniffed around the empty room. More like a warehouse than anything. All concrete and grimy windows, which let in a little light but not much visibility. The detective kept her weapon drawn, but she motioned Carlyle forward.

There was definitely something going on here that Carlyle hadn't been let in on, and she didn't know what to make of that. She figured it wasn't malicious, but that didn't mean it didn't make her nervous.

Carlyle watched as the dogs headed for the stairs.

"You can't let them go up there," the detective said.

Carlyle gave the order to stop, and both dogs sat obediently. Right there at the bottom of the stairs.

"You sure they can't go upstairs?"

"You have reason to believe they scent something upstairs?"

Carlyle pointed to both of them, sitting at attention, waiting for the okay signal. "Clearly."

The detective nodded. She pulled her radio to her mouth. "Hart. The dogs want upstairs. Call it in. See if someone can expand that search warrant for us."

The return came back staticky but affirmative. The detective still held her gun, her eyes focused on the stairs. She had a frown on her face.

She wanted up there. She *suspected* something up there.

Carlyle wondered if she could just…go. She wasn't a cop. Search warrants didn't matter to her. But then one of the dogs let out two low *woofs*. Carlyle frowned. It wasn't one of the normal search responses, but she thought Cash had told her something about that indication one time. A long time ago. When he'd first been introducing her to all the dogs.

She looked at the dog who'd made the noise. Colby. Colby hadn't always been search and rescue. Or she had, but it had been for something else… What was it?

When Carlyle remembered, her body went a little cold. "Detective, I think we better get out of here."

"Why?"

"These dogs are trained for search and rescue, but this one in particular also has some training with finding drugs, weapons and explosives." Carlyle didn't know the exact signs for all of those, but she knew the dog's reaction just…wasn't good.

"All right."

Carlyle signaled the dogs out of the building, she and the detective following. But just as they reached the doorway something…exploded. Loud and bright, and then the ceiling rained down on them.

Hot. Bright. *Hell*. Something—or *somethings*—crashed on top of her. Painful, but nothing heavy or sharp enough to do real damage. She hoped.

The dogs were out, and Carlyle was about to jump forward to follow them, but she heard swearing and looked behind her. The detective was on the ground, conscious, but when she tried to get up, she swore even harder and didn't manage. That's when Carlyle noticed she had something stuck in her leg.

But worse, all around them were flames. The entire upstairs had exploded and collapsed, and none of the sounds the fire and building were making could be good. The roof was crumbling. Carlyle had to get them out of here. She grabbed the detective's arm. "This might hurt, but it's better than staying put." Then she dragged her out through the doorway.

They'd likely sustained some burns, and if the blood dripping on the ground was anything to go by, she had a bit of a head wound. And *maybe* dragging the detective was hell on her stitches from the other day. But she was on her own two feet and of sound mind.

She managed to drag the detective away from the flames. She thought—hoped—she heard sirens in the distance but mostly it was just the crackle and creak of a building going up in flames.

Carlyle kept dragging Laurel, but she was running out of steam. She managed to make it around the corner before she stumbled a little bit and fell on her butt. She scooted her back against the brick building and the detective did the same.

"Well, thanks. Probably saved my life, Ms. Daniels."

"Any time."

"Your head's bleeding."

"Yeah, so's your leg. Don't look at it," Carlyle immediately told her, because the giant piece of debris sticking out of the woman's leg was about to cause Carlyle to lose her lunch, and she'd seen worse, she liked to think.

But yikes.

"Don't worry. Been hurt once or twice. Know the drill." But the detective closed her eyes, leaned her head against the wall. Then she swore. Loudly. "This better not put me off the damn case."

Hart came running up to them, crouched in front of the detective, worry all over him. "You okay?"

"Yeah, thanks to her."

"Paramedics are on their way with fire, plus another unit." Hart looked at the detective's leg, blanched, swallowed, but didn't shake or faint. He looked over at Carlyle. "Anything beside that gash on your head?"

The old stab wound throbbed, but she didn't think that was relevant. Besides, her heart was beating too hard, and her limbs were too shaky to really take stock. "No. Where are my dogs?"

"They ran straight for the truck, so we leashed them up with the others. That okay?"

Carlyle nodded. She didn't want to have to tell Cash what happened. "Yeah, listen. I better get them back to the ranch." Of course she felt about as sturdy as a dead tree branch, but no one needed to know that.

"No. You'll get checked out. Sit tight. I've got some phone calls to make. Do you want to call someone from the ranch to come pick up the dogs?"

Carlyle nodded. "I left my phone in the truck though."

"Use mine," Detective Delaney-Carson said, holding out her cell phone, but before Carlyle could make the call, the detective grabbed Hart by the pants' leg.

"Hart," the detective said, sounding like she was trying to be more firm than she actually *sounded* firm. "Don't you dare call my husband."

"Grady'll kill me if I don't."

"Yeah, well. The price you pay for being my partner, I guess. He'll find out soon enough, hopefully once I'm all bandaged up. You tell him now? *I* kill you."

But there wasn't any more to say because an ambulance pulled up. One EMT went straight for the detective and one for Carlyle. They poked and prodded at her head, asked her too many questions to count. And fully ignored her when she said she was fine.

"We'll transport you both to the hospital in the same ambulance. Easier that way. You need a stretcher, Detective. Ms. Daniels, you can walk on your own accord if you feel up to it."

Carlyle nodded, then steeled herself to look at the detective. But they'd removed the debris and there was bloody gauze over her thigh.

She was conscious though. Talking to the EMT with the stretcher, every bit the in-charge detective even after what had happened.

What *had* happened?

Carlyle got one last glimpse of the building. Something had exploded on that top floor they weren't allowed in. And that was fishy. But the detective had been acting weird. Like she knew something she wasn't letting on.

Once they were all loaded up in the ambulance, Carlyle didn't make her phone call. She looked at the detective. "That thing off?" she said, pointing to the body cam.

The woman reached up, switched something on it. "Now it is."

"Detective, you know what happened in there, don't you?"

"I think you earned the right to call me Laurel. And maybe be the namesake of our next kid."

"Jeez. Isn't three enough?"

"We make cute babies."

It *almost* made Carlyle laugh. "I bet."

The detective—*Laurel*—sighed. "We have some theories. I'll tell you about it. Make your phone call first."

WHEN CASH'S PHONE RANG, he didn't recognize the number, but with Carlyle off searching for things with his dogs, he couldn't just ignore it. So he answered, with a pit of dread in his stomach. "Hello?"

"Hey."

"This isn't your number."

"No, it's the detective's. I'm helping her out with something, but we've got to leave the dogs behind. Can you come pick them up? Detective Hart will have the truck and the dogs at the Sheriff's Office."

"What are you working on?" Cash asked.

"I can't explain just yet. I will tonight though, promise."

"Carl—"

"Really, Cash. It's fine. I promise. We just need the dogs picked up. I'll be home tonight, and I'll be able to explain everything. Just too many…people around right now. Okay?"

He didn't like this at all, but he understood why she might not be able to talk. But then why not text? "You sure you're okay?"

She laughed, and *that* sounded more like her. "Yeah, I'm sure. If I was in some kind of trouble, I'd be too busy fighting my way out of it to call you."

Fair enough, even though the idea made him frown. "Okay, I'll come pick up the truck. Zeke's still out here, he can drop me off. He was talking about doing some more poking around Bent anyway."

"Oh, he doesn't need to do that."

"Why not?"

"Listen, I've got lots of stuff to tell you guys, but can you just stay away from Bent for now? It's not dangerous, I promise. I just want to make sure we aren't messing with this case. That detective was right. We need to make sure she can build a case."

Now he was *really* worried. "Carlyle, I have never once heard you admit someone else was right."

"I didn't say the *male* detective was right. Then you'd really have to worry."

Which was fair enough, and almost made him want to laugh if he could around the little weight of worry in his stomach. But she was a grown woman, and everything she said made *sense*, even if it didn't land right.

"Just get the dogs back to the ranch," she said. "I'll call you when I need a ride if I can't hitch one home with one of the cops."

"Car…" He couldn't get over the feeling she was holding out on him. That something was *wrong*. But she'd called the ranch…home, and that felt…important. "All right. Just promise you'll call. And come home soon."

"I promise. By dinner. Get the dogs. We'll talk soon. Bye."

"Bye." He pulled the phone away from his ear, trying to tell himself everything was fine. If there was a problem, she would have at least hinted at one. She'd only hide something to protect him, and he couldn't think of what she'd be protecting him from.

But he was damn well taking Zeke with him. First, he hunted down Mary to make sure she'd keep Izzy within someone's eyesight at all times. Then he found Zeke and explained the phone call.

"Since when is she about listening to detectives' orders?"

"I don't know," Cash said. "I don't like it."

"Yeah, me neither," Zeke said. "All right. Ready?"

Cash nodded, but before they could make way for the door, Hawk entered the room with a phone to his ear. He made a stopping motion to them, and though Cash felt impatience snapping, he waited. And so did Zeke.

When Hawk finally pulled the phone away from his ear, his expression was blank. Cop blank. "I just got called into a fire. There was an explosion. One Bent County detective and one civilian were hurt and taken to the hospital."

Cash was already moving—and so was Zeke, swearing a blue streak.

"You can't just go tearing off—" Hawk called after them, but they were outside and in Zeke's truck before he finished.

"Hold on," Zeke muttered, and then he drove like a bat out of hell for the hospital.

Cash only wished he'd go faster.

Chapter Thirteen

Carlyle managed to downplay her injuries to the nurse. There was enough confusion that she didn't even have to take her shirt off. They just cleaned up her head—no stitches this time—and let her go with a little printout about painkillers and what to look for.

Carlyle knew she should head out. Call Cash to pick her up. Or maybe call Chloe so she didn't have to tell Cash about this at all. Maybe if she took off the bandage before she got back to the ranch, he wouldn't even know.

But she hadn't gotten much out of Laurel about what the detective knew in the short ambulance ride, and Carlyle was determined to return to the ranch with more information than when she'd left.

So, she poked around the hospital until she figured out where Laurel had gone—she'd had to be admitted due to the severity of her injury. Carlyle waited until the hallway was empty and no one appeared to be in her room, then slipped in.

Laurel looked up from where she'd been messing with the IV in her arm and frowned a little at Carlyle. "Are you supposed to be in here?"

"Are you supposed to be trying to take that IV out?"

"That is *not* what I was doing."

"Uh-huh."

"You get the green light or are you sneaking off?"

"Green light. Just a little scrape on my head," she said, pointing to her bandage and ignoring the throbbing pain in her side. "You need surgery?"

"Still some discussion on that. I'll riot," she muttered irritably. And since Carlyle understood the feeling so well, she smiled.

"No one out there?" Laurel asked, jerking her chin toward the door.

Carlyle shook her head. "Pretty empty."

"Okay, come here so I can talk softly. I don't think anyone would be listening, but we're not going to be too careful with small towns where everyone knows everyone. Pull up that chair."

Carlyle did as she was told and was grateful when Laurel didn't beat around the bush.

"I'm going to tell you a few things. I shouldn't name names, but I'm going to because your people probably need to be on the lookout, and because I don't know how long I'll be stuck here. Hart will keep working on your case, and he's as good as me. I should leave it at that, but I figure you and yours will poke around anyway, so why not poke in the right direction?"

"That sounds very un-cop of you."

Laurel smiled. "I would have been highly insulted by that when I first started out, but these days, I'll take it as a compliment. I feel like we're on the cusp of something. It's complicated, and I haven't been able to untie all the little knots yet. But there's a correlation between Bryan Ferguson, Tripp Anthony and Butch Scott."

Carlyle hadn't heard of Butch before, but Scott was Chessa's last name.

"Chessa's brother," Laurel confirmed. "Half-brother, anyway, according to his birth certificate. And Butch's stepmother owned that building across from Rightful Claim. Where we found Chessa's body. Butch and Bryan were stepsiblings once upon a time, and Butch, Bryan and Tripp all graduated high school together. Not uncommon out here, and I haven't gotten far enough to know if they were ever friends, kept being friends, but the ownership of that building was suspect."

"Even more so now."

"Yeah."

"Look, Hart will keep tugging on the line. I might need a day or two to talk my way around doctors and my husband to get back on the case, but we're not going anywhere. We're going to solve this."

The door flew open. "Speak of the devil," Laurel muttered. "Run. Hide. Save yourself."

The man did look a bit like a devil. He was *very* large, one arm nearly covered in tattoos. He had a beard, and his hair was a little wild. He looked like he would tear down the foundations of the earth, and Carlyle had enough experience with men—particularly the protective sort—to see it was about the fact his wife had been hurt, and there was nothing he could do about it. So he was just going to be…loudly and impotently angry about it.

"What are you doing here?" the detective—*Laurel*—demanded of the man who was her husband. "You are supposed to be on kid duty."

"And now your sister is. What the hell, princess?"

Princess? People really did have secret lives you couldn't guess at.

"Grady, this is Carlyle. Carlyle, my husband."

"Don't pull that polite BS with me," the man grumbled as he strode to the other side of Laurel's hospital bed, but he looked over at Carlyle and gave her a nod. "Hi."

"Hey."

"I assume the two guys yelling in the waiting room who I used as a diversion belong to you."

Carlyle blinked. *Two* men. Her brothers? Well, no reason to feel bummed about that. She *had* lied to Cash about where she was. Well. Only sorta. She was fine. Cleared and on her way out.

But apparently, first she had to deal with her brothers and how they'd gotten wind of her situation. "I guess I should go...put a stop to that."

But the man's attention was already back on his wife, and Carlyle could still see all that anger, but she could also see the gentle way he took Laurel's hand, and that anger was just love and worry all tangled up in something that might feel useful.

She supposed that's what married people with three kids who wanted another one did. Carlyle didn't know what to do with the weird feeling in her gut, so she went to find her brothers.

But it wasn't them out at the nurse's station yelling. Well, one of the angry men in the waiting room was. The other one was Cash.

It was an odd realization, to see some of that violent anger in his eyes that had been in the detective's husband's. Like she might matter to him *that* much.

And something inside of her—something she'd shored up so many times in her life, plugged all the cracks and holes, fought tooth and nail to keep it intact—came crumbling down.

The tears spilled over, and she walked over to Cash. Her breathing hitched, and she didn't want to sob, but she was a little afraid that noise that came out of her was exactly that. As he turned, he frowned, but pulled her into his arms.

She supposed it was all of it. Explosions and tangled webs of people they hadn't figured out. Cash in her bed and Izzy's not-so-subtle disapproval. That look in his eyes. The detective and potty chairs and tattooed husbands and debris sticking out of her leg, all because she wanted to find the truth.

God, Carlyle was so tired of people getting hurt to find the truth. Her whole life. The *whole* of it.

"Hey." She heard the surprise in Cash's voice, but he held her there, tight and close, rubbing a comforting hand up and down her back. "It's okay. You're okay," he murmured.

And the silly thing was, she knew that, but it made everything better when he said it.

IN A TURN of events Cash didn't quite know what to do with, Zeke handed him the keys to his truck. "You take her home. I'll get the dogs."

Cash had figured he'd have to fight him on it. Zeke was the more formidable brother, mostly because Mary had Walker wrapped around her little finger. Walker had been threaded into the Hudson family and ranch life. Zeke kept himself apart.

But this was an acknowledgement of…something. So, Cash handed the keys to the dog truck over to Zeke. He had a million admonitions to offer about how to drive with the dogs, how to leash them properly, how to make everything okay.

But in the end, he offered none. Zeke would figure it out. The important thing was getting Carlyle back to the ranch where she could rest. The woman was *crying*, despite the fact she was on her own two feet and seemed to be okay.

Carlyle sniffled into his shoulder, then gradually pulled herself back. Zeke put his hand on her shoulder, and she looked over at him.

"You really okay, kid?" he asked, with a gentleness Cash had never heard out of him.

She nodded. Didn't give her brother a hard time for calling her *kid*. Cash and Zeke exchanged a worried look over her head, but what was there to do?

Zeke left and Cash led Carlyle back out to the parking lot. He'd never seen her cry like that, never expected to. She brazened through everything, and he knew there were deeper feelings under all that bravado, but he hadn't expected a... breakdown, he supposed.

They climbed into Zeke's truck without saying a word. She'd stopped crying, but the evidence of it was all over her face. He'd *planned* on chewing her out for not telling them what was going on, but now he didn't have the heart to. So he just...drove.

She laid her head on his shoulder the whole way back. She didn't say anything, and while he occasionally opened his mouth to say something, in the end, he just kept it shut. Sometimes, comfortable silence was the best medicine.

When he pulled up to a stop in front of the ranch, he made a move to get out, but Carlyle didn't. She just sat there staring at the house.

"Everything okay?"

She didn't look at him, but she answered his question. "You haven't even been mad about me not telling you the truth."

"You seem upset enough without me adding to it."

"That's nice."

"Is it?"

She finally looked over. "Yeah. Because I probably would have been a jerk about it if the situation was reversed."

"I'm beginning to think you're a big old softy, Carlyle. And not a jerk at all."

She let out a little huff of a sound, *almost* a laugh. "That's nice that you think that."

"That's me. Mr. Nice."

"But you're hot too, if it makes you feel better."

It was his turn to laugh. She was sounding more and more like herself, even if he didn't know what to do with that.

"You need some rest. I assume they gave you instructions for dealing with that?" he said, finally addressing the bandage on her head.

"Yeah, in my pocket."

"So, we'll go take care of it."

"I need to tell everyone some stuff Laurel, the detective, told me. About the case, about the connections."

"Come on, Car. You're beat."

"Yeah, but the detective who was on your side is in the hospital, and I have information that we should be looking at." She leaned toward him, across the center console. So serious, so...*worried*. "Being beat can take a back seat." She pushed herself out of the truck, hopped down before he could rush around to stop her.

He frowned. "You have to take care of yourself."

"If there's anything I've learned, it's sometimes the only way to take care of yourself is to see the damn thing through so it can stop hanging over your head. This is too big to tiptoe around. We've got to dive in, no matter how we feel."

If nothing else, she was back to her normal go-getting self, but... That was not him. Not anymore. He'd left all that *dive in* thinking behind when Izzy came along. But that was the extreme again.

Maybe what the two of them needed most from each other was the balancing act. The compromise. "All right. We'll compromise. I'll get Jack and whoever else is within reach right now. Get this over with. Anyone who doesn't make it, Jack will spread the info. You've got fifteen minutes, then you're in bed. And you're going to hand over those instructions."

She frowned, but she eventually slid the paper out of her pocket as they entered the house.

"Sit," he said, pointing to the couch. "I'll be right back."

He went through the house, found Jack, Anna with Caroline on her hip, and Walker standing in the kitchen over a pan of brownies.

"She's in the living room," Cash told Walker before he could make the angry demand that was clearly on the tip of his tongue.

Walker left quickly.

"Where's Iz?"

"She and Mary are up in Mary's room going over nursery colors," Anna said. "It's keeping her occupied. What's going on? Zeke already called and said Carlyle's okay."

"Come on out to the living room. Carlyle will explain. Anyone else around?"

Jack shook his head. "Palmer and Louisa are up at their house site. Grant and Dahlia are still out visiting her sister. Hawk's dealing with the fire."

"We'll do this just us then. Fill in everyone else after the fact."

"Hawk should be home soon," Anna said. "We can needle him for more information on the fire."

Cash nodded as they walked out to the living room. Walker sat next to Carlyle, who was rolling her eyes. A good sign, Cash thought.

Once everyone got situated, Carlyle jumped right into it. "Did any of you know Chessa's brother?"

"Chessa only has sisters," Cash replied.

"Laurel said—"

"You're on a first-name basis with the detective now?" Walker interrupted suspiciously.

"Yeah, saved her life and all."

"Jesus," Cash and Walker said in unison.

But Cash couldn't think about lives in danger. He had to focus on the problem at hand. "Chessa doesn't have a brother." *Didn't* have a brother, he reminded himself internally. Because she was gone this time. Really gone. Such a strange ribbon of grief and relief every day over that, and he wasn't sure he'd ever fully come to terms with it. Which made him think of Izzy upstairs with Mary, worried about how things would change, how she would fit. Knowing the answer had never been Chessa, and now never could be.

"Laurel said it was a half-brother. And this half-brother's stepmother owned the building that exploded."

As if on cue with the word *exploded*, Hawk came in.

"What can you tell us?" Anna demanded.

"Not much, yet. Sent some things away to be tested." He took Caroline from Anna, kissed the baby's head. "What I can say is, the explosion set at the building Carlyle and the detective were searching was deliberate."

"Obviously," Carlyle muttered.

"And we...found some human remains in the debris."

An echo of shock went through the room, and Cash was glad Izzy wasn't here to hear that. Maybe she'd have to know eventually, but for right now they could stick to one murder.

"We'll do some tests there too. Determine if the fire was the cause of death or something before."

"I don't think it was the fire," Carlyle said. "The detective and I were in the building. I think the police were in and out of the building before I got there. They only had a search warrant for the downstairs, but... We would have heard someone upstairs. The dogs would have sensed someone upstairs, right?"

She looked at Cash, so he nodded. "They might not have reacted to it though, if they were searching for the scent."

Hawk nodded. "It's all good information to have. The police are tracking down the property owner. Luckily, they already had contact with her regarding the search warrant so it's just a matter of finding her. I've done what I can do today in terms of the fire. Now, it's a bit of a waiting game until tests come back and more questioning is done."

"There's more though. This half brother you guys apparently didn't know about, Butch Scott—"

"Butch Scott. Wait. We know Butch Scott. I thought they were...cousins or something?" Anna said, looking at Cash.

"That's what she always told us."

"Maybe he was," Carlyle said, as if this strange mistake didn't mean anything. "More important, Butch Scott and Bryan Ferguson were stepbrothers at one point."

All eyes turned to Jack. His expression was not as cop-cool as Cash had expected it to be.

"I had some news of my own I wanted to share once we got everyone together. Bryan didn't show up for work tonight. No one knows where he went." He looked up at Hawk. "Do you have any more information on that corpse in your building?"

Hawk took a breath. "The initial consensus is adult male, but most identifying characteristics had been burned away. Until the tests are run. One happenstance missing person doesn't mean it'll be Bryan."

"But it could be," Jack said firmly.

Hawk nodded. "Yeah, it could be."

"Laurel said she and Hart would keep trying to untangle the connections, but she also sort of gave me the go-ahead to try our hand at it. She wants to figure out who did this almost as much as we do."

"So, that's what we'll do," Jack said.

Chapter Fourteen

"So, let's get started," Carlyle said. Even though her head and side throbbed. Even though her eyes felt weirdly prickly. Even though she kind of wanted to crawl into her bed and cry for a hundred years.

But that was a feeling to be avoided, so why not go whole-hog on this? Familiar territory, all in all. Push down the emotional garbage and focus on the danger, on solving the mystery. What else could matter?

"No, you're going to bed, Car."

She was about to argue with Cash—no one got to tell her what to do and so on and so forth, but Walker gave her the subtlest shake of the head. And she had no idea *why* that made her feel something close to ashamed. Like maybe he understood what it felt like…to deal with the garbage rather than the danger. Like, maybe just maybe, that's why he had a wife and a kid on the way.

Because he'd let the garbage go.

She didn't know why everything suddenly felt *different*. Like that unbelievable explosion—ranking pretty damn low on the list of traumatic events on her life—felt like it had detonated something inside of her.

Or maybe it was watching that detective—so sure of herself, so professional, so kick-butt—be worried about potty stools and be happily married to a husband who looked like he'd move heaven and earth to reverse time and not have her hurt, even though she was in this dangerous job.

Cash helped Carlyle to her feet, and she didn't fight him. She felt like spun glass, and the wrong move would shatter her—like she had in the hospital. If she cried in front of him twice in one day, she was quite certain she would literally die of embarrassment.

So she just let herself be led away, and tried to turn off all the vulnerable parts of her brain. Disassociate. Find some detached place to be.

But she just kept seeing Laurel's husband storming into her hospital room. Walker shaking his head at her. Cash angrily standing in that waiting room demanding to see her.

"I keep thinking you're feeling more yourself, then you get real, real quiet. I know they checked you out, but are you sure you don't have a concussion?"

"Not a concussion." *Just a mental crisis.*

He pulled the instructions he'd taken from her out of his pocket. "It says you can take a shower. Let's do that."

"Together?"

He laughed. "As enticing an offer as that is, *you* are resting tonight. Shower. Are you hungry? I can go hunt you down a snack. Then, *sleep*. Lots of sleep. No staying up late. No getting up early."

"Sure, Dad."

He winced, which *almost* brought her some joy. Not *everything* inside of her had been rearranged today if she could enjoy making him uncomfortable, and that was a relief.

"Go on," he said, not rising to the bait. "Can you handle the shower on your own?" He looked over the paper once more. "Don't wash your hair," he instructed.

She plucked the paper from his hands. "I'll handle it."

He opened his mouth, then shut it. "Okay, you can handle it."

She thought that was going to be that. He'd turn and leave, and she could take her shower in peace and figure out how to shore up all these cracks in her armor. Put all these rearranged pieces of herself back in the right order so that she didn't want to cry. So she didn't want to ask him ridiculous things like *where is this going? Will you ever love me like that detective's husband loves her? Like Walker loves Mary?*

But Cash didn't walk away. He kept *talking*. "But sometimes, you let other people handle it. Because I can't take that scrape on your head away. Or the fact you got *stabbed* to save my daughter. So you could just let me do this. You take a shower, I'll get you some food, and you'll give me a bit of room to fuss over you before you go to sleep."

Fuss. She hated to be fussed over. Wasn't that why she was always saying the shocking thing? When her brothers had gotten all soft over her, it had made her miss her mother so much she thought she wouldn't survive the *weight* of it. "I really don't want to cry in front of you again," she said, because if *anything* made her brothers run, it was that.

Cash, on the other hand, shrugged. Unbothered. "I have a kid. I can handle tears. It's one of my few talents."

It was true. At the hospital he'd just held her. Let her not talk. He'd just…acted like it was a perfectly fine and normal thing to do to cry. He was just doing all this *taking care*, and what had she done for him? What *could* she do?

She sucked at taking care. The only thing she was good at was diving into things headfirst—like this afternoon with the detective, which hadn't gone well at all.

And she'd had to watch the detective's real life. That man's expression when he looked at his wife. Love and worry and just this perfect picture of *life*.

Like what Mary and Walker were building. Like so many of the people here, and she'd sworn to herself she never wanted all that, but now she was *surrounded* and…and…

God, she had to make this stop. And she knew how. Face it head-on. Freak him out so he bailed. "We need to have the talk."

Cash's eyebrows drew together. "What talk?"

"The talk. The you-and-me talk. The…what-the-hell-are-we-doing talk. Because there's just…all these threads, and we can't keep knotting them."

He studied her like he was afraid she'd suffered the concussion he was so worried about, when she knew her head was just fine. Even if her words weren't. Even if *she* wasn't, at the heart of things.

"I know I'm doing this wrong. Hell, that's how I do things, so why not? You just dive right in."

"Get in the shower. I'll get you something to eat. You'll rest and—"

"I don't want that! I don't want *this*!" She pointed a little erratically at herself because she had no words for what she felt. Only this anxiety-fueled gesture. Only this need to put a stop to all this before…before…before…

She didn't know before *what*. Just *before*.

"Car, I'd love to follow, but I just plain don't."

"I know that. You think I don't know that?" She was off the rails, and she didn't know how to get back on them except to explode everything. "I don't need you to tell me you're in love with me. I just need to know that you could be, eventually. That…eventually… That… It's just… You've been married. Had a kid. I haven't. And I never thought I'd want something so…boring. But I guess, I think, maybe I do. Not like, *today*. Just…someday. So, we should be on the same page about that, because there's too much tangled and rooted here to just…bump up against that someday in the future and need to walk away."

For a moment, he stood there like a statue. An awful statue. Because she couldn't read what he thought of any of that, and so she had the space to think of all the worst-case scenarios she'd just introduced.

Because that's what you do, Carlyle Daniels. Create worst-case scenarios.

But when he spoke, his voice was strangely…raspy. Like each word held such great weight it scraped against his throat.

"Hawk came in and said a civilian had been hurt, and we knew it had to be you. I just…went dark. Hollowed out. I know fear. I've lived with that bastard most of my life, and this was that. The kind you just… It takes over. You are reminded you have *no* control."

She'd been there—more times than she could count. So many times she'd given up on the idea of control a long time ago.

"Your brother asks me about love," he said disgustedly. "Fair enough, I guess, but then my *daughter* asks me. Now you…and I don't know." He raked his fingers through his hair, leaving it unruly. "My track record sucks. My…radar sucks."

She didn't understand where he was going with this, and she wanted to poke and prod more about her brother and Izzy asking him about *love*, but something about his panic eased her own. "*You* don't suck."

He sighed and met her gaze. Not quite so panicked, but she didn't know what had taken over. Something…resigned. "I'm glad you think so. But… You have to understand. A while back, I figured that was it. I made my mistake, was going to pay for it forever, so that was *it*."

Ouch. Well, she hadn't expected it to be that quite cut-and-dried, but now she had to get rid of him so she could cry in peace. "That's all you had to say. We don't have to drag it out." She moved for the bathroom door—because like hell she'd cry again. "We don't have to—"

But he stepped into the bathroom doorway so she couldn't answer, his expression stormy. "Would you shut up and let me finish? You think *you're* panicking? I know how wrong this can go, and I've got a daughter to think about. My panic wins."

"I actually prefer to win," she grumbled, crossing her arms over her chest.

He made a huffing sound, almost like a laugh. But then he got all serious again. "Carlyle, I don't know how to answer all your questions. I'm still…sorting everything out. But let's start with that I am not sitting here thinking… *I could never marry or have kids with this woman.* It's certainly not some… off-the-table thing."

That was not romantic. It really shouldn't be romantic. Was her bar so low? Or was it she just understood how much that must…mess with him. How much *she* must mess with a man who cut off everything he could for so long.

So she nodded. "Well, I guess that's all I was asking."

"Maybe you should ask for a hell of a lot more," he said, looking downright *sad*.

They really were just two messed up, messy people. But she didn't mind that, didn't think it was too terrible. Not when they really wanted to…be good people, help people. Maybe they had a lot of stuff to work through, but they weren't *bad*.

So maybe all this *more* everyone kept talking about wasn't *more* at all. It was just having the kind of self-awareness to know what she really wanted—outside of what anyone else thought.

"You know, I don't have a kid. I think that makes fear different. It must. But I've also been pretty well acquainted with fear most my life. I know far too intimately how tenuous it all is. How little control *anyone* has. So no, I don't need to ask for *more*, Cash." She moved forward and wrapped her arms around him and squeezed tight—even though it sent a bolt of pain through her side. "Not from you. I think you're physically and psychologically incapable of giving less than you've got."

He ran a hand down her back. "I hope that's true."

But she didn't hope. She knew.

Just like she knew she couldn't rest. They couldn't rest until they found something. Because they were all in danger until this mystery got solved.

But for a little while, she'd give him what he asked for. The space to fuss. And she'd try really hard not to hate it.

CASH FINALLY CONVINCED Carlyle to get into the shower, then he went to the kitchen and put together some food on a tray like Mary usually did. It wasn't as nice as when Mary did it, but it would get the job done.

Fuel. Carlyle needed rest and fuel. And once he made sure she got those things, he could go figure out this whole Butch Scott thing. And once he did *that*, maybe they could figure out the personal stuff.

He had to breathe through the tightness in his chest. A panic born of…well, failure. Everything with Chessa had been such a spectacular failure. Here he was twelve years later, still dealing with it. Even though she was dead. It wasn't that he thought Carlyle was like that. It was more… Well, he supposed he couldn't help but blame himself for not finding a way to make things work with Chessa, for not finding a way to get through to her.

Intellectually, he knew better. Love didn't solve addiction. It couldn't erase the marks of an unsteady and abusive childhood. Even if he'd been able to find it within himself to love her, he couldn't change her.

But the guilt stayed. Because he'd wanted a better outcome for Izzy, and for her mother.

So, for the time being, he'd turn his attention to trying to figure out who killed Chessa. Maybe that could ease some of his guilt, and then…then he could really think about what a future with Carlyle looked like.

The future and thinking about it scared the living daylights out of him ever since he'd first dropped Izzy off at kindergarten.

He shook it all away. Focused on the task at hand. That's what had gotten him through for the past few years. One step before the other.

So he took the tray of food to Carlyle's room. She was sitting at the window, looking out at the night sky. That must have been what she'd been doing the night someone had been at Izzy's window. Had that wistful, sad look been on her face then too?

He wanted to find some way to take that wistfulness, that sadness away. She deserved so much more than *this*. But didn't they all? Maybe *deserved* just flat-out didn't matter. Maybe there was only making the best out of what you had.

And the fact she was here. Carlyle being whole and wholly her was a best. A bright spot. "All right. You should eat."

She turned to look at him, then her eyes dropped to the tray. She swallowed, hard. "I thought you'd have Mary put something together."

"She and Izzy had their heads together ordering stuff for the baby. Didn't want to interrupt. Sorry if it's not up to par." He set it on the table within reach of where she was sitting.

She shook her head, her eyes bright. "It's great. I'm… I'm pretty used to doing everything on my own. I guess it's been easy to let Mary swoop in because she's just…her."

"It's what she does."

"Yeah, and it's what you do too, I'm starting to realize." She reached forward, picked up a piece of cheese. "But I also know that means you'll try to tell me to eat, to sleep, and it's not going to happen. You're not doing the work without me. Either we both sleep or we both work. The end. But I think we need to work. I think we need to figure out who this half-brother you didn't know about is."

"I knew about him. Chessa just claimed...less of a familial connection. Which makes sense. Chessa's parents were a bit of a mess. She used to say her father had impregnated half the county. He was an addict himself. Abusive."

"I'm not going to feel sorry for her. Even if she's dead. Anyone who'd sell their daughter doesn't get my sympathy. I don't care if it's the addiction talking."

Cash knew he would always have a complicated relationship with feeling sympathy and grief toward Chessa. But he'd always found some comfort in that his family got to just wholesale hate her, blame her. It was simple for them, and even though he couldn't partake, it felt good it could be simple for someone.

And this felt good in a different way. Because no matter what Izzy thought or worried about, Carlyle was so wholly on her side. Always.

"I'm not asking you to feel sorry for her. I'm just trying to make it clear. She could have half siblings everywhere. It doesn't necessarily mean Chessa had a relationship with Butch, or knew they were siblings. Even with the same last name."

"But they were. So maybe *he* did, even if she didn't?"

"Maybe. I don't remember meeting him. He was more Anna's age. I think that's why she remembered the name. I'm sure he was trouble like the rest of the Scotts. Nobody really had a chance, growing up like that."

"I imagine Jack is already looking into what kind of trouble he's been in," she said, continuing to eat.

"Yes. Palmer will be doing his own searches too. So there's no reason for you to—"

"From here on out, we're in this together, bud. No more independent work. So, unless you're planning on taking a break, I'm not either."

He sighed. She was pale, and her hair was in a messy knot on her head as she'd followed the instructions and had not washed it. She looked in desperate need of that break. "*I* haven't been stabbed and nearly exploded, Carlyle."

She shook her head, unmoved. "Lucky you. Doesn't change anything."

He sighed. There would be no getting through to her, so he supposed he had to just give in. But not without conditions. "You finish your food. Drink some water. Take something for that headache I know you're pretending you don't have. Once you do all that, we'll join Jack and Palmer downstairs. But not before you take a little care of yourself."

"I always take care of myself," she replied, that typical flash of defiance in her eyes.

He crouched next to her seat so they were eye to eye. "It's not *yourself* anymore, Car. Got it?"

She held his gaze for a very long time. Then she nodded. And leaned forward and pressed her mouth to his, gently. Cash let the kiss linger, until she pulled away.

"That goes both ways, Cash. You got that?"

"Yeah, I think we both got it."

Chapter Fifteen

When they went down to the living room, there was what Carlyle could only describe as a war room set up. They were treating it like one of their cold cases.

Palmer had joined the fray, sitting in a chair with a laptop in his lap. Zeke was back from picking up the dogs and was conferring with Grant over a bulletin board on wheels they must have rolled out once she'd gone upstairs. Anna rocked Caroline in the corner chair, while telling Grant to add things or take things off the bulletin board. Hawk stood closer to the entryway, speaking into his phone in low tones.

When Zeke spotted Carlyle enter the room, he scowled. "You should rest."

"There's no point. I'm not going to sleep knowing you all are down here working this out." She walked over to the bulletin board, ignoring the way Zeke's glare was now aimed at Cash.

Honestly. *Men.*

"What have you all come up with in the past hour?"

Jack was the one who took the reins first. "It's looking more and more like Ferguson was the body in the building. We'll need dental records to confirm, but no one's seen him, and everything Bent County would release to Brink leans toward Ferguson."

"No whereabouts on Chessa's half-brother?" Carlyle asked.

Jack shook his head. "They're looking, thanks to Detective Delaney-Carson. But he likely knows he's being looked for, so that'll make it more difficult."

Carlyle stared at all the seemingly disparate events on the bulletin board. "What's the endgame here? We have a failed kidnapping, a murder—probably two—and an explosion. What is the goal?"

"Maybe there isn't one," Anna replied, considering. "Just destruction? Pain? They wanted to frame Cash, like Izzy said. So maybe that's it?"

But they were doing a really bad job of framing Cash, Carlyle thought to herself, frowning at the bulletin board as she tried to find a thread that made any sense. Maybe they couldn't have predicted her as an alibi for Chessa's murder, but they had to know he'd have one for the explosion. Unless there was something about that which would point to Cash?

"Some guy messes with *my* sister, I'm going to mess him up." Zeke looked over at Cash pointedly.

"I hardly *messed* with Chessa," Cash said darkly. "Quite the opposite."

"It wouldn't have to be true. Could have just been how Chessa framed things to her brother."

Carlyle rolled her eyes. "But Cash didn't think she had much of a relationship with this Butch. Chessa claimed him as a cousin when they were together. It's possible they didn't even know or care they were related. Just because they had the same father named on their birth certificate doesn't mean much—as you and I both know." After all, the name of the father on her birth certificate had not been accurate.

"Maybe something changed in the past few years," Grant suggested. "Maybe they didn't know about each other a decade ago or didn't care. But something brought them together more recently and they figured the connection out?" Grant pointed at a paper tacked to the bulletin board. "Butch Scott has had trouble with the law since he was a minor. As an adult, a lot of the charges deal with drugs. Could be they started to run in the same circles."

"Then how does Bryan Ferguson get messed up in this?" Jack said. He'd apparently at least accepted his employee was part of it, but Carlyle got the feeling Jack didn't believe in Ferguson having full-on involvement. Maybe because he'd likely ended up dead.

Maybe Jack was right, to an extent. He knew Ferguson. Had worked with him. Been his boss. Jack was hardly the type to believe in someone who didn't prove they were trustworthy. Carlyle wasn't even sure he trusted *her*.

"Whether intentionally or not, we know Ferguson helped Tripp get Chessa out of jail on bond that night last year. Or at least kept it from Jack for as long as possible," Cash said. "Whether it was true or not, Chessa said Tripp was her boyfriend at the time. Chessa escapes, Tripp dies. But Chessa doesn't just escape, she disappears. She lies very low for a *year*."

"And that was abnormal?" Carlyle asked Cash, but it was Anna who answered.

"She never went more than a few months without demanding money from somebody around here."

"Did you all pay her off?"

"At first," Cash said, clearly unhappy that he had. "But once the drug addiction became evident, we cut it off. She never stopped asking though. Until this all happened. I figured she was just…finally aware enough that she'd crossed that final line. She'd engaged in actively harming one of us, talked too freely of getting her hands on Izzy. I thought maybe she'd figured out nothing good was going to come from messing with us."

Carlyle shook her head. She was no addict expert, but she understood patterns. "If she stayed away that long, she had access to money to buy drugs, or just access to the drugs themselves. That pattern doesn't stop because someone finally becomes self-aware. Especially someone who paints themselves a victim. She didn't realize anything. She found a steady mark."

"Butch Scott?" Anna suggested.

"Maybe."

"Well, we can't do anything with that information until the cops find him. And you're not going off in the middle of the night to search, so I guess it's bedtime."

Carlyle didn't even bother to acknowledge Zeke had spoken. She was studying Butch's rap sheet. She tapped the end of it. "He's also kept his nose clean for the past year almost. After *years* of not going more than four months without getting some kind of arrest." She looked at Jack. "We want to find out where he is, sure. But we also want to know where they *were*. Them both going quiet makes me think they were together."

"Together not getting into trouble?" Grant asked dubiously.

Carlyle shook her head and looked at Zeke. Because she knew he had to be thinking the same thing she was. "Sure, you can stay out of trouble by not finding any, but that's not their MO. So the other option is they found someone to *hide* their trouble. Someone—or *someones*—who could hide it *for* them."

"You're suggesting Ferguson kept them from getting in trouble," Jack said, and though his voice was detached, even Carlyle could tell this was eating at him.

As much as Carlyle wanted to go easy on him, because she was that softy Cash had accused her of being and didn't want to hurt Jack worse than he was hurting himself, they had to follow the truth to find the truth. "He knew the ins and outs of Sunrise Sheriff's Department, didn't he? And likely Bent County too."

Jack didn't reply, but that was reply enough.

"You guys searched his apartment when you looked for him?"

"Bent County did," Jack said. "They're making sure Sunrise is staying as far away from this as possible."

Carlyle nodded, thinking. "What about other property he owned? Or Tripp Anthony? Just because he's dead doesn't mean he doesn't connect to the big picture here."

"Tripp lived on our property, in the cabin Walker stayed at when he first came here. Before that, he lived at home with his parents in Hardy," Anna said. "They would have been the ones in charge of everything when he died. And he's been dead this whole time."

"Still, it wouldn't hurt to look into what he had. Into *his* known associates, as well as Bryan's. Find those little connections that might lead to bigger ones. The cops are going to do what they can, and I know Laurel wants to get to the truth of this, but she's been hurt."

"So, we pick up the slack," Zeke said.

Carlyle nodded, turning her attention to Jack. "You know how they'll go about it. How they'll approach these connections. We need to do it differently. So we're not just treading the same water. Where are they going to look first?"

Jack was quiet for a moment, but eventually seemed to relent. "They'll focus on Butch. How he relates to the case, to Chessa—only to Ferguson if and when he's identified as the dead man. But right now? They're going to focus on finding Butch and getting info about him."

Carlyle nodded, because she'd figured as much. "Okay, so let's focus on Ferguson. And Tripp, to an extent. Let them focus on the Butch angle, we'll focus on this one."

"I'll text Brink to look into any property Ferguson *and* Tripp might have had access to," Jack said. "Maybe it leads us to something before this started, but it won't stop anything. Ferguson being dead means whoever killed him will know we'll look into him. They won't be anywhere that ties them to him."

"If they're smart," Carlyle agreed. She studied the bulletin board, because so many things didn't add up. It was possible everyone was just so clever that even the Bent County detectives and this group of trained investigators couldn't see their pattern, but Carlyle was beginning to wonder if it didn't make any sense because it was scattershot. Because there was no *solid* goal.

She glanced at Cash.

Except maybe…revenge.

CASH BOWED OUT of the discussions a little early to go put Izzy to bed. He wasn't surprised exactly that Carlyle had decided to come with him. He'd thought the case and wanting to crack it would come first, but she walked away without a backward glance.

For her, Izzy was a priority too. And that mattered a great deal.

"She's going to ask about the bandage," he said to Carlyle. It was his first instinct to hide it, or lie to Izzy about it, but as much as Izzy was *his* daughter to care for and protect, it was Carlyle's injury, because she'd gotten messed up in his life. Maybe it was her call on this one.

"She didn't know I was at the hospital?"

"I doubt Mary told her or she would have insisted on seeing you a lot earlier. They've been so happily busy with baby stuff, I didn't want to interrupt."

Cash didn't know why that made Carlyle frown, but he didn't have a chance to ask because they'd reached Mary's open door.

Not only were Mary and Izzy sitting next to each other, heads practically touching as they looked at something on Mary's laptop, but Walker was sitting in the armchair in the corner flipping through a pregnancy book. Copper was curled in the corner, but he lifted his head when Cash and Carlyle stepped in the room. Walker eyed Carlyle though didn't say anything.

"Time for bed, Iz," Cash said.

Izzy rolled her eyes, but she got up at the same time. "It's summer. Why can't I stay up late?"

"It's late enough. And you've got chores in the morning, just like the rest of us."

She groaned, but before she left the room, she turned back to Mary. "*I* like the name Levi."

"We are not naming our kid after some boy band singer," Walker said from his spot in the corner. Clearly this little argument had been going on for a while now.

"He plays the *drums*, Uncle Walker," Izzy said with the kind of contempt only a twelve-year-old girl can muster. Walker hid a smile.

"Oh, Levi Jones?" Carlyle said, perking up. "He's *hot*."

Izzy nodded emphatically and Cash couldn't stop himself from pulling a face, but Carlyle grinned at him, and it was nice to see these parts of her back. The clearheaded investigator she'd been downstairs. The mischievous woman who liked to tease.

He liked the softer sides of her too, hoped she'd get more used to those coming out, but he knew she was *feeling* her best when she could cause a little discomfort. He had no idea why he found that so damn attractive.

They got Izzy through her bedtime routine, and Cash tucked her in while Carlyle waited outside the door.

"How come she has a bandage on her head?" Izzy asked, surprising Cash that she'd noticed and hadn't said anything to Carlyle. He'd been ready to let Carlyle take the lead on this, but Izzy was asking out of earshot.

"She just had a little accident when she went to help the detective." Which was mostly true. "She's good. I promise." And that was the important part. She was good.

Izzy nodded, but she was chewing on her lip. Clearly still worried. Cash brushed some hair off her forehead. He couldn't promise everything would be fine like he wanted to. "We're getting to the bottom of everything. One step at a time. We'll get there." He kissed her forehead, then moved to leave the room, Copper settled into his dog bed under the window.

But Izzy spoke before he'd made it to the door.

"You know, if you and Carlyle got married and had a baby, that'd be okay."

He froze. Inside and out. What the hell was he supposed to say to *that*? Except maybe no more days with Mary baby planning.

Cash had to clear his throat to speak as he turned to look at her, but he couldn't see her expression in the dark. "Ah, well, it's a bit…soon for all that, Iz."

"That's okay. But I like babies, so…"

"I… Okay," he agreed, because he didn't know what else to do. Because that was *quite* the one-eighty from earlier. Because this whole Carlyle thing wasn't even a *week* old, and everyone was already throwing all this at him. "Night, Izzy. I love you."

This was why people didn't live with their families into adulthood.

He stepped into the hallway, closing the door behind him.

Carlyle studied him. "Looking a little pale," she said, as if concerned, but he saw the amusement in her eyes.

"You heard her, didn't you?"

She laughed, hooked her arm with his and leaned into him as they walked down the hallway to his room. "Yeah. Don't worry, I'm sure I went a little pale too. I do not know that *I* like babies. Particularly coming out of me."

Cash only grunted. They walked into his bedroom, still arm in arm, but once inside his room, he pulled his arm away from her. He pointed at her.

"Now, no funny business."

She grinned, sliding her arms around his waist. "Aw, come on. Just a little." That grin stayed in place, and he saw a kind of relaxed happy that hadn't been in her eyes all day. Understandably. But there were shadows under her eyes and that bandage on her head.

"You need your rest." But he dropped his mouth to hers, because good in the midst of bad was starting to become… not the distraction he always feared, but a foundation to get through the bad.

Still, he bundled her into his bed, and it didn't take much for her to fall asleep. She was exhausted and injured. He was a little exhausted himself apparently, because the next thing he knew he woke with a start, not quite sure what it was that had woken him up. Carlyle was curled up next to him and as he lay there and listened to the sounds of the house in the dark, he didn't hear a thing. He glanced at the clock. Four in the morning.

Early yet, even before Mary's usual ungodly wake-up call, but Cash knew he had lots to do today, and there was no point trying to get another hour's sleep when he'd likely lay there and make too many mental to-do lists to count. Might as well get up and start the *do* portion of his day.

Palmer and Zeke had handled the dogs last night, but the truck would need cleaning out. There was paperwork to do from yesterday's events with the dogs—he'd have to have Carlyle write up a report for what had happened. Much as he didn't want her to have to relive the explosion part, it was important to keep records of everything the dogs did outside the ranch.

He slid out of bed, being careful not to wake Carlyle. She stirred a little, but rolled over and was quickly breathing evenly again. Swiftie stayed put on her side of the bed. He grabbed his clothes, his phone, then carefully eased out of the room.

Clearly, everyone in the house was still asleep, which was good. Often, in the middle of danger or investigations there was always someone up and about, putting too much time and worry into it. But everyone upstairs was paired off now, and there were kids and kids-to-be in the house besides Izzy. Life—real life—was starting to take over all the ways they'd isolated themselves since their parents had died.

Except for maybe Jack, who very well could be awake in his room working on something, but Cash hoped he was asleep.

It was dark and still as he walked downstairs. Not even the telltale sound of a baby crying or a rocking chair creaking. He decided to forgo coffee. He didn't want to chance waking anyone up, particularly when a lot of them had likely been up too late looking into Bryan Ferguson.

Cash disengaged the security system so he could step outside into the cool, dark morning. On a normal morning, he would have left it off, knowing people would be coming and going for the rest of the day, but it was early and dark enough he thought it best to reengage the system once he was out. The cameras always ran no matter what, but the alarms were usually only in place overnight.

Once that was taken care of, he turned and looked out into the dark night around the ranch. He lifted his face to the sky. The moon was a tiny sliver above his cabin in the distance, clear and bright despite its diminished size. The sky sparkled and pulsed. And for a moment, Cash just stood there and absorbed this odd time of night, this quiet.

Home. This had always been his home. Through good times and very bad times, Hudson Ranch had been the roots that had kept him tethered. Izzy had come along and only sunk those roots deeper—but he'd only been able to do that for her because of his family and this place.

He didn't let himself wallow in self-pity as a rule. It always felt too close to going down Chessa's line of thinking about the world, but Cash realized he'd gotten very bad about counting his blessings. He had shrunk his world down to Izzy and just Izzy. He *knew* he'd been lucky in the face of tragedy, but he hadn't *felt* it in a long time.

Even with the danger going on around them, he felt that gratitude in this moment. He'd had this place, this foundation to keep Izzy safe all these years. And he could manage all the years to come.

A streak of a shooting star flashed across the sky. Like a good omen.

He was ready for a few good omens. He'd been white-knuckling it for so long, and there was a part of his brain telling him to keep at it. There were murders and explosions. Now was not the time to *relax and enjoy.*

But for all the *wrong*, there was good. His daughter. His

family. His dogs and business. And the surprising detour that was Carlyle Daniels. A good reminder of what he'd realized himself last night. No matter the bad, the foundation of good was how you muddled through.

Between Bent County, the Sunrise Sheriff's Department, his family and the Daniels siblings, they would get to the bottom of this. He'd long ago stopped depending on answers for a great many things—when your parents disappeared into thin air never to be heard from again, that was the life lesson.

But today, he was going to believe they'd find this problem's answers. He'd give Izzy the answers about her mother's death that he'd never been able to find about his own. No matter what it took.

He set out across the yard, heading for the dog barns. He'd get his chores done early, then move into investigation mode. They could afford a full break from training for a day or two, as long as the dogs got exercise.

So focused on this plan of action, he almost didn't stop his forward progress even as his gaze went over the dark shadow of his cabin. But a few steps beyond the cabin, the image of it, the wrongness of *something*, caught up with him.

He paused, frowned, then turned back toward it. He'd seen…something. Probably just the reflection of the moon. But could they be too careful right now?

He retraced his steps silently. He studied the shadowy cabin. Everything was barely visible in the dim light of the moon and stars. It was all dark now. No light. No flash of anything. Definitely just a random reflection, he told himself. Mentally urging himself to move on.

But his body didn't listen. It was rooted to the spot as he squinted through the dark at the cabin. He didn't see anything this time, but…he *heard* something. A rustle, an exhale. *Something*.

He should go back to the house and get a gun. He should text one of his brothers. There were a lot of things he should do, but the closer he got to the cabin, the more he could discern that the noise was a voice. Someone was inside the cabin. *Talking.* He couldn't make out words, but a window or door must have been open because he could hear the tone and tenor of the voice.

Normally, that would have sent him back to the house immediately. Normally, he would have made all the right choices in this moment.

But the voice clearly said, "You have to." In a voice he *recognized.*

It wasn't possible. It couldn't be possible.

But he *knew* that voice.

So he moved toward the cabin, rather than away like he should.

Chapter Sixteen

Once Cash reached the porch, he could tell the front door was cracked open. It was too dark to determine if it had been forced or not, but it didn't matter when he knew that voice. It was clearly coming from inside, and they were either talking to themselves or their audience was completely silent.

Cash crept up the stairs, listening to every word that was spoken. It couldn't be possible, but…

"I told you it was a bad idea." There was a beat, the speaker clearly listening.

Then it dawned on him. She was on the phone. Had the flash of light he'd seen been a phone screen?

"You're the one who had to do the explosion," she said, her voice getting louder in frustration. A frustration he was so well acquainted with.

Was this some dream? A break with reality? Everyone had said she was dead. *Dead.* People he trusted. People he loved. Everyone certain she was murdered. There were cops who thought *he* was a suspect.

But that was Chessa's voice. He knew Chessa's voice. Maybe they hadn't spent much time together in the past few years, but her voice had haunted him for years. He had listened and watched for her vigilantly for so long now, it was hard to believe he'd be wrong. He couldn't imagine anyone sounding this much like her and not *being* her. Or talking about explosions—the one that was clearly connected to his current predicament.

Cash crept closer to the door. Maybe if he could get some glimpse at the person talking, he could convince himself there was no possible way—

But the door swung open, and he had to jump back to avoid being smacked in the face by it.

The woman who stepped out into the night was… It was Chessa. Maybe it was dark, but the moon and stars offered *some* light. Maybe someone out there looked *a lot* like her in the shadows. But he knew this woman, and even in the dark he just knew it was…her. Short and slightly built. That I'll-mess-anyone-up posture he'd once found attractive, when he'd wanted to see *everyone* messed up.

Chessa wasn't dead. No matter what anyone had said. She was *here*.

"We've got company," she said into the phone at her ear. She didn't seem surprised to see him. Just sort of grim about it. She shoved the phone in her pocket. "Where's your posse?" she asked dismissively, the shadow of her chin jerking toward the house.

Just like always. Such a *Chessa* movement and statement. It was *her*.

Cash couldn't get over the pure shock of it all. Even now. Standing here, staring at her. It was real and he didn't know how to process it.

He didn't think she was high. He'd spent that first year of Izzy's life learning the signs in Chessa. There was a *movement* to her when she was high. Tonight she seemed still, controlled and stone-cold sober. That was honestly more of a concern than her being alive. High Chessa was volatile and dangerous, but Sober Chessa used all that rage and trauma to cause true, focused damage.

"You're alive," he managed to say, no matter how pointless that sounded in the quiet night around them. "How the hell did you convince people you were dead?"

She made a noise, not quite a laugh, but sort of amused. "I can't believe that worked. Pays to have friends on the inside."

"Ferguson?"

She didn't act surprised he knew. "Poor guy. All *riddled* with guilt with pulling one over on his little cop buddies. He was going to break. Had to take care of it." She sighed like she was upset over a broken nail. "Oh well. He did what we needed."

"Who's *we*?"

"Wouldn't you like to know?" She shook her head. "You really thought you'd ever be rid of me, baby?"

Sometimes, it made his skin crawl that she was Izzy's mother, but this was beyond all of those old guilts and frustrations. She had somehow convinced an entire law enforcement agency she was dead. But she wasn't, and she was *here*, sneaking around the ranch.

"What are you doing here, Chessa?" he asked, doing his best to sound bored instead of enraged.

"What do you think? I'm going to get my hands on her. I'll never stop trying. *Never*." She moved forward, but Cash didn't see any kind of weapon on her. She just poked her finger into his chest.

He would never understand. She hadn't wanted to be a mother, hadn't wanted to stick around. She'd *left*, and he hadn't made that hard on her so he couldn't ever understand this need to keep popping back up. To keep trying to *hurt* the daughter she didn't want.

Because she was a damn wound every day of his life. And Izzy's.

But her poke turned into a shove, almost like she couldn't quite stop herself, and he was still reeling from her being *alive* that it landed hard enough that he stumbled back.

"I'm going to take her," Chessa said, giving him another push, though he was ready for it this time. He held his ground.

"Why do you think it's going to go differently this time?" And it made him uneasy, because she might not be the most rational person on the planet—high or sober—but Izzy was just as protected as she always was, and Chessa had never once succeeded at getting her hands on their daughter.

Chessa didn't respond to his question. Instead, she lunged at him. A terrible attempt at a tackle, but then she kicked his shin, and he went down just enough that she jumped on top of him.

It was all so...surreally ridiculous. Cash wasn't quite sure how to proceed, except to protect himself from her weak attempts at punching and kicking. She was short and never'd had much meat on her bones, but she seemed nothing but skin and bones now.

He had the height and the weight to easily stop her blows. He couldn't fathom why she was trying to fight him when he had the physical upper hand. He rolled over on top of her, pinning her hands above her head. She stopped moving, but he could see the way she grinned up at him in the breaking light of dawn.

"You won't hit me, Cash. All that noble Hudson blood. You won't do anything except sit there and take it." She lifted her leg, clearly trying to land a knee, and failing as she tried to free her arms from his grasp. "I'm your daughter's mother. You wouldn't do *anything* to hurt me."

"That's where you're wrong, Chessa. Because I'd do anything and hurt any damn person to protect my daughter."

"I'm counting on it," Chessa said, then she smiled up at him and it was clue enough for what was coming. But he wasn't quite fast enough. The blow hit him from behind, from someone much bigger than him. It didn't knock him out, though it hurt like the devil, but it did knock him off Chessa.

And before he could get to his feet, she rolled over and jabbed something sharp and painful into his thigh.

And then everything went black.

CARLYLE COULDN'T BELIEVE how long she'd slept, or that she'd slept through Cash leaving the room. She was usually a light sleeper, but she supposed the past few days had really taken it out of her.

She sat up in Cash's bed, then yawned and stretched as she blinked at the bright sun streaming through the windows. Her body hurt. All over. She lifted her shirt to peek at her stitches.

She frowned a little. They'd bled through the bandage she'd slapped on last night after she'd showered. Maybe she should have mentioned something at the hospital the other day, but she had just wanted to get out of there.

And she definitely didn't want to go *back*. So, she'd just slap another bandage on and hope the problem went away. Because there was too much to do today. Way too much.

And Cash had let her sleep the entire morning away. She was going to have to have a talking to with that man. She didn't mind being taken care of *a little*, but not when so many important things were going on. Hopefully, there'd been some kind of break in the case.

If there wasn't, well, she was damn well going to find one.

She slid out of bed with a wince. Her head wasn't too bad, but man, her side was really killing her. She'd need to take something for the pain when she changed the bandage. All of her supplies were down in her room, so that'd be the first stop.

She let Swiftie out. "Have you been up here the whole time?" she asked, giving the dog a pat on the head as she walked out into the hallway.

But she stopped abruptly. Izzy was coming out of her own room down the hallway. She came to the same abrupt halt.

A deep, awkward silence ensued as Izzy studied Carlyle, then the door behind her. Swiftie trotted past Izzy to head downstairs, likely to be let out.

Carlyle didn't know how to sit in an awkward silence, so she cleared her throat. "Uh, you sleep in too?"

"No. I was just up here to get Caroline her doggy," Izzy said, holding up the stuffed animal.

"Your dad isn't…in there," Carlyle said. God knew why. She might love this little girl, but she hardly owed her an *explanation*. She definitely wasn't going to tell a twelve-year-old everything had been perfectly hands-off. Last night at least.

Izzy frowned. "He isn't? I haven't seen him all morning."

"I'm sure he's just…out doing chores." It was the only explanation, but it was strange Izzy hadn't seen him at *all*. He usually made a point of eating breakfast with her. "Did you text him?"

Izzy shook her head. "We all thought he was sleeping in, so we were leaving him to it."

Because they'd likely known *she* was in the room, allegedly with him. The whole family, no doubt. *We all.* Oh, Carlyle wasn't ready to think about *we all*. She knew they all *thought* things, and that was easy to brazen through when it wasn't *true*. But it was true now and…

She blew out a breath. Well, she was going to have to deal with it, wasn't she? *She'd* been the one to bring up all that future junk. She could hardly get a little gun-shy now that they had an audience.

Carlyle pulled her phone out of her pocket. She sent Cash a quick *where are you* text, then forced herself to smile reassuringly at Izzy. "I bet he's out with the dogs. I just have to grab a few things then I'll go look for him if he doesn't answer."

Izzy chewed on her bottom lip, but she nodded. They headed downstairs and Izzy trailed after her to her bedroom. Carlyle didn't want Izzy to worry, so she decided to forgo the bandage and the painkillers and just grab her work boots and a hat to hide the bump and bandage on her head.

"Have you eaten break—" But before she could shoo Izzy out of the bedroom and to the kitchen, Izzy practically leapt forward.

"Carlyle! You've got blood on your shirt."

Carlyle looked down at her side. Damn stitches. "Oh, that's nothing."

"That's where you had your stitches," Izzy said, frowning so deeply a line formed on her forehead. "Carlyle, you need to go to the doctor!"

Carlyle shook her head. "Nah. I'm good. I just need to change the bandage. No worries. I'll just…"

Izzy took her hand and pulled her into the little half bathroom attached to her room. She grabbed a washcloth and ran the hot water. "It could be infected," she said, sounding very adult. Her expression was very stern. Carlyle could certainly physically move past the girl, but she found herself standing in the bathroom, feeling like a child herself.

"It's fine."

Izzy sighed very heavily. "Lift your shirt," she instructed.

Carlyle wasn't much for taking orders, but coming from a *child* she really didn't know how to be a jerk in response, so she did as she was told.

Izzy tutted over the bloody bandage, carefully removed it and threw it in the trash. She gently washed away the blood, sighed over the broken stitches, then applied a new bandage over the gash with adept hands. She had Mary's cool, collected nature about her, and the calm, authoritarian voice Cash used with the dogs.

"You really should go to the doctor if that's not better by tomorrow." She looked up at Carlyle very sternly.

Carlyle could only smile and brush a hand over Izzy's flyaway hair. No wonder she was crazy about her. "You're something, kid."

Izzy's mouth curved a little. "I could be an EMT when I grow up. Help people in emergencies. Sometimes I help the vet when he comes out, but that just makes me sad. The animals don't know what you're saying to them, but people know you're trying to help them. So, I think I'll do that. I'd be good at it."

"Bet your ass you would." Carlyle had no problem seeing her do just that.

This caused Izzy to give her a full-blown smile. But it died quickly. "What if my dad is having an emergency? What if—"

"He has his phone. His dogs. And his brain. I can't promise you he's not… Let's just focus on finding him, and we'll go from there. But no matter what, he's going to be okay." Which she also couldn't promise, but she needed it to be true for herself just as much for Izzy. He had to be fine. He *would* be fine. He was Cash.

Izzy nodded and they walked toward the kitchen. Carlyle slid her arm around Izzy's shoulders, gave them a reassuring squeeze. Again, the move was as much for the girl as it was for herself.

Mary was sitting at the kitchen table with Walker. They

both looked up at their entrance, but then Mary frowned. "Where's Cash?"

"He was up early. Really early. I haven't seen him since. Are we sure no one's seen him out and about this morning?"

Mary blinked once, then smiled over at Izzy. "Caroline probably wants that, honey," she said, pointing to the stuffed animal still in Izzy's hand.

"I'll get it to her in a second. So *no one* knows where Dad is?" she demanded, looking at Carlyle, then back at Mary and Walker.

"I'm sure he's out doing chores," Carlyle managed to say, but he hadn't texted her back. So she was getting less and less sure. Still, where would he have gone? People didn't just... disappear.

She thought of the Hudson parents and had to swallow the lump of fear that lodged in her throat.

"He didn't get coffee this morning," Mary said quietly, pointing to the carafe. "His mugs—kitchen and travel—are still right there." She looked over to Walker, who nodded.

"I'll grab Palmer to look at the security footage. Grant and I will go find him," Walker said, making it sound easy. Light and casual as he got to his feet. "Probably hip-deep in dogs somewhere," he said, and flashed Izzy a grin. He gave his wife a quick squeeze on the way out.

Mary nodded. Her expression was calm, but she wrung her hands together in a sign of nerves as Walker strode out of the kitchen.

"The uncles will take care of it," Izzy said, sounding so calm and collected just like her aunt, but Carlyle saw the terror in her eyes, so she didn't argue. She took Izzy's hand in hers.

"Yeah, besides, if he's with the dogs, we all know he's fine. Those dogs are fierce."

Izzy swallowed and nodded, but her gaze was worried and

she stared at the back door. If he'd left, it would be on the security footage. If he was out there on the ranch, Walker and Grant would find him.

If he was in trouble… Well, the Hudsons and the Daniels would come together to get him out of it.

No matter what.

Chapter Seventeen

Cash came to in the dark. His head pounded. His stomach threatened to heave out its contents. He felt fuzzy headed and a little drunk. But he hadn't been drinking. He'd been…

He tried to cast back and remember. Tried to lift a hand, but he couldn't move at all.

He was tied up. To a chair. He looked around, even as his vision seemed to swim. Inside his cabin. That was good, even if nothing else was. Like the roiling nausea in his gut, the complete immobility. None of that was *good*, but he was in his own kitchen, which meant help was not that far away.

He took a breath, trying to steady himself. Bad but not terrible. He could work with this. He would have to.

"This might just be the *best* day," Chessa said.

He turned his head toward her voice. She was smiling at him. Her eyes were bright now, her movements jerky. How he'd gotten in this predicament was a little fuzzy, but he remembered her. Alive. She'd been sober before, but now it was clear she'd taken a hit of something.

Behind her, rifling through his kitchen pantry was a big man.

"Butch, right?" Cash managed. His mouth was dry and trying to speak caused a coughing fit he immediately regretted.

The man didn't respond. Not to him. Not to Chessa. He

just opened a jar of peanut butter and gave it a little sniff. As if satisfied by the smell, her re-capped the jar and tossed it into a bag on the ground. While Chessa moved around the kitchen, not doing anything. Just moving.

"I'm getting tired of waiting for him," she said, clearly aiming those words at Butch. That guy had to be Butch. Even though Cash had known of him, maybe seen him a few times, he had no clear recollection of what her cousin or half brother or whatever he was looked like, but they had to be in this together.

"You're always tired of waiting," Butch grumbled. "And it never got you anywhere, so why don't you shut up and let me handle it?"

She scowled at the man's back. Cash watched as her eyes darted toward the knife block on the counter, then back at the man. But she didn't make a move to grab the knives. She just turned to face Cash once more.

She sauntered over to him, got her face real close to his. "Maybe you'd like another hit?" she said, smirking. "A little lighter this time, so you don't pass full out. You never were one for the hard stuff, were you?"

He remembered now. The pain in his leg. She'd shot him up with something. "You were bad choice enough," he managed to say.

She reared back and slapped him across the face. It stung, and made the other side of his head throb, but the blow was hardly terrible and did little. He raised a condescending eyebrow at her.

"Feel big and important?" he asked her, working to keep his voice calm in the face of her increasing agitation so he didn't start coughing again.

She was clearly going to hit him again, but Butch grabbed her arm before she could swing. "Knock it off."

Chessa tried to wrestle her arm away from Butch, but he held firm. "I warned you." His voice was stone-cold. "You start acting this way, you won't get another hit. You'll end up as dead as everyone thinks you are."

Cash was very familiar with the look of seething hate on Chessa's face, but she stopped struggling. "How much longer?" she demanded of Butch through clenched teeth.

"Long as it takes. That's how we stay out of jail, remember?"

She groaned and jerked her arm out of Butch's grasp, but she didn't say anything more, or do anything. Just stood in the corner of the kitchen, and when she couldn't stand that, simply began to pace. She complained, but quietly and under her breath.

Cash kept his gaze on her as he surreptitiously pulled at the cord that tied his arms and legs to the chair. Tied tight with almost no wiggle room. Likely Butch's doing. He was definitely the one in charge and worked with a clearer head and less explosive anger than Chessa.

Which might keep Cash alive longer, but it definitely meant he had less of a chance of escaping. He knew what buttons to push when it came to Chessa. Less so of Butch.

"So, who are we waiting on? You've killed Bryan Ferguson, and I'm sure you're aware the police figured out that you all connect."

Butch didn't react, but Chessa kind of jerked at that, then whirled around so her back was to Cash. Butch went back to his pantry perusal and didn't say anything.

"They also know this is bigger than Bryan. It connects back to Tripp."

This time Butch paused what he was doing and looked over his shoulder at Cash. "Please, keep talking." He smirked. "The more information, the better."

Cash didn't scowl, though he wanted to. "It's just not going to be rocket science to figure out the connection. Especially once they get ahold of your stepmother."

"Good luck there," Chessa said with a snort, earning her a glare from Butch.

Cash filed that away. Whatever Butch didn't want Chessa going on about was important. Information that could help. Once he got out of here.

Because he *would* get out of here. This was his house, his land and everyone who loved him was within arm's reach.

"This can't end well for you guys," Cash said.

"Don't worry about our plans, honey. We're going to be just fine. You, on the other hand? We're going to—"

"Shut up, Chessa. I'm warning you," Butch said, tossing a box of crackers into his pack. "Not another word."

"You think she's going to be quiet?" Cash said, forcing himself to laugh. If there was one thing he had on his side, it was the certainty that Chessa had a short fuse. "She can't control herself when it comes to anything."

Butch made a little noise, kind of like a laugh himself. "Women," he muttered.

"You've spent twelve years trying to beat me, Chess. You've never won."

"I've won. I'll *win*! Once I make this trade—"

"Hey!" Butch yelled, the volume of it hopefully traveling outside. *Please someone be outside.* "I told you to shut the hell up."

But Chessa was on a roll. Because high or not, controlling her anger had never been in her skill set. She moved toward him, hands in fists.

"You paint yourselves the heroes, but people hate you. They're going to be so happy to think you're a bad guy. Just look at your parents. Someone hated them so much, they got rid of them without a trace."

"I said that's enough," Butch said angrily. He walked right over to Chessa. Cash braced himself for the blow he thought was coming to her, but it was worse. Butch put his hands around her throat. "You can't shut up. I'll make sure you never talk again." Then he clearly squeezed because Chessa started clawing at his arms and struggling. Her face started to turn purple as Butch choked her.

Cash couldn't just...watch her be killed. No matter what she'd done, who she'd been, this wasn't right. He tried to jerk his body enough to move the chair, to do anything. "Hey! Knock it off!"

Butch didn't pay him any mind. Cash looked around the kitchen, desperately hoping for some inspiration in how to get out of this, how to stop Butch, how to...

Then he saw the phone on the counter kind of shake. He couldn't hear it vibrating over Chessa's gurgles, but any sort of distraction would help.

"Hey! Isn't that your phone ringing?"

Butch looked over at the counter and sighed. He let go of Chessa and she dropped to the ground, gasping for air and pawing at her neck. Alive. Somehow, still alive.

Cash didn't feel relief, exactly. But he pushed all feeling away. He had to focus. Butch had answered the phone, but he didn't say anything besides *yes* or *no*.

Cash pulled at the bonds again. Tight. Too tight. He couldn't really move the chair. The only way he was going to get out of this was to wait it out. To somehow survive until...

Hell, he didn't know. But he wasn't about to give up.

"It's time," Butch said to Chessa. "But if you don't watch your step, we're leaving the girl behind and maybe your corpse. No trade."

Chessa sneered at Butch, but she got to her feet on shaky legs. "Whatever," she muttered, her voice raspy.

The girl. Why did it always come back to Izzy? "How the hell do you think you're going to get your hands on Izzy? I'm *missing.* You think my family is just going to...what? Leave her home alone? Leave her unprotected? She's got an *army* keeping her safe. You'll never get your hands on her." He said it because it was true, and because it was a reminder to himself. No one was going to let Izzy get hurt.

"We have our ways." Then Chessa pulled out her phone and held it up, like she was taking a picture of him. "Smile, honey. We're about to send your family on a very wild goose chase."

WALKER AND GRANT walked into the kitchen a little while later, and they didn't need to speak for Carlyle to know they hadn't found Cash. Palmer was still looking through security footage, she assumed.

And Cash hadn't texted her back.

But she'd sat at the table and forced herself to eat, if only to keep Izzy company. Anna and Caroline had joined them in the kitchen, pretending not to be worried, but Anna's gaze kept tracking out the window.

Grant's gaze skirted over Izzy, but Walker dove right in. "There's no evidence he ever let the dogs out this morning."

"But he had to. He always does," Izzy said, grabbing onto Carlyle's arm.

"I'm going to go get Palmer," Anna muttered. She passed off Caroline to Mary and left the kitchen.

Izzy leaned into Carlyle and Carlyle held her tight, trying not to let her mind zoom ahead. One step at a time. If he hadn't let the dogs out, something had stopped him. It would be on the security footage. Palmer would have found something, and they'd know how to proceed.

But before Palmer came in or Anna returned, Jack strode in through the back door in his Sunrise SD polo. "Anything?" he demanded.

Mary shook her head. "No."

Jack didn't say anything to that, and Carlyle couldn't read his expression. She supposed Jack, more than any of them, had the most practice keeping a blank expression in the face of potential trauma.

There had to be something to *do*. Something that wasn't just sitting around *waiting*. Carlyle was about to insist upon it when Anna returned, Palmer at her heels.

"He left the house just after four," Palmer said grimly. "Turned off the alarm, then reset it. The footage loses him between the house and the dog barns. There's no sign of him on the barn cameras."

"What about the cabin?"

"The cameras at the cabin are wired. The wires were cut sometime yesterday. But there's no evidence of anyone getting on the property from any of the entrance points."

There was a little chorus of swearing.

"The ranch is just too big to ever be fully secure," Palmer said. "But the fact we've had this kind of trouble multiple times suggests someone knew enough about the setup to circumnavigate it."

"Chessa," Izzy said, her voice wavering.

"But Chessa is dead," Anna pointed out.

"Yes, but she knew the place," Palmer said. Like the rest of them, he glanced at Izzy as if not quite sure how much to say. "She was also allegedly friends with Tripp before he died. He was our ranch hand. He knew the place *and* the security quite well. They might both be dead, but they might have passed along some information to someone who's not."

"We'll start a search party," Jack said. "We know he left

on foot. If he got waylaid by someone, the chances are they were on foot as well unless we find tracks. So, we'll split up. In threes. Izzy will stay here with Mary, Dahlia, the baby, some dogs and…" He looked over everyone. "Carlyle."

"Uh-uh. No way."

"You're injured, and we need someone here who's good with a gun."

He was full of it, but as much as she wanted to go look for Cash, Izzy was gripping her hand with such force it almost hurt. The little girl needed her, and Mary might be good at comforting, but Jack was right. Carlyle knew her way around a firearm, and how to protect.

This would be the best thing she could do for Cash, so she nodded.

Jack started deciding groups, but his phone trilled, and he pulled it out of his pocket with a frown. Then swore. Viciously.

But then he looked from Izzy to Mary. "Mary, why don't you take—"

"No," Izzy shouted, jumping to her feet. "What happened? You know something. Don't take me away." She looked up at Carlyle, tears in her eyes but a stubborn set to her mouth. Carlyle wrapped her arm around her shoulders.

"Tell us, Jack."

Jack's mouth hardened, but he nodded. "Someone just texted me a picture of Cash. They're asking for a ransom. So he's fine. He's alive." Carlyle knew Jack said that just for Izzy. "They just want us to pay money to get him back."

"Money, but why?"

Jack didn't answer her. "I'm going to forward Hart the text. And Brink and have her bring some Sunrise officers out here so we can decide how to proceed."

Carlyle and everyone—but Mary—pushed in close to Jack

to see the picture on his screen. How to proceed? Someone had Cash and...

In the picture he was tied up. He had a big bruise on his head and for a moment, a fleeting, terrible moment, she thought he must be dead. But he was scowling. Scowling at the picture-taker.

"They said they're in a hotel in Hardy. They've given me a money drop off point."

"They're not going to give him up," Grant said in a low voice, meant just for the adults.

Carlyle agreed with him, but she wasn't sure what else could be done. They wouldn't just give an address that could be surrounded. "He won't be at the place they're saying. They know you'll go to the cops."

Jack nodded. "No doubt, but we'll have to at least begin to play it their way."

"I want to see," Izzy said, trying to reach up and take the phone from Jack.

"There's nothing to see, sweetie. It's just a picture to show us he's alive and well. They can't get a ransom if he's not. The police will take it from here. It'll be okay."

But Izzy didn't drop her hand. "Let. Me. See."

Carlyle looked from the girl to the picture. It wasn't that bad, and it was clear he was alive. She wasn't sure Izzy needed this stuck in her head, but sometimes knowing was better than the unknown.

"Let her. It'll be better. She won't wonder. She'll know." And they'd find a way to get Cash back here, so this terrible picture wouldn't have to be anyone's last memory. Carlyle swallowed the heavy lump in her throat.

Jack sighed deeply, but then lowered himself into a chair. He motioned Izzy over, then put his arm around her reassuringly as he tipped the phone screen toward her. "He's going to be okay, Izzy. We're going to make sure of it."

Her chin wobbled, and her eyes filled with tears, but then her eyebrows drew together. "That's not a hotel. That's not Hardy."

"What?" Carlyle demanded…along with everyone else.

"Look." Izzy pointed at the bottom edge of the screen, and everyone leaned closer. "That's our kitchen. In the cabin."

Carlyle couldn't figure out what Izzy was pointing at. The picture was mostly just Cash's face, with very little hints at the room around him. She did see a little pink dot behind his ear. Carlyle looked around at the other adults at the table. They were all frowning too.

Izzy pushed Jack's hand out of the way and used her fingers to zoom in on the picture. "There," she said, pointing to the tiny pink dot nearly completely hidden behind Cash's ear. "That's my fairy stained glass thing that hangs in the kitchen window. I *know* it is."

Carlyle let out a breath. It was a stretch, a real reach. She looked behind her, out the kitchen window. The cabin was right there across the yard. She moved over to the window along with everyone else.

"You think they could be in there *now*?" Carlyle asked. She wanted to run across the yard right now and find out, but they all clearly knew on the off chance Cash *was* in there, they had to be very, very careful.

"Why though?" Jack asked. "Why hold him here so close to all of us?"

"Because they told you to go to Hardy," Carlyle said. She didn't want to say the rest in front of Izzy, but maybe it was best if the girl knew. "This isn't about Cash, or not only about him. What has Chessa said she wanted every single time?"

Anna swept a hand over Izzy's hair. "Chessa's dead," she said, once again.

"Sure, but that doesn't mean what she was after just stops. Especially if she was working with people. Butch. Bryan. Whoever. What purpose does it serve to send you off property when we know he's not? To put fewer people on Izzy. Because what were you going to do before the picture, Jack? Have two people and some dogs stay here with Izzy while the rest of you scattered."

Jack said nothing, but she could see a flash of irritation in his eyes. Not because she *was* right, but because he hadn't seen it himself.

"All right. We wait for the police to get here. We surround the cabin. We—"

"That'll take too long and put Cash too much at risk. We have to be sneaky," Carlyle insisted. "We can't go about it the way you normally would. This is about Cash and Izzy, but it's also kind of about you guys as a whole, right? Cash was the one to kick Chessa out, to refuse to pay her, but you all played a role in that. And if Chessa knew you, and passed that along to whoever is part of that, then she knows what you'd do."

"Chessa would have to think about someone besides herself for more than five seconds to know what we'd do," Anna said darkly.

But Jack's gaze never left Carlyle. "What do you suggest then?"

"I think we should give them what they want."

Chapter Eighteen

The response to Carlyle's suggestion was loud. Carlyle let out a sharp whistle to stop it. "Let me finish! Calm down. You guys. Seriously? I am not suggesting we put Izzy in danger. I'm suggesting we lay a trap. Let them think you've gone to Hardy, that we've scattered. Let them think you've handled this in the typical Sheriff Jack Hudson fashion, and then pull the rug out from under them."

"We need to make sure they're still in the cabin first," Grant said. "There's no point to this if they've moved location."

"My phone," Izzy said. "We can track Dad's phone with my phone. But I don't know where Dad puts it at night."

"I do," Mary said, and she hurried out of the kitchen.

Carlyle gave Izzy a squeeze. "Good thinking, kid."

Izzy nodded. She was clutching Carlyle's arm for dear life, but she was holding up. And that was what was holding them all up, Carlyle thought. They couldn't fall apart when they had to come together. They couldn't dissolve when Cash needed them to be strong.

Carlyle looked out the window. She could see just the edge of the cabin. What she really wanted to do was run across the yard, beat down the door and deal with whatever.

But it just didn't make sense. Whoever had Cash had a plan. Whether they had him in that cabin, in the hotel in Hardy or somewhere completely else, they wanted something. And this would never end until they got to the bottom of what.

And who.

If Chessa was still alive, Carlyle could believe this was all about Izzy. But with her dead, that made less and less sense.

"Did they ever find the stepmother who owned the building?" she asked Jack.

He shook his head. "She's been reported missing by a friend."

"Missing? Not like she took off?"

"It's unclear, but there's some speculation something happened to her, rather than that she's avoiding questions about the explosion."

Carlyle sucked in a breath. Another murder? What could possibly be worth all of this? It didn't add up or make any sense.

Jack's phone rang, making everyone jump. "It's Hart," he muttered, then put the phone to his ear and walked out of the kitchen. Likely so he could speak freely without worrying about Izzy's reaction.

Mary reentered with Izzy's phone. "Here." Mary handed the phone to Izzy. Izzy immediately began to poke away at the screen. She held out the little map that popped up. "He's somewhere close on the property. That means he's in the cabin!"

"He could have left it behind," Anna said gently. Phrasing it in such a way it sounded like that would have been Cash's choice, not his kidnapper's.

"He could have, but I think we know he didn't," Carlyle said, working to keep her words calm. "If Izzy's phone tracks it on the property, and Izzy recognizes the background of that picture, chances are high he is in the cabin. Right *now*. We need to move forward with that plan."

Jack returned. "Hart is on his way. He's going to have a

few men on standby at the entrances and exits of the ranch. He didn't think it sounded like a good idea to run code onto the ranch."

"You need to make it look like you're sending out your search teams," Carlyle said. "Mary and I will invite Hart inside when he gets here."

"We're not going anywhere," Jack said resolutely. "If Cash is in the cabin—"

"You don't have to *go*. You just have to make it look like you did. Make it look like Izzy is a sitting duck. But she won't be. Look, we could barge in there and get him out—God knows I'd like to—but we don't know what or who we're dealing with. We have to be more careful. Why not draw them out?"

"Because that takes time, Carlyle." She knew Jack wanted to say more—that it might be time Cash didn't have, but Carlyle refused to believe that. If they were holding him, demanding ransom, they'd keep him alive.

"Cash can handle time," Carlyle insisted. Because he had to. "We have the upper hand if we draw them out. We go in there guns blazing, they do. So we need to do something with the dogs too."

Jack didn't have a response to that. He was scowling, so clearly he didn't agree with her, but maybe he realized they really had no other options.

"Three of you go out together, armed and watchful, and saddle the horses like you're going on a search," Carlyle instructed. "The most likely thing is they're in that cabin, watching. Waiting for us to scatter. We have to act quickly."

There was a pause. Just about everyone in the kitchen—except her brother—looked to Jack. Carlyle wanted to be frustrated, but she understood the family's habitual looking to him to be the leader, to have the final say.

"Walker, Palmer and Grant. Go saddle up four horses. Walk them across the yard to the back of the house. Out of sight of the cabin. We'll tie them up there. Then we'll fan out and form an inner perimeter, out of sight. Any dogs not in a kennel or in the barn, get them there. Carlyle's right. We can't risk them posing a problem."

"Everyone should be armed," Carlyle said. "Every single person." She gave a meaningful jerk of her chin toward Izzy.

This earned Carlyle another glare from Jack. But then he sighed. His telltale sign of giving in. "All right. Palmer?"

"Got it." Palmer disappeared, likely to go gather the firearms in the house from their locked safe.

"I think it should look like as few people are with Izzy as possible, and that Izzy is within as close as reach to the cabin as possible. When Hart gets here, the two of us open the door. Together. And let him in."

"Don't you think we should hide somewhere?" Mary said, worry in every inch of her expression. "We have a great offense—all these people. There's nothing wrong with a little defense."

"We want to draw them out," Carlyle told her, with a gentleness she probably wouldn't have used with anyone else. "They need to get a glimpse of Izzy. They need to think they have this in the bag. The more they think they can easily take her, the better chance we have of doing this cleanly."

Mary didn't say anything to that, but Carlyle watched her reach out for Walker's hand as she placed her other over the slight bump of her stomach.

"You all need to go pretend to search, however Jack wants that to look. Mary and Dahlia can watch the cabin from upstairs with Caroline. Any kind of binoculars you've got—see if you can get any glimpse inside. Izzy and I stay down here and wait for Hart."

There was another pause. Then Palmer returned with the guns. It was the strangest tableau, everyone standing in the Hudson kitchen, watching as guns were distributed to different people. Palmer hesitated at Izzy, but he handed her the one she'd been practicing with all the same.

"I know you know how to use it, Iz, and we trust you to. But remember, there are a lot of adults around here who can and will handle things. This is just a last resort."

Izzy took the gun and nodded. "I know."

Palmer let out a breath then turned to the remainder of the people in the kitchen. "We should move. The sooner we draw them out, the sooner Cash is safe."

Jack nodded and then everyone began to disperse. Most everyone left out the back door, leaving Carlyle, Izzy, Mary and Dahlia in the kitchen.

Carlyle pulled her phone out of her pocket. "I'm going to start a group call. That way we can all listen and communicate."

"Good idea."

Carlyle started the call on her phone, then shoved it into her pocket on speaker. They all separated, each going to their designated spots. Carlyle took Izzy into the living room, but the girl kept looking over her shoulder.

"Aunt Mary usually isn't scared," Izzy murmured, watching the staircase even though Mary had long disappeared.

Carlyle crouched to be eye level with Izzy and waited for the girl's gaze to meet hers. "There isn't anything wrong with being scared. This is scary. But we're going to fight, even if it's scary."

"I just want my dad to be okay."

"I know. We all do. So, he's going to be. Come on. Let's watch for Hart." She held Izzy's free hand and pulled her over to the big front window. They watched the lane that led up to the house without saying anything.

"I don't want to just sit around waiting, Carlyle," Izzy said, a frustrated and determined look on her face that concerned Carlyle almost as much as Cash being held so close without anyone understanding the situation.

In any other time in her life, Carlyle would have jumped in headfirst, but she was responsible for Izzy. Cash would never forgive her if she messed that up, and Carlyle would never forgive herself. So, for the first time in her life she had to go against her instincts and just stay put.

"I don't either, but sometimes... Man, I learned this one the hard way, but sometimes you've got to let other people help you out. You try to do everything on your own, everyone gets hurt."

Izzy didn't say anything to that, but a little cloud of dust started at the ridge. Then the police car appeared. Carlyle squeezed Izzy's hand. "We've got so much help."

The cruiser pulled to a stop at the front porch and Hart got out. He had a hand on his gun, and it was clear even though he was in detective plain clothes, he was wearing Kevlar underneath.

Carlyle pulled Izzy toward the door. She opened it, and fully stepped out herself. She then pulled Izzy behind her, so hopefully if someone in the cabin was watching they'd catch a glimpse of the little girl and know she was at Carlyle's side.

"Come on in, Hart."

"Where's Jack?" he asked as he followed Carlyle inside.

Carlyle explained her theory on what these people wanted. She described the Hudson plan of keeping out of sight but close enough to know what was going on. She even explained where everyone in the house was and why she had Izzy with her.

Maybe she hadn't always trusted these cops, but now she had no choice.

"You're going to leave," she told him. "Drive all the way out. Then walk back in. Form an outer perimeter with your guys, and Zeke because he'll be here soon enough. We've got the inner. You start making a tighter and tighter circle, but the main directive is to stay out of sight from the cabin. They'll come out. Likely just one at first, but they'll come out. It's got to be more than one, so you don't want to intercede until we're sure there's no danger to Cash."

"This *is* my investigation."

"And this is my home. And the people I love," Carlyle replied. "My plan's good. The best you're going to get."

Hart glanced down at Izzy, who—to Carlyle's pride—had a lifted-chin, stubbornly defiant expression on her face. She shouldn't be holding a gun, worried about her father's life, but here she was, holding up. Holding true.

"All right. Here." He unhooked a radio from his vest. "You'll be able to hear us communicating with each other. Anything bad goes down inside, you radio out. Just press this button and talk."

Carlyle nodded. It was a good addition to her plan. Not that she was going to admit that to him.

"Anything strikes you as off, you're going to radio us, okay?"

She nodded. "I've got everyone else on a group call in my pocket. We'll do our best to communicate everything to everyone."

"Okay. I'm going to run code off the property, make it look like I'm off to Hardy and the address. Sound good?"

Better than good, but she only nodded. "You trust your guys on the perimeter?"

"With my life," Hart replied.

She hoped to God it wouldn't come to that. She opened the front door once more, letting Hart out then closing the door and locking it.

"Now what?" Izzie asked.

"Now, we have to wait."

Izzie nodded, but she was chewing on her bottom lip. A telltale sign something was bothering her.

Well, why wouldn't she be bothered? Her father was being held against his will in their home.

"It's going to be okay," Carlyle said. She would move hell and earth to make it okay.

Izzy nodded, but when she looked up at Carlyle, the expression in her eyes had Carlyle's stomach sinking.

"Carlyle, I think there's something I need to tell you."

CASH WAS FEELING worse and worse, the headache so bad he wished he could scoop his own brain out to stop the throbbing. Whatever Chessa had shot him up with was a hell of a drug.

Butch had finished with the pantry and was now stationed at the kitchen window. He hid behind the curtain but was watching through a gap. Cash couldn't quite turn his head enough to see out the gap himself, but he kept trying.

Chessa moved around. When it was clear Butch was getting agitated with her, she'd disappear into the living room for a bit, but she always came back. Edgy and pacing.

Cash could see the oven clock and knew it was creeping closer to ten in the morning. He'd been gone too long now. His family would be looking for him. It made no sense why they were keeping him this close to the people who could easily overtake *two* people. Even if they were armed.

"Finally," Butch muttered as the sounds of sirens filled the air.

Cash tried to turn in his seat again, but the bonds were too tight, cutting into his skin. Sirens, yes. But he frowned as the sound went from loud to soft—like the emergency vehicles were leaving the ranch, not coming toward it.

"Go on then," Butch said, jerking his chin at Chessa.

Chessa flashed Cash a self-satisfied grin then slipped out the back door. Cash tried to angle his head so he could see out of the kitchen window, but he couldn't manage it. Where did Chessa think she was going? What had those sirens been? He wanted to demand answers, but even if Butch gave them, Cash could hardly trust them to be true.

"You really think you can trust her to do anything?" he said instead to Butch, because it was a valid enough question. "Particularly when she's on something?"

"Not my rodeo, buddy," Butch muttered.

Cash frowned. Why would Butch pretend like he wasn't involved when it was clear he was? "This is a lot of work and effort if this isn't your rodeo."

"You have no idea the reward," Butch said with a harsh laugh. "Don't worry though. You won't be alive long enough to find out."

But he *was* still alive. For hours on end. Which meant they needed him alive for *something*. "I'm still alive, so…" Cash attempted a shrug despite his bonds. "I guess I'm not too worried about this alleged demise that's coming."

Butch spared him a glance. "For as long as we need you, you'll live. But that isn't much longer."

Chapter Nineteen

Carlyle slowly crouched down and put her hands on Izzy's shoulders. "What do you need to tell me?"

"I... I didn't think it mattered. It was...my little secret. And I would have told everybody, but I didn't think it would—"

"Iz, slow down. Take a breath. Just tell me. Tell me what you've been keeping a secret."

"There's a tunnel."

"A *what*?"

"A tunnel," she repeated, and her eyes were full of tears, her shoulders shaking underneath Carlyle's hands. "Between the cabin and the house. You just have to go into the cellar at the cabin, which is kind of creepy. Then there's this...tunnel. It comes here, through the basement. I don't go there much, but sometimes I just wanted to see... I just wanted to... I don't know. But if Dad is in the cabin, maybe we can get to him through the tunnel. The cellar opens right by the back door."

"Why didn't you tell anyone else?"

For a moment, Izzy didn't say anything. She looked at Carlyle's pocket, where the phone on speaker was, and chewed her bottom lip.

"It was somewhere I could go that nobody knew about. It was just mine. Just for me and I got to make all the choices there and..."

Carlyle could hear Jack saying something over the speakerphone, but she couldn't focus enough for the words to make sense. She could only try to work through what Izzy was telling her.

A tunnel. To the cabin. To *Cash*.

"Show me," she said to Izzy. Because if she could get to that cabin undetected... They could stop this. "Just show me where the tunnel starts in the basement and—"

"That won't be necessary."

Carlyle jerked Izzy behind her and faced down a woman with a gun. The lady was short, wiry and looked really... rough. The look in her eye was maniacal enough it made Carlyle's whole body run ice-cold. But she held Izzy behind her. No matter what, she'd keep Izzy safe.

"Carlyle," Izzy said in a small voice. "Why did everyone say she was dead?"

Carlyle stared at the woman and realized those blue eyes were familiar because they were the same shade and shape as Izzy's.

Chessa. Not dead, like everyone had said, but here. Alive and with a gun.

"Because Hudsons *lie*, Izabelle," Chessa said, pointing the gun at Carlyle's chest.

"No we don't!" Izzy shouted, trying to come out from behind Carlyle, but Carlyle held her firm. Maybe she didn't know why, but she knew Chessa wanted Izzy, and that sure as hell wasn't going to happen.

"I don't know what you think you're doing, Chessa, but it isn't going to work," Carlyle said, very calmly as she tried to think of what she could do to get Izzy out of here. Up the stairs. To Mary or Dahlia. She couldn't start shooting until Izzy was safe.

Then Carlyle could do what needed doing. But the staircase was on the other side of Chessa.

Whose finger was curled around the trigger of the gun.

"I don't need you," she said to Carlyle. "I thought Butch should have killed you when he had the chance." So Butch had been the attempted kidnapper. "He's so finicky and weird about things. So mad when I killed that two-bit cop. But he got to off his stepmother, didn't he?" She closed one eye, the gun clearly pointed at Carlyle. She was going to shoot, and Carlyle's only chance at survival was really that she was a bad shot.

Or help.

Because when the gunshot went off, it wasn't Chessa's gun. Or Izzy's or even Carlyle's. Chessa jerked and stumbled face-first onto the ground. Carlyle kept a hard grip on Izzy, keeping her behind her, but moving quickly forward to rip the gun out of Chessa's hand.

She made a low moaning sound as she writhed on the floor, but she didn't get up. Carlyle went ahead and lifted Izzy straight up off the ground and hurried her to the stairs where Dahlia sat on a stair, shaking.

"God, I hate guns," she muttered as Carlyle shoved Izzy at her. Dahlia wrapped her arms around Izzy, even though her arms shook.

"It's okay," Carlyle said. She gave Dahlia's arm a squeeze and looked her straight in the eye. "Hey, you saved the day. Take Izzy upstairs. Be with Mary this time. Lock the door."

"Carlyle—"

But Carlyle wasn't listening. There was a tunnel in the basement. And Cash on the other end.

She looked at Izzy. "Stay safe." Then she ran.

CASH HEARD THE *pop* of what could have only been a gunshot. Somewhere far off, but distinctive enough to know it was a gun. A gun.

Cash looked at Butch, who gave nothing away. He just kept looking out the gap in the curtains.

The minutes that passed were interminable, but as Cash watched Butch, the man's expression began to change. From neutral to more and more irritated. He looked at the clock on the wall more than once.

"Chessa late?" Cash asked.

"Shut up," Butch replied, standing. He walked over to Cash.

Cash didn't know why he didn't stay quiet, didn't know why he was dead set on pissing off the big guy when he was tied to a chair. Maybe Carlyle had gotten to him after all. "Big surprise that Chessa messed everything up."

Butch leaned in and Cash used it as his chance. Maybe he couldn't escape his bonds, but if he could knock Butch out or incapacitate him in some way, then at least there was no threat he'd die.

He used his head to land the hardest blow to Butch's nose that he possibly could. Pain radiated through his own skull on contact, but Butch outright *howled*, and blood spurted from his nose. Butch swore a blue streak as he stumbled back and landed on his butt.

Fury blazed in his expression, and he scrambled over to what Cash had assumed was just a bag of food pilfered from his pantry. But Butch pulled out a gun.

Well, that wasn't good. But he couldn't work up much fear over the radiating pain in his head, the blurred vision. Maybe he'd given himself a concussion? But he was about to get a gunshot wound for the trouble.

"I wouldn't," a female voice said from the kitchen entry-way.

Cash could only stare as Carlyle appeared. Butch whirled, but Carlyle was faster. She shot and Butch stumbled back, crashing into the kitchen counter. Carlyle moved over to him while Butch made terrible, pained moans.

She grabbed a knife from the block on the counter and began to saw at the ties around Cash's wrists behind the chair.

"Izzy?" he asked.

"Mary and Dahlia have her."

"They're working for someone. There could be more people out there."

"Cops and your entire family have the whole ranch surrounded." The bonds on his arms fell away and he nearly gasped in relief. "The ransom attempt wasn't the smartest move. No one fell for it. We're safe. She's safe."

She cut the ties at his feet then helped him up. She studied his face. "That's a hell of a knock," she said. He didn't know if she was seeing the mark from hitting Butch, or from earlier, but it didn't matter.

Somehow she was here, and Izzy was safe, and Butch...

Cash wasn't steady on his feet, but he used the counter and the wall to balance as he walked over to where Butch sat.

Butch had pushed himself against the wall. His complexion was gray. Blood poured out of his nose and the bullet wound in his stomach. His eyes were glassy, but they looked from Cash to Carlyle with a kind of resigned hate.

"Who sent you?" Cash demanded. "What do you want with my daughter?"

Butch looked at him, then Carlyle, then at the gun she held pointed at him. Cash didn't expect an answer. But Butch surprised him.

"Rob Scott."

Cash frowned. "I never had anything to do with Chessa's father. Neither did she."

"Yeah, and that was fine and dandy when she didn't have anything to offer him, but then he got into selling and Chessa helped him out. Got him customers. Worked in a little prostitution ring. She kept talking up how much money she could get for Izzy, how much you'd wronged her. Eventually, he decided to fund her delusion, but she's a loose cannon. I tried to tell him that, but he didn't care if it came with a payday."

"That's a nice story that leaves you completely out of it," Carlyle said while Cash reeled over all of that…truly awful information.

"I don't see anything wrong with wanting to make a profit. I'm not fool enough to use the product like her." He jerked his chin like he was aiming it at Chessa even though she wasn't there. "I'm just muscle. I do what I'm told. And I didn't kill anyone, so what? I'll do a few years' jail time. I ain't worried about it. Probably cut me a deal if I tell them everything. That's the only reason I'm bothering to tell you anything. I don't have any loyalty to Scott."

"Then why work for him?"

"Why not? The money's good, the women are better." He shrugged, even as rivulets of blood flowed out of his nose and stomach. Even as he sat there knowing that even if he survived, he was going to jail. "Better than busting my ass at some minimum-wage job."

Cash didn't see how, but he didn't have to. The sirens were getting closer. "Go open the front door, Car."

Carlyle opened a drawer, pulled out some dish towels. "Push that in there. If he doesn't die, he can testify."

Cash supposed she was right, so he did as he was told. Butch just stared at him. Not with hate, not with interest. Cash stared right back.

"She isn't right, you know," Butch said, then he grunted in pain as Cash pushed harder to stop the bleeding. "You crossed her. She'll never let it go. And now that you got in Rob's way? That's two lunatics with you on their hit list."

Cash supposed, deep down, he'd known that even if he

couldn't understand it. In Chessa's mind, he was the villain, and Izzy was hers for the taking. "That a warning, Butch?"

"Nah. Just the truth. I hope it hangs over your head for the rest of your life."

Before Cash could say anything to that, two EMTs rushed in with a stretcher. They pushed Cash out of the way and went to work on Butch, but Carlyle was dragging in another one. "He needs one too," she said, pointing at him.

The EMT walked over to him, took one look at his head and nodded. "Yeah, you've earned yourself a hospital trip."

"Is he good enough to go with me?"

Cash looked behind the EMT to see Detective Hart, but the EMT took him by the chin, moved his head this way and that. Asked him to follow her finger with his eyes. "Yes. But straight to the hospital."

Hart nodded and the EMT released him and strode over to where they were working on Butch. Carlyle led him outside and to the Bent County police cruiser Hart must have been driving.

"I'll go with and—"

Cash cut her off. "Stay here. With Izzy. Please?"

She took a breath, studied him, then nodded. She leaned in, pressed her mouth to his. "Like glue, Cash."

"Thanks."

She helped him into the back of Hart's cruiser, gave his hand one last squeeze, and then didn't just walk off to the cabin, but jogged. He knew she'd keep her promise.

"You up to telling me what happened?" Hart asked as he started the engine.

"Yeah, let's get this over with."

Chapter Twenty

Carlyle woke up feeling fuzzy headed. She was too warm, and under a blanket that smelled like strawberries.

When she blinked her eyes open, she realized she'd fallen asleep with Izzy in Izzy's bed in the kids' room. Izzy was curled up next to her, her fingers wrapped around Carlyle's wrist. For a moment, Carlyle could only watch the girl sleep.

Her heart ached in a million ways, for a hundred reasons. She nearly cried, then and there, but she'd hate to have Izzy wake up to tears.

Because the bad stuff was over now. She didn't know the prognosis on Chessa, or Butch for that matter, but she knew that Izzy was safe. Butch had been happy to rat out who was behind it, and there was no way any of them would be let out of jail for a very long time.

Carlyle would do everything in her power to make certain.

Izzy stirred next to her, yawning as she blinked her eyes open. She met Carlyle's gaze then sat straight up. "Do you think Dad's home?"

Carlyle sat up too and swung her legs over the side. "If he's not, you and I are going to the hospital and demanding to see him."

"Demanding?"

"Oh yeah. Or sneaking into his room. We'll work it out."

Izzy *almost* smiled at that, and they both got up off the bed and walked out into the hallway, the two dogs trailing behind them. Carlyle had no sense of what time it was, or even what day at this point. When they walked down the stairs, Izzy gripped her hand.

They both looked at where Chessa had been, and Carlyle figured she was holding onto Izzy as much as Izzy was holding onto her at this point. They were about to head for the kitchen, but a noise in the living room had them changing course, and as they walked through the hallway, they caught sight of Cash walking in the front door, flanked by Jack and Grant.

"Daddy!" Izzy tried to run over to him, but Carlyle held her firm for a minute.

But Cash nodded, so Carlyle let her go. The little girl raced over to Cash, who knelt to catch her. It was Grant standing behind Cash that clearly kept him from being knocked over by Izzy.

Carlyle stayed where she was, the lump in her throat making it impossible to speak anyway.

"Let's get Cash sitting down," Grant said, helping Cash back up to his feet while Izzy clung to him.

"I'll fill everyone in on the case once we get situated," Jack offered.

There was a bit of a commotion then, people talking at once as the big group of them settled into the living room. Carlyle figured she'd go stand next to Walker, but as she passed the couch where Cash and Izzy were situated, Izzy reached out and gave her arm a tug, so Carlyle had to take a seat right next to her.

With her arms wrapped tight around Cash's arm, she laid her head on Carlyle's shoulder. Like they were a little unit. Or could be.

"We're questioning Chessa's father," Jack said. "Zeke talked to some of his contacts at a federal agency. It looks like they can build a particularly big case against him—beyond just this. Especially if Butch makes it and testifies, which is looking possible."

"How did Chessa make everyone think she'd been murdered?" Cash asked. His voice was a little raspy, and it looked like he hadn't slept, but he looked...relaxed. Because his daughter was right here.

He moved his arm over Izzy's shoulders, resting his hand on Carlyle's. Carlyle had to blink back the tears stinging her eyes.

Because it was over. Really over. Sure, there were legal steps left. If Chessa survived the gunshot wound, she could still be a threat if she didn't get much jail time. It wasn't some perfect happy ending.

But with so much of the danger neutralized, a happy ending felt like so much possibility Carlyle just wanted to weep.

Jack's expression was grim. "We're still working on identifying the body that was originally ID'd as Chessa's. It looks like they fake-identified the body as Chessa with the help of Ferguson and Rob Scott. Hart's theory is the body is one of her fellow—" Jack's gaze landed on Izzy "—coworkers," he finally said.

So, another prostitute. Carlyle supposed it made sense that Chessa and her father could manipulate things with a woman who worked for them, who they probably knew enough about to hide her identity.

"Butch and Chessa will be under guard at the hospital until they make a full recovery—if they do. Then they'll be transported to jail. Chessa's awake and eager to turn on everyone. The information Butch gave you corroborates much of what Chessa said, and Chessa claims Butch killed his stepmother.

Police are looking into that too, but even without full coop-eration, they'll all be on the hook for first-degree murder. They'll be locked up for a long while."

"What about this tunnel?" Cash asked.

"As far as we can tell, they were old cellars that were con-nected," Jack said. "Old enough I'm not even sure our par-ents knew about them. They were sealed off, kind of, it looks like, until…"

"I found the one in the cabin when I was mad one day," Izzy said, looking at her lap. "Messing around in the cellar because Dad told me not to. Then I found the tunnel entrance and it was like a book, and I was mad, so I kept it a secret. Then it just became this…thing I did whenever I was mad. Whenever everyone was talking about stuff or doing stuff they were hiding from me. I didn't unseal the other side though. I tried, but I couldn't do it." She looked up at Jack, like she was desperate for him to believe her.

"No, that definitely looked more recent. I think the kid-napping attempt might have been a distraction in more ways than one. It's possible Chessa and Butch have been hiding out in the cabin since after that night."

Carlyle absorbed that like a blow. Painful, but what could you do? It was over, and they'd survived.

"I'm sorry," Izzy said, her voice so small it was a wonder anyone but Carlyle and Cash heard her. "I didn't tell anyone because… I just wanted to feel like… I just wanted to have something nobody knew about. That no one could protect me from. I'm sorry…"

"I'm sorry too, Iz," Cash said, pulling her close. "Sorry you felt like you needed that."

Izzy nodded and snuggled into him. He glanced at Carlyle over Izzy's head and smiled. "We'll all get a little better at…

talking to each other instead of trying to save each other, all on our own. Day by day."

Carlyle managed to smile back, even though she was overwhelmed with too many emotions to wade through. "Yeah." Because that was life. Day by day. Doing their best to do a little better. And she'd finally found a really good place to make her home, and good people to expand her family.

Danger or no, she was exactly where she wanted to be with the people she wanted to be with—all who'd worked together to keep each other safe and sound, no matter what threats were hurled at them.

What more could anyone ask for?

AFTER A FEW DAYS, Cash couldn't say he felt back to one hundred percent, but he felt more in control of his body. Felt like he'd dealt with what had happened, mostly.

Carlyle had handled working with the dogs for the past few days, with only moderate supervision from him as everyone was always fussing at him to rest. Then they ate their family dinner, put Izzy to bed together and came out onto the porch to watch the sunset, with Swiftie never leaving Carlyle's side for long.

It was a nice little routine. Rocking on the porch swing, her head in his lap as night slowly crept over the world.

Tonight, he was staring at his cabin. The place he'd raised his daughter, and then been held against his will.

"I don't think I can ever live there again." He twisted a lock of Carlyle's hair around his finger.

"So why not bulldoze it and start over?"

"Seems like a waste of a house."

"Sounds therapeutic to me. We can take a sledgehammer to it together. Have a destruction party."

Cash laughed, even though it hurt his head a little. "I'll keep that in mind."

And it was amazing, really. How she made everything feel infinitely possible. All those doors he'd closed and locked on himself, she'd busted open just by being her.

So, he figured tonight was as good a night as any. "You know I'm in love with you, right?"

She didn't say anything at first, but she did smile up at him. That brash, cocky smile that had first made her seem like some foreign beacon of light he couldn't resist.

"Yeah, I figured as much."

"You going to admit you're in love with me yet?"

She made a considering noise. "What's in it for me if I do?"

"Good question."

"I guess a hot guy in my bed," she said thoughtfully, as though she were ticking off points on a list.

He gave her a disapproving look. "Or my bed."

"And you're pretty decent when it comes to housework. That's a plus." She sat up and squinted out at the sunset as if considering.

He shook his head. "If you say so."

"And I like a man who can be a good dad to his daughter. If you couldn't, no amount of hotness could make up for it."

"You've got quite the criteria there."

"And the dogs. They can sense evil, so since they love you, you must not be evil."

"I'm glad the dogs are what convinced you of that."

She laughed then looked at him, her blue-gray eyes twinkling with mischief. "You're a pretty good package, Cash."

"Great," he muttered, because he knew she was messing with him, and he knew she got a kick out of it when he acted messed with.

She leaned her head on his shoulder and sighed. "I love you, Cash."

They watched the sun slip behind the horizon, not thinking about how everything would be happy and easy from here on out, but that no matter what was thrown at them, they'd always have that love.

* * * * *

TWIN JEOPARDY

CINDI MYERS

To Gini

Chapter One

"Look right down there in that gully. Just to the left of that tree branch that's sticking up out of the gravel. See that flash of white? I'm sure that's bones."

Eagle Mountain Search and Rescue volunteer Vince Shepherd moved in closer beside the couple who had summoned the team to this remote mountain trail above Galloway Basin. He squinted toward the spot the man had indicated. Yes, that definitely looked like a long bone. A femur, maybe? And was that a rib cage? His heart pounded with a mixture of hope and fear.

"They sure look human to me," the female half of the pair, a sturdy brunette who wore her hair in a long braid, said.

Search and rescue captain Danny Irwin lowered the binoculars he had focused on whatever was down there in the gully. "It's worth checking out," he said. "Thanks for calling it in."

"Looks like a pretty gnarly climb down there." The male hiker, red-haired and red-bearded, frowned into the gully. "Lots of downed trees and loose rock."

"We'll figure it out," Danny said. Tall and lanky, with shaggy brown hair and a laconic manner, in another context he might have been mistaken for a surfer instead of a registered nurse and search and rescue veteran. He looked past them to the gathered volunteers—only six responders, since this had been deemed a nonemergency call and not everyone was free on a Friday morning. "Three of us will make the hike down," he said. "The other three need to monitor the situation up top, in case any of us get into trouble."

"I'll go down with you." Vince stepped forward. He was one of the newer members of the group, but he had done a lot of hiking and climbing before he joined up, and he wanted to get a closer look at those bones. Part of him dreaded seeing them, but better to know the truth sooner rather than later. It was a long shot that those bones had anything to do with his sister, but what if they really did belong to her?

"I'll go too," Hannah Gwynn said. A paramedic, Hannah served as the team's current medical officer.

"If you hike down from the top end of the gulley, it's not that steep." Sheri Stevens, on summer vacation from her teaching position, looked up the mountainside. "You won't need to rope up or anything."

"Yeah, we just have to pick our way around the dead trees, boulders and loose gravel swept down by spring runoff," Danny said. He looked to Vince. "You ready to go?"

"Yeah."

They left Sheri, along with Grace Wilcox and Caleb Garrison, to monitor the situation up top. The hikers who had called in the find elected to head back down the mountain. Danny led the way, picking a path through the debris-choked gully. The July sun beat down, but at this high elevation the warmth was welcome. Wildflowers carpeted the meadows alongside the gully, and if it weren't for the reason for their presence here, it would have been an enjoyable outing. The climb wasn't physically challenging, but it was tedious and frustrating, requiring frequent backtracking and constant readjustments to the unsteady footing. "How did those bones ever end up down here?" Vince wondered out loud as he clambered over a fallen tree trunk, then skirted a large boulder.

"They might have washed down from farther up the mountain," Hannah said. She hopped over a mudhole, then pulled aside a fallen branch to clear a better path.

Danny stopped to gauge their progress, then pulled out his handheld radio. "How much farther do we have to go?" he asked.

"You've got about five hundred feet," Sheri replied. "You'll know you're close when you see that big branch sticking up. It's got most of the bark peeled off of it. The bones are just beyond that."

"I may need you to direct us when we get there," Danny said. "There's so much debris down here it's hard to distinguish details."

They squeezed through a tangle of tree limbs, then trudged across a section of mud, boots sinking with each step, before scaling a jumble of granite slabs. "Guess I'm getting my workout in for the day," Vince said, as he hauled himself to the top of what he hoped was the final slab. From here, he had a view down the gully. "I think that's the tree Sheri was talking about." He pointed toward a jagged branch, the bare wood shining white in the sun.

"I see a path through to there," Danny said. He hopped down from the slab and set out again, shoving aside knots of brush as he went. Hannah followed, with Vince bringing up the rear.

"You're almost there," Sheri radioed. "Look uphill."

A few minutes later, Danny stopped. "We're here," he said, and crouched down to examine something on the ground.

Vince hung back. "Is it human bones?" he called.

Hannah moved in closer and leaned over Danny's shoulder.

"It's a skeleton, all right," she said. "Kind of small. Maybe a child?"

For a moment, Vince stopped breathing. Valerie had been ten when she disappeared from the family's campsite above Galloway Basin. A four-foot dynamo with sandy-brown curls cut short, she had a dimple in her left cheek that matched Vince's own. He forced himself to move forward until he was standing beside Hannah, looking down on a small rib cage, and a heap of arm and leg bones.

Danny moved up the gully a few steps and began shifting a pile of rocks. After a few seconds, he stood once more. "It's not a human," he said. "It's a bear."

"What?" Hannah looked up from her scrutiny of the bones.

"The skull is right here." Danny pulled out something from among the rocks and held it up. The skull was oblong, with a prominent jaw, one oversize canine tooth jutting from one corner of the mouth.

"A bear?" Vince staggered a little. Not Valerie.

"Kind of a small one." Danny leaned over the skeleton once more. "See, if you look closer, you can tell the femur is too short to be human, and the shoulder blades are a lot wider."

"You're right," Hannah said. "I guess I was thinking 'human' because that's what the hikers called in, and at first glance it's similar."

"Maybe a cub that didn't make it through a hard winter," Danny said.

Vince was dimly aware of their conversation. A bear. Not a little girl. Not Valerie.

"It really did look like a human from a distance." Hannah hugged her elbows. "I can't say I'm sorry we don't have to try to transport a skeleton out of here."

Danny dropped the skull. "That's it, then. Let's get away

from here." He pulled out his radio. "We're headed back up," he said. "The bones weren't human, but a bear's."

Hannah started to move past Vince but stopped. "Are you okay?" she asked. "You look like you don't feel so hot."

"I'll be okay." He ran his hand over his face. "I guess I was trying to prepare myself for the worst, and now…"

Hannah's eyes widened. She gripped his shoulder. "Oh my gosh, Vince. I didn't even think! You thought this was Valerie, didn't you?"

No sense lying about it. "I knew it probably wasn't," he said. "But our camp wasn't that far from here, and after all these years, we're still waiting for her to be found."

Danny had ended his radio transmission and joined them. "Is something wrong?" he asked.

Hannah squeezed Vince's arm. "I'm sorry," she said. "I should have remembered."

"No reason you should have," he said. "It was a long time ago." Fifteen years. Most of his life.

Danny was watching him, a puzzled look on his face. "Something I need to know about?" he asked.

"My sister." Vince cleared his throat and focused on pulling himself together. After this long, he hadn't expected to feel so emotional. "My twin sister. She disappeared on a family camping trip in the mountains the summer we were ten." He looked past Danny, toward the mountains rising around them. "Not that far from here. She was never found, so when I heard bones had been spotted up here, I couldn't help wondering…" His voice trailed away.

"That's rough," Danny said. "Do you have any idea what happened to her?"

"None. Maybe she fell or had some other kind of accident, but lots of people looked, for days, and we never found any sign of her."

"I was a little older than you, but I still remember the posters around town and people volunteering to help search," Hannah said. "It really is scary how someone can just vanish up here."

"Sometimes they get found years later," Danny said. "There was that woman about ten years ago. She had disappeared skiing three years before, and her remains were found in a bunch of avalanche debris."

"You must think about Valerie every time you're up here," Hannah said.

"I do," Vince said. "And pretty much every time I'm up here, I look for her." Though that wasn't the sole reason he had joined search and rescue, it had been one consideration.

"I hope someone finds your sister one day," Hannah said. "I'm sorry it wasn't today."

"Really, I'm okay now. It was just kind of a shock." He shrugged, trying to appear steadier than he felt. "Like you said, now we don't have to haul a body bag up out of this gully." He didn't wait for them to answer, but turned and began retracing his steps. For a brief moment, when he had first looked down on those bones, a wave of dizziness washed over him, a mixture of profound relief that they would finally know Valerie's fate and gut-wrenching grief at proof that she really was gone. No matter how improbable it would be for her to still be alive after all this time, as long as they didn't have a body, they were able to cling to a sliver of hope that she was still walking around somewhere and maybe one day they would be reunited.

Finding out the bones weren't even human resulted in the kind of nausea-inducing whiplash experienced on roller coasters and bungee jumps. A few deep breaths and a little physical exertion, and he'd be all right again. Valerie was still gone. Probably dead. They would likely never know what happened to her. It was a reality he had grown used to, even if he had never fully accepted it.

"I HAVE AN idea for a series of articles I want to do." Tammy Patterson, the *Eagle Mountain Examiner*'s only full-time reporter, stood in front of editor Russ Saunders's desk, notepad in hand. Russ cast a jaundiced eye on anything he considered "too fluffy," so she would have to pitch this right.

Russ removed the cigar from the corner of his mouth—he never smoked the things, just chewed them. Tammy suspected he had adopted the habit when he first took helm of the paper when he was fresh out of college, thinking it made him appear more mature and even jaded. Now he actually was mature—north of fifty—and definitely jaded. "What's your idea?" he asked.

"This year is the twenty-fifth anniversary of the founding of Eagle Mountain Search and Rescue," she said. "I want to run a series of articles that looks back on some of their most dramatic callouts and daring rescues."

"Why would our readers care?" This was the question he always asked.

"People love reading about local heroism, not to mention danger, the outdoors and even unsolved mysteries."

"How is this going to contribute to our bottom line?" This was Russ's other favorite question, and one she had also anticipated.

"We'll ask local businesses to buy space for messages or special ads that celebrate Eagle Mountain Search and Rescue's anniversary. They get to advertise their business and support a favorite local organization."

He leaned forward, elbows on the desk. "How many articles are you talking about?" he asked.

"Six. One every other week for three months."

She could practically see him running through the calculations in his head. "When can you have the first article ready?" he asked.

"Two weeks. I want to start with the search for Valerie Shepherd." Before he could ask, she rushed on. "She was a ten-year-old girl who disappeared on a family camping trip in the mountains fifteen years ago. Never a trace of her seen again. Search and rescue was part of the largest wilderness search in local history. That search really ushered in a new era for the group, with a turn toward more professional training and organization."

"I remember," Russ said. "Local family. Wasn't she a twin?"

"Yes. Her brother, Vince, works for the county Road and Bridge Department. Her parents are in Junction."

"You'll talk to them for your article."

"Of course. And search and rescue has agreed to give me access to their archives. And there are lots of photos in our files we can use."

"Sounds good," Russ said. "But don't let this take precedence over your regular news coverage."

"When have I ever done that, Russ?"

He chomped down on the cigar once more and spoke around it. "You're not a slacker, I'll give you that."

Smiling to herself, Tammy moved back to her desk. Working for the only paper in town, which came out once a week, was a great way to feel like she always knew everything going on. But the sameness of reporting on the school board and county commissioner's meetings, as well as perennial wrangles over building codes or the budget amount to devote to promoting tourism, could get old. It was good to have something exciting and interesting to write about. The fifteen-year-old mystery of a missing girl definitely wasn't going to be boring.

Chapter Two

"You're Vince Shepherd, right?"

Vince accepted the beer from the bartender at Mo's Pub and turned to see who was addressing him. A young woman with a cascade of blond curls and a friendly smile eyed him through round wire-rimmed glasses. "I'm Vince," he said, wary. "Who are you?"

"I'm Tammy Patterson. I'm a reporter for the *Eagle Mountain Examiner*." She offered her hand, nails polished bright pink and a trio of rings on her fingers.

"Sure. I've read your stuff." He shook her hand. What did a reporter want with him?

"Do you have a minute to talk?" she asked.

He sipped the beer. "Talk about what?"

"I'm working on a series of stories about Eagle Mountain Search and Rescue, to celebrate their twenty-fifth anniversary. I have a few questions for you."

"Okay. Sure." He could talk about search and rescue.

"There's a spot over here where it's a little quieter." She led the way to a booth near the back of the crowded bar.

"I haven't been with the group that long," Vince said as he slid into the padded seat across from her.

"What group is that?" she asked. She was searching in an oversize black leather tote bag.

"Search and rescue. You said you were writing about them."

"Oh. I didn't know you were a member of SAR." She pulled out a notepad, a pen and a small recorder and laid them on the table in front of her. "That's even better."

He sipped more beer and frowned. "If you didn't know I was with SAR, why do you want to talk to me?"

"I want to talk to you about your sister. Valerie."

Valerie again. It wasn't that he never thought about his missing twin, but after fifteen years she wasn't on his mind every day. But today she had taken up a disproportionate space in his head, what with the callout about the bones that morning. And now this reporter was asking about her. "Why do you want to talk about Valerie?" he asked.

"I want to write about the search for her fifteen years ago. It was the largest wilderness search in county history, and as a result of that search, Eagle Mountain Search and Rescue instituted a lot of new policies and adopted a more professional approach to their operations."

"You know she was never found," he said. "It's not exactly a feel-good story."

"No, but it's an enduring mystery."

He braced himself for her to say that people were always interested in mysteries. That was true, but when it was your own family tragedy at the center of the mystery, it was tough to think of it as entertaining. But she gave him a direct look, her blue eyes showing no sign of guile. "It doesn't hurt to bring the case to the public's attention again. You never know when someone might have seen the one thing that could help you find out what happened that day."

"Do you really think there's a person out there who knows something they've never talked about?" he asked. "I'm pretty sure the sheriff's department—not to mention my parents—talked to everyone they could find."

"There was another camper in the area that day. No one ever found and talked to him."

"How do you know about him?"

"One of the news stories from the paper's archives mentioned law enforcement was looking for the man."

"He was backpacking, like us. It's not like he could have smuggled my sister out in his pack or anything. The general consensus was that Valerie fell or had some other accident. It's pretty rugged country, and there are a lot of places a little kid could get lost."

She glanced at her notes. "I plan to meet with the sheriff, and search and rescue has agreed to let me review their logs and other information in the archives about the search. And I want to speak with your parents."

"Let me call them first."

"That would be great." She smiled, and he felt the impact of the expression. How could someone put so much warmth into a smile? "I'll wait until I hear from you before I contact them. But it would help a lot if you could tell me about that day. I'd like to know more about Valerie and what she was like, and what your family was like before that day."

"I was only ten when it happened."

"She was your twin. You must have memories of her."

"I do."

She leaned toward him, her voice gentle. "I'm not trying to cause you pain, opening up old wounds. But Valerie is at the center of the story. I want to try to show my readers how her loss affected not just her family but also this town. I have a quote from the newspaper stories at the time. One of the volunteer searchers said that before Valerie disappeared, everyone thought of the wilderness as safe—not without risk, but a haven from the kinds of crimes that happen in cities and towns. That sense of security was taken along with her."

"We don't know that her disappearance was a crime."

"No. But because her body was never found—not a single trace—the possibility remains that someone took her. It's every family's worst nightmare, isn't it?"

"Yeah." A nightmare. One from which they had never completely awakened.

Fifteen Years Ago

"Come on, Vince. Race me to that big red rock up ahead." Valerie turned around and walked backward along the trail, thumbs hooked in the straps of her blue backpack, her legs like two pale sticks between the frayed hem of her denim shorts and the folded cuffs of the striped knit socks she wore with her green leather hiking boots. She had had what their mom deemed a growth spurt that summer, and was now three inches taller than Vince and all angles. Except for the corkscrew curls that stuck out from the green bandanna she had tied around her head.

"I don't want to race," he said. He didn't even want to be on this trip, lugging a heavy pack up into the middle of nowhere instead of hanging out with his friends at Trevor Richardson's birthday party, which was going to be a pool party at the rec center in Junction. Some of the boys—including Vince— had been invited to spend the night, with sleeping bags in the Richardsons' basement rec room, where they planned to stay up all night eating junk food and watching horror movies.

But Vince's parents had put an end to that prospect, insisting Vince needed to come on this trip. "We've been planning it for weeks, and family comes first," his mother said when Vince had protested.

So here he was, with the straps of his backpack digging into his shoulders and Valerie doing her best to be the kid who was *soooo* happy to be here. Instead of sympathizing with her twin, she was purposely making him look bad.

"How can anybody be such a grumpy-pants when we're surrounded by all this gorgeousness?" Valerie turned to face forward again and raised her arms in the air like she was auditioning for *The Sound of Music* or something.

No one answered her. Instead, their dad said, "I think there's a good spot to camp up ahead, off to the left in the shelter of that dike." He pointed toward a gray rock wall that stood out from the rest of the more eroded mountainside. An amateur geologist, Dad liked to use these trips to talk about various rock formations and how they had come to be. Usually, Vince found this interesting, but how could that stuff— much of which he had heard before—compare to the lost prospect of swimming, pizza, and a sleepover with unlimited junk food and horror movies?

"Awesome!" Valerie raced toward the campsite, pack bouncing. Vince brought up the rear of the group. When he got there, Valerie had already scaled a flat-topped chunk of granite. "There's another camper over there!" She pointed straight ahead. "Looks like a guy with a blue dome tent."

"Come down and help set up camp," their mother said. She was already pulling the rain fly and a bag of stakes from her pack while their father unpacked the folded tent. They each carried their own sleeping bags and pads, and the food for the weekend was divided among them.

"I'll help with the tent," Valerie said.

"Vince can help with that," their father said. "Why don't you see if you can find firewood? I thought I spotted some dead trees on the other side of the trail."

Valerie raced off to gather wood while Vince reluctantly helped his dad assemble the tent. "There will be other parties," his father said.

"Not like this one." Vince pounded a tent stake into the hard ground. "And there will be lots of other camping trips."

"Maybe. But you and your sister are growing up fast. In a few years you'll have jobs, then you'll be going away to college. It won't be as easy for the four of us to get away. These trips are important, though you may not realize how important until you're older."

"Trevor's party was important to me."

His dad paused in the act of feeding one of the collapsible tent poles through the channel in the top of the tent. "I can understand that. And maybe insisting you come with us wasn't the fairest decision, but it's the one I made. It's too late to go back, so you might as well try to make the best of it. Maybe we'll do something for your birthday to make up for it. I can't promise a pool party, but you could invite your friends to spend the night and watch movies."

"Really?"

Dad smiled. "I don't see why not."

Vince grinned. Wait until the guys heard about this! Then his elation faded. "What about Valerie?" He and his twin always celebrated together, usually with a joint party, featuring games and cake and ice cream.

"The two of you are old enough for separate celebrations, I think. I'll talk to your mom."

"Thanks!" By the time they had finished with the tent, he was feeling better. He helped spread the pads and sleeping bags inside, then emerged to find the light already fading, the air cooling. He retrieved a fleece pullover from his pack. "Find your sister and tell her to come back to camp," his mother said.

He crossed the road and hadn't gone far before he met Valerie staggering toward him, arms full of dead tree branches.

She was dropping more than she was transporting, and he hurried to take half the load from her.

"I met our neighbor," she said when both loads were balanced.

"Who?"

"The man who's camped over there." She nodded up the road. "He was looking for firewood too, but he said I could have this and he would look somewhere else."

"What's his name?"

"He didn't say. He just smiled and left. He had a nice smile." Her dimple deepened at the recollection.

"You're not supposed to talk to strangers," Vince said.

"I didn't say anything. He did all the talking."

"That's hard to believe. You never shut up."

She hip-checked him. He did the same to her. "You are such a dork!" she said.

"You're the champion dork."

"I'm number one!" she shouted, and ran ahead of him.

They raced into camp. Mom smiled at them. "As soon as the fire is going, I'll start supper," she said.

"What are we having?" Valerie asked.

"Sausage spaghetti."

"And s'mores for dessert?" Valerie asked.

"Yes."

"Yay!" Valerie shouted.

"Yay!" Vince echoed.

They ate all the spaghetti and the s'mores, then lay back by the campfire and watched for shooting stars. Vince counted five of them streaking across the sky in the space of half an hour. Valerie nudged him. "Admit it, you're glad you came," she said.

"I wish I could have done both—the party and this."

"Yeah. That would have been fun. But I'm glad you're here."

He fell asleep there on the ground, and his father woke him to go into the tent, where he burrowed into his sleeping bag beside Valerie. She lay curled on her side, the rhythm of her deep breathing lulling him to sleep.

He woke early the next morning when she crawled over him on her way to the door. "What are you doing?" he whispered, then glanced toward their parents, who slept side by side a few inches away.

"I'm going to get wood and start a fire." Valerie pulled on one green boot, then the other, then ducked out the tent flap and zipped it up again.

He lay down again and must have fallen back asleep. Next thing he knew, his mother was shaking him. "Vince, have you seen your sister?"

"Huh?" He raised up on his elbows and looked around. Valerie and his dad were both gone from the tent, and his mother was dressed in tan hiking shorts and a blue fleece, her brown hair pulled back in a ponytail.

"Valerie isn't here. Do you know where she went?" Mom asked.

"She got up early and said she was going to get firewood." He sat up. Bright sunlight showed through the open tent flap. "What time is it?"

"It's after eight. When did she get up?"

"I don't know. Really early, I think." He had that impression, anyway.

"Get up and get dressed. We need to look for her."

When he crawled out of the tent, he noticed the firepit was empty and cold. "Valerie!" his mother called.

"Valerie!" His dad echoed from the other side of the dike.

Vince climbed onto the granite slab and shaded his eyes, searching for movement or a flash of color. His father joined him. "Do you see anything?" Dad asked.

"No. Yesterday, she said there was a man camped over here, but I don't see anyone."

"Come on. We need to spread out and look farther away."

They searched for an hour. Vince peered into canyons and climbed atop rocks, but there was no sign of Valerie. "I'm going to hike back to the car and go for the sheriff," his father said. "You stay with your mother and keep looking."

His mother pulled him close. Her eyes were red and swollen from crying. "Where could she have gone?" she asked. "Did she say where she was going?"

"No. She just said she was going to get some wood."

"How can she have just vanished?"

But she had. None of them would ever see her again.

Chapter Three

Tammy met with Sheriff Travis Walker on Monday morning. When she had first moved to Eagle Mountain, the handsome dark-haired sheriff was considered one of the most eligible bachelors in town. Now the married father of twins, he had a reputation for being an honest, hardworking lawman who had run unopposed in the last election. Not long after Tammy had started work at the newspaper, she had been attacked by a pair of men who had been preying on women in the area. She had escaped unharmed, and Travis had been gentle, but firm, in digging out all the information she could remember about her attackers.

As she waited in his office, she studied the photo of his smiling wife, a baby in each arm. It probably wasn't easy being married to a man who had to face his share of danger, but Lacey Walker looked happy. Tammy felt a pinch of jealousy as she stared at the photo. She wanted that kind of happiness—that settledness of having a mate who loved you and children who were part of you. So far, that had eluded her.

"Hello, Tammy." She turned as Travis entered the office. He settled behind the desk, the chair creaking as he sat back. "Sorry to keep you waiting."

"I haven't been here long."

"I had a copy of the Valerie Shepherd file made for you.

There's not a lot of information here." He handed a single file folder across the desk.

"I spoke with Vince Shepherd Friday," she said. "He told me the consensus was that Valerie must have fallen and either been killed instantly or so injured she wasn't able to cry for help."

"By all accounts, she was an active, adventurous little girl," Travis said. "There are a lot of steep drop-offs, deep canyons and unstable rock formations in the area."

"But if that was the case, don't you think someone would have found her? According to the accounts I've read, there were literally hundreds of people searching for her for weeks. And yet not one item of clothing or any part of her remains has been found."

He shrugged. "If she ended up deep in a canyon, or in a cave or rock crevice, her remains might never be discovered."

"What about the other camper who was in the area? A single man."

"I can only tell you what's in the file, since I wasn't part of the force then. The notes you'll find in there indicate that while Valerie mentioned seeing a man camping a short distance away from the Shepherd family, no one else in the family actually saw him, and no one else we talked to saw him either."

"Do you think she was making him up? Was she like that?"

"I don't know. I'm mentioning it as one possibility."

She opened the file folder and began flipping through the notes and reports inside, scanning each page. She stopped at one report. "This says a deputy spoke to a couple of hikers who saw a man with a backpack in the area. He was alone, and they never saw him again."

"He might be the man Valerie saw, or he might be someone else," Travis said. "The department put out an appeal asking anyone who had been in the area that day to come forward, but no one ever did."

She closed the file and looked at him again. "Were there ever any suspects?"

"None," Travis said.

"What about the family? Could one of them have done something to Valerie and hidden it from the others? I know it's horrible to think about, but it does happen."

"There are copies of interviews with each family member, as well as background information from neighbors and teachers who knew them. Everyone agreed that Valerie was a loved, well-cared-for child. The parents and her brother were devastated by her loss."

"Whenever I write stories like this, I always hope someone will come forward with new information," she said. "We usually run a box at the end of the article that asks anyone who might have information to contact the sheriff's department."

"I'd be happy to hear from anyone who could shed more light on what happened that day, but I think it's doubtful that will happen."

"Probably not. Of course, the main point of the article is to highlight the efforts of search and rescue that day. Can I get a quote from you about that?"

"My understanding is that prior to Valerie's disappearance, the group was a loose-knit band of volunteers without the formal structure they have today. They worked with local law enforcement, but they weren't under the direction of the sheriff's department, as they are today. Today Eagle Mountain Search and Rescue is a professional, highly trained organization I would consider one of the best in the mountain west."

She scribbled the quote in her notebook. "That's great," she said. "Exactly what I'm looking for."

He flashed one of his rare smiles. "I'm glad I could help."

She left the sheriff's department and was walking back to the newspaper office when a voice hailed her. She turned and was surprised to see her younger brother, Mitch, striding toward her. Mitch had inherited their father's darker, straighter hair, which he wore long and pulled back in a ponytail. Dressed in fashionably cut jeans and a loose linen shirt, he looked ready to make a deal on Wall Street or—a more likely scenario—sell a luxurious vacation home to that Wall Street denizen.

"How's the real estate business?" she asked as Mitch drew even with her.

"I just came from a showing I hope will result in a sale of a ranch over near the county line," he said. "Now I have time to kill and thought I'd see if you wanted to grab lunch."

"I do if you're buying," she said. She nudged him with her elbow. "Seeing as you're about to earn a big commission and everything."

"It's not a done deal yet," he said. "But I can buy my sister lunch." He hugged her briefly. "How are you doing?"

"I'm doing okay."

"Not better than okay? Are you still upset about Darrell?"

"No, I am not upset about Darrell." Not anymore. Breaking things off with him had been the right decision, she knew. He wasn't interested in ever settling down and she was ready to look for something long term. "Ending things between us was sad," she said. "But I know it was the right thing to do."

"You'll find someone else," he said. "Maybe a handsome, wealthy, single, straight man looking to make his home in Eagle Mountain will walk into my office this afternoon and I'll introduce him to you."

"Please do," she said, and laughed.

"Where should we have lunch?" he asked.

"Let me drop this off at my office, then you can pick," she said, holding up the file folder.

He gestured at the file. "Something you're working on?"

"I'm writing about the search fifteen years ago for a little girl who went missing."

"How old was this girl?"

"Ten."

The lines across his forehead deepened. "Why are you writing about something that happened that long ago?"

She explained her planned series of articles focusing on Eagle Mountain Search and Rescue.

"And she was ten, huh?"

"Yeah, I know." The same age as their older brother, Adam, when he had been killed by a speeding car. "I interviewed the girl's twin brother Friday. When he talked about feeling lost after she was gone, I knew exactly what he was going through." She had been nine when Adam was killed, Mitch seven. Young enough to not fully comprehend how someone could suddenly be gone. Old enough to see the way their family changed forever on that day.

"Did you tell him about Adam?" Mitch asked.

"No. It's not something I talk about with anyone but you." Her mother, the only parent left now, had long ago stopped talking about her eldest son, the memories too painful.

"Yeah, me either."

She left the file on her desk; then she and Mitch walked over two blocks to the edge of the park and a food truck that sold tacos and other Mexican street food. She and Mitch had just settled at a picnic table with their purchases when Vince and two other men in the khaki uniform shirts of Eagle Mountain Road and Bridge took their place in line. "Hey, Tammy," Vince said.

"Hi, Vince. How are you?"

"Can't complain." Then he was called to place his order, and he turned away.

"Who is that?" Mitch asked.

"Vince Shepherd. Valerie's brother."

"Is he single?"

"Why? Are you interested?"

He made a face. "I was thinking for you."

It was her turn to scowl at him.

"I'm just saying," he said. "The two of you seem to get along well."

She laughed. "Saying hello to each other doesn't tell you anything about how we'd get along."

He held up both hands in a defensive gesture. "Don't blame me for wanting you to be happy."

"I am happy," she said. Maybe not the level of happiness she craved, but life wasn't all bliss and she didn't expect it to be. She touched her brother's wrist. "I'm fine, Mitch. You don't have to worry about me."

"Just don't go stirring up trouble with this article."

"Oh, please. There's nothing about this article that could cause me trouble. I'm not an investigative reporter digging up dirt in a big city." Maybe in another life, she would have chosen a more exciting career, but being the sole reporter at a small-town paper suited her. It was comfortable and safe, and that's what she craved—most of the time, at least.

"I DIDN'T KNOW you knew Tammy Patterson," Vince's co-worker, Cavin, said when the three of them were seated at a table a short distance from where Tammy and her friend were eating.

"We've met." Vince poured salsa onto his tacos.

"I heard she split up with the guy she was dating," the third man at the table, Sandor, said.

Vince stared at him. "How do you know these things?"

"My wife works at the salon where Tammy gets her hair cut. She knows everything there is to know about half the female population in town. And then she comes home and tells me everything."

"The scary thing is, you remember it," Cavin said.

Sandor shrugged. "People are interesting."

"If you say so." Vince bit into his taco. He glanced over at Tammy. She was pretty, in a friendly, down-to-earth kind of way. All those soft curls. She was laughing with the guy she was with.

Cavin nudged him. "Caught you looking," he said.

Vince focused on his food once more. "She and that guy look pretty cozy, so I'd say she isn't available," he said.

"That's her brother," Sandor said. "He's a real estate agent over at Brown Realty. He helped us find the house we're in."

Vince couldn't help himself—he had to look at the pair again. Maybe a family resemblance was there. Tammy rested a hand on the man's forearm and smiled into his eyes. He felt a pang. What would it be like to have a lunch with a grown-up Valerie like that? To have someone besides your parents who had known you your whole life, who had seen life from a similar perspective and had the same frame of reference? He would never know.

Cavin shifted the conversation to a discussion of parts he needed to order for one of the county graders, and Vince turned his back on Tammy and her brother. Maybe he wasn't cut out for relationships. He didn't like getting too close to people. That was okay. Everybody was different, and he was happy enough. Most of the time.

"As we say goodbye to our friend Paul, it is with great sadness, as well as gratitude for having him in our lives. Though his physical body is gone from us, his memory endures, and we will hold him in our hearts forever." The black-suited man from the funeral home who had agreed to lead this graveside burial looked across the open grave at the trio of mourners. "Go in peace," he said. "And I'm sorry for your loss."

"Thank you." Valerie choked out the words, then cleared her throat, pulling herself together. Paul never liked it when she cried. It was the one thing she did that ever made him angry. She turned away, not wanting to see them shovel dirt onto the coffin.

"It's hard to believe he's gone."

She glanced at the speaker—Bill, who had played on the local softball team with Paul. "I guess so," she said. Though after staring at his dead body, slumped in his favorite chair in front of the TV, she hadn't any doubts that he had died. An asthma attack, the coroner had said.

"I mean, he was so young," Bill continued. "Only forty-five."

Thirty-nine, she silently corrected. But he told everyone he was older because of her. She hadn't realized herself until she had found papers with his real age on them one day when she was sixteen. It made sense, though. No one would have believed he was her father if they knew he was only fourteen years older. Not that it was anyone's business.

"I know there's not any formal wake or anything, but do you want to get coffee or something?"

She stopped walking. So did Bill. He shoved his hands in the pockets of his baggy suit and hunched his shoulders the way tall people sometimes did, as if trying to look smaller. He was thin and bony, and already losing his hair despite the fact that he was still in his twenties. He wasn't bad looking, but his cloying infatuation with her was grating. "No thank you," she said. "I don't feel like company."

"Well, sure. Of course." He took a step back. "Maybe another time."

She walked alone to her car and drove back to the house that had been home the past fifteen years, in a drab suburb of Omaha, Nebraska. She had been happy here while Paul was alive. Happy enough. Happy as a person could be who had been abandoned by the people who were supposed to take care of her. As Paul had often reminded her, she was lucky he had come along when he did, to look after her.

But now Paul was gone. She had no one.

She was alone now. Free to do whatever she wanted. Paul had left her a little money—several thousand in cash he kept in the safe in his bedroom closet, as well as the house and ample funds in the bank accounts they shared. She would take that money and spend some time making things right.

Chapter Four

Monday night, Vince called his parents. He had been putting the conversation off since he had talked to Tammy on Friday, but it was time he let them know. Though they had moved to Junction several years before, they still subscribed to the *Eagle Mountain Examiner*, and he didn't want them surprised by Tammy's request for an interview. Besides, she was waiting on him before she could finish the article.

His father answered the phone and put the call on Speaker right away. "Hello, Vince," he said. "Your mother is right here. How are you doing?"

"I'm okay, Dad. How are you and Mom?"

"We're fine," his mom answered. "A little tired. We played golf today—a full eighteen holes. With Barb and Ray Ferngil. Do you remember them? Ray used to work with your dad."

Vince had no idea who they were talking about. "You had beautiful weather for a game," he said.

"We did," his dad said. "I like living near a good course."

"Did you just call to chat, or did you need something?" his mom asked. "Not that we don't love to hear from you, but you don't usually call on a Monday night."

"A reporter here in Eagle Mountain is doing a series of articles on the local search and rescue organization," he said.

"One of the articles is going to be about the search for Valerie. I just wanted to warn you so it didn't come as a shock."

"Oh." One short, sad exhalation from his mom that made his chest tighten. He hoped she wasn't going to start crying. She hadn't done that in a long time, but it always unsettled him.

"Did this reporter talk to you about it?" his dad asked. "Is that how you know?"

"Yeah. She interviewed me. I think it's going to be a good story. Apparently, the search for Valerie was a catalyst that transformed the rescue group into a professional organization."

"Well, good. Good." He could picture his dad nodding in that thoughtful way he had—lips pursed, brow furrowed.

"She wants to talk to you and Mom too."

"Well…" Now he pictured his father looking at his mother, gauging her reaction to the request.

"Of course we'll talk to her," his mom said. "Maybe someone will come forward who remembers something about that day that got overlooked. Or the article will inspire people to look for her while they're hiking in that area."

"Maybe so, Mom. Though after such a long time, I don't think we can hope for much."

"You never know. Maybe…maybe Valerie will see the article and get in touch."

He winced. His parents—especially his mother—had never given up hope that Valerie hadn't died that day but that she had been taken, perhaps by the mysterious camper no one had ever identified. "I don't know about that, Mom," he said.

"I know you think I'm foolish, but it's not such a far-fetched idea. There have been other missing children who were discovered as adults. And I still say if Valerie had died that day, someone would have found her. You may not remember, but they literally had people spaced two feet apart in long lines, searching every inch of the area around our campsite for miles. How could they have not found her if she was still there?"

"I didn't mean to upset you," Vince said. "I just wanted you to know."

"We appreciate that," his dad said. Gone was the cheerfulness with which he had started the call. Now he sounded tired. Old.

"I'll let you know if I hear anything else," Vince said. "I'd better go now."

"Goodbye, son." This from his dad. In the background, he heard a sound he thought might have been his mother, crying.

He ended the call and leaned against the sofa, head back, eyes closed. For years, his mom had sworn that if Valerie was dead, she would know it. "She's my daughter," she said. "That's a bond that doesn't break."

Once, years ago, she had pressed Vince to admit that he still felt his sister was alive too. "She's your twin," Mom said. "You're halves of the same whole."

"We're not identical twins, Mom."

"Oh, you know what I mean."

"I'm sorry, Mom, I don't."

"You don't feel Valerie is still alive somewhere?"

"I don't know, Mom."

Her face crumpled, but she pulled herself together. "Do you feel like she's gone, then?" she asked.

"I don't know, Mom."

When he thought of his sister, he didn't feel anything. Just…empty. Not a wrenching loss or a sense that she was just away for a while. There was a void where his sister was supposed to be, and he didn't expect anything would ever fill it.

AT THE THURSDAY-EVENING meeting of Eagle Mountain Search and Rescue volunteers. Vince settled on one end of the sofa in the hangar-like building that served as search and rescue headquarters, next to newlyweds Jake and Hannah Gwynn. When he wasn't volunteering with SAR, Jake was a deputy with the Rayford County Sheriff's Department, which put him on the scene for many of the accidents SAR responded to. After seeing the volunteers in action, he had decided to join their ranks. And it had been one way to guarantee he would see more of Hannah.

"All right, everyone. Let's go ahead and get started." Danny, clipboard in hand, walked to the front of the room, and conversation among the volunteers died down. "First up, I want to introduce our newest volunteer, Bethany Ames."

A slender young woman with a mass of dark curls stood and waved. She had a heart-shaped face and an upturned nose, and a dimple in her cheek when she smiled. "Bethany is new to the area and works at Peak Jeep and Snowmobile Rentals," Danny continued. "Everyone, introduce yourselves later." Bethany sat, and Danny consulted his clipboard again. "Next, most of you already know that this summer marks the twenty-fifth anniversary of the founding of Eagle Mountain Search and Rescue."

"Happy birthday to us!" Ryan Welch called out while several others responded with whistles or clapping.

"Will there be a cake?" someone else asked.

"Cake is always welcome," Danny agreed. "We'll see what we can do. In the meantime, the *Eagle Mountain Examiner* is planning a series of articles about the organization, focusing on several of our missions over the years, as well as sharing how the group has grown and changed."

Murmurs of approval greeted this news.

"The first article is going to run next week. Most of you

know Tammy Patterson, the paper's reporter. She's starting the series with a feature about the search for Valerie Shepherd fifteen years ago."

A number of people turned to look at Vince. "Are you okay with this?" Jake asked.

"I already spoke with Tammy," Vince said. "It's fine."

"Valerie was never found," Tony Meisner, the volunteer who had been with the group longest—over twenty years—said. "Why start with that mission?"

"Because that search—and the failure of anyone to find Valerie—changed the way the group organized and trained," Danny said. "After that, we formally operated under the direction of the sheriff, we required more training, restructured the command system with new roles, and sought accreditation with the Colorado Search and Rescue Association."

Tony sat back. "Okay, that makes sense. Still seems a bummer to start with such a sad case." He looked over at the sofa. "No offense, Vince. I always felt bad we didn't find your sister."

"It's okay," Vince said. "I know everyone tried their best." He didn't remember that much about the actual search for Valerie. His parents had kept him home, perhaps fearful that he might wander off and come to harm. But he had seen the appeals for people to help with the search, and photographs in the paper showing lines of volunteers marching across the area where they had camped.

"This series is going to be great publicity for the group," Danny said. "We want to take advantage of that by stepping up our fundraising."

Groans rose up around the room. "I know, I know," Danny said. "Nobody likes begging for money. But the work we do is expensive—equipment constantly needs replacing and supplies replenishing. Training costs money, and then there are the everyday expenses, like gas for vehicles and utility bills for this building and the occasional meal to keep you people from resigning. We rely on donations for the bulk of our funds."

"I guess when people read this article and think about how great and wonderful we are, we might as well be there with our hands out," Ryan said.

Many in the group laughed. Danny smiled. "The paper has agreed to print a coupon people can use to mail in a donation, as well as information about how they can donate online. We're also going to have our usual booth at the community Fourth of July celebration," he said. He held up the clipboard. "I've got the sign-up sheet here. We've also been asked to participate in something the city is calling First Responders Fun Fair."

"What is that?" Sheri asked.

"The Elks Club is hosting their usual carnival games, but this time they're asking fire, sheriff's, EMS and SAR personnel to man the various games, with all the proceeds from ticket sales split among the four groups. Last year they took in almost five thousand dollars in proceeds, so it's a significant addition to our coffers."

"Sure, we can do that," Eldon Ramsey said.

"I have a sign-up sheet for the carnival as well. Everyone needs to come up and choose your time slots." He set the clipboard aside. "No training tonight, but we do need to pull out and inspect all the climbing gear and reorganize and replenish first aid supplies. Sheri and Tony are in charge of the climbing gear, while Hannah and I will oversee the first aid supplies. We each need people to help, so spread out and let's get to work."

Vince was trying to decide who to work with when Bethany approached. "Hi," she said. "Have you been with search and rescue long?"

"About six months," he said. "So I'm still a rookie too."

"It's a little intimidating being around so many experienced volunteers." She scanned the room. "I don't have any special skills, but Danny said I didn't need them, just a willingness to work and follow direction."

"You'll do fine," Vince said. "Everyone here pitches in to help the newbies learn the ropes."

Her expression sobered. "I was sorry to hear about your sister."

"Um, thanks." She was looking at him with those big, dark eyes, her expression a familiar one—mixed curiosity and pity. He never knew how to respond to that, so he was relieved when Tony approached. "Come help with the climbing gear," he said. He glanced at Bethany. "I know Hannah could use another hand with the medical supplies."

"Sure. Thanks." Bethany touched his arm. "It was nice talking with you, Vince," she said, and hurried away.

Vince and Tony moved to the closet that held the ropes and hardware used in climbing. The steep canyons and high peaks of the terrain around Eagle Mountain meant that many of their rescue operations involved climbing or rappelling, and a significant part of volunteer training focused on the skills needed for these activities. Sheri and Tony began laying out ropes, and she explained how to inspect the colored braided strands for damage and excessive wear.

Vince accepted a coil of rope from Tony. He realized the veteran was the only one here tonight who'd been part of the search when Valerie disappeared. "Did you help look for my sister?" he asked.

"I did." The lines around his blue eyes deepened. Lean and muscular, Tony had the weathered complexion of a man who spent a lot of time outdoors, his neat beard and blond hair beginning to show streaks of gray. "We went out every day for a week."

"What was that like?" Vince asked. "I mean, what about it led to so many changes for the group?"

Tony considered the question for a long moment, then said, "It wasn't that we were disorganized, but we hadn't had any formal training. We knew some basic principles, but the training we get nowadays teaches us about the psychology of searches. People who are lost have patterns of behavior. Most people tend to stick to trails or roads, even animal trails. In the mountains, they tend to move up, to try to get a better view of terrain. They may believe no one is looking for them and they have to walk out of a situation to be found, which may lead them to keep moving, even if they're disoriented and have no idea where they are. Today we use mapping techniques and even mathematical formulas to determine the most likely area a person will be located, and focus the search on these areas first. We didn't have any of that kind of data fifteen years ago—we just tried to search as wide an area as possible, with no precision."

"Does it seem odd to you that no trace of her was ever discovered?" Vince asked. "Not a piece of clothing or a bone or anything?"

"One thing I know now that I didn't know then was that children will sometimes hide from searchers or refuse to answer when people, even family members, call for them," he said. "They're afraid of getting into trouble. We might have walked right by your sister and not known she was there if she didn't respond to our calls. Then too, there's a lot of country up there, much of it rough and pretty inaccessible. Most people who die in the back country are found eventually, but not everyone. I'm sorry."

"We always wondered if she was taken."

"That happens too," Tony said. "But who took her? There was no one else up there."

"Valerie said there was a man camped near us. None of us ever saw him, but we didn't look. And she wasn't one to make things up."

"Then maybe that's what happened. If it is, I'm sorry about that too."

Vince knew the statistics. Children who were taken were almost always killed unless they were kidnapped by a relative, and he was pretty sure that hadn't happened to Valerie. He didn't like to think of his sister ending up that way, any more than he wanted to believe she had fallen into a crevice in the mountains and been killed. He had long believed she had died, but he wanted to know how. Wasn't that human nature—to not like unanswered questions?

IN THE FOUR years Tammy had been reporting for the *Eagle Mountain Examiner*, she had written feel-good pieces about local citizens; straightforward accounts of town council and school board meetings; reports of burglaries, fires and murder. She had even written a first-person report of her own escape from a pair of serial killers who had terrorized the area one winter. While some of these stories had been tougher to write than others, none had affected her as much as her recounting of the disappearance of Valerie Shepherd.

More than one volunteer had teared up as they spoke of the search for the little girl. "She used to come into my store with her mom," said the owner of the local meat market. "Such a grin on her face. She was an impish kind of kid—always up to something. Her twin brother was quieter, following her lead. We couldn't believe she would just vanish the way she did."

"It hit me hard," another volunteer admitted. "I wouldn't let my own kids out of my sight for a long time after that. To think of anything like that happening here, where we always felt safe. It was hard to believe things could change that suddenly—one minute she was there, the next she was gone."

But Tammy knew how suddenly life could change. The day Adam had been killed, the three of them—Adam, Mitch and her—had been playing in the front yard, kicking a soccer ball back and forth, when the ball had rolled into the street. "I'll get it!" Adam called, and ran after it.

He didn't see the car race around the curve. And the driver didn't see Adam until it was too late. One minute he had been there with them, laughing and playing. The next moment he was gone. A hole was torn in their family that could never be repaired. They had done their best to heal, but they all carried the wound inside them.

She had seen the same kind of damage in Vince Shepherd when she had interviewed him. He knew what it was like to walk through life with an empty space in your heart or your soul that could never be filled. Tammy coped by avoiding thinking about Adam and what had happened that day. But talking to Vince and to the volunteer searchers had forced her to feel all those feelings again—grief and anger and confusion. How could something like that happen? How could a person who was practically part of you suddenly not be there?

She had wanted to ask Vince if he was like her—if he coped with the loss by avoiding thinking about it. She had apologized for bringing him and his family any pain, but was an apology enough?

That was why she turned up outside Vince's condo at eight thirty on a Wednesday night, a fresh copy of the latest issue of the *Examiner* in her hand. She rang the bell to his unit and shifted from foot to foot, jittery with nerves. What if he hated what she had written?

Footsteps sounded on the other side of the door, and then

Vince stood on the threshold, a wary expression on his handsome face. His hair was damp, curling around his ears. The T-shirt that clung to his chest and abs was damp too, as if he had pulled it on hastily, along with the jeans. His feet were bare. "I didn't mean to disturb you," she blurted, feeling her face heat. "I just wanted to give you this." She thrust the paper at him. "Everyone else will see it in the morning, but I wanted you to read it first."

He unfolded the paper and scanned the headlines, stopping at the story that filled the front page below the fold. "'Search for Missing Girl Shaped EMSAR Future.'"

Tammy bit her lower lip and forced herself to remain still as he read. She had rewritten the lede so many times she had memorized it. *When ten-year-old Valerie Shepherd vanished from the mountains above Galloway Basin on a sunny summer Saturday, she changed the family who loved her forever. But she also changed the community of Eagle Mountain. And her disappearance spurred the transformation of Eagle Mountain Search and Rescue from a group of dedicated amateurs to the highly trained professional-quality organization they are today.*

Vince glanced up from the paper. He didn't look upset, which was a relief. "Come on in," he said, and took a step back.

"Okay. Sure." She moved past him, the scent of his soap—something herbal—distracting her, not to mention the realization that mere inches separated her from his seriously ripped body. How had she not noticed this the other night? He hadn't been wearing a clinging, wet T-shirt, but still, how had she missed those shoulders?

She pushed the thought away and moved into a small living room furnished with a sofa, matching chair, coffee table and a large wall-mounted television. He slipped past her, picked up the remote and switched off the TV. "Have a seat," he said.

She settled on one end of the sofa. He took the other, the newspaper spread out on his lap. "Thanks for bringing this by," he said.

"I figured people might mention the article to you, and you'd want to know what's in it."

He nodded and looked down, reading again. She gripped both knees and pretended to study the room, but she was almost entirely focused on Vince, attuned to any reaction he might have to her words.

He was a fast reader. Or maybe he was skimming. Not many seconds passed before he looked up again. "It's good," he said. "All the stuff about search and rescue is interesting. I didn't realize all the emphasis on training was relatively new."

"Part of that is because there's a lot more training courses available now."

He glanced back down at the paper. "I didn't know so many people still think about Valerie. I always figured my mom and dad and me were the only ones who remembered her."

"I didn't have to remind anyone about what happened," Tammy said. "As soon as I said her name, they remembered. And everyone asked if I knew anything more about what happened to her."

"I guess no one came up with any new information? I mean, the article doesn't mention anything."

"There's nothing new. I'm sorry."

"I guess it would be surprising to think anything else would come to light after all this time."

"Will you share that with your parents?" She tapped the paper. "I should have brought a copy for them too. I wasn't thinking."

"It's okay. They have a subscription. They're looking forward to the article. Dad said they enjoyed talking to you."

"I enjoyed talking with them." Though, in some ways, it

had been uncomfortably like talking with her own mother—the familiar sad and wistful expressions, along with the way they second-guessed every action that day. If they had done this instead of that, maybe they could have prevented what had happened.

"My dad said you were empathetic. I guess that's an important quality for a writer."

She looked away, then forced her gaze back to him. No reason not to tell him. "I had a brother, Adam. He died when he was ten. I was nine. We were playing in the front yard of our house—me and Adam and our brother, Mitch—and our soccer ball rolled into the street. Adam ran after it and was hit by a car."

"Then you know what it's like," he said. "Everything is fine, and the next second, nothing will ever be the same again."

"Yeah." The lump in her throat startled and embarrassed her. After all this time, she didn't cry about Adam. What good would that do? But her eyes stung and her chest tightened. She clenched her fists, digging her nails into her palms. "What happened to Adam was terrible," she said. "But at least we know what happened to him." There was a grave her mother visited, though Tammy never did. The Shepherds didn't even have that.

"That was your brother with you at lunch the other day, right?" Vince asked.

"Yes. Mitch."

"It's nice that he's here in town. I always wondered if it would have been a little easier if I had had a sibling. Someone else for my parents to focus on. Someone else who had the same story I did."

"It was comforting having Mitch, especially right after

Adam died, when my parents were struggling. He and I made sure to look after each other."

"I would have liked that, but I got used to being on my own. And my folks pulled themselves together after a while."

"They seem like great people."

"What about your parents?" he asked. "Do they live near here?"

"My dad died five years ago. But my mom is here. She and I share a house, actually."

"I don't think I could live with my parents again."

"My mom is a pretty good roommate."

Silence. He was looking down at the newspaper again, and she started to feel awkward. She stood. "I won't keep you. I just wanted to drop that off."

He set aside the paper and rose also. "Thanks."

He followed her to the door. When he had first invited her inside, hope had flickered that maybe they could connect on another level. As friends. Maybe even potential dates. Not that she was eager to rush into anything, but Vince was single, good-looking and close to her age. She couldn't deny a certain attraction, and while lost siblings maybe wasn't the most solid foundation on which to build a relationship, it did give them something in common.

Now all she wanted to do was get out of his condo. Everything felt too awkward and forced. She shouldn't have told him about Adam. It was too personal. Too close to home. She hoped he hadn't thought she was using her tragedy to get close to him. The idea made her queasy. "Good night," she said, and reached for the doorknob.

He put his hand over hers. He had big hands, and calluses on his fingers, the roughness registering against her skin, making her hyperaware of his physical presence. He wasn't an overly large man, but he was muscular and fit—so *male*.

She would never write that in an article. The only reason she was even thinking it now was because he had her stirred up and confused. He looked into her eyes, and though she didn't move, she felt knocked off-balance. Such an intense look. Staggering. "Thanks for telling me about Adam," he said.

"I don't talk about him much," she said. "But I thought you'd understand."

"Yeah, I do." His gaze flickered to her lips, and she wondered if he was thinking about kissing her. Entirely inappropriate, and yet she fought to keep from leaning toward him, inviting his touch. *Okaaay.* She needed to get a grip.

"Good night," she said again. "I'll, uh, see you around."

She did turn the doorknob then, and he moved his hand away and stepped back. "Good night."

She managed to walk all the way to her car without breaking into a run or melting into a puddle. In her car, she sat and took deep breaths. What the heck had just happened in there? She had gone to Vince's condo to give him a copy of the newspaper, not to bare her soul or fall madly in lust. If he had felt even half of what she had, he was probably thinking she was the most unprofessional reporter he had ever met. Or worse, did he think she was chasing after him? She closed her eyes and rested her forehead against the steering wheel. Please, no, not that. She was not desperate, and she wanted nothing to do with a man who thought she was.

As for telling him about Adam, that hadn't been a bid for sympathy. She had wanted him to know she sympathized with that special brand of grief they shared. She was just being friendly, but too many times that kind of thing got misinterpreted. It had happened to her before. Once, when an intern at the paper arrived in town after a long day of travel, clearly exhausted and famished, she had invited him to dinner at her place. He had misinterpreted this as an attempt at seduction, which had embarrassed them both and made for an awkward six months as they worked side by side. Vince's father was right—she was an empathetic person. Too empathetic.

She straightened and started the car. Maybe she had embarrassed herself again tonight, but she would get over it. She had survived worse—what was one more injury to her dignity?

Chapter Five

All day Thursday, people stopped Vince to comment on the article in that day's paper. People expressed sympathy over the loss of his sister. Many wanted to hear Vince's take on what had happened that day, or hoped to glean details that hadn't been revealed in the article. "I never knew you had a sister," Sandor said as he and Vince made repairs to a guardrail that afternoon.

"It's not something I talk about." Vince shoved on the guardrail support to bring it into line. "Tighten that bolt there."

Sandor began tightening the bolt. "I wonder what happened to her. I mean, you think after all this time, they would have found something."

"You'd think. Okay, shove rocks up against this post to keep it upright. Then we'll pack the dirt down around it."

"I wonder if it was, like, aliens or something."

Vince stared. "Aliens."

"Yeah. I mean, what if she was abducted by aliens?"

"I don't believe in aliens."

Sandor frowned. "You don't? But there are a lot of stories…"

Vince shook his head. "Finish setting that post. I'm going to check the other side of the bridge."

No one else mentioned aliens, but several felt compelled

to share their theories, most involving kidnapping, or maybe, they said, Valerie had run away. Vince listened to them all, then found somewhere else he needed to be. It wasn't as if he hadn't already thought of all these things over the years—except the aliens. But without proof, he would never know what happened to his sister.

He arrived at his condo a little after five, ready to take a shower, have dinner and a drink, and binge TV. He was walking up to his door when a neighbor called out to him. He braced himself for sympathy or speculation as he waited for Tasha Brueger to reach him. "Hi, Vince," she said. "I just wanted to tell you there was a young woman here about an hour ago. She was asking about you."

"Who was she?"

"She didn't tell me her name. She just stopped me and asked if I knew when you'd be home. She was standing here at your front door. I guess she'd been ringing the bell and not getting an answer. I told her you usually got home a little after five."

He couldn't imagine who would be looking for him. Another reporter, maybe? "What did she look like?"

Tasha—who was a foot shorter than Vince's six feet and had to tilt her head back to look up at him—tugged on one long brown curl and pursed her lips, deep dimples forming on either side of her round cheeks. "She was just sort of average, you know? Dark hair, pulled back in a ponytail. Not too tall, not too short. Not fat or skinny. She wore sunglasses. I had to go pick Sammy up from practice, so we didn't talk long."

"Thanks." He turned back to his door, and Tasha hurried away. Could the woman looking for him have been Tammy Patterson? The description didn't really fit her, and if Tammy wanted to talk to him, why not call or text?

He let himself in and dropped his backpack by the door. He wasn't sure if Tammy would ever want to see him again.

Last night had ended awkwardly between them. That was all on him—he'd been caught so off guard by the intensity of his attraction to her that he had frozen. He considered himself a pro at keeping things casual when it came to women. His default setting for relationships might be summed up as "don't bother getting too close." But Tammy, with her warm smile and earnest expression—as well as the revelation about her brother's death—had cut through his carefully manufactured defenses with breathtaking ease. He didn't have to explain his feelings to her because she had experienced them herself.

Whether it was that understanding or her soft curves and cloud of blond curls, he had been bowled over by the desire to touch her. To kiss her. To discover what it would be like to be close to her. He thought she might be feeling a little of the same, but he couldn't be sure. If he had actually done any of the things his mind insisted on picturing, she might have slugged him. He knew plenty of women, but he couldn't say he knew *about* them. Would things be different if he had a sister to ask?

He shed his clothing as he walked down the hall and hit the shower. He closed his eyes and let the hot water beat down and willed himself not to think about anything for just a few minutes.

Half an hour later, he was in the kitchen, staring into the open refrigerator and trying to decide what to make for dinner, when his phone rang. It was a local number, so he answered. "Hi, Vince. It's Tammy." She sounded out of breath. Anxious.

"Hey. What's up?" Did he sound cool or just not too bright?

"Would it be okay if I came by your place for a few minutes? I have something I need to show you."

"Is everything okay? You sound upset." Or at least, less than thrilled by the prospect of yet another awkward visit with him.

"I'm just…confused. Anyway, I think you need to see this."

"What is it?"

"I'd rather show you than talk about it."

"Okay. Sure. Come on by."

"I'll be right over."

He ended the call and closed the refrigerator, then leaned back against it, no longer hungry. Tammy had sounded rattled. He hadn't known her long, but she had struck him as a calm person. Someone who didn't panic easily.

He rubbed his jaw, and the scratch of whiskers made him wonder if he should shave. Would she think he was trying too hard?

He didn't have much time to wonder. Five minutes later, his doorbell rang. He opened it to Tammy. She was a little pale and a lot agitated. "Sorry to bother you again," she said as she rushed past him into the condo.

"No problem. Did you stop by earlier, before I got home?"

"What? No. No, I just left the office."

"Okay. What is it you need me to see?"

She looked around the room. "Can we sit down?" Without waiting for an answer, she started for the sofa.

"Do you want a drink or something?" he asked.

"Not now. Maybe after." She sat, then took an envelope from her purse and set the purse on the floor beside her. "Someone put this through the mail slot beside the door of the newspaper office this afternoon," she said, and tapped the envelope. "No one even uses that slot anymore—it's a relic from when the building was occupied by the electric company and people used the slot to leave their payments. But every once in while we get a Letter to the Editor dropped off that way. When I came in about five o'clock and saw the envelope, that's what I thought this was. A complaint or something like that."

He sat beside her, angled toward her, their knees almost

touching. "Whatever it is has you upset," he said. "Is it a threat or something?"

She thrust the letter toward him. "Read it," she said.

He took the envelope. It was a blank, white business-sized envelope, unsealed. He opened it and slid out a single sheet of white paper. The message on it was typewritten.

Nice article about the search for Valerie Shepherd. But you got a few things wrong about that day. More than a few things, actually. I don't blame you. You were sold a bunch of lies. I think people lie more than they tell the truth, especially when the lies make them look better. Maybe one day we'll meet and I'll tell you what really happened.

He scanned the brief message. This was what had Tammy so upset? This rambling from a person who couldn't possibly know what had happened? He glanced up from the sheet. "It's just someone babbling about lies," he said.

"Look at the bottom of the page," she said. "At the signature."

He let his gaze travel to the bottom of the sheet of paper, to a cursive scrawl in black ink. The hair on the back of his neck rose as he stared, and he had trouble breathing. No. He was letting his imagination run away from him. It didn't really say what he thought it said.

"It's signed *V*," Tammy said. "*V* for *Valerie*?"

"It can't be Valerie." Vince looked and sounded calmer than Tammy felt. She wasn't one to overreact, but those chilling words about lies—and the single *V* at the bottom—had combined to set her heart racing and her adrenaline flooding. She had been alone in the newspaper office, with no one to offer a different perspective, so she had called the one person she was sure would know the truth. Except, now that she was here, she felt more foolish than frightened.

Vince dropped his gaze to the letter again, his eyes tracking the words across the page. Then he set the sheet of paper aside on the coffee table in front of them. "No one lied that day," he said. "At least, my parents didn't lie, and I didn't."

"Maybe the letter writer means someone else." Tammy wet her dry lips and glanced at the letter as if it was a spider she needed to keep an eye on in case it came any closer. "Maybe there's someone who saw what happened to Valerie and never spoke up."

"Then why not come forward and tell us what happened?" His voice rose on the last words, anger edging out the calm she suspected must have been an act. Of course he was upset. Having someone impersonate his sister must have been a horrible jolt.

"I'm sorry," she said. "I should have realized it was a fake. I didn't mean to upset you."

"It's okay." He blew out a breath. "You didn't expect this, but I should have. Every time any new publicity about Valerie's disappearance comes out, people like that come out of nowhere." He nodded at the letter. "I don't know if they're mentally ill or running a scam, or maybe both. I can't tell you how many times my parents have dealt with this kind of thing."

"How horrible for you all."

"It was. For months after she first went missing, they would get calls from people who promised to find Valerie—for a price. So-called psychics and private detectives. My parents spent a lot of money paying off various people. They wanted so badly to believe it was Valerie that they lost all common sense. I'm betting this is more of the same."

"That makes me sick," she said. "What is wrong with people?"

"You're a reporter and you ask that?"

She let out a shaky laugh. "I guess I don't let people like that take up any more headspace than necessary." She glanced at the letter again. "Should I throw it away?"

"File it. Just in case this person decides to cause trouble." His expression grew troubled again. "I wonder if they were trying to shake me down too."

"What do you mean?"

"When I got home today, my neighbor told me a woman had stopped by looking for me. I thought it might have been you, but you said you hadn't been by. Now I wonder if it was the person who wrote the letter."

"You would know if the person was Valerie?"

"I hope I would. Though after fifteen years, who knows? Anyway, a scammer would claim to know Valerie or to be her 'representative'—a friend, or a lawyer."

"You do know how these things work, don't you?"

"Unfortunately, I do." He stood. "I wouldn't worry about that letter, though. If you ignore these people, they move on and look for an easier victim."

She tucked the letter back into the envelope and returned it to her purse. "Sorry to disturb your evening."

"No. That's okay. I didn't have any plans." He shoved his hands in the pockets of his jeans. "I was getting ready to make dinner. You want to stay and eat with me?"

"Oh, uh…"

"Sorry, you probably have plans."

"No. I'd be happy to stay. I can help too."

"Then come into the kitchen, and let's see what we've got to work with."

Together, they assembled a meal of pasta, chicken and vegetables. As they worked, they talked about everything but

Valerie—his love of climbing, her passion for gardening, his experience with search and rescue, and her volunteer position working with high school journalism students.

"Are you seeing anyone?" she asked when the conversation lulled. Maybe the question was a bit forward, but she was dying to know. And she hadn't seen any sign of a romantic interest around his place.

He didn't look up from draining the pasta. "No. Are you?"

"No. I broke up with a guy a few months ago."

He dumped the pasta in a bowl and carried the bowl to the table. "Is that good? Bad?"

"A little sad." She sat in the chair across from him at the table. "We'd been together awhile. But it wasn't working out." They had fallen into a pattern of fighting more than they got along. "Breaking up was the right thing to do."

"But lonely when you're used to having someone around," he said.

Was that the voice of experience speaking or just someone who was very empathetic? "I've managed to avoid long-term relationships," he continued. "I'm not the easiest guy to get along with."

"You haven't thrown up any red flags for me." Her cheeks warmed. She hadn't meant that to sound like she was sizing him up for potential-mate material. "I mean, I haven't noticed any upsetting tendencies—a bad temper or substance abuse, or narcissism."

He laughed. "According to several exes, I don't trust people, I don't confide in people and I don't care enough about people."

"Harsh."

"Yeah, well, who's to say they haven't been right? Not everyone has to be part of a couple."

"You're absolutely right." She raised her wineglass. "To being happy with yourself."

"To being happy with yourself." He smiled, and his gaze met hers, and something lurched inside her, an internal shift that signaled she might be even happier with a certain untrusting, unconfiding but definitely not uncaring man.

Chapter Six

Elisabeth couldn't believe how great it felt to be in the mountains again. Was it possible she had been missing this without even realizing it? Amid all this bare rock and immense sky, anything seemed possible, as if the world truly had no limits. She continued up the trail, climbing higher and higher, thighs burning, lungs straining for breath. Obviously, she needed more time to acclimate to the altitude, but she was in pretty good shape, considering she hadn't spent much time on athletic pursuits.

She stopped and assessed her surroundings. There was a flat-sided dike jutting up from the adjacent rock like a jagged tooth. And there was a big boulder, lichen spattering the surface in green and white and orange. She climbed the rock, scrambling a little for purchase, and stood atop it. She stared at the clump of pinions below, in a kind of trance for a long moment.

She snapped out of it and turned to face the dike. She pulled out her phone and took a few pictures to document the scene; then she headed back down the trail. She met only a few people on the way down—a couple and a larger group of friends. No little kids. Did families not come backpacking up here anymore?

Back in town, she grabbed a decent veggie wrap from the

coffee shop at the Gold Nugget Hotel, then walked down the street to a real estate office she had spotted earlier. She stopped on the sidewalk outside Brown Realty to study the flyers tacked to the window, all for overpriced vacation homes, luxury condos and one huge ranch that was listed for over a billion dollars. Did people really pay those kinds of prices to live here? If that was the case, she might stick around a little longer and meet some of those wealthy people.

A chime announced her arrival as she pushed open the door. A man who was the sole occupant of the place looked up from behind the desk and smiled. "Hi," he said. "Can I help you?"

He was maybe a little older than her, his long dark hair pulled back in a ponytail. He wore a tailored white shirt, sleeves rolled up to reveal strong forearms, and dark jeans that definitely hadn't come from the nearest discount store. Paul would approve of this man's style. "I'm looking for a place to rent in town," she said. "Just for a couple of months. A house or condo. Something nice."

"We have several beautiful vacation properties available for short-term rentals." The man stood and extended his hand. "I'm Mitch."

"I'm Elisabeth." His fingers were cool against hers, his grip firm but not crushing. And he looked her in the eye with a direct gaze. A sizzle of attraction raced through her. No ring on his finger.

"Have a seat, Elisabeth, and I'll show you what we have available." He sat also, and swiveled the computer monitor so they both could see it. "Do you have a particular location in mind?"

"There's a condo complex by the river. Riverside. Do you have anything there?"

"We do have a few units available in that property," Mitch said. "Though they require a six-month lease."

"If they're vacant, maybe we can negotiate something shorter."

"I can't promise anything, but why don't we take a look?"

He bent over the keyboard, typing with two fingers, but rapidly. She studied him, feeling the sizzle of awareness again. Maybe there were advantages to sticking around town that she hadn't yet considered.

"Here are some interior shots of one of the units," he said. "It's a top floor, corner unit, so a little more privacy. As you can see, it has updated appliances and a modern, airy interior. You'd be close to the river and the hiking and biking trails, and just a few minutes from town. Another few minutes to the highway and access to both Junction, an hour to the north, and the miles of trails in the backcountry. Hiking and jeeping in the summer, rock and ice climbing, winter skiing. Fly-fishing, photography, camping—we offer everything in the way of outdoor adventure."

He spoke with a natural enthusiasm that helped negate the salesman's spiel. "I like the condo," she said. "Could we drive over there and take a look?"

"Of course. Do you want to see any others before we go?"

"No. That's the one I want."

"What about the six-month lease?" he asked.

"I'm sure we can work something out." She could always agree to the lease, then leave whenever she wanted without paying the rest of the rent. She knew how to disappear so that they would never find her to sue for the rest of the money.

"Let me forward the phones and lock up here, and I'll be set," he said.

She waited by the entrance while he took care of these tasks, then followed him out the door. After he had locked up, she moved closer and slipped her arm through his. "After we see the condo, maybe you can show me around town," she said. "Then I'd love to buy you a drink."

Extra heat sparked in his smile, and he covered her hand with his own and squeezed it. "That sounds like a great idea, Elisabeth."

"I'm full of great ideas." So many, and so few people to truly appreciate her greatness. But she had learned to never sell herself short. Other people had failed her, but that was no reason to ever fail herself.

SUMMER SATURDAYS WERE busy days on the backroads and trails around Eagle Mountain, which meant they were also busy for search and rescue volunteers. The first call that day came in just before 11:00 a.m. A young man had fallen from the rocks above Rocky Falls. "The family member who called in the accident says the young man—fifteen—is responsive but in pain," Danny told the volunteers who assembled at search and rescue headquarters. "He thinks the boy—his nephew—might have broken bones."

"How did he happen to fall, do we know?" volunteer Chris Mercer asked. An artist who wore blue streaks in her dark hair, Chris had several years' experience with SAR but wasn't an elite climber or a medical professional. She was simply dedicated and hardworking, willing to do the mundane driving, fetching, carrying and following orders that made up the bulk of a volunteer's efforts.

Danny grimaced. "He climbed up onto the rocks to pose for a picture and slipped."

"The rocks behind the sign that says 'Danger: Do Not Climb on Rocks'?" Harper Stevens asked.

"Yep." Danny raised his voice to address them all. "Let's hustle, everyone."

As they were loading their gear, Bethany slipped in next to Vince. "Hi." She flashed a smile, her eyes not meeting his. "This is the first call I've been on. I'm a little nervous."

"That's natural," Vince said. "Just do what you're told and pitch in whenever you can." He handed her a plastic bin full of climbing helmets. "Find a place to stow these in the Beast there." He pointed to the specially outfitted Jeep used for rescue operations. "I'm going to get more supplies."

"I think you have an admirer," Ryan said when Vince returned to the supply closet for another load. "I saw the new girl, Bethany, making eyes at you."

"'Making eyes'? Seriously, what does that even mean?" Vince slung a coil of rope over one shoulder.

"Bet she'd go out with you if you asked her," Ryan said. "Just saying."

He glanced back and saw Bethany standing where he had left her, still watching him. He quickly turned around. "Not interested," he said. Bethany was cute and probably really sweet, but there was no spark there. Not like when he looked at Tammy. "Come on," he said. "Let's get this stuff loaded so we can head out."

The young man who had fallen got off lucky, with a broken leg and some cracked ribs. The search and rescue team climbed the trail to the top of the falls and identified a point from which Hannah and Ryan Welch could be lowered on ropes to the teen, Lance. At first, he denied climbing on the rocks, though eventually he admitted to ignoring the signs and boosting himself up on the boulder for a selfie with the waterfall in the background. "Am I going to be, like, disabled or something?" he asked, his expression stricken.

"You should heal just fine," Hannah said as she fitted his leg with a splint. Once the leg was stabilized, she and Ryan fitted him with neck and back braces and a helmet, then helped him into a litter and wrapped him up warmly.

Meanwhile, up on the trail, Vince worked with Eldon, Tony and Sheri to rig a rope-and-pulley system for getting their patient back onto the trail. Once they had lifted him safely out of the canyon, another group of volunteers took over to transport him to the waiting ambulance. The family—his mom, dad, uncle and sister—followed the litter team down.

As the remaining volunteers disassembled the rigging and packed up to return to headquarters, Vince paused to look over at the sign that cautioned people against climbing on the rocks. "I feel like someone should write in 'We really mean it' underneath there," he said.

"It wouldn't work," Eldon said. He stuffed a brake bar into a carrying bag. "Kids that age think they're invincible. I did."

Unlike many of his peers, Vince had never known that feeling of invulnerability. What happened to Valerie had made him too aware of all the ways things could go wrong.

The group returned to SAR headquarters and were unloading gear when a second call came in. "Hikers with a medical emergency," Danny relayed after speaking with the emergency dispatcher. "Mount Wilson trail. A man with chest pains and a woman who's collapsed."

The words were like a shot of adrenaline through the group. They hurried to reload the search and rescue Jeep, as well as several personal vehicles, with equipment and personnel for an urgent ride to the Mount Wilson trailhead. "They're within a mile of the top," Danny directed as they unloaded the vehicles and distributed gear for the trek up the slope. "A thirty-eight-year-old woman and a forty-six-year-old man. No history of heart trouble, but he's reporting chest pain and dizziness and disorientation."

"What about the woman?" Hannah asked.

"The report on her is that she's unable to continue hiking."

"I don't like the sound of either of those," Hannah said.

A solemn team started up the mountain. Tony and Sheri elected to jog ahead with an AED and first aid supplies. Caleb Garrison was next with a canister of oxygen, while the others followed as quickly as they could, spread out along the steep trail to one of the most popular peaks in the region. Other hikers on their way down squeezed over to the side to let them pass when they recognized the blue windbreakers with *Search and Rescue* emblazoned on the front and back. "Good luck!" some called after them.

It took two hours of hard hiking to reach the couple, who were stretched out to one side of the trail, a few concerned onlookers gathered around. Sheri, Tony, Caleb and Hannah were arranged around them, the man receiving oxygen while Sheri spoke with the woman. Vince slipped off his pack, which contained another canister of oxygen and various first aid supplies, and fished out his water bottle.

"What's the story?" he asked Harper, who had arrived ahead of him.

"Hannah doesn't think he's having a heart attack, but he'll need to be checked out at the hospital to be sure," Harper said. "Mostly I think they weren't well prepared for a hike like this and they overdid it. They don't have hats or sunscreen or enough water. They're sunburned and dehydrated and dealing with the altitude and exhaustion."

The couple did look miserable. They were sipping water and listening as Sheri and Danny addressed them each in turn. They were probably hearing about how most of their problems could have been prevented with simple precautions like sunscreen, water and an easier pace. But that didn't help them now. For that, they would get a free ride down the mountain in litters carried by Vince and his fellow volunteers, and a checkup at the hospital to ensure they truly were all right.

The trip down the trail was equally as solemn as the hike up, but without the urgency. Even a small adult was a heavy, awkward burden to carry. After consultation, Danny declared that the woman would walk down—with Bethany and Harper on either side to steady her, if need be—and her husband would be transported on the litter. His chest pains had subsided, but no one wanted to chance their return. The litter was fitted with a large wheel to support part of the weight and help it roll along the ground, but it still required a volunteer at each corner to help steady and balance it. The position was awkward and uncomfortable, and volunteers switched off every half mile.

Meanwhile, the woman moaned and complained the whole way down. Vince decided that as much as maneuvering the litter made his back and knees ache, he preferred that duty.

The sun was sinking behind the mountains by the time they made it to the trailhead. The couple headed off in an ambulance, and the volunteers reloaded their gear. Some of the group announced they were going out for beer and pizza. "Are you going out?" Bethany asked as Vince was shouldering his pack to head to his car.

"Not tonight," he said. All he wanted was a hot shower and to stretch out on the sofa, where he would likely fall asleep. "But you should go, if you want. It'll be a great way to get to know people."

She looked over toward the group—Ryan and Eldon, Caleb, and a few others. "I don't know."

"Suit yourself." He shrugged on the pack and headed out. He drove to his condo, parked, and collected his mail before he walked to his door and unlocked it. Inside, he shed his shoes, pack and SAR windbreaker, then stood sorting through the mail. Mostly junk, but a colorful postcard caught his eye. A larger-than-life cartoon Viking stood beside an impossibly buxom and equally cartoonish female Viking. *Welcome to Williams's Valhalla-Land!* proclaimed large green letters above them.

Vince stared, heart pounding. He and Valerie and their parents had stopped at this roadside attraction, somewhere in Minnesota or Michigan, on a road trip to visit his dad's brother and his family on the Upper Peninsula the summer before Valerie disappeared. Somewhere, pasted into an album tucked into his parents' bookshelf, was a photograph his mother had snapped of him and Valerie, posing with these same cartoon Vikings.

He flipped the card over and read the message, in loopy cursive handwriting: *Hello, Vince the Viking. I bet you're surprised to hear from me. V.*

Chapter Seven

"Slow down, Mitch. I can hardly understand you, you're talk-ing so fast." Tammy juggled her phone and the salad she had been carrying to her kitchen table when her brother called Saturday evening.

"I met this great girl—*woman*. Her name is Elisabeth. She came into my office looking for a rental, and we hit it off. We had drinks afterwards, and we're going to have dinner tomorrow night."

Tammy sat at the table. Her brother wasn't normally this effusive. In fact, he rarely talked about the women he dated. "Wow, she must be special," she said.

"I think so." She could hear the smile in his voice. "I hope you'll meet her soon."

"You said she was looking for a rental. Is she new in town?"

"She's here for several months, but I'm hoping to talk her into staying longer."

"Where is she from?"

"Somewhere in the Midwest, I think. We didn't talk about that."

"What *did* you talk about?"

He laughed. "She asked a lot about me, and about Eagle Mountain. But she told me a few things about herself. She said her father just died and left her some money, so she's taking the opportunity to see more of the country. And she likes to hike—we talked about checking out a few of the local trails while she's here."

"It sounds like the two of you really clicked."

"We did. I've never met anyone who is so easy to talk to. I tried to talk her into having dinner with me tonight too, but she said she had things she needed to do. I thought at first maybe I had come on too strong, but then she said she'd love to go out with me tomorrow night, so that was a relief."

"I'll look forward to meeting her." She took a bite of salad and chewed, angling away from the phone as Mitch told her more about the wonderful Elisabeth.

Her phone beeped, and she checked the screen. "I have to go, Mitch," she said. "I have another call coming in, and I need to take it."

"A breaking news story for the paper?" he asked.

"Someone connected with an article that I need to talk to." Not a complete lie.

"All right, then. I'll talk to you later."

"Have fun tomorrow night." She ended the call and answered the incoming one. "Hey, Vince," she said.

"Do you still have that note that was supposedly from Valerie?" he asked.

"I think so. Why?"

"Because I got a postcard today." His voice broke, and the silence that followed made her think he was struggling to pull himself together.

"Vince, are you all right?" she asked.

"The postcard—it had something on it only Valerie, or someone who knew us, would know about," he said.

She sat up straighter. "Do you think Valerie sent my note and your postcard?"

"I don't know what to think. I mean, if she is alive, why not just pick up the phone and call? Or come to see me in person?"

"Have your parents heard anything? It seems like she would want to contact them too."

"If they have, they haven't told me about it. And I'm too afraid to call and upset them. What if this is just another scam?"

"Maybe you should contact the sheriff's office," she said.

"Maybe. Before I do that, could you come over, and bring the note you received? Or I could come there. I thought we could compare the signature and decide if it's the same person."

"The note is at the newspaper office," she said. "Why don't you meet me there?"

"Great. I'll see you in a few minutes."

She ended the call, then sat for a moment, her salad untouched. The reporter side of her was intrigued by the turn this story was taking. But she hadn't missed the pain in Vince's voice. She wanted to protect her friend while still getting to the bottom of what could be major news.

VINCE WAITED ON the sidewalk outside the newspaper office. A few people passed on their way to the pizza place at the end of the block, but otherwise this part of town was quiet. The sun had set, but it wasn't yet full dark. The silhouettes of the mountains above town stood out against the gray sky. The tops of those peaks were miles away, yet they looked almost close enough to touch.

He slipped off his backpack and felt in the side pocket, where he had tucked the postcard. His sister couldn't have sent it, could she? Why now, after so many years? And why be so vague?

A blue Subaru zipped around the corner and pulled to the

curb in front of Vince. Tammy got out. She looked harried, her cheeks flushed, her blouse half-untucked and her hair a little mussed. "I hope you haven't been waiting long," she said.

"Not long." He waited behind her while she unlocked the door, then tapped a code into the alarm keypad beside it.

"Come on back here to my desk." She moved through the office, flipping light switches as she went, until she reached a large desk crowded with a desktop computer and stacks of notebooks and loose sheets of paper. "The letter is in the file here," she said, and pulled open a bottom desk drawer. She rummaged among the contents of the drawer, then stood, waving a piece of paper. "I never throw anything away," she said. "As you can tell by the state of my desk."

She sank into the desk chair, and Vince sat in a straight-backed wooden chair across from her. She set the letter on the desk between them and smoothed out the folds. "Could I see the postcard you received?" she asked.

He opened the backpack and handed the card to her. She smiled as she studied the cartoon on the front, then turned it over to read the message on the back. "'Vince the Viking'?" she asked.

He grimaced. "The summer before Valerie disappeared— when we were both nine—we took a family trip to the Upper Peninsula to visit my dad's brother, Ricky. On the way, we stopped at every tourist attraction my dad could find—wind-mills and arrowhead collections and little museums." He nodded to the postcard. "And Valhalla-Land."

Tammy's smile vanished and her eyebrows drew together. "It would be a wild coincidence for someone who didn't know about that trip to send this to you out of the blue."

"I think so," he said. "And it's not just Valhalla-Land. After the trip, Valerie and I called each other 'Vince the Viking' and 'Valerie the Viking' for weeks afterwards. No one else would know that. I mean, my mom and dad would, if they even remember. And maybe Uncle Ricky. But they wouldn't pretend to be Valerie."

Tammy turned the postcard over. "This is postmarked in Junction, but it could have been mailed here in town. All our mail is routed through the Junction office. But that's a long way from Valhalla-Land."

"Whoever sent it must have brought it with them," he said.

"Could you order something like this online?" Tammy asked.

"Even if you could, you would have to know its significance to me and Valerie." He sat back, legs stretched out in front of him. "I'd forgotten all about that little pit stop on a long-ago vacation until I saw that card."

She laid the card beside the letter on the desk and leaned over to study it more closely. "It's signed the same way as my note—just the single V," she said.

"I thought so too. But if it's Valerie, why not sign her whole name?"

"Do you think your parents still have a sample of her handwriting?"

"Probably. But she was ten. A person's handwriting changes as they get older, doesn't it?"

"I don't know." She sat back. "Do you think you should contact your parents? I'm sure if we go to the sheriff's department with these notes, they'll want to talk to your parents as well."

Vince blew out a breath. "I don't want to upset them, but better me than a call from a sheriff's deputy." He took out his phone.

His mother answered on the second ring. "Hello, Vince," she said, cheerful. Glad to hear from him.

"Hi, Mom. I'm not interrupting anything, am I?"

"No, I'm just sitting here trying to read this book that isn't all that interesting. It's for my book club, and it's supposed to be a big bestseller, but I must not be the intended audience."

"Is Dad there?"

"No, he had a meeting. Do you want me to ask him to call you tomorrow, or can I help you with something?"

He took a deep breath. He saw no way to ease into the subject. "Have you gotten any letters from someone claiming to be Valerie?" he asked.

"You mean recently?"

"Yes."

"No, dear. Years ago we received a couple of letters that were vague and rambling. We showed them to someone from the Center for Missing and Exploited Children. They told us they were almost certainly a scam. Other parents had received similar letters."

"I didn't know," he said.

"You were still young. We didn't see any reason to involve you. Why are you asking about this now?"

He glanced across the desk at Tammy. She was watching him intently. "I got a postcard from someone who sounded like they could be Valerie," he said. "It was just signed with the letter V."

"Oh my. I'm sure it's because of the article in the paper. It was a good article, of course, but this kind of attention seems to bring out the worst in people. What did the postcard say?"

He picked up the card. "Do you remember that summer we went to Uncle Ricky's place?"

"The summer you were nine. That was a fun trip."

"We stopped at a place called Valhalla-Land. With a bunch of Viking stuff."

"Oh my, yes. So kitschy. But you kids loved it."

"Valerie and I called each other Vikings for weeks after that."

His mom laughed. "I'd forgotten about that, but you did. Vince the Viking and Valerie the Viking. But what made you remember that?"

"This postcard has a picture of Valhalla-Land. And on the back, it says 'Hello to Vince the Viking.'"

His mother drew in her breath sharply but said nothing.

"Mom! Are you okay?"

"I'm... I'm fine. Just a little surprised. It's such an odd thing to write. And how would anyone know about that?"

"I don't know. The reporter who wrote the story for the paper, Tammy Patterson, received a note too. Hers was more generic. All about how she got things wrong in her story and 'You were sold a bunch of lies.' She and I think we should show these to the sheriff, just in case someone is trying to scam us. But I wanted to talk to you first."

"Yes, you should show them to the sheriff," she said. "Not that it will do any good. No one ever caught any of the other people who tried to swindle us. There are some evil people in this world who will take advantage of a family's grief."

"Tomorrow we'll talk to Sheriff Walker or one of his deputies," Vince said. "I'll let you know what they say."

"I'll tell your father when he gets in. It's odd. And upsetting. What if this really is Valerie, reaching out to us after all these years?"

"Why send teasing notes?" he asked. "Why not just show up and say, 'Here I am'?"

"I don't know. Maybe it's a kind of game. Valerie did always like games and teasing. The day she disappeared, we thought she was hiding from us, playing a joke."

"If she's alive, she's twenty-five," Vince said. "Too old for silly games."

"I don't know what to think," his mom said.

"I'll let you know what the sheriff says."

They said good-night, and he ended the call. He felt worse than ever.

"Do you want me to go with you to the sheriff's department tomorrow?" Tammy asked.

"They'll want to talk to you too." He looked around the room, at the silent computers and framed front pages of past issues of the *Eagle Mountain Examiner*. "Are you going to write about this for the paper?"

He couldn't read her expression. Was that hurt in her eyes? "Not unless something comes of it that's newsworthy," she said.

"What would that be?"

"I don't know. If they catch someone trying to scam you."

"Or if Valerie actually is alive and well."

"People do show up sometimes," Tammy said. "There was a case last year where a woman had been living in Europe with her kidnapper for years. I'm not trying to get your hopes up," she hastened to add. "I'm just saying that's one possibility."

"Yeah. I guess we'll find out." He stood. "Thanks for meeting with me. I'll let you know in the morning when I can go with you to the sheriff. I need to check my work schedule."

He left the building. She followed, locking up behind them. "Do you want to go for a drink?" she asked. "Or coffee?"

"No. I need to go home."

"All right. I'll see you tomorrow." She hesitated, then patted his arm. "I'm sorry my article pulled this person—whoever they are—out of the woodwork. Especially if it's someone who wants to hurt you."

"It's not your fault. And maybe it *is* Valerie." He didn't believe that, but it was something positive to cling to, at least for a little while. Over the years, he had thought about what it might be like to see his sister again, but after so long it was hard to picture her as anything but the rambunctious ten-year-old she had been. A grown Valerie would be a stranger to him. She would still be his sister—his twin. But they would have lost so much of their shared history. Would she even be someone he liked? Worse—would she like him, or what he had become in her absence?

Ten years ago

"I LEFT DINNER for you in the refrigerator. Leave the plate covered and heat it in the microwave for three minutes." Mom fussed about the kitchen, wiping down the counter and putting stray glasses and silverware in the dishwasher as she talked. "If you need anything, call the Wilsons next door for help. Don't open the door to strangers. And don't stay up too late watching TV. You know you have school tomorrow."

"Mom, I know how to look after myself. I'm not some little kid," Vince protested. At fifteen, he towered over his five-foot, two-inch mom, and was the same height as his dad. Any day now, he'd probably start shaving.

"I know, dear." His mom stilled, looking as if she wasn't happy about this news. "I just want you to be careful. I couldn't cope if anything happened to you."

Inwardly, Vince cringed, though he tried not to show how much he resented statements like this. He got it—his parents had lost one child and were terrified of losing another. They were hyperprotective of him, so much so that even leaving him alone for a few hours while they enjoyed a rare evening out with friends was a big deal. But none of his friends had as many rules and curfews as he did. It wasn't fair. But the one time he had tried to point this out, his mother had gotten all teary and said it wasn't fair that Valerie disappeared and they never knew what happened to her. After that, he gave up trying to reason with his parents and settled for breaking their rules whenever he could. Tonight, for instance, his friend Jackson Greenway was coming over. Their plan was to smoke a joint and watch a porn video Jackson had stolen from his older brother Parker, who was nineteen and had his own condo. They were going to order pizza and maybe call these sisters Jackson had met. His parents would be horrified if they knew any of this, which was kind of the point.

He hugged his mom. "Don't worry," he said. "I'll be safe here. You and Dad have a good time."

She gave him a wobbly smile and patted his back. "You're a fine son," she said. "Your father and I are so proud of you. You know that, don't you?"

He had done a lot to make his parents proud. He made good grades and was a top player on a regional youth lacrosse team. When he did break the rules, he made sure not to get caught, and he had never gotten into serious trouble. It didn't make up for Valerie being gone, but it was something.

He waved from the front door as they pulled out of the driveway, then slipped out his phone and called Jackson to tell him the coast was clear.

Twenty minutes later, Jackson's mother's Camry eased down the street, the throbbing bass from the stereo rattling the windows. Six months older than Vince, Jackson had his driver's license, and his parents let him borrow his mother's car whenever he wanted, as long as he topped off the gas tank.

Jackson—taller even than Vince, with long, thin arms and legs and blond hair past his shoulders—parked at the curb, then exited the car with the pizza box in one hand and a DVD and a bag of weed in the other. "Are we ready to party?" he asked.

"Ready." Vince held the door open wide. "We have the place to ourselves for at least four hours."

"Sweet!" Jackson breezed in and set the pizza on the bar that separated the kitchen from the living room. "And look what I got to go with our pizza." He fished in the pockets of his baggy cargo shorts and pulled out two cans of beer. "I snagged them from the garage refrigerator on my way out. My dad will never miss them."

"Let me grab some plates for the pizza," Vince said. "I'm starving."

They had popped the tops on the beer and were digging into their first slices of pizza when the Shepherd's house phone rang.

"Don't answer it," Jackson said. "It's probably just some phone solicitor or a politician asking for your vote."

"I have to answer it," Vince said. "It might be my mom, with some last-minute instruction about dinner or something." He moved to the phone on the kitchen wall and picked up the receiver. "Hello?"

"Hello? Vince, is that you?"

A cold shiver raced up his spine. "Hello?" he said. "Who is this?" His mind played tricks on him sometimes. He would be in a crowded hallway at school and would think he'd heard Valerie's voice, only to turn around and discover it was some-one else. Once, after a lacrosse game, he had followed a teen-age girl all the way to the parking lot because something about how she looked from the back was so familiar. Then she had turned around and spotted him, and he had to pretend he was merely retrieving something from his car.

"It's Valerie. Don't you remember me?" The person on the other end of the line began to sob. "I need you to help me, Vince."

"Where are you?" he asked. Then: "Who are you, really?"

The line went dead. Vince stared at the receiver in his hand.

"Dude, your face went all white," Jackson said. "You're not going to faint, are you?"

"How do you call back the last number you talked to?" he asked.

"Star-six-nine." Jackson's chair scraped loudly against the floor as he shoved it back and stood. "What's going on? Who was that on the phone?"

"I don't know." He punched in *69 and waited while the phone rang. And rang. And rang. After ten rings, he hung up.

Jackson was standing beside him now. "You don't look so hot," he said. "Who was that calling?"

"She said she was Valerie."

Jackson's eyes widened. "Your dead sister?"

"We don't know for sure she's dead, but yeah. She knew my name, and she said she was Valerie."

"Did it sound like her? What you remember?"

"It did." But was that because it was her, or because he wanted it to be her? "I think you'd better go," he said. "I need to call my parents."

He thought Jackson would argue, but instead, he patted Vince's back. "I can stay here if you want. You can tell your folks you called me for moral support. We'll hide the beer and stuff before they get home."

"Thanks, but I'll be okay by myself."

Jackson gathered up the beer and pizza, the pot and the DVD, and said goodbye. When he was gone, Vince braced himself and called his dad's cell phone. "I had a call just now," he said. "From someone claiming to be Valerie. She said she needed help, and she started crying. It sounded real." A sob broke free on the last word. He couldn't help it.

"We'll be right there," his dad said.

His parents came home right away. Vince had pulled himself together by the time they arrived, but he could tell his mom had been crying. Her eyes were red and puffy, and when she hugged him, she held on too tightly, for a little too long.

He told them about the call, and they contacted the local police and the FBI agent who had worked with them when Valerie first went missing. The cops arrived, then two FBI agents. They matched the number from the call to a pay phone in Nebraska, then said the pay phone had been vandalized, probably before that call was made, though they couldn't be sure.

They never heard from the caller again, and everyone agreed it had likely been a scam. But for months afterward, Vince replayed the call in his head. Valerie's voice, begging him to help her.

Chapter Eight

"We can take this into evidence, but without more context, there's not a lot we can do." Sheriff Walker faced Tammy and Vince across his neat desk Sunday morning, the letter and postcard side by side on the almost-empty expanse of oak. "Unfortunately, it's not unusual for twisted people to prey on the families of crime victims this way."

"We don't know that Valerie's disappearance was a crime." Vince flushed when Travis turned to look at him.

"That's true," Travis said. "But it's a crime to pretend to be someone else for the purpose of extorting money or other compensation."

"The letter writer hasn't asked for anything," Tammy said.

"Not yet." Travis considered the letters once more. "If you receive any other correspondence like this, handle it as little as possible. We might be able to recover prints or DNA."

They promised to keep the sheriff informed of any developments and left his office. Outside, on the sidewalk, Vince pulled out his keys. "I have to go," he said. "I promised my parents I'd have lunch with them."

"Before you go, there's something I need to say." Tammy had been rehearsing this little speech all morning, and she needed to get it out before she lost nerve.

He stopped and turned to face her, expression wary.

"You asked me last night if I'm going to write about this," she said.

"Have you changed your mind?"

"No." She shook her head. "Not unless you want me to. If you think it will help us find who did this, I will."

"No. The last thing I want right now is more publicity. It draws out the scammers."

"I'm your friend, Vince," she said. "First. Reporter, second. I want to make sure you understand that. I want you to feel free to talk to me without fear of what you say ending up in the paper." Having him believe anything other than that hurt more than she wanted to admit.

"Thanks," he said. "I appreciate it."

"Good. I wanted to make sure you knew that."

Embarrassed now, she turned and led the way down the sidewalk toward the lot where they had parked their vehicles. They hadn't gone far before she spotted a familiar figure. "Hey, Mitch." She waved.

Her brother stopped and waited for her to catch up. She turned back to Vince. "Vince, this is my brother, Mitch. Mitch, this is Vince Shepherd."

The two men shook hands. "How's it going?" Vince asked.

"I'm headed over to Riverside Condos." Mitch glanced at Tammy. "Elisabeth signed a lease on an empty unit there, and I want to make sure there's no problem with the paperwork."

"Vince lives at Riverside," Tammy said.

Mitch grinned. "Then you'll see me around. At least, I hope you will."

"Mitch is so gone on his new client," Tammy said.

"Elisabeth is a special person," Mitch said. He checked his watch. "Gotta run. Nice to meet you, Vince."

Mitch loped away. They were at their cars now; Tammy

turned to Vince. "Let me know if anything else happens," she said. "Because I'm your friend. Not because I'm a reporter."

He took a step back, hands in his pockets. "Thanks. Um, maybe we could have dinner later."

She fought back a grin. "I'd like that."

"Just…as friends," he added.

"Sure." It wasn't all she wanted, but it would do. For now.

AS A ROOKIE with just a few months of search and rescue experience under his belt, Vince saw every call as a new challenge. Though veterans might approach another auto accident or fallen hiker as the type of incident they had competently dealt with dozens of times before, Vince's mind raced with a review of everything he had learned about the protocol for this type of emergency, and the awareness that one misstep could potentially jeopardize someone's life.

No one was looking at their mission Tuesday evening as routine, however. Rescuers lined the road above Carson Canyon and followed the beam of a handheld spotlight until it came to rest on a pickup truck snagged in an almost-vertical position on the sharply sloping canyon wall. The truck's front end was smashed, the windshield shattered, the back bumper and half the rear-cargo area extending out into the darkness beyond—a canyon that was easily a hundred yards deep. "It looks like the front axle is snagged over that boulder." Danny lowered the binoculars he had been using to survey the scene and handed them to Tony. "See what you think."

"I don't see anything to secure chains to," Ryan said. "How are we going to stabilize the wreck enough to make it safe for us to go down there?"

"Shine that light into the cab," Tony said.

Grace, who was holding the light, shifted the beam to illuminate the cab.

"Looks like at least two people in the vehicle," Tony said. "Still secured by seat belts. They're not moving, so they're either dead or unconscious."

"We need to get a wrecker out here," Caleb said. "They could hook onto the frame with chains and it wouldn't go anywhere."

"One of us will have to climb down and hook it up," Eldon said. "We've done it before."

"We've done it before," Ryan said, "but not to a vehicle in that kind of precarious position."

"And not in the dark."

"Let's get some lights out here," Danny said. He took out his phone. "I'm going to call for a wrecker. But I want you to start rigging for the rescue. Approach it as if we don't have a wrecker available. You need to secure the vehicle, get the rescuers down safely, and lift out the driver and passenger."

"See if a helicopter is available," Sheri said. "It might be easier to lift the victims out by air than to try to drag them up this steep slope."

Danny acknowledged this and spoke into his phone. Ryan turned to Vince. "Come help us with the rigging."

"Could I help?" Bethany spoke up.

"Have you done any climbing training yet?" Ryan asked. "Not yet."

"Then it's probably better that you help with setting up the portable work lights. Everything will make more sense to you after you've got a little more training under your belt."

"Oh, uh, sure." She gave a wobbly smile and hurried away.

Ryan smirked. "Don't say anything," Vince warned. He wasn't in the mood for teasing—no matter how good natured—over the new girl's infatuation with him.

Ryan held up his hands. "I didn't say a thing."

Ryan, Vince and several others set to work constructing

the intricate series of ropes, chains, anchors, pulleys, knots, brake bars, carabiners and other hardware to construct a spiderweb of lines that would enable volunteers to travel safely up and down the steep slope.

Two trucks from the highway department pulled up with a bank of work lights that did a better job of illuminating the accident scene. Close on their heels, Bud O'Brien arrived with his largest wrecker, which featured a long boom that could extend over the canyon. A portly man in his late fifties with a wad of chewing tobacco puffing out one cheek, Bud peered over the edge at the smashed truck. "I can get it out of there," he said. "But one of you will have to hook it up."

Danny delegated Ryan and Eldon to make the initial climb down. Once the vehicle was secure, Tony and Sheri would follow, with Caleb and Vince on standby if they needed more assistance. "We'll need to package the victims for transport on the helicopter flying in from Delta. The chopper will set them down in the road, and we'll transfer to an ambulance."

"Any response from the truck?" Vince asked.

"Nothing," Danny said. "I tried hailing them and got no reply. I thought I saw movement earlier, but it's difficult from this distance to be sure." He looked past Vince. "I think Bud has the wrecker in place now." He raised his voice. "All right, everybody. Let's do this!"

Vince positioned himself across from Caleb to monitor the rigging as first Ryan, then Eldon descended. He found himself holding his breath as Ryan neared the vehicle. One false move might send the truck plummeting the rest of the way into the canyon. From here, he couldn't see the people inside. Maybe it was a good thing they were unconscious, since that made it less likely they would move about and possibly dislodge the vehicle.

With Ryan in place just above and behind the truck, Eldon

started his descent. Vince watched carefully, trying to absorb everything. Maybe one day he would be the one setting the rigging or even making the descent. He had a little experience climbing, though nowhere near the training Sherri, Ryan and some of the others had completed in high-angle rescue.

When Eldon had almost reached Ryan, Danny signaled to Bud, who began lowering the heavy cable and hook from the boom, which was extended out over the canyon. Eldon snagged the hook, then prepared to crawl beneath the truck.

Bud radioed down. "Be sure to attach that to the frame, not the axle."

"Understood," Eldon said. "That truck better not slip and take me with it."

"We've got you," Caleb called over the radio. Eldon and Ryan were both attached to safety lines tethered to anchors at the top of the cliff.

A cheer rose up when Eldon emerged from beneath the truck, thumbs up. Then he and Ryan approached the truck's cab, one on either side. They had to hold on to the vehicle in order to balance on the narrow ledge. Ryan cleared away broken glass and leaned into the driver's side of the vehicle. A moment later he leaned out again. "A driver and one passenger. The driver is unconscious, lacerations on his head and face. The passenger is female. No pulse. We're going to need the Jaws down here to get them out."

The mood among the volunteers sobered at the news that the passenger was dead, but they set to work securing the hydraulic extractor, more commonly known as the Jaws of Life, for cutting into the truck to make it easier to free the driver and passenger. They attached the tool to a line, and Tony and Sheri took it down when they descended.

"This is the scariest thing I've seen," Bethany said as she and Vince watched their fellow volunteers work on cutting the truck cab apart. "One slip and the whole truck might go over, and everyone down there with it."

"Part of me is glad I'm not down there," Vince said. "But it's hard to be up here too, wishing I could do more to help."

"Somebody has to be up here, making sure nothing goes wrong with the rigging," she said.

"You're right." He glanced below again as Tony and Eldon eased the driver from the truck cab onto a backboard. "I'll be glad when everyone is up top safely."

"I hear you."

Someone called to Bethany, and she moved away. Vince relaxed a little. Bethany was nice, but her obvious interest in him made him uncomfortable. She hadn't said or done anything out of line, but every time he turned around, she was either standing next to him or watching from across the room. Others besides Ryan had noticed. He didn't want to be rude to her, but he wished she would back off a little.

He focused again on the scene below. The volunteers fitted the driver with a helmet, neck brace and an oxygen mask and strapped him into a litter. They had a radio conversation with Danny, who, in addition to being the search and rescue captain, was also a registered nurse.

A heavy throb signaled the arrival of the rescue helicopter. The beam from its searchlight had them shielding their eyes from the glare. The chopper swept in, then hovered over the crash site and lowered a cable. The team below had affixed lines to the litter and attached these to the cable from the helicopter. At a signal from Tony, the helicopter rose and ferried the injured man to the middle of the closed road, where another team of volunteers helped lower the litter to the ground, unfastened it from the cable and carried it to a waiting ambulance.

The helicopter headed for the canyon again, this time to

retrieve the black bag containing the body of the passenger. This second transfer accomplished, the volunteers collected their gear and ascended, one at a time, up the canyon walls. Vince, Caleb and Chris monitored the climbers. As soon as everyone was up top and out of their climbing harnesses, they began the tedious chore of disassembling all the rigging and putting everything neatly away, ready to be used in the next emergency.

"How did the passenger die?" Caleb asked Tony as they disconnected various pieces of hardware from the climbing ropes they had used to assemble the rigging.

"Can't say for sure," Tony said. "But maybe a broken neck. The driver had a head injury. I think he may have banged his head into the window. Everything in the vehicle was thrown around. I think it was a pretty violent descent."

Vince shuddered, imagining. This was the first call where the real threat of danger had superseded the adrenaline rush of helping someone out under challenging conditions. Today, there had been a real threat of harm to everyone involved. His worries over a couple of annoying notes seem petty in contrast.

THE PASS WAS closed by the time Tammy arrived. She had to park half a mile from the accident scene and hike up the road in the dark, past the line of cars waiting to get over the pass when it reopened, then past parked vehicles belonging to search and rescue volunteers, highway department employees and local law enforcement.

The accident site was lit up like a movie set, halogen lights on tall stands ringing a section of roadside and shining down into the canyon. Tammy stopped to take a picture, struck by the contrast of the bright lights and the shadowy cliffs. She was tucking her camera away when someone brushed past her. A slim, dark figure was running down the mountain, away from the accident. Tammy stared after the woman—she was sure it was a woman, though she had seen the figure for only a few seconds. Nothing about her was familiar, though.

She moved closer. Deputy Shane Ellis, who was standing beside his patrol vehicle, watching the search and rescue team work, waved in greeting. Tammy took out her camera once more and moved closer, in time to get a shot of volunteer Ryan Welch begin his descent into the canyon. She took a few more photographs of other volunteers. She didn't see Vince, but he would be easy to miss in the crowd with so many people milling around in the darkness.

She joined Shane by the sheriff's department SUV. Shane—a former professional baseball player who had surprised everyone by becoming a sheriff's deputy—nodded at her. "Good to see the local press reporting the latest news," he said.

She took out a notebook and pen. "What happened here?" she asked.

"It looks like a pickup truck came around that curve with too much speed." He pointed ahead of them, to a sharp curve on the highway. "He slid on loose gravel and went over the edge. The canyon walls are really steep in this section, and he must have had quite a ride. But he got lucky. The undercarriage of the vehicle hung up on a boulder."

"The driver was a male."

"We don't know for sure. And there appears to be at least one passenger. But until search and rescue takes a look, I don't have any more information."

She scribbled notes she hoped she would be able to read when she sat down tomorrow to write the story. "I saw Ryan Welch descending into the canyon," she said.

"He and Eldon Ramsey are going down to stabilize the vehicle so rescuers can free the people inside the truck and assess their injuries," Shane said. "Bud O'Brien has his biggest wrecker out for the job."

The boom wrecker, lit up by the spotlights, would make an excellent shot for the paper. And Bud might like to have one to hang in his office. She started to move closer to take more photographs when Shane's next words stopped her. "I heard you got a note that was supposedly from Vince Shepherd's long-lost sister."

"I turned it into the sheriff," she said. "Do you know if he's learned anything more about whoever wrote it?"

"I don't think so," Shane said.

"Then I don't know any more than you do." She pushed away from the side of the SUV. "I'm going to get more photographs and talk to some of the rescuers."

She fired off a dozen more pictures, then climbed onto a boulder, which gave her a birds-eye view into the canyon. A couple of scraggly trees partially blocked her view of the wrecked truck, but she could see enough to feel a little queasy at the prospect of anyone trying to work around the smashed-up vehicle.

The loud chop of helicopter rotors drowned out the rumble of the wrecker's engine and the conversation of the volunteers. The rescue helicopter swept in and hovered on the edge of the canyon, the backwash from the rotors flinging loose gravel at onlookers and whipping back their hair. People tried to shield their eyes, but none of them looked away as a cable slowly lowered from the belly of the chopper. A few tense minutes later, the cable rose again, a litter bearing the figure of a person, wrapped like a mummy. A cheer rose from the crowd when the litter was safely inside.

Moments later, the cable lowered again. This time the trip was faster, as was the return journey. Another litter rose, but this one carried no securely wrapped figure—only a black plastic bag. The body bag meant one of the occupants of the truck hadn't made it.

Tammy moved in to speak with SAR Captain Danny Irwin. "Was there just the one fatality?" she asked.

"Yes. The passenger," Danny said "But the driver—a man—has a good chance of making it."

"Do we know who they are?" she asked.

Danny met her gaze. "We checked for ID, but I can't reveal that until their families are notified."

"Just tell me if they're locals," she said.

"They are not," he said.

Some of the tension that had been building since she had gotten the call about the accident lessened. The fatality was a tragedy, but not as wrenching as if it had been someone she knew. "What can you tell me about the rescue efforts?" she asked.

Danny straightened. "This was a highly technical rescue that put our training to the test," he said. "The truck was in a dangerous position, and our volunteers risked their lives to stabilize the vehicle and free the driver and passenger from the wreckage. This rescue involved everyone on-site, from those doing the climbing and rendering medical aid, to the volunteers who monitored the rigging, to those who provided backup support. This was an example of the teamwork Eagle Mountain Search and Rescue is known for."

"I got some great photos," Tammy said. "Everyone who lives here already knows how lucky we are to have such a great search and rescue group, but this kind of thing reminds them how awesome you all are."

"We're not doing it for the glory," Danny said. "But all that training and equipment isn't free. Anything that might net a few more donations is welcome."

Laughter from a group just beyond them distracted her. She looked past him. Was that Vince?

"Looking for someone?" Danny asked.

"Vince Shepherd. Is he here tonight?"

Danny looked around. "Vince is here somewhere."

"I'm sure I'll find him." She hurried away before Danny could ask why she wanted to speak with Vince. Even she wasn't completely sure of the answer to that question, except that she liked Vince a lot. She wanted to know him better. And she wanted him to like her.

She hadn't seen him since they had parted company after their interview with the sheriff Sunday morning. He hadn't followed up on his dinner invitation. She had picked up the phone to text him half a dozen times but had stopped herself from following through on the impulse. She wasn't going to chase a man who wasn't interested in her. Whatever happened between them would have to happen in its own time. If it didn't, well, maybe it wasn't meant to happen at all. Was that the coward in her, making excuses? Maybe so, but she was reluctant to let go of the notion that a real love should be strong enough to overcome the obstacles life put in its way. If it wasn't, what was the point? Life was so fragile and fleeting, why risk grabbing hold of something that was even more unreliable?

VINCE SHOVED THE last duffel of supplies into the back of the search and rescue vehicle known as the Beast. Six volunteers had snagged a ride to the scene in the specially outfitted Jeep, but he wasn't one of them. Instead, he and the rest of the crew had driven their personal vehicles. He had left his truck parked down the road from the accident site.

"I'm parked right behind you." Grace Wilcox fell into step beside him. Grace had been with the team a few months longer than he had, but he didn't know much about her, except that she was an environmental scientist and she was dating a new deputy with the sheriff's department.

"That was an amazing rescue tonight," he said.

"I'm in awe of people like Sheri and Ryan, who make those dangerous climbs," Grace said. "And in the dark. I'm literally just learning the ropes, and I don't ever think I'll be that skilled and confident."

"How did you get involved with search and rescue?" he asked.

"I like helping others and making a difference." She flashed a smile. "And it gets me out of my own head. I could easily turn into a hermit if I didn't force myself to get out and be part of the community. This is a good way to do that. And I'm learning new skills, getting into shape—I love it. Even when the rescues are hard or dangerous. It's all important, and how often do any of us get to do something that's really important?"

"I guess you're right." He had joined search and rescue because he remembered how hard they had worked to help find Valerie. Even though they hadn't succeeded, the memory of those dedicated volunteers had stuck with him. And though he had never mentioned this when he applied to be a volunteer, he had hoped that time spent in remote locations in the mountains might lead to him uncovering a clue about what had happened to Valerie. He had imagined that would mean finding her body, or at least something that had belonged to her. That hadn't happened, but until the mystery of her disappearance was solved, he would never let go of the hope of finding a solution.

"The new girl seems really nice," Grace said.

"Bethany? Yeah, she's nice."

"She's shy, like me, but I can tell she's trying to come out of her shell."

"I guess so." Maybe he was reading too much into her attention to him. Some people were just friendly.

"Hey, what is that all over your truck?"

Grace's steps faltered, then stopped. Vince stopped also, and stared at his truck. The moon had risen, and even in that silvery light, he could tell something was wrong with the paint job on the truck. It was too splotchy. He broke into a run and stopped when his boots crunched on broken glass. Every window in the truck was shattered. The windshield was still holding together, though a spiderweb of cracks spread out from a spot centered over the driver's side.

"Is that red paint?" Grace spoke from beside him.

Vince crunched toward the truck until he could touch the dark stain across the hood. His finger came away red and sticky. He stared, realizing something was scrawled amid the broken lines of the windshield glass—messy words in the same red paint.

YOU THOUGHT I WAS DEAD, DIDN'T YOU?

"What's that at the bottom?" Caleb had joined Vince and Grace. "It looks like a check mark."

"It's not a check mark," Vince said. He stared at the two slashes of paint meeting at the bottom. "It's a *V*." *V* for *Valerie*.

Chapter Nine

Tammy headed back down the hill toward her car. She searched groups of people she passed, hoping to spot Vince. She would say hello, and they could make small talk about the accident. Maybe they could firm up dinner plans.

A crowd had gathered on the side of the road up ahead. Curious, Tammy pushed through the clot of people and was startled to see Vince standing in front of his truck. Several people were shining flashlights on the vehicle, revealing a broken window and splashes of red paint. Tammy stared at the message on the windshield: YOU THOUGHT I WAS DEAD, DIDN'T YOU? V.

Deputy Shane Ellis, along with Colorado State Patrol Officer Ryder Stewart, moved in alongside Vince and began talking to him. Tammy snapped off a few photographs of the scene, then joined them. "Hello, Vince," she said during a lull in the conversation.

"Hey, Tammy." He resumed staring at his truck. "I can't believe this happened."

Tammy turned to Shane. "Who did this?" she asked.

"We haven't found anyone who saw anything," Shane said.

"Everyone was focused on the accident, and it was dark," Ryder said. "The road was closed, and there weren't a lot of people along this stretch where the volunteers parked their cars. We've got a shoe impression where a person stepped in the paint. It may have been the perpetrator, or maybe someone who was trying to get a closer look." He studied Tammy's tennis shoes. "The print is about your size."

"No paint on me or my shoes." She extended her leg so he could examine the sole of first one shoe, then the other. "So you think a woman did this?"

"It's a possibility," Ryder said. "But only *one* possibility."

"Someone could have parked on the other side of the closure and hiked up the road like I did," she said. "If they waited until everyone was up at the accident site, maybe when the helicopter arrived and was making a lot of noise and attracting everyone's attention. Then they smashed the windows, wrote the message and tossed the paint, and left before anyone saw them."

"That could be how it happened," Ryder said. "Do you know something about it?"

"I got to the accident site a few minutes before the helicopter arrived," she said. "While I was walking up the road, a woman ran past me. I didn't get a good look, but I'm pretty sure it was a woman—slender and not too tall, dressed in dark clothing. I noticed her because she was running—and away from the accident, not toward it like everyone else."

Vince was focused on her now. "What color hair did she have? Did you get a look at her face?"

"No. I was focused on getting to the accident scene. And she was moving pretty fast."

"Did you see where she went?" Shane asked.

"No, I didn't," she admitted.

"The message is signed *V*," Vince said.

"Do you think it's Valerie?" Tammy asked.

"I don't know what to think," he admitted.

"Both of you need to come down to the department and

give a statement," Shane said. "Meanwhile, we'll go over the truck for evidence."

"I can give you a ride to town," Tammy said.

Vince looked glum. "Why would anyone go after my truck? And why the cryptic message?"

"I don't know," Tammy said. "Maybe the sheriff can figure something out." She didn't believe that. Whoever was pretending to be Valerie, she hadn't provided them with evidence of her motive, other than to harass Vince. "Do you have an ex who is angry with you? If she knows about Valerie, she might be hiding behind the name as a way of unsettling you."

"It's unsettling, all right. But no, I don't have any exes, angry or otherwise. I told you, I'm not the best at relationships."

She wanted to reassure him that he was just fine, that no one was an expert at these things, but what did she know? Better to focus on being his friend. If something more developed, that would be good, but better not to force it.

Vince slid into the passenger seat of Tammy's Subaru, the image of his vandalized truck still fixed in his mind. *You thought I was dead, didn't you?* Of course he thought Valerie was dead. Hundreds of people had searched for her immediately after she went missing, and they hadn't found one clue as to what happened to her. No one had heard from her in fifteen years. She had disappeared in the high mountains, where people died in accidents every year. One wrong step or a slip could send a person plummeting off a cliff or into a deep fissure in the rocks, and no one would ever see them again.

Whoever was doing this couldn't be Valerie. She would have no reason to taunt him this way. The real Valerie would be happy to see him again.

But a scammer would demand money, and that hadn't happened yet.

Which left someone who was doing this in order to torture Vince and his family. A person who enjoyed making other people suffer. Was it someone he knew or a stranger who had read the article in the *Examiner* and decided to focus on him? "Has anyone contacted the paper about the article you wrote?" he asked Tammy.

"What do you mean by *contact*?" she asked. "A few people complimented me on the article. And some people asked what else I had planned for the series."

"I'm thinking maybe someone saw the article and fixated on it as a way to harass me," he said. "I've heard of people who enjoy psychologically torturing others. Some of the calls my parents received soon after Valerie disappeared were made by people like that. They would say things like 'Your daughter is being tortured, and you'll never see her again.'"

"That's so cruel," she said.

"It is. I'm trying to figure out if the person who sent that postcard and vandalized my car is like that. They've decided for whatever reason to target me, and Valerie's story is a convenient one to hide behind." The idea made sense—more sense than the possibility that Valerie had suddenly shown up again after all these years.

"You should tell the sheriff that," she said. "There might even be someone who contacted your parents before who has resurfaced."

At the sheriff's department, Tammy left with Shane to give her statement while Jake Gwynn escorted Vince to an interview room. They had scarcely settled into chairs across from each other when Travis entered. "I might have a few questions after you've given your statement to Jake about what happened tonight."

Vince took him through the events of the evening, from when he had first parked his truck on the side of the closed highway to his arrival back there two hours later, and the vandalism he had seen. "You're sure the note was signed *V*?" Jake asked. "It couldn't have been some random paint drip?"

Vince thought back to the message on the windshield. "I'm pretty sure it was *V*," he said.

"Do you know who *V* might be?" Jake asked.

"I think it's someone who is trying to make me think the message was written by my sister, Valerie." Vince looked to Travis. "Maybe the same person who sent that postcard."

"You don't believe this really is Valerie?" Travis asked.

"How could it be? If she's still alive, why haven't we heard anything for fifteen years? And if she was kidnapped and suddenly escaped, you'd think she'd be thrilled to see us again. She wouldn't hide and try to frighten us."

Travis scooted his chair closer and looked Vince in the eye. "Did you have anything to do with your sister's disappearance?"

"What? No!"

"Is it possible Valerie might have thought you had something to do with the accident or whatever happened that day?" Travis continued. "Maybe you were playing and she slipped and fell, and you were too afraid to tell anyone. Or you dared her to do something and she took the dare and was hurt."

"No! I was in the tent, asleep, when she disappeared. I saw her leave the tent, then fell back asleep. By the time I woke up, my parents were already searching."

Travis's expression gave nothing away. Vince glared at him. "Do you think this is Valerie? And that she's exacting revenge for something I did to her?"

"I think it's always a good idea to look at every possibility," Travis said.

"If this is my sister, where has she been all this time? And why couldn't hundreds of people searching for her find any trace after that day?"

"I don't know," Travis said. "But I'm doing my best to find out. Is there anything else about tonight, or about the postcard or the message left on your truck, that makes you think of anything or anyone?"

"No. I've gone over and over it in my head, and I can't think of anything, except that this is another scammer or one of those people who likes to torture others. My parents got calls like that after Valerie disappeared. Is it possible this is one of those people and the article in the *Examiner* shifted their focus to me?"

"Do you know the names of any of those people?" Travis asked.

"I don't think so, but I'll ask my parents." Although that would mean involving them in this, and he had been hoping to avoid that. "Maybe you have something in your files on the case," he said.

"I haven't found anything, but I promise I'll take a look." Travis stood. "Jake will print your statement and you can sign it, then you're free to go. Call us in a day or two, and we'll let you know when you can have your truck."

"I hate to think how much it's going to cost to restore the truck," he said.

Travis didn't comment on this, merely said good-night and left the room. Vince waited for the printout of his statement, read over it and then dashed off his signature. It wasn't until he was walking down the hall that he wondered how he was going to get to his condo. But when he stepped into the lobby, Tammy rose from a chair by the door. "I waited to give you a ride home," she said.

"Thanks."

He didn't say anything else until they were seated in her car. "Are you going to write about my truck being vandalized for the paper?" he asked.

"I don't know," she said. "I have to work on the story about the truck accident and the rescue." She glanced at him, then back at the road. "Why?"

"I'd rather you didn't," he said. "I don't want to upset my parents, but most of all, I don't want to give whoever this is more attention."

"If we do run anything, it's most likely to be a line item in the sheriff's report. But it isn't my decision to make. That would be up to my editor."

"You don't have to give him the photos you took," he said.

"No, I don't." She fell silent, and he worried he had hurt her feelings.

"I'm not trying to tell you how to do your job," he added. "And I'm grateful for all the help you've given me. I'm just trying to sort out how to handle all of this."

"I know." She turned into the parking area for his condo and pulled into an empty space. She unfastened her seat belt but kept the engine running. "I'm sorry about your truck," she said. "That has to feel like a personal attack."

"It does," he agreed. "That message—'You thought I was dead, didn't you?' As if I betrayed my sister by believing she was no longer alive."

"Even though a lot of people share that assumption."

"I'm angry that I'm letting some sick person get to me this way," he said.

"Don't beat yourself up for being human." She reached over and took his hand. Her skin was cool and smooth, her touch firm and comforting. "I wish I could do more to help."

"You're doing a lot just being here." He turned toward her,

and she surprised him by leaning over and pressing her lips to his.

He leaned into the kiss, pulled by attraction and need. Then, just as suddenly, she pulled away. The kiss was brief, but the impression of it lingered. She gave a nervous laugh and didn't meet his gaze. "Call me if you need anything else," she said, and fastened her seat belt.

That seemed the definite signal for him to leave. "I will," he said. "And thanks for everything."

He got out of the car and forced himself to walk up to his condo without looking back. He was relieved to find no nasty notes on his door. He sank onto the couch and leaned forward, elbows on knees and head in his hand. His lips still tingled from that kiss. He liked Tammy. He liked being with her. He was attracted to her, and it would be fun to explore that attraction. But was now the time to get involved with anyone, with everything stirred up over Valerie?

Though, when he looked at his life closely, he recognized that Valerie had been his excuse for not getting serious about anyone all his life. Since his twin had vanished all those years ago, he had grown used to being alone. Valerie wasn't half of him, but she was part of him. She was part of his life even though she was no longer in it, and he didn't know how to explain that to someone else. Valerie wasn't dead, but she would never be truly gone either. He had always wondered if finding her body would make it easier to finally lay her to rest.

Instead, he was grappling with someone who claimed his sister was still alive and wasn't happy with him. Valerie was still taking up too much room in his head and his life to make it possible to be there for someone else.

Chapter Ten

Wednesday morning, Tammy sat at her desk in the office of the *Eagle Mountain Examiner*, reviewing the photos she had taken the night before. She was supposed to be selecting the image from the rescue to run with the story she had already turned in. But her attention kept returning to the shots she had taken of Vince's vandalized car. *You thought I was dead, didn't you?* And that slash of a *V* beneath. If it was possible for a painted message to look angry, this one did.

She replayed those few seconds when the figure had run past her in the dark—slender body, long hair—and something about the way they moved had made Tammy certain it was a woman. Who would be running away from the accident, unless it was the person who had vandalized Vince's car?

Tammy had arrived at the scene after all the rescue personnel were in place. Law enforcement was either stationed at the highway barricade or near the accident site. Could one of them have seen the same fleeing woman?

She stood and walked to the open door of Russ's office. He was hunched over his desk, frowning at his computer monitor, but looked up at her approach. "What?" he asked.

"I'm going out to do background interviews for a story I'm working on," she said.

"Go." He waved her away and returned to scowling at the monitor.

She slung her handbag over one shoulder and headed on foot to the sheriff's department. It was the kind of perfect summer day that made tourists congratulate themselves on having chosen such an idyllic spot for a vacation—sunny but not hot, with cloudless turquoise skies and blooming flowers everywhere you looked.

The atmosphere was less sunny in the lobby of the sheriff's department. Office Manager Adelaide Kinkaid looked up from her command center at the front desk, her expression stern. "What can I do for you, Ms. Patterson?" she asked.

"I'd like to speak to the sheriff," Tammy said.

"Sheriff Walker does not have time to speak with the press," Adelaide said, her response to every request Tammy had ever made to speak with the sheriff.

"Then I need to speak with one of the deputies who responded to the accident at Carson Canyon last night."

Adelaide's eyes narrowed. "What do you need to know?"

"I need to clarify a couple of facts for the article I wrote." Pause, and an earnest expression. "I would hate to get anything wrong."

Adelaide's frown tightened, but after a few seconds, she picked up the phone and asked a deputy to come to the lobby to speak with "the reporter from the *Examiner*." As if everyone in town didn't already know Tammy was the sole reporter—well, except for the high school student who covered school sports each year, and Russ, who did write his share of news stories.

Deputy Jamie Douglas smiled when she saw Tammy. Tammy returned the smile. She and Jamie were friends, and she didn't have to worry about her friend being evasive. Jamie glanced at Adelaide. "Come on back, and we'll talk at my desk," she said.

As they walked down the hallway to the crowded bullpen where Jamie shared a desk with other deputies, the two friends exchanged the usual pleasantries. "How is Olivia?" Tammy asked.

"We think she's going to start crawling any minute now," Jamie said of her three-month old daughter. "And she's growing like crazy. Nate says she's going to be tall like him, but I think it's too soon to tell." They arrived at Jamie's desk. "Adelaide said you had some questions about the accident last night?"

"Yes. I wanted to know who was working the barricade where they closed the highway."

"I was."

"Did anyone try to get past you? On foot, maybe?"

"No. You and the rescue personnel are the only people we let through."

Maybe the woman she had seen had slipped through before the barricade went up. "Did you see anyone leaving the area?" Tammy asked. "Anyone you didn't recognize, or who wasn't authorized to be there?"

"No. Why?"

She explained about the running woman who had passed her as she hiked up the hill.

"I didn't see anyone like that," Jamie said. She looked over Tammy's shoulder. "Dwight, come here a minute."

Deputy Dwight Preston joined them. "Hi, Tammy."

"Dwight, did you see anyone come or go past the barricade last night who you didn't know? Anyone who wasn't with search and rescue or highway patrol?"

"There was the other reporter," he said.

"What other reporter?" Tammy asked.

"With the *Junction Sentinel*. She said the couple in the truck were from Junction, and she was covering the story."

Tammy's heart raced. "What did she look like?"

"About your height. Slender. She was wearing dark jeans and a dark shirt and a baseball cap. I couldn't see her hair."

"Did she give a name?" Jamie asked.

"No. She just said she was a reporter with the *Sentinel*. She had a camera and a notebook, so I let her through."

"Were the couple in the truck from Junction?" Tammy asked.

Jamie and Dwight looked at each other. "I'll check," Jamie said, and turned to her computer.

"Is something wrong?" Dwight asked.

Tammy explained about the running woman. "It sounds like it could have been the same woman," Dwight said. "Maybe she was in a hurry to get back to town and file her story."

Jamie looked up. "The couple was from North Carolina," she said.

Tammy thanked them and hurried back to the newspaper office. From there, she telephoned the Junction paper and asked for her friend, Tyler Frazier. "Hey, Tammy!" he greeted her. "This is a nice surprise."

"Hey, Tyler. I'm trying to locate a reporter there at the paper. She was here in Eagle Mountain last night, covering an accident we had where a couple's truck went off the road and over a cliff."

"Sounds like a wild story, but I don't think we would have sent a reporter to cover it," he said. "That's pretty far out of our coverage area."

"Would you mind checking for me?"

"Okay. Hold on a second."

He put her on Hold. A song that was popular when her parents were teenagers came on, and Tammy hummed along as she studied the photos of the vandalized truck once more. She had taken one of the red footprint, left when someone—the vandal?—had stepped in the red paint. Red like blood. She shivered at the thought.

Tyler came back on the line. "No one here went down to Eagle Mountain yesterday to cover an accident or anything else," he said. "What did this reporter look like?"

"Female, young, slender, about my height. Maybe with long hair." The woman who had run past her had had long hair.

"That doesn't sound like anyone we have on staff," Tyler said. "Sorry I can't help you."

She hung up. Someone had posed as a reporter in order to get past the highway barrier. Had she done so specifically to get to Vince's truck? But why? Why target him?

The phone rang, the screen showing a familiar name. "Hello, Mitch," she said.

"Come have lunch with me," Mitch said.

She started to tell him she was too busy. Truthfully, she wasn't in the mood to socialize, even with Mitch.

"Please. Elisabeth will be there, and I want you to meet her."

"All right." She couldn't pass up the chance to meet the woman who had captivated her brother.

"Meet us at the Rib Shack at twelve thirty."

When she arrived at the barbecue stand near the river, she spotted Mitch already in line. Next to him was a slender, dark-haired woman about her height, whom he introduced as Elisabeth. The woman's smile was warm, her handshake firm. "It's nice to meet you," she said.

"It's good to meet you too," Tammy said. "And welcome to Eagle Mountain. Mitch tells me you're new in town."

"Yes. He's been helping me get settled." She gave Mitch

an adoring smile, which he returned. Tammy had never seen her brother this besotted. Why was that unsettling?

"What brought you to Eagle Mountain?" Tammy asked. "We're not exactly on the beaten path."

"I had a friend who used to live here," she said. "She raved about how beautiful it is, and I can't say she was wrong."

It was their turn to order. When they had collected their food, they carried it to a picnic table in the shade of a towering blue spruce. Elisabeth and Mitch settled across from Tammy, sitting so close their shoulders touched.

"Elisabeth, where are you from?" Tammy asked.

"Nebraska."

"Oh, do you have family there?"

Elisabeth's expression saddened. Something about her was familiar to Tammy, but she couldn't place her. "Not anymore. My father passed away recently, and I'm all alone."

"I'm sorry to hear that. You don't have other family?"

"No one close, no." She glanced at Mitch. "Not everyone is lucky enough to have a close sibling."

"Are you in Eagle Mountain for long?" Tammy asked.

"I hope so." She beamed at Mitch, and he beamed back. Why did this set Tammy's teeth on edge? Was she jealous that Mitch was happy and she wasn't? No. She wasn't like that. And Elisabeth seemed perfectly nice.

"Mitch tells me you're a reporter," Elisabeth said, her attention on Tammy once more. "That must be such interesting work."

"It is."

"What are some of the stories you've covered?" She propped her chin on her hand, eyes laser-focused on Tammy.

Tammy shifted, uncomfortable under that intense gaze. "Last night I covered an accident. A truck went off the road and plunged over a cliff, but it was caught halfway down on a boulder. Search and rescue had to make a dangerous climb down to stabilize the truck and retrieve the accident victims."

"That certainly sounds dramatic," Elisabeth said.

"It was." She studied the other woman more closely. "You weren't up there near the accident scene last night, were you?"

"Who, me?" Elisabeth looked amused. "Why would you think that?"

"I thought I saw you up there." Tammy couldn't be sure, but Elisabeth might have been the figure who ran by her.

Elisabeth chuckled. "It wasn't me." She leaned into Mitch. "I was otherwise occupied."

"Elisabeth was with me last night," Mitch said. He put his arm around her shoulders.

"It must have been someone else, then." Tammy focused on her lunch, though she scarcely tasted the spicy barbecue.

"You wrote that article about the little girl who disappeared, didn't you?" Elisabeth said.

"Yes."

Elisabeth glanced at Mitch. "I read it when I first got to town. It's hard to believe anyone could just vanish that way."

"It happens more often than you would think," Mitch said. "There's a lot of hazardous country. It's easy to get lost or have an accident."

"I would think parents of a child would keep a closer eye on them." Elisabeth popped a french fry into her mouth.

"Apparently, Valerie slipped out of the tent early in the morning, before the rest of the family was awake," Tammy said.

"Well, the parents would say that if they wanted to cover up their own guilt, wouldn't they?"

Before Tammy could question this odd assertion, another local real estate agent stopped by their table to say hello.

Mitch introduced Elisabeth, who smiled warmly and leaned closer to Mitch.

When the other man left, Tammy gathered up the remains of her lunch. "I'd better get back to work," she said. "It was nice meeting you, Elisabeth."

"You too." Elisabeth linked her arm with Mitch's. "I'm sure we're going to be seeing a lot more of each other."

Tammy took the longest route back to the newspaper office, trying to walk off her mixed emotions about her brother's newest girlfriend. Was it the swiftness with which the relationship had progressed that unsettled her? She clearly wasn't the woman who had impersonated a reporter from Junction last night, or the person who had run past Tammy and maybe vandalized Vince's car. Tammy hadn't dared press for more details, but her brother's smug expression seemed to imply that he and Elisabeth had spent the entire night together.

Back at the office, she got to work on an article summarizing the most recent town council meeting and rewriting a press release from a local charitable organization.

Hours later, she was gathering her things to leave when the receptionist, Micki, a high school student who worked from one to six most afternoons, came over to her desk. "Someone just put this through the mail slot," she said. "It's addressed to you."

Tammy accepted the envelope and stared at her name in crooked block print across the front. The printing looked familiar. She worked her thumb beneath the flap and teased it open. The message inside was typed.

Dear Tammy
As a reporter, I'm sure you're interested in the truth. I read the article you wrote about the disappearance of Valerie Shepherd and feel the need to set a few things straight.
   Despite what the Shepherds have told everyone for

years, Valerie did not simply wander off. Her parents—
and her brother, Vince—deliberately left her in those
mountains to die. That was the whole reason they even
went into the mountains that weekend. The family had
other things to do that weekend, but Mr. Shepherd insisted they had to go. He couldn't wait to get rid of the
difficult child in the family. I guess he thought life would
be easier with only Vince, his perfect son, to contend
with. If not for the kindness of a stranger who found
her, Valerie would have perished. The truth is, her family didn't want her anymore. Fortunately, she ended up
with someone who did want her.

This is the truth you need to let the public know about.
V.

Chapter Eleven

Vince read the letter through twice, heart hammering wildly. "It's not true," he said. "My parents and I didn't abandon Valerie. My parents were crushed by her disappearance. We've never stopped hoping she would be found."

"Why would anyone write these accusations?" Sheriff Walker tapped the corner of the letter, which was laid out on the table in the interview room at the sheriff's department. After Tammy had telephoned to tell him about the note, Vince had agreed to meet her at the sheriff's office, a place that was becoming all-too familiar to him after his recent visits. Travis sat on one side of the table, his brother, Sergeant Gage Walker, standing behind him. Vince and Tammy sat side by side across from him, not touching, but close enough that he could sense the rise and fall of her breath. This note had clearly unnerved her, and seeing her so upset had shaken him.

He forced his attention back to the sheriff's question. "I don't know." He stared at the single *V* typed at the bottom of the letter.

"It sounds to me like someone's pretending to be Valerie," Tammy said.

"It's signed the same way as the message left on my truck's windshield," Vince said.

"Did your sister sign her name that way?" Travis asked. "A single *V*?"

"No. But we were only ten when she disappeared." He tried to think but drew a blank. "I can't say I'd ever seen her sign anything."

"The letter writer refers to Valerie in the third person," Tammy said. "She doesn't say 'I did not simply wander off,' but '*Valerie* did not simply wander off.'" She shrugged. "I don't know if that's significant. It's just an observation."

"Maybe she likes to refer to herself in the third person," Travis said.

"Or maybe this isn't Valerie." Vince shook his head. "Of course it isn't Valerie."

Gage spoke for the first time. "Why do you say that?"

"Because even if Valerie is alive, she has no reason to want to hurt me. We were twins." He looked down at the table and swallowed past a lump in his throat. "Losing her was like losing part of myself."

"She's been gone a long time," Gage said. "Maybe she thinks you didn't do enough to find her. Or she blames you for whatever happened to her."

"But what could have happened to her?" Vince asked.

Gage and Travis exchanged a glance, though he couldn't read the meaning behind that look. It was the kind of coded expression couples or siblings shared—the kind of communication he and Valerie had once enjoyed. "At the time your sister disappeared, both you and your parents mentioned another camper in the area," Travis said.

"Valerie said there was a man camped near us," Vince said. "I never saw him, and when we searched the area for him, we never saw any sign of him."

"Was it like her to make things up?" Travis asked.

"No. I believed there was a camper and he left early."

"Maybe he took Valerie with him when he left," Gage said.

"I know my parents thought so," Vince said. "They urged law enforcement to look for the man, and I believe they tried to find him. But no one else reported seeing him, and we didn't have much to go on—just a man with a blue tent."

Tammy leaned forward, her expression eager. "Do you think Valerie was kidnapped by this man and, after fifteen years, managed to escape and come looking for her family?" she asked.

"It's one possibility," Travis said. "Though that's not to go any further than this room."

Tammy shrank back at his stern look. "Yes, sir," she said.

Travis slid the letter into an evidence bag. "Or maybe this is a hoax." He regarded Vince for a long moment. Vince tried to remain still, to not reveal how unsettled the sheriff's scrutiny made him. "Are you sure you can't think of anyone who might want to harass you?" Travis asked. "An ex–romantic partner or someone you worked with? A former neighbor or classmate? Maybe another family member?"

"No one," Vince said.

"You can't think of anyone who has any reason to be unhappy with you?" Gage asked.

Vince shrugged. "No. I guess I'm not the kind of guy to upset people." The truth was, he seldom got close enough to anyone to upset them—or to make much of an impression at all. He had friends. He had dated several women. But he couldn't say any of those relationships had the depth he thought was required to end up with someone wanting to wreck his truck—or his life.

Travis stood and Gage moved away from the wall. "Those are all my questions for now," the sheriff said.

Vince followed Tammy out of the interview room, down the hall and onto the sidewalk. She stopped at the corner and hugged her arms across her chest. "That was frustrating," she said. "I was hoping the sheriff would have more answers."

"Do you think Valerie could be the one doing this?" he asked. "Sending those notes and vandalizing my truck? Has she been alive all these years and we didn't know?"

Tammy angled toward him, her expression soft with concern. "There have been other cases, of children who were abducted and turned up alive years later," she said.

"Then why not just contact me and tell me the truth?" Frustration made knots in his gut. "Why attack my truck and accuse me of helping to get rid of her?"

"It does feel like there's a lot of animosity in those letters— and what was done to your truck…" Tammy rubbed her hands up and down her arms as if she was cold.

It did. The idea that his sister—his twin whom he had loved without even having to think about it—would *hate* him this way felt dark and ugly.

They resumed walking, he assumed back toward the newspaper office. This time of day, the sidewalks were full of tourists and locals, running errands or visiting the shops and restaurants. He and Tammy had to walk close together, shoulders bumping frequently, in order to have a conversation. "What was Valerie like as a girl?" Tammy asked. "I mean, her temperament and attitudes? Was she like you or the opposite? Or somewhere in-between?"

He considered the question. Valerie had been such an essential part of his life that he had taken for granted she would always be there—until she wasn't. And at ten years old, he hadn't spent much time thinking about how other people felt or how they were different from him. But he had had a lot of time since then to examine everything he knew about his sister. "Valerie was more outgoing than I was," he said. "More daring. She would talk to strangers in public or wander off on her own when we were in the park or out shopping."

"Then she wouldn't have been afraid, necessarily, of a stranger who approached her?" Tammy asked.

"No. I mean, our parents and teachers had talked to us about stranger danger. Valerie was smart. I don't think she would have gotten into a car with someone she didn't know. But if a person struck up a conversation with her, she would have been friendly. And she liked attention. I guess she was kind of a show-off."

"Did that bother you when you were a boy? That she tried to get attention?"

"No. I didn't care. I wasn't interested in having people pay attention to me."

"Did she have a temper? Was she quick to anger or to take offense?"

"Oh yeah." He remembered. "She would get so mad sometimes. Her face would turn red, and she would stomp her foot." He almost smiled, picturing her rage over not being allowed to do something she wanted to do. "It's not fair!" she had howled, furious about not getting her way.

"But she could be sweet too," he said. "That weekend of the camping trip, I was upset about missing a friend's birthday party. Valerie tried to make me feel better. She even told my dad she thought I should be allowed to go to the party. And though she teased me about being afraid of things she wasn't—spiders and steep mountain bike tracks and things like that—she was never too hard on me."

"The two of you were close, then?"

He shrugged. "We were twins. And we didn't have any other siblings or cousins who lived nearby. The two of us were kind of a team."

"It must have been hard for you when she disappeared."

"For a long time, it didn't feel real," he said. "I kept thinking the door would open and she would be there, laughing and telling us all it had been a joke, that she had merely been hiding."

"Cruel joke," Tammy said. "Would she have done something like that?"

"Maybe," he said. "It would have been better than the truth—that we never knew what happened to her."

But what if the person who was harassing him now did turn out to be Valerie? Would that be worse than believing she had died? He couldn't wrap his head around the answer. "I'd like to know what happened to her," he said. "And I want whoever is sending these letters and whoever attacked my truck to be found and stopped."

"I want that too," Tammy said. She rested her hand on his shoulder. "And I'll do everything I can to help you."

It was the kind of thing any person might say, but he could sense the sincerity behind her words. She cared. The idea touched him—and unsettled him too. He had spent years keeping his distance from people. If you didn't get too close to people, you wouldn't be too hurt when they left you. He understood that not everyone wanted to live that way, but it had worked for him so far. Why should he change now just because one curly-haired reporter was getting under his skin?

Fifteen years ago

"IT'S MY TURN to hide. You have to find me!" Before Vince could protest, Valerie slapped his shoulder and ran away.

Annoyed, he closed his eyes and began to count. "One, two, three…"

He hated when it was his turn to find Valerie. She never failed to choose the best hiding spots. Impossible spots, like the gap between the cushions and the underside of their hide-a-bed sofa in the den, or in the rafters of the garage. He could spend hours searching for her with no luck, except he often gave up long before then.

Not that it was better when it was his turn to hide. She always found him, usually within ten minutes. Then she would crow about how terrible he was at this game. Which was why he never wanted to play. But today he had made the mistake of promising to play whatever Valerie wanted, never thinking she would choose hide-and-seek on such a hot afternoon. It had to be near ninety degrees out, and the sun was beating down. Maybe that wasn't hot to people like his aunt and uncle from Texas, but here in the mountains, with no air-conditioning in their house, ninety degrees was sweltering.

He reached fifty and decided that was enough. He was supposed to count to one hundred, but with Valerie, he needed any advantage he could grab. He opened his eyes and looked around, searching for any clue as to which direction she had run. He didn't see any footprints in the rocks and grass that made up the empty lot behind their house where they were playing. No flash of the bright red T-shirt she was wearing. The shed door wasn't ajar. Would she hide inside one of the parked cars?

He hurried to his mom's Chevy and opened the rear door. A blast of heat pushed him back. Valerie had better not be in there. She'd roast. He forced himself to stick his head inside and look around, but no Valerie.

No Valerie in the shed either, or behind any of the trees or bigger boulders that ringed the lot. Their rule was that they had to stay within the lot, which was bordered on two sides by wooden fencing. The back side gave way to a steep drop-off. Vince approached this and looked over. It would be just like Valerie to slide down there, thinking it would be a stealthy hiding place, and not be able to get back up. But there was nothing in the gully below but more trees and rocks.

He turned around and faced the house. He hadn't heard a door open or close, but Valerie might have managed to slip inside if she had been quiet. She was good at stealth. Better than he was. He was going through another growth spurt, and everything he did was clumsy. Squinting in the bright sunlight, he moved toward the house. He approached the back door, then looked under the steps. There was a shadowed hollow there where Vince had hidden once. It had taken Valerie over fifteen minutes to find him that time. She had even said it was a good hiding place.

But she hadn't decided to use it this time. He moved along the house, looking behind the lilac bushes, their blooms spent brown twigs now.

Something scrabbled in the loose mulch behind him, and he whirled, heart pounding. He stared at the ground beneath the lilacs. What was down there? He didn't see anything, but something had made that noise. "Valerie?" he asked, tentative.

Fingers gripped his ankle, hard, and yanked. Vince screamed and staggered back, arms flailing. Raucous laughter brought him up short.

Valerie, cobwebs draped across her hair like old lace and a smudge of dirt across one cheek, crawled out from beneath the porch. "Oh my gosh, that was great!" she shrieked, doubled over with laughter. "You screamed like a little girl!"

"You're supposed to be hiding, not attacking me!" he yelled.

"You walked right past me!" she said. "I couldn't resist. Your ankle was right there!"

He stared at the gap in the foundation she had squeezed into. "You have spiderwebs in your hair," he said.

She swept her fingers through her wavy locks, and the sticky webbing clung to them. "There are spiders under there too," she said.

He shuddered. "That's disgusting."

"No it's not. I'm not afraid of a few bugs." She lifted her chin. "I'm not afraid of anything."

Vince envied his sister's fearlessness. He was afraid of so many things—spiders and falling, not catching a fly ball in Little League, failing a math test and being stuck in fourth grade forever. "I bet you're afraid of dying," he said. "Everyone is afraid of that. Even adults."

Valerie shrugged. "I'm not."

"Liar."

She leaned forward and slapped his shoulder. "Your turn to hide. And pick a good place." Then she closed her eyes and started counting out loud. "One, two, three…"

Vince ran. He thought about leaving the yard and heading down the street to his friend Brett's house. That would make Valerie mad, but she'd either tell their mom—in which case, Vince would end up grounded—or she wouldn't tell anyone, but would exact her own revenge, like putting ants in his underwear drawer or putting dog poop in his bed. She had done both of those things before, and Vince had ended up punished when his mother found out. "Valerie wouldn't do something like that," she had said.

And Valerie had played the innocent like a pro, looking at him with wide, hurt eyes. Later, she had sidled up to Vince in the hallway, after his mother had sentenced him to spend an hour every day after school pulling weeds in the flower beds, and whispered, "That'll teach you to try to get the better of me."

Vince ran to the shed and hid behind the lawn mower and paint cans. It wasn't the best hiding place, but it was a good enough spot to sit and think in the moments before Valerie came to find him. He would think about all the things he could do to get back at Valerie, but wouldn't. If she hadn't been his sister, he would have admired her daring instead of being jealous of it. And when it came down to it, he would rather have her on his side than angry with him.

Chapter Twelve

Thursday afternoon, Tammy sat at her desk in the *Examiner* office and paged through the folder of information she had assembled about Valerie Shepherd's disappearance. She had all the original newspaper articles and notes from search and rescue about their role in the hunt for the missing girl, as well as the copy of the sheriff's department file that Travis had given her.

She stopped and reread the initial interview with Victor and Susan Shepherd, then took out a highlighter and ran it over the section where they talked about the camper Valerie claimed to have seen. "Right after we got to camp, Valerie climbed up onto a boulder and said she could see another camper nearby. Someone with a blue dome tent," Susan said. Her husband hadn't even heard this remark. The most information came from Vince, who said Valerie told him she met the man when she went to collect firewood. He had given her wood he had gathered and smiled at her. "She said he had a nice smile," Vince had said.

The sheriff's deputies had asked every person in the area that day if they had seen a lone male camper or backpacker, or one with a little girl who matched Valerie's description. No one had seen him. Appeals to the public who might have seen such a man had yielded nothing.

A man with a nice smile. Had the smile won Valerie over enough that she had gone with him? But where? Vince and his parents swore they had never seen the man, who, if he had been real, had seemingly vanished without a trace. Valerie had risen before the rest of the family and gone out to search for more wood. Had she encountered the man again and he had spirited her away in those early hours before anyone else was on the trail? It was possible, but if that was the case, where had they gone?

She continued reading through the file and came upon a single paragraph from a statement taken from a woman and her boyfriend six months after Valerie's disappearance. They had seen a man with a backpack on a trail near the one the Shepherds had taken, on the day before the Shepherds' camping trip. They described him as medium height and build, brown hair, early to mid-twenties. He wore jeans and a black T-shirt and hiking boots, and had a blue backpack. They hadn't spoken to him and had only come forward after seeing repeated appeals for information about a lone male hiker. "But it was the day before the little girl disappeared, and on a different trail," the woman—Jennifer—had said.

A handwritten note at the bottom of the page stated they were unable to obtain any further information about this man. A second note, in a different colored ink and different handwriting, contained just two words: *probably unrelated*.

That was the last entry in the slim file. Tammy closed the folder and stared into space, hoping for inspiration but finding none. Her stomach growled, and she decided maybe she would think better after lunch.

She walked down the street and was waiting in line for a booth at Kate's Café when a voice behind her said, "Tammy Shepherd? That is you, isn't it?"

She turned to find Elisabeth slipping in behind her. Tammy

glanced past her, expecting to see Mitch. Elisabeth laughed. "Mitch is showing a big ranch over near Delta," she said. "I'm on my own. And it looks like you are too."

The pause after these words was so weighted Tammy felt it pushing against her. "We should have lunch together," she said.

"I'd love that." Elisabeth linked her arm with Tammy's. "It will give us a chance to get to know each other better."

The server arrived to escort them to a booth along the side, and Tammy focused on the menu. But after a few moments, she became aware of Elisabeth studying her. She looked up. "You don't look like Mitch, do you?" Elisabeth said.

"He takes after my dad," Tammy said. "I look more like my mom. Though people say there's a resemblance."

Elisabeth shook her head. "I don't see it. Though maybe some family traits run stronger than that. For instance, my brother and I looked just alike. People thought we were twins."

"Oh. How many siblings do you have?" It seemed a safe enough topic of conversation.

"None. At least, not anymore. He died. My whole family is dead." She smiled, the expression so at odds with her words that Tammy was taken aback.

The server arrived to take their orders, providing a reprieve. Tammy tried to gather her thoughts. When they were alone again, she asked, "Have you been enjoying your time in Eagle Mountain?"

"I have. This morning I went shopping. There's a boutique in the Gold Nugget Hotel. Lucky Strike—do you know it?"

Tammy knew of the boutique, though its prices were beyond what she could manage on her reporter's salary. The styles displayed in the boutique's front windows were more upscale than what she usually wore. She dressed for comfort, ready to race out to the scene of an accident or to interview someone at a construction site or mine. Elisabeth, in her short skirt and heels, looked straight out of a magazine spread. There was no missing the way heads turned to follow her when she crossed a room.

"You're the first newspaper reporter I've ever met," Elisabeth said. "I thought that was one of those jobs that didn't exist anymore."

"People are still interested in the news," Tammy said.

"On television and online, maybe. I thought printed news was going the way of the dinosaurs."

This wasn't the first time Tammy had heard similar statements. "Not our paper," she said. "There's no other source for local news."

"Then you enjoy your job," Elisabeth said.

"Yes." The hours were long and the pay wasn't the best, but reporting was what she had always wanted to do. "The work offers a lot of variety," she said. "And I end up knowing about everything going on."

"What interesting things are going on in Eagle Mountain?"

"Everyone's gearing up for the Fourth of July. It's a big holiday here, for the locals and the tourists. There's a festival and a parade and fireworks."

"It sounds charming."

Tammy couldn't tell if *charming* was a positive or a negative to Elisabeth. "Do they do anything special for the Fourth where you're from?" she asked.

"Different places have fireworks." Elisabeth unrolled her napkin and spread it across her lap. "Mitch told me the two of you have a sibling who died. That's too bad, isn't it?"

Was that a question or an observation? Tammy was saved from having to reply by the arrival of the server with their food. She focused on the food, pondering a way to take the conversation in a less personal direction.

"Do you have a boyfriend?" Elisabeth asked.

Tammy had just taken a large bite of her sandwich and almost choked. She chewed and tried to think of an answer that wouldn't beg elaboration when Elisabeth added, "I saw you with a cute guy outside the sheriff's department. Tall, dark and handsome."

Tammy's face warmed. "That was just a friend."

"Uh-huh." Elisabeth gave her a knowing look. "Does your *friend* have a name?"

"Vince."

Elisabeth poked at her salad with her fork. "What's he like?"

"He's a great guy."

"And you like him a lot. I can tell."

"I do." There was relief in admitting this out loud, an easing of pressure. "But I'm not sure how he feels about me."

"Hmm. Then maybe you should ask him."

Tammy made a face. "I don't want to put him on the spot." And risk scaring him off.

"Okay. Then why not try a little experiment?"

"What do you mean?"

"Turn up the heat and see how he responds."

Tammy flashed back to the one kiss she and Vince had shared. There had been plenty of heat there, but nothing had happened since. "I don't know..."

"Oh, come on," Elisabeth said. "Just try a little seduction. If he goes for it, you'll at least know he's attracted to you physically. That's a place to start."

"Thanks for the suggestion, but that's not my style. Say, how long are you going to be in town? Mitch mentioned you weren't sure when you first moved here."

"I'm still not certain, though this place is growing on me. And I like your brother. He and I have really clicked." The way she said the words—and the smile that accompanied them—left no doubt that Mitch had responded well to any seduction Elisabeth had directed at him.

But Tammy could have guessed that, seeing how besotted her brother was with this gorgeous woman.

Her phone buzzed, and she slipped it out of her pocket and checked the screen. Where are you? Russ had texted. She imagined the irritation behind the words. The editor wasn't known for his patience. "I have to get back to work," she said. She took out her wallet.

"Oh no." Elisabeth raised a hand. "This is my treat."

"Oh. Thanks. At least let me get the tip."

"It's all taken care of." She pulled out a sleek black credit card.

"Thanks. And I'll, uh, see you soon," she said, and made her exit. No one, she was sure, watched her as she hurried away.

Lunch had been…unsettling. Elisabeth had been friendly and the two women had gotten along, but Tammy realized she still didn't know anything about her brother's new girlfriend—except that startling revelation about a dead brother and two dead parents. Though she had mentioned when they first met that her father had recently died. Elisabeth had deflected any questions about herself, each time turning the conversation back to Tammy.

Maybe Elisabeth was a private person who didn't like to talk about herself. Tammy could respect that. But she wished she and her brother's girlfriend had connected better. Mitch liked her so much that Tammy wanted to like her too.

Some people take longer to warm up to than others, she reminded herself. If Elisabeth did decide to remain in Eagle Mountain, the two of them would have plenty of opportunities to get to know each other better.

VINCE WAS JUST stepping out of the shower Saturday morning when his phone alarmed with an Amber Alert for a missing teen. He was reading through the description of a fifteen-year-old male who had walked out of his family's home the night before when he received the call-out for search and rescue.

Fifteen minutes later, he gathered with other volunteers at search and rescue headquarters. "We're looking for Nicholas Gruber," Danny told the assembled rescuers. "Five feet nine inches tall. Blue eyes. Brown hair. Last seen wearing jeans and a black T-shirt and black running shoes." He lowered the phone from which he had been reading the description. "Apparently, Nicholas had a fight with his mom and dad last night and stormed out. He has done this before, and he always returns in the morning after he's had time to cool off. When he didn't show up this morning, they contacted all his friends, but no one has seen him."

"They must be worried sick," Carrie Andrews said. Vince remembered that she had two children of her own.

"The Grubers live on County Road 7, near Coal Canyon," Danny said. "Nicholas left the house on foot about nine o'clock last night. The sheriff wants to get Anna and her search dog, Jacquie, out there first to see if the dog can pick up the trail. We're on standby to assist in a ground search if they don't find him."

Everyone shifted to look at volunteer Anna Trent and the black standard poodle at her side. The dog, Jacquie, wore a blue vest with *Search Dog* in large white letters on the side. "We're ready," Anna said.

"You and Jacquie can ride with me," Deputy Jake Gwynn said.

He, Anna and the dog left, and the others moved in closer to Danny and Deputy Ryker Vernon. Bethany was there, standing next to Harper, across from Vince. She caught his eye and he nodded, then quickly looked away. He really didn't want to encourage her attention. "We've established a staging area for search volunteers at the lumber mill about a mile from the Grubers' home," Ryker said. "If you'll make your way there, you'll be handy if we need you to help search or if we find Nicholas and he's injured."

While several volunteers piled into the Beast, Vince opted to drive his own vehicle to the lumber mill. Or rather, the car his mother had insisted on lending him when she learned of the damage to his truck. The white Ford Escape was newer and more luxurious than Vince's truck, but he missed his own vehicle, which was still at the sheriff's department impound yard, awaiting the completion of their investigation. Vince wasn't pressuring them to give it back because he doubted he had the funds to pay for the work the truck would need to restore it.

Set back off the road in a stand of tall Douglas fir, the small mill specialized in deck railings, rustic benches and other rough-cut lumber projects. Though the saws were silent today, the smell of fresh sawdust hung in the air. Vince parked beside Ryan Welch's pickup and opened the driver's-side door to let in the scented breeze.

Ryan came over to stand beside Vince and was soon joined by Caleb and Eldon. "I hope Anna and her dog find the kid," Eldon said.

"He's probably just hiding out somewhere," Ryan said. "I did the same thing a couple of times when I was his age— blew up at my parents, then just had to get away for a while."

"Yeah, I guess I did too," Eldon said. "But I'd go stay with my aunt—my dad's younger sister. And she would call my dad and let him know where I was."

"I would go and stay at a friend's house for a couple of days," Caleb said.

The others looked at Vince, who shifted uncomfortably. "I guess I was lucky," he said. "I never fought with my parents." Even if he had, after what had happened with Valerie, he wouldn't have walked out on his mom and dad. It would have worried them too much not to know where he was, even for a few hours.

A loud whistle split the air, and they all turned toward the sound. Danny was standing in the bed of a pickup, motioning for everyone to gather.

"Anna and Jacquie found Nicholas," Danny said when everyone was assembled around the truck. "Apparently, he got disoriented in the darkness and slipped or fell into the canyon. He's okay, except he thinks he broke or sprained his ankle. We're going to have to get him out."

Relief that Nicholas was alive and not in imminent danger energized the group. They gathered equipment and set out to hike to the spot where the teen had fallen. A middle-aged man and woman, both with short hair in shades of brown, were already there. The man lay on his stomach, his attention focused on the boy sprawled fifty yards below. The woman sat beside the man. They both looked up as the rescuers approached. "We're Nicholas's parents," the woman said.

"We're with Eagle Mountain Search and Rescue." Danny introduced himself and shook hands with each of them. "If you could wait back there, away from the edge, we'll have your son with you in no time."

"All right." Mr. Gruber glanced down into the canyon. "He's barely hanging on down there. Are you sure you can get to him without him falling?"

"We'll take care of him." Danny put a hand on the man's shoulder and gently urged him farther back.

The rescuers moved in, the challenge of what they needed to do quickly apparent. The soil along the edge of the canyon was loose, crumbling and raining down onto the boy below repeatedly as they worked. "How are you doing, Nicholas?" Danny called down.

"I'm worried I'm going to fall," came the thin, strained reply. "My ankle's hurt, and every time I try to move, more rock falls."

"Stay still and hang on," Danny instructed. "We need to get things set up here, then we're going to come down to get you."

"Okay. But hurry." Nicholas's voice trembled with fear, but Vince thought he heard determination too.

They were forced to establish an anchor on a tree across the road and ended up using a shovel to dig to more compacted soil before Eldon began the initial descent. Vince helped with the rigging, monitoring the ropes and pulleys and passing whatever equipment Ryan requested as he helped first Eldon, then Danny to descend. Vince found himself holding his breath as the men searched for solid hand-and footholds, the descent slowed by the need to continually reroute to more stable ground. No wonder the kid had fallen.

"I wonder if I'll ever be able to do anything so dangerous."

Vince looked back and found Bethany standing there. She was focused on the scene unfolding below. Then her gaze shifted to him, and the brief, shy smile he had come to associate with her flashed across her face. "I've been doing a little climbing in Caspar Canyon. Sheri and Hannah and some of the others held a kind of clinic for female volunteers."

"That's good," he said.

"At least I know the names of everything now so I can help with the gear."

"You'll get more comfortable the more time you have in." Vince remembered his early days with the group, when he had been overwhelmed by the magnitude of the job they did and uncertain where he fit in with the team.

Bethany was focused on the rescue efforts again, which gave Vince time to study her. She had her dark brown curls pulled back in a low ponytail, and exertion or the breeze in the canyon had reddened her cheeks. She wasn't beautiful, exactly, but cute, in a girl-next-door kind of way. Valerie had been like that. In fact, she and Bethany had the same hair and the same dimple in one cheek. His heart stumbled in its rhythm at the thought, and he stared harder, waiting for some spark of recognition. But nothing happened.

He cleared his throat, and Bethany shifted her attention to him once more. "How long have you been in Eagle Mountain?" he asked.

"Two months."

"Do you have family here? Friends?"

"No. I came for the job at Peak Jeep." She shrugged. "I was ready for a fresh start."

"Why search and rescue?"

"I was looking for a way to get to know more people. And I wanted to do something that would make a difference. Oh, look. They've reached the boy."

Nicholas had been huddled against the ground, one hand over his head to shield him from the worst of the debris that rained down, though more than one fist-sized rock struck his back and many smaller pebbles or dirt clods peppered him.

But now the two rescuers reached him and established themselves on either side of him, and he slumped between them. Eldon fitted the boy with a helmet and harness while Danny assessed his physical condition. "I'm going to fit the ankle with an air boot and give him something for the discomfort," Danny radioed up to Sheri, who was serving as incident commander. "I can't find any other injuries, though he's a little dehydrated from being out here all night. We'll give him some water, and the paramedics can take charge once he's up top."

They sent down more lines, and with a volunteer on either side, Nicholas began the slow ascent. Once he slipped and cried out, but the safety gear arrested his fall, as it was designed to do, and the trio started up again.

Mr. and Mrs. Gruber had gradually moved closer and closer to the edge of the drop-off and were waiting to embrace their wayward son as soon as he stood, somewhat shakily, before them. "I'm sorry," Nicholas said. "I didn't mean to scare you."

His mother wiped at the tears streaming down her son's face, then dashed away her own. "You must have been frightened too, falling in the dark and spending the night not knowing where you were," she said.

"I was worried I'd never get to see you again," Nicholas said, and fought back a sob.

Paramedic Merrily Rayford approached. "We need to get you to the hospital to take care of that ankle," she said. "Mom and Dad can follow in their car."

Vince moved in to help with the ropes while Bethany cleared a path to the waiting ambulance. "That was pretty intense," Vince told Eldon as his fellow volunteer stepped out of his harness.

"Good ending, though," Eldon said.

"Bet he won't be so quick to storm out of the house next time," Ryan said.

"Or maybe his folks will pay a little more attention to how he's feeling," Caleb said.

Vince helped load the equipment, then headed for his car and drove back to his condo. He parked and looked up to find a familiar shapely figure standing in the glow of the light over his front door.

Chapter Thirteen

Vince's heart beat faster as he made his way to the front door. Tammy waved and held up the pizza box she was carrying. "Hey," he said as he drew closer.

"I heard about the rescue," she said. "I thought you might be hungry."

The aroma of pepperoni and cheese made his mouth water. "Thanks," he said, and fished out his keys. "Come on in."

He unlocked the door and she followed him inside. "I hope you don't mind me stopping by," she said.

"Of course not. It's always good to see you."

"I didn't know if you had other plans. After all, it's Saturday night."

"No plans," he said. "Just let me put away this gear."

"I'll meet you in the kitchen."

When he reached the kitchen, she was bent over, sliding the pizza into the oven. She glanced over her shoulder at his approach. "I thought I'd warm it up a little."

"Good idea." She was a little more dressed up than usual, in a pink top that showed a hint of cleavage and a bit of lace. She smelled good too. He wanted to nuzzle her neck and inhale deeply.

He slipped past her and turned away so she wouldn't see the

erection this thought had aroused. "How did you hear about the rescue?" he asked as he took plates from the cupboard.

"I have an emergency scanner. It's handy for news stories."

"I'm surprised you weren't there, covering this one."

"Russ lives two houses down, so he volunteered to take it. Didn't you see him there?"

"I wasn't paying attention. I was focused on the rescue."

"Of course. How is the kid who fell?"

"He's going to be fine. And maybe less quick to run away the next time he and his parents don't see eye to eye."

"That's what happened? He ran away?"

"He probably just wanted to take a walk and let off steam, but he got disoriented in the dark and ended up falling into the canyon. The road is pretty narrow, and the soil on the edge was crumbling. It kept collapsing as we were working, trying to set up the rigging to bring him up."

"Sounds like it was a happy ending, though."

"Yeah."

She took the pizza from the oven and carried it to the table. Vince helped himself to a couple of slices. "What happened today made me think about Valerie," he said.

"Oh?"

"This kid was a few hundred yards from his house. When he first fell, he must have shouted for help, but those trees and the dirt and everything absorbs sound. Apparently, no one heard him. And though his parents said they searched for him, they couldn't see him where he was and couldn't hear him. I wonder if something like that happened with Valerie."

"I guess it could have happened that way," she said. "Though you would think, with so many people searching for her, they would have found something."

"Not if she ended up in a deep crevice or a long way from where she fell."

"That's terrible to think about."

It was, but he had tortured himself for years with speculation about his sister's fate. No need to pull Tammy into that. "Did you ever get into fights with your parents and leave the house to cool off when you were a teen?" he asked, thinking about his conversation with his fellow volunteers.

She plucked a piece of pepperoni from the pizza and popped it into her mouth. "I wanted to a few times," she said. "But I never did. My parents had lost one kid. They were terrified of losing another. It made them overprotective, and I chafed against that. But at the same time, I didn't want to hurt them. At least, not any more than they had already been hurt."

"Yeah. It was like that for me too," he said.

She set aside a pizza crust. "I can hardly remember anymore what Mom and Dad were like before my brother died," she said. "Their pain was part of them, like my mom's curly hair or my dad's cleft chin."

"Yeah. I guess you never get over something like that."

"Were your parents overprotective too?"

"Not exactly." It made sense that having lost one child, a parent would hold even more tightly to the offspring left behind. But it hadn't been like that in his house. How to explain it to her without making his parents sound like terrible people? "Losing Valerie was such a blow they kind of, I don't know, checked out for a while," he said. "They couldn't cope. I knew they loved me—and they tried, they really did. But it was like they were in so much pain they didn't have more of themselves to give. I was kind of on my own."

"Oh, Vince."

He winced at the sympathy in her voice. "It was okay. Most of the time, anyway. Birthdays were hard."

"Because it was her birthday too."

"Yeah. When we took that camping trip, my dad tried to

make up for me missing my friend's party by saying that when it was my birthday, I could have a sleepover. Not a joint party with Valerie, the way it usually was, but a celebration just for me and my friends. But that never happened."

"Did they not celebrate your birthday at all?" Tammy asked.

"There were always presents and a cake. But there was too much sadness. It was like a weight, pressing us down." He shrugged. "I don't celebrate my birthday anymore. I can't." That day could never be only about him anymore.

"I'm sorry," she said. "But I get it. I always felt like I didn't just lose my brother when Adam died. Our whole family lost itself. We couldn't be the same family we were before, and we never figured out how to completely put ourselves back together."

"You can't," he said. "That one piece is always missing."

They ate in silence for a while, but it wasn't uncomfortable. Tammy was the only person he had ever known who truly understood what growing up had been like for him. And he knew what things had been like for her too. He felt closer to her right now than he had to anyone.

"You look nice tonight," he said.

She smiled, and her cheeks blushed a little pinker. "Thanks." She glanced down at the pink shirt. "I had lunch Thursday with my brother's new girlfriend, Elisabeth. She's always perfectly put together. I guess she inspired me to make a little more effort with my appearance."

"You always look good," he said.

Their eyes met, and in that moment he felt so…whole. As if he didn't need anything else but to be here, right now, with this woman.

They finished eating and carried their dishes in the sink. She started to turn on the water, but he put his hand on her arm. "Don't worry about those now," he said. "Let's go into the living room and talk."

They sat side by side on the sofa, but instead of saying anything, she leaned over and kissed him. Her lips were soft, their gentle pressure making him aware of every sensation firing in his body at her touch. She pressed her palm to his chest, over his heart, every hard beat reverberating through them both.

He pulled her close, clinging to her like a drowning man, a wave of longing almost pulling him under. He kissed her hard, then drew back a little to look at her. She stared back. Was he reading her true feelings in that look or his own emotional turmoil reflected back at him? "I really, really like you," he said.

She looked amused, and slid her hand down his chest to the waistband of his jeans. "I really like you too."

Words failed him as she traced the top of his waistband with one finger. "I want you, Vince," she said.

"Yes." He smothered any reply she might have made with another kiss, and followed eagerly as she lay back and pulled him down with her. He slid one hand beneath her shirt, gliding over the satiny skin of her stomach and up to cup one full breast. He fought the urge to tear at her clothing, wanting to see and feel all of her at once. Only now did he realize how much he had been holding back. "That first day we met, I was attracted to you," he said, nuzzling her neck. "Your perfume drove me wild."

"I don't wear perfume," she said.

"Maybe it's something else, but you smell amazing." He inhaled deeply and smiled. Vanilla, floral and definitely sexy. "Maybe it's just you."

"Mmm." She wrapped both legs around him, pulling him even closer, and for a long while, conversation ceased as they lost themselves in playful discovery.

Finally, flushed and a little out of breath, she pushed against him. "Why don't we go into the bedroom?" she suggested.

He levered up on his elbows. He must have been crushing her. "Good idea," he said.

"Oh, I'm full of good ideas." The knowing smile that accompanied the words sent a fresh jolt of heat through him. Wanting something this much was exhilarating. And a little terrifying. *You've done this before*, he reminded himself as he took her hand and pulled her toward his bedroom.

That was true, but he wasn't sure getting it right had ever mattered so much.

TAMMY WASN'T A WEEPER. Sappy commercials and sad novels didn't make her tear up the way they did many of her friends. But lying here in Vince's bed had her blinking against a stinging in her eyes. Vince cared so much. He cared about her and how she felt. "Is that good?" he asked as he moved down her naked body. "Do you like that?"

"Everywhere you touch me feels good," she said. "Just keep doing what you're doing. I'll let you know if there's anything I don't like."

But there wasn't anything about him she didn't like—from the sculpted muscles of his arms and shoulders to the strong curve of his thighs, to the smile that pulled at his lips as he traced the lines of her body with his mouth, proof that he liked what he was discovering.

He had taken out a condom without her having to ask, and when they came together, he was gentle, holding back. She stroked his shoulders. "It's okay," she said. "You can't hurt me."

"I don't want to be too rough," he said, his voice ragged.

"You won't be."

He was less careful then, and she was soon caught up in

the intensity. There was something erotic about seeing him like this, on the edge of control, and knowing she had brought him to this point. She had never been this aware of her partner's desire in the midst of her own, and that knowledge acted like a multiplier, heightening every sensation. They found a rhythm, hard and deep, and she gave herself up to it, riding the waves of sensation, not even minding as tears slipped out of the corners of her eyes as she reached her climax.

He trembled in her arms, and she held him tightly as he found his own release. They lay together for a long moment, not speaking, his weight heavy but still feeling good.

Finally, he levered off her. "I must be crushing you," he said, and moved to lie beside her.

"No, it was wonderful." She idly stroked his hair. "You're wonderful."

He didn't say *You're wonderful too*, or any clichéd response. Instead, he rested his head in the hollow of her shoulder and his hand across her stomach, cradling her as if she was so precious he couldn't find the words.

"I WISH WE could stay here like this all day," Vince said the next morning after he and Tammy had made love again. They lay in a tangle of sheets, sunlight pouring through the thin sheers over the bedroom window.

"We'd have to send out for food," she said. "And coffee."

He sat up. "I'll make coffee," he said. "And breakfast. But then I have to leave. I promised my dad I'd play golf with him today, and he likes to get an early tee time."

"My mom is making Sunday dinner for my brother and his girlfriend," Tammy said. "I need to be there too."

Vince pulled on his jeans, then looked over his shoulder at her. "I'd rather be with you."

That look—a little possessive, a lot lustful—sent a tremor

through her. "I'd rather be with you too," she said. "But family is important."

"Of course it is." He opened a dresser drawer and pulled out a shirt. She began dressing also. Even if he had never put it into words, she figured he felt the same obligation she did. It wasn't enough that they be their parents' children. They had to try to make up for their missing sibling, impossible as that might be.

They parted at his front door with a passionate kiss. "See you later?" he asked.

"For sure."

She had texted her mother the night before to let her know she was spending the night "with a friend" and expected a full interrogation, and maybe a lecture, when she walked in. Instead, the only thing her mother said was, "I need you to set the table while I finish the rolls. Use the wedding china."

Tammy set down her bag and followed her mother into the kitchen. "This is just a casual dinner," she said. "You don't need to use the wedding china." The service for twelve had been a wedding gift from Tammy's great-grandmother, and was only used on holidays and special occasions. The rest of the time, it was displayed in a large buffet on one side of the dining room, dutifully removed and hand-washed each quarter to prevent a buildup of dust.

"This is the first time Mitchell has brought anyone home for dinner." Her mother began shaping dough into rolls and arranging them in a buttered pan. "I want everything to be special."

"You don't have to worry about impressing her, Mom," Tammy said. "She should be worried about impressing you."

"Just looking at Elisabeth, you can tell she comes from money." Mom plopped another roll in the pan. "She's used to fancy things."

"Did Mitch tell you that—that she comes from money?"

She paused in the act of shaping another roll. "No, but it's obvious. Those clothes she wears didn't come from the discount store, and I'm sure her haircut cost at least a hundred dollars."

"If Elisabeth likes Mitch, it's not because he has money," Tammy said, trying to quell her annoyance. "It shouldn't matter what kind of plates we serve dinner on."

"Still, I want to make a good impression."

Tammy went to the buffet and began removing four plates. "If I'd known this was going to be such a big deal, I would have invited a friend," she called back to her mother.

"You can invite your friend some other time," her mother said. "Today, I think the focus should be on Mitch and Elisabeth."

The excitement in her mother's voice set off alarm bells. Tammy returned to the kitchen. "What's going on?" she asked. "Is something happening I should know about?"

Her mother smiled—something she did so seldom the transformation of her features shocked Tammy. "I don't know for sure, but Mitch hinted around that he's serious about this young woman. I think he might propose soon. She could be part of our family before long, and I want her to feel welcomed."

"He's only known her a couple of weeks," Tammy said. "She hasn't even said if she's going to stay in town."

"If they marry, of course she'll stay in Eagle Mountain," her mother said.

Tammy returned to the dining room and tried to process this turn of events as she set the table. Her mother could be wrong. She might be reading more into the relationship than was there.

Then again, Elisabeth's eagerness to have lunch with

Tammy last week could have been a way of reaching out to someone she saw as a future sister-in-law. A shudder went through her at the thought; then she immediately felt terrible. If her brother loved Elisabeth, Tammy would learn to love her too.

By the time Mitch and Elisabeth arrived, the table was set with the wedding china and fresh flowers, and the aromas of the Sunday roast and fresh-baked rolls perfumed the air. Elisabeth wore a sleeveless summer sheath in cherry-pink linen, with matching high-heeled sandals. Tammy, dressed in jeans and a T-shirt advertising a defunct local band, reminded herself she had nothing to be defensive about. "It's good to see you," she said.

"Everything looks lovely, Mrs. Patterson," Elisabeth said.

"Not as lovely as you, dear," Mrs. Patterson said. She had changed into slacks and a gauzy top Tammy had never seen before.

"Elisabeth always looks great," Mitch said, and pulled her closer. She smiled up at him, a pleased-with-herself look. Though maybe that was Tammy projecting. She was beginning to realize this wasn't going to be their usual laid-back Sunday meal.

For the next hour, Tammy's mother and brother remained focused on Elisabeth, showering her with compliments and asking her about herself. But while she revealed the same details Tammy already knew—she was from Nebraska and her family had all died—that was all they got. "What kind of work do you do?" Mrs. Patterson asked.

"Oh, I've done a lot of different things," Elisabeth said. "I helped my father manage his investments."

"Do you mean, trading stocks and bonds?" Tammy asked. "Or real estate?"

"Something like that." Elisabeth turned to Mitch. "Mitch

had an exciting week. He thinks he's found a buyer for a big ranch near Delta."

Mitch looked pleased. "The deal isn't final yet," he said. "But it's looking promising."

"It would be the largest commission you're earned yet, wouldn't it?" Elisabeth said.

"Yes, it would."

"I could steer you toward some sound investments, if you're interested," Elisabeth said.

Was she legit, or was this some kind of scam? Tammy wondered, then immediately hated herself for thinking it. Her brother was smart enough to see through a scam, even through the rosy lenses of infatuation. And Elisabeth was allowed to be beautiful, charming and good with money.

"What about you, Tammy?" Elisabeth asked. "Did you report on anything particularly interesting this week?"

"The county commissioners agreed to buy a new grader for the road crew," Tammy said. "And the Elks Club has sold almost all of the tickets for the Fourth of July Jeep raffle."

Even Elisabeth's laugh sounded delicate and feminine. "You have to love what passes for news in a small town, don't you?"

"It's reassuring to know there's very little serious crime around here," Mitch said.

"I suppose so," Elisabeth demurred. "Though personally, I never minded a little more excitement."

"Then we'll have to make our own excitement," Mitch said.

Elisabeth smiled at him. "That's an excellent idea."

When the meal ended, Tammy offered to do the dishes. Better to work off her bad attitude scraping plates than risk taking her annoyance out on her brother's girlfriend.

She was loading the dishwasher when Elisabeth came into the kitchen, a stack of dessert plates in hand. "These were overlooked on the side board," she said, and set them in the sink.

"Thanks," Tammy said.

"Let me help," Elisabeth said.

"No. Go back in with Mitch and Mom. I wouldn't want you to risk getting that beautiful dress dirty."

But Elisabeth made no move to leave. "How's it going with your friend—Vince?" she asked.

Tammy cursed her inability to hold back a blush. "It's going well."

"Did you do what I suggested? Turn up the heat a little?"

Tammy nodded.

"Didn't I tell you?" Elisabeth grinned, and Tammy couldn't help but grin back.

"What are you two plotting in here?" Mitch came in. He stood between them, one arm around each of them. "It's good to see my two favorite women getting along."

"Don't let Mom hear that," Tammy said. "She might feel snubbed."

"My two favorite young women, then." He released his hold on Tammy but took Elisabeth's hand. "Did Elisabeth tell you she's decided to stay in Eagle Mountain?"

"No. That's good news?"

"Of course it's good news," Mitch said. He turned to Elisabeth. "You were asking about my childhood. Mom pulled out her photo albums. You're going to get a laugh out of some of these shots."

They left, still holding hands, and Tammy returned her attention to the dishes. Whatever it was about Elisabeth that set her teeth on edge, she needed to let it go. She was a pleasant woman who had gone out of her way just now to be friendly. Tammy would return the favor. She wanted Mitch to be happy, and if Elisabeth was the one who made him happy, Tammy needed to find a way to tolerate her, even if she doubted she could truly love her.

Chapter Fourteen

Once every couple of months, Vince's dad invited Vince to play golf. He didn't have his father's love for the game, but he enjoyed the time they spent, just the two of them, walking the course and talking. Most of the conversations were superficial, but he still relished these moments with the man he admired most in the world.

"When do you think you'll get your truck back?" Dad asked after they had teed off that Sunday afternoon.

"I don't know. The sheriff's department hasn't completed its investigation." He hooked the shot, and the ball went sailing into the rough. "Do you and Mom need your car back? I could borrow one from a friend."

"No, you keep it as long as you like." They trudged toward Vince's wayward ball. "I was just wondering. Do they have any idea who did it?"

Vince lined up his shot and took it, hitting the ball back onto the fairway. "No. The sheriff asked if I thought it could be Valerie."

He expected his dad to be shocked or to protest that that wasn't possible. Instead, he looked thoughtful. "I've often wondered if she is still alive somewhere."

"Why do you think that?"

"Take your shot, son."

Vince's heart wasn't in the next strokes, but he managed to keep the ball on the fairway and eventually in the hole.

His dad led the way to the next tee box. "Why do you think Valerie is still alive?" Vince asked again. Had his dad been keeping something secret from him all this time?

"I suppose because we never found her," he said. "And because she's my daughter. It's a fanciful idea, I guess, but if she's dead, wouldn't I feel it? I know your mother feels the same way."

What did Vince feel? Valerie was his twin, yet he had long ago accepted she was dead. But what if she wasn't?

He waited until his dad had taken his shot before he spoke again. "If Valerie is alive, why not contact us?" he asked. "Why write cryptic notes or mess up my truck?"

"Maybe she's under someone else's control and this is her only way to communicate." He swung and connected with the ball, sending it straight up the fairway. He was so calm that Vince realized he must have spent a lot of time thinking about this possibility.

"Dad, she'd be twenty-five years old now. How could she be under someone else's control?"

"Someone could be threatening her, forcing her to do these things."

"But why? No one has asked for money. No one has tried to physically harm us. It's just…annoying." He took his stroke and sliced the ball to the right.

"And a little frightening." Dad put his hand on Vince's shoulder, a rare moment of physical closeness from his normally undemonstrative father.

"Yeah, it is frightening," Vince admitted. "I keep wondering what's going to happen next."

"If they want something, you'll find out," his dad said.

"Scammers are experts at the long game, reeling people in slowly."

"Is that what happened with you and that guy who claimed to be ex–special forces? The one you and Mom paid all that money to?" That had been a particularly elaborate scam, and a costly one. The man claimed Valerie was being held prisoner in a Mexican brothel, and that, with funds for their expenses, he and some other former military friends could rescue her.

His dad looked rueful. "I thought I was smart enough to see through all the liars by that time. Valerie had been missing five years, and I thought I had heard it all. But this man was a pro. He presented just the right image. I resisted him for a long time, but then he sent pictures—photographs of a young woman he claimed was Valerie. We could only see her from the back—that should have been my first clue this wasn't legit. But she had the same hair, and we could see the resemblance. He said if we paid for him and a team to fly down there, they promised to get her back. We wanted so much to believe, and he counted on that."

Vince's chest hurt, listening to this sad tale, even though he had known the basic outline for a long time. "I think anyone would have done the same in your shoes," he said.

They played through the next hole, the heaviness of their memories wrapped around them. After Vince's next shot, his dad said, "I never told your mother this, but I thought I saw Valerie once."

Vince's breath caught, and he stared. "Where? When?"

"Seven years ago. I had a work meeting outside of Omaha, Nebraska. A group of us visited a casino on the Missouri river one evening. There was this cocktail waitress—pretty, young, very friendly. I noticed her, but I wasn't paying any particular attention to her. Then one of the guys nudged me and told me she obviously liked me because she kept staring at me. I looked over, and she caught my eye and smiled. And—I recognized her. It was Valerie."

"In a casino in Omaha? Dad, why did you think it was Valerie?"

"Her eyes, and the way she looked at me. I hurried toward her, but she darted away. I spent the rest of the night searching for her. I even went back the following day and asked the manager about her. He said they didn't have any employees that fit the description I gave them. But I know what I saw."

"What did you do?" Vince asked.

"I took an extra day after the conference. I went back to the casino, then spent hours driving around the area. I guess I thought I might spot her again, but if she didn't want to be seen, there were a million places she could hide. I finally convinced myself that I must have been mistaken. I went back home and tried to forget about her. But I've always wondered."

"If Valerie is alive, I have to think she would want to see us," Vince said. "We're her family."

"I like to think that too, son. But we don't know what she's been through in the time she's been apart from us."

She isn't alive, he wanted to say but didn't. If it made his father feel better to believe his daughter wasn't dead, Vince wasn't going to dissuade him. But that kind of hope felt to Vince like a chain holding them all back. Valerie was dead. Until they accepted that, they could never move on.

MONDAY, TAMMY TRIED to focus on work, but her mind continually drifted to thoughts of Vince, replaying the two amazing evenings they had spent together. She thought she had been head over heels for a man before. The giddy sensation of wanting to be with someone every minute wasn't new. But things with Vince were different. More intense, yet less stressful. They connected in a way she hadn't known was possible, and didn't feel any pressure to hide the "weird" side of herself from him. She hadn't realized how much she was holding back in other relationships until she got close to Vince.

"What are you grinning about?" Russ asked as he passed her desk that afternoon.

She immediately assumed a sober expression. "Nothing," she said.

"What are you working on?" he asked.

She glanced at her computer screen, the cursor blinking on the beginning of an unwritten paragraph—the same position it had been in for the last half hour. She started to repeat *Nothing* but thought better of it. "I'm writing that piece about the women's club rummage sale," she said. "And I'm finishing up my next piece about search and rescue."

"Don't forget the planning commission meeting at six."

She groaned. "Nothing ever happens at those meetings."

"Then why are they having a meeting?" he asked.

"So they can table making a decision on land-use codes—the same thing they've done the last three meetings."

"They can't table a decision forever," Russ said. "And when they reach a conclusion, our readers will want to know what it is."

She sighed. Russ was right, of course. And she did have the meeting on her calendar. It was just that she would 100 percent have preferred to spend the evening with Vince.

But the meeting did give her an excuse to text him. Though they hadn't made definite plans for tonight, she sensed that spending every night together was becoming a habit neither was in a hurry to break.

Can't get together tonight, she typed. I've got to cover the planning commission meeting.

She pressed Send and waited, not exactly holding her breath but unable to look away from the screen.

The phone vibrated, and a small thrill raced through her as she read his reply. Too bad. Guess I'll have to sit at home alone and think about my plans for next time we get together.

She started to type a reply asking for more specifics about what he had in mind but became aware of Russ watching her. "You're grinning again," he said.

She frowned and turned the phone so the screen was definitely out of Russ's line of sight. Looking forward to seeing you again, she typed. TTYL.

The meeting that evening proved as boring as she had anticipated, though the commission did spring for pizza from Mo's to feed themselves, Tammy and the two locals who showed up. At least she didn't have to listen to them debate the exact definition of *agricultural use* on an empty stomach.

By nine o'clock everyone in the room seemed to have had enough. The committee had agreed on some definitions and tabled other decisions until the following month. Tammy gathered her belongings and drove home. She debated dropping by to see Vince but decided instead to call him when she got in.

Her mind played out possible avenues for such a conversation as she climbed out of her car and headed up the walkway to her house.

Then something—or rather, someone—hit her with such force she was knocked off her feet. She didn't even have time to scream before her attacker landed on top of her and began pummeling her.

Chapter Fifteen

For a moment Tammy couldn't fight back or even breathe. She forced her eyes open, trying to see who was hitting her, but could make out only the shadowy outline of a figure dressed in dark clothing. Her attacker grabbed her hair and forced her head back, then rammed it into the dirt.

Pain rocketed through her and freed her from her momentary paralysis. She shoved against her assailant, then brought her knee up, hard, between the other person's legs. The reaction wasn't the one she had expected. Her attacker grunted, then laughed.

Whoever this was, Tammy realized they weren't much bigger than her. Another shove pushed them off her. She kicked out again, this time connecting with the other person's shin. She grabbed for any hold she could find and wrapped her hand around an ear and pulled hard.

This time her attacker screamed—a high-pitched wail of rage. They staggered up and began kicking at Tammy, who rolled away, then shoved to her knees.

By the time she got to her feet, whoever had assaulted her was running away, feet pounding hard on the pavement. Tammy stood, staggering a little as a wave of dizziness rocked her. The front door creaked open. "Tammy? Is that you?" her mother's voice asked.

The words forced her into action. She hurried to the door and gently urged her mother back inside. "Let's go in, Mom." She followed her mom into the front hall and locked the door behind them.

Mrs. Patterson stared at her daughter. "You're bleeding!" she said. "What happened?"

Tammy turned to the mirror by the door. Blood trickled from her swollen lip, and her hair was sticky with clotting blood. One eye was starting to swell, and her shirt was torn. "Someone attacked me right in our driveway," she said.

"We need to call the sheriff." Her mother looked around, as if searching for a phone.

"Yes. You'd better do that."

While her mother dialed 911 and talked to the operator, Tammy went to one of the front windows and peered out. Hers was the only vehicle visible near the house, and she could see no sign of her attacker, though the darkness past the circle of light from the porch was so intense she could scarcely make out anything.

"They're sending a deputy right away." Her mother came to stand beside her. "Let me clean up that cut," she said.

"No, thanks. I'll be okay until after the deputy gets here. They may want to take pictures or something." Was that only in cases of rape? Had that been the attacker's intent? This felt like violence for the sake of violence. Someone wanted to hurt her.

Deputy Declan Owen knocked on the door approximately ten minutes later. The handsome dark-haired deputy was relatively new to the Rayford County Sheriff's Department, but he had impressed Tammy as smart and professional. He studied her battered face for a moment when she opened the door, then said, "Why don't we sit down somewhere, and you can tell me what happened."

She led him to the living room, where they sat on either end of the sofa. Her mother took the armchair nearest Tammy and perched on the edge of the seat, hands knotted together. "I drove home from the planning-commission meeting, parked my car and started up the walkway," Tammy said. "Then someone attacked me. I hit the ground hard, my attacker on top of me, pummeling me. We wrestled for a few minutes, then I managed to fight them off and they ran away."

"Did you see your attacker?" Declan asked. "Can you describe them?"

She shook her head. "It was dark, and I think they were wearing dark clothing. I think they even had something covering their face, like a balaclava."

"How big a person? Did they say anything? Could you tell if it was a man or a woman?"

"Not much bigger than me," she said. "I think that's why I was able to shove them off. And I think... I don't think it was a man. They felt—softer. Like a woman. And...and I kicked them hard between the legs, and while they didn't like it, it didn't exactly disable them."

Declan made more notes on the pad in his hand. "Did they say anything?"

"Not a word."

"Do you have any idea who this was?"

"No. I don't know why anyone would attack me. Especially another woman."

"Anyone who might be upset by an article you've written lately?"

"No. I haven't written anything controversial lately. And when people get upset by an article, they write angry letters to the editor. Or they tell me to my face what I did wrong. This person just started hitting me without saying anything."

"Could it be a jealous girlfriend or wife who thinks you're involved with their husband or boyfriend?"

"No. I haven't been dating anyone." She blushed. "Well, I'm sort of seeing Vince Shepherd. But he doesn't have a girlfriend, or a wife." Not that she knew of, anyway.

Declan turned to Tammy's mom. "Did you see anything unusual this evening before Tammy came home?" he asked. "A strange car in the neighborhood, maybe someone who stopped by the house, looking for her?"

"No. I didn't know anything was going on until I heard a scream. I went to the door to see if Tammy had fallen in the dark or something."

"Did you get a glimpse of her attacker?" Declan asked.

"I'm sorry, no." Her mother frowned at Tammy. "I didn't know you were dating anyone."

"Vince and I are taking things slow," she said. She turned to Declan. "Have there been any other attacks like this?"

"No," Declan said. "Is there anything else you can tell us about the person who attacked you? Did they have long or short hair, or anything that stood out to you?"

"I think they had their hair covered, perhaps by the balaclava. I didn't feel any hair. Whoever it was, they were strong—and angry." She touched her swollen lip. "I need to clean up and get some ice on my face."

Declan stood. "I'll talk to your neighbors and see if any of them noticed anyone hanging around who shouldn't be in the area. Let us know if you think of anything else."

Tammy walked with him to the door. As soon as he was gone, her mother started fussing. "We should go to the hospital," she said. "You might need stitches."

"I'll be okay, Mom. I'm going to take a shower, then go to bed." The fight had left her exhausted, and in no mood to talk to anyone. Not even Vince.

"I'm going to call Mitch and ask him to come over."

"Mom, no. He's probably with Elisabeth."

"I don't care. I'll feel a lot safer with him here. She can come with him, if she likes."

Tammy studied her mother's placid expression. "You like her, don't you?"

"I like that she makes your brother happy. That's what I want most for both of you children."

"Do you worry that she's not right for him?"

"The most unlikely couples can make a good match," her mother said. "As long as each partner has an equal stake in making things work. Otherwise, there's going to be trouble ahead."

Tammy retreated to her bathroom. If she let herself, those terrifying moments on the ground with her assailant would replay themselves over and over and in her mind. Instead, she thought about Vince. The two of them seemed equally matched. And they were both equally hesitant to be hurt. Did that bode well for their future or mean they were condemned to never get close enough to last?

THE SEARCH AND rescue training Tuesday evening was mandatory for rookies like Vince, who were preparing for their SARTech II certification test. He took a seat at the end of a table, next to Grace Wilcox. Bethany turned to smile at him. "Hi, Vince," she said.

"Hey." The intensity with which she studied him unnerved him. He didn't want to be unfriendly, but he didn't want to encourage her attention either.

"Don't you have anything better to do on a Tuesday night?" Grace Wilcox asked as Eldon slipped past them to settle on her other side.

"It never hurts to refresh my memory," Eldon said. He

picked up a pencil and slotted it behind one ear. "Plus, May is out of town at an art show, and there's nothing good on TV. I might as well be here."

Danny moved to the front of the room. "Let's get started, everyone. Somebody dim the lights." He hit the button for the first slide. "We're going to start with some definitions."

A loud creak from the door interrupted him. Everyone in the room turned to see Tammy slip inside. "Sorry I'm late," she said, and took a seat at the back of the room. She had her head down, hair falling over one eye. Vince sat up straighter and tried to get a better look. Normally, he expected her to smile and maybe search the room for him, but she wasn't doing that. Was something wrong?

"It's okay," Danny said. "Let's get started with the first section."

They took a break after the first hour, and Vince made his way toward Tammy. He stopped short when she turned to look at him. One eye was swollen shut, and her lips were puffy. "What happened to you?" he asked. At the sound of his voice, everyone who hadn't already been looking their way turned toward them.

Tammy's face reddened. "Somebody jumped me outside my house last night when I got home from the meeting," she said. She put a hand on his arm. "I'm okay. Really."

"Who was it?" Eldon asked.

"I don't know," she said. "It was dark and I didn't see a lot, and they never said anything. I fought them off, and they ran away. Apparently, none of the neighbors saw anyone suspicious in the area." She put a hand to her face. "I know I look terrible."

"You look fine." Vince hesitated, then put an arm around her. "But I hate that you were hurt." He leaned closer and spoke more softly into her ear. "Why didn't you tell me?"

"I didn't want to upset you," she said. "You've got enough on your mind right now."

"Not too much to care about what happens to you," he said.

This made her smile, though she immediately winced, probably because her lip hurt.

"Are you thinking of joining search and rescue?" Bethany asked. She had moved up on Vince's other side and was studying Tammy with that piercing way of hers.

Tammy looked grateful for the change of subject. "No. I told Danny I wanted to write more about the training you guys undergo, and he suggested I attend the class tonight."

"It's an overview of the general knowledge we need to have," Danny said. "Though there's a lot more that goes into wilderness rescues."

"So I'm learning," she said.

"Is that your next article, about training?" Caleb asked.

"No. I'm going to write about the Denise Darling case."

A buzz arose as several people asked about Denise Darling, and others rushed to explain. Danny, being the most senior volunteer present, gained the floor. "She was a thirteen-year-old girl who disappeared during a youth hiking trip seven years ago," he said. "She became separated from her group and got lost. She was found eight days later, almost ten miles from the place she had last been seen."

"Was she alive?" Bethany asked.

"She was alive." Vince hadn't realized he had spoken loudly enough to be heard until everyone turned to him. "I remember the story," he added. "It was all anyone talked about for a while." And he remembered it because of Valerie. When Denise Darling had been found, his mother had burst into sobs. Not because she wasn't glad that a girl had been restored to her family, but because the same thing had never happened to them. Why wasn't Valerie ever found?

"I wonder what became of her," Danny said. "She did an amazing job of taking care of herself—better than most adults under similar circumstances."

"I'm still trying to locate her for an interview," Tammy said. "If I do, I'll let you know."

Danny checked his watch. "We'd better get back to work, or we'll be here all night."

Vince tried to focus on the material, but he kept looking back at Tammy's battered face. Who would hurt her that way?

He hoped the notes he was taking would help him cram for the SARTech test, because he had been too distracted to absorb much information tonight. As soon as Danny turned the lights up, he was out of his chair and headed for Tammy. She smiled at his approach. "Don't look so worried," she said. "I really am all right."

"Where did this happen?" he asked.

"Right in front of my house. I think the person might have been waiting for me. Either that or they followed me home from the planning-commission meeting."

"You're not making me less worried," he said.

She took both his hands in hers and squeezed. "Mitch is staying at the house for a while," she said. "I guess it does feel safer having him there."

"You're welcome to stay with me whenever you like."

"I like that idea." She rose on tiptoe and pressed her lips to his. He wrapped his arms around her and turned it into a proper kiss.

A shrill whistle sounded. "Hey, get a room!" someone shouted, followed by raucous laughter.

They pulled apart. "Why don't I follow you home?" she said, and reached for her car door. She immediately recoiled, and let out a moan.

"What is it?" Vince took her arm. "What's wrong?"

She pointed, and now he saw that something red was smeared across the car door and windshield. He leaned around to examine the windshield and went cold all over when he read the message scrawled in the same red across the glass: *Next time you won't be so lucky. V.*

Chapter Sixteen

"It's not blood." Paramedic Hannah Gwynn cleaned the red goo from Tammy's hand. A crowd had gathered around the Subaru, and someone said the sheriff's department was on the way. Another volunteer had switched on the outdoor spotlights on the side of the building, flooding the gravel parking area with yellow-tinged light.

"I think it's stage blood." Jake Gwynn leaned closer to the car to study the smears of red. "It smells sweet, like corn syrup."

"Why would someone leave you a message like that?" Eldon asked.

"It's because of me," Vince said. His face was pale, the muscles along his jaw tight, as if he was grinding his teeth. He had both hands shoved in the pockets of his jeans and kept sneaking looks at Tammy, though he wouldn't directly meet her gaze.

Her hands clean, she moved to his side and took his arm. "This isn't your fault," she said.

"This was done by the same person who trashed my truck," he said. "It's probably the same person who attacked you last night."

"You can't know that," she said.

"The signature is the same." He pointed to the message on the side window.

She read the threatening words again, freezing when she came to the single *V*, like a check mark near the driver's-side windshield wiper. "I didn't notice the V before," she said.

"The message does seem to be referring to your previous assault," Jake said. "And I'm no expert on graffiti, but this looks similar to the writing on Vince's truck."

"At least they didn't smash my windows." She was trying to make a joke, but the effect was spoiled when her voice broke on the final words.

The crunch of tires on gravel signaled the arrival of a sheriff's department SUV. Sergeant Gage Walker exited the vehicle and strode toward them. Tammy had interviewed Gage many times for cases she had reported. Though similar in appearance to his brother, the sheriff, Gage was more easygoing and less intimidating. He nodded to Tammy, then studied the red-smeared car and the sinister message. Then he turned to the crowd. "I'll talk to the rest of you in a bit. Meanwhile, give us some room, will you?"

The others moved away, herded by Jake. Gage turned back to Tammy. "Tough way to end the night," he said.

"It sure is."

"Any ideas who's behind this and the attack on you last night?" he asked.

"None."

"I think it's the same person who trashed my truck," Vince said. "The same person who sent those notes about Valerie."

"*V*," Gage said. He stepped back and took a few photos of the car, then turned to Tammy. "Why threaten you?" he asked.

She glanced at Vince. Their relationship wasn't exactly a secret, but she also wasn't sure where they stood. "Tammy and I are friends," he said. "Good friends. If this 'V' has been watching me, they've seen us together. Maybe they think hurting Tammy is a way to get back at me."

"I read the report on your assault," Gage said. "You told Declan you thought your assailant was a woman?"

"Yes." Vince frowned at her. Something else she hadn't told him. But again, she hadn't wanted him to worry. If V and her attacker were the same person, did that mean it was Valerie? Or someone pretending to be her?

"Why would V want to get back at you?" Gage asked.

"I'm not sure whoever this is has a reason," she said. "Or at least, not one that would make sense to us."

"In some of the communications, V seems to be assuming the role of Valerie," Vince said.

"Any chance this is your sister?" Gage asked.

"The sheriff asked me that too," Vince said. "I don't know. Valerie disappeared fifteen years ago. Why appear out of nowhere now, and why try to hurt me?"

"When you came here tonight, did you see anyone or anything out of the ordinary?" Gage asked.

"No. And I was looking. After what happened last night, I was spooked."

Gage took her through her steps that evening, from the time she left the newspaper office until she drove to search and rescue headquarters, and verified that she was the last person to arrive at the meeting.

"No one arrived or left after you?" Gage asked.

"No one," she said.

"I didn't see anyone come or go," Vince said.

"All right. We'll process the scene and see if we come up with anything," Gage said. "You'll need to leave your car here. Do you have someplace safe to stay tonight? And what about your mother? Is she home alone?"

"My brother is with her. He's moved in temporarily."

"I'll see that Tammy gets somewhere safe," Vince said. He straightened and took his hands from his pockets. "Do you need anything else?"

"Not right now," Gage said. "I may have more questions later."

"I have a backpack in the car I'd like to grab," she said.

Gage slipped on a glove and opened the back door of the vehicle, and waited while she leaned in and took out the backpack. "Check to verify nothing is missing," he said.

She did so, pawing through the notebooks, extra camera battery, tape recorder and other tools of her trade. "Everything looks okay."

"You're free to go, then."

Vince led her a little ways to the white Ford Escape he was driving these days. "It's my mother's," he said by way of explanation.

Tammy stashed her pack in the back seat, then slid into the passenger seat. Vince drove without speaking, not to her home but to his condo. "I'd feel better if you stayed here tonight," he said. "You can call your mother and brother to let them know you're okay."

"I'd like that." Spending the night alone, even with her brother and mother in other parts of the house, would be too uncomfortable. Even though Vince might be right and the attacks on her might be because V was targeting him, she felt safer with him beside her. If V came around again, it would be two against one.

He carried her pack into the house. Once inside, he pulled her close. "I felt awful when I saw you tonight, hurt." He brushed his lips across her swollen eye, then barely touched her wounded lip. "When I think I could have lost you—" His voice broke.

"You didn't lose me. I'm okay and I'm right here." She

kissed him. It didn't hurt. Instead it felt good, the way his strong arms around her felt good. The kiss ended, and she looked into his eyes, trying to judge what he was feeling. "I'm sorry I didn't tell you about the attack right away. It was just…a lot to process. I wanted time to think."

"You think it was a woman?" he asked.

"I think so. She wasn't much bigger than me, and she didn't feel like a man."

He loosened his hold on her a little. "What do you want to do now?" he asked.

"I can think of a few things." She smiled. "But first, I want to take a shower." Her hand was still slightly sticky from the fake blood, and she wanted to wash away the whole experience.

"Let's take one together," he said.

"Mmm." A pleasant heat washed through her at the thought. "Let me call my mom first so she doesn't worry."

She was surprised when her brother answered the phone. "Mitch, why are you answering Mom's phone?"

"She's in the bathroom and I saw the call was from you. What's up?"

Maybe it was better not to have to explain everything to her mother. "I'm staying with a friend tonight," she said.

"Do you mean, Vince Shepherd?"

"How do you know about Vince?"

"Elisabeth told me you and he had something going on. I'm cool with that, as long as he treats you right."

"I don't need your permission to date someone," she said.

"I'm just saying I think Vince is okay. Don't be so touchy."

"Is Elisabeth there with you?"

"No. She said she had something else to do tonight. To tell you the truth, I think she was uncomfortable with the idea of being here with you and Mom. She thinks the two of you don't like her."

"That's not true," Tammy said. "We hardly know her."

"Yeah, well, it's okay. I'll see her tomorrow."

"And I'll see you tomorrow," she said. "Make sure Mom knows I'm okay."

"Have a good night."

She ended the call and pocketed her phone. "Everything okay?" Vince asked.

"It's fine." She moved closer. She didn't want to talk about her brother or Elisabeth or anything outside the safety of these four walls. She wrapped her arms around him. "What about that shower?"

VINCE LAY AWAKE after Tammy had fallen asleep. He might never think about his shower the same way after tonight. Something about steam and soap and slick skin… It had been just what he needed after the shock of seeing her battered face, then reading the sinister message written in what he was sure was supposed to resemble blood on her car.

His phone vibrated, then the first notes of the ringtone sounded. He lunged for it, silencing it before it could wake Tammy. Then he sat on the side of the bed and checked the screen as the phone continued to vibrate in his hand. Unknown number. Which usually meant spam, but he'd better check in case it was a search and rescue call from one of the team members.

He spoke softly. "Hello?"

"Vin, Vin, Vinnie, Vince."

The singsong chant sent a cold shock through him. "Who is this?" he snapped.

"'Vince and Tammy sitting in a tree, *k-i-s-s-i-n-g*.'"

"Who is this?"

"You know who this is. Or have you forgotten your sister so soon? The twin Mommy and Daddy gave away. You thought you would all be happier without me. But I can't let that happen, can I?"

"Valerie?" He choked on the name as fear and disgust—that someone would stoop to impersonating his sister—warred with hope that she was alive. "Is that you? Where are you?"

"Closer than you think. But I'll never tell."

"Valerie, I—" The phone went dead. He stared at the screen, then hit the recall button. Nothing happened.

"What is it?"

He glanced back to find that Tammy had rolled onto her back and was looking at him. "Crank call," he said, and set the phone aside.

"You said, 'Valerie.'" She sat up now and put a hand on his arm. "Tell me."

He told her about the call. The whole experience had been surreal, but talking about it solidified the details in his mind. He hadn't dreamed it. "Did it sound like Valerie?" she asked.

"I don't remember what she sounds like. It was so long ago. But she used to sing that rhyme, about kissing in a tree."

"I used to sing that rhyme. It's something kids do."

"She started out the call saying 'Vin, Vin, Vinnie, Vincent.' She used to do that too, when she was trying to annoy me."

She leaned against him, soft and warm against his back. "We should call the sheriff."

"What are they going to do? Add this to their growing file of harassment?" He lay back down and pulled her close. "I don't want to deal with them now. Do you?"

"No." She laid her head on his shoulder.

"I had another call from Valerie once," he said. "Or someone claiming to be her. I was fifteen and home with a friend. My parents were out, and when I answered the phone, the person on the other end said she was Valerie and needed me to help her. Then she hung up. It sounded just like her."

"Oh, Vince, what did you do?"

"I told my parents and they called the police. They traced the call to a broken pay phone somewhere in another state. I remember being angry at Valerie for teasing me that way. My parents finally persuaded me that it had to be a cruel joke. This was probably the same thing."

"Whatever it is, it's horrible," she said. "But we'll get through it. Together."

"Yeah." He tightened his arm around her. As if that was all it took to protect them both. "I'm scared," he said. "Then it feels silly to be scared of someone who writes vague notes and makes prank calls."

"It's like being harassed by a ghost," she said. "That's pretty scary."

"I don't believe in ghosts," he said. "Whoever is doing this is a real person."

"I don't know what to tell you, except that I'm here for you."

"As long as you don't get hurt again. You should think about keeping your distance from me, at least for a while." He had to force the words out, but keeping her safe was more important than his own feelings.

"No way." She squeezed him tighter. "I'm sticking with you."

"I'm that irresistible, am I?"

"You are."

"I'm never going to be able to sleep now," he said.

"Me neither. What should we do instead?"

"We could play cards," he said, his voice teasing.

Her arm snaked around his waist. "I have a better idea."

"Tell me about it."

"I'd rather show you. After all, they say actions speak louder than words."

He rolled forward and pressed his body against hers. "Then I'm ready to hear everything you have to say."

ON WEDNESDAY, Gage Walker stopped by the *Eagle Mountain Examiner* office. Tammy's stomach gave a nervous shimmy when she spotted him standing in the doorway in his neat khaki uniform. "Hello, Gage," she said. "Can I help you?"

"I'm dropping off the weekly sheriff's report." He held up a single sheet of paper. The report—a summary of the number and types of calls made by the department during the previous week—was one of the paper's most popular features. People seemed to delight in reading about calls to chase bears out of people's gardens or put cows back into pastures. They speculated on who might be behind the more serious entries, from drunk driving arrests to domestic violence calls. But the report was usually delivered by a civilian clerk or a duty officer, not the force's second-in-command.

Gage approached Tammy's desk and handed over the report. "Any more word from V?" he asked.

"No. She hasn't contacted me." It seemed easier to refer to V as female since that was how she thought of her since the attack.

"What about Vince? Has he heard anything?"

"I don't think so." She had never been a proficient liar, and she was sure Gage would see through the falsehood. She had tried to persuade Vince to tell the sheriff's department about the late-night call from someone pretending to be Valerie, but he had refused, convinced they wouldn't be able to do anything.

"Did you find any fingerprints or DNA on my car?" she asked, hoping to divert Gage's attention.

"No. Not on Vince's truck either." He held up a finger. "But that's not for the paper."

"I know, Gage. I'm not writing about either incident."

"I just want to be clear. Tell Vince to get in touch if he hears anything else from V."

"I will." She stood and walked with him to the door. "I guess I'll see you at the Fourth of July festivities tomorrow?"

"I'm on duty in the morning," he said. "In the afternoon, I'm working the Elks' Fun Fair."

"I'll stop and say hello. Maybe get a picture for the paper."

When she was sure he was gone, she went into the back room, where old issues of the paper were stored, and pulled out her phone. When Vince answered, she said, "Gage was just here. He was asking if I had heard anything from V."

"What did you tell him?"

"I told him no. That wasn't exactly a lie, since she didn't call me. But then he asked if you had heard from her. I lied about that too."

"It doesn't matter. It was just a prank call. We haven't heard from her again."

"You're working the Fun Fair tomorrow, right? So is Gage. He'll probably ask you about V."

"My parents will be with me. I'll tell him I don't want to talk about any of this with them there. He'll respect that."

"Okay. I'll see you later, then."

"I'm making fajitas for dinner."

"Then I won't be late."

Though it wasn't official, she had all but moved into Vince's condo. Her mother hadn't even objected when she stopped by the house to get her clothes. "I feel better knowing you have a man to protect you," she said.

The feminist in Tammy resented the implication she couldn't look after herself, but the realist admitted having a strong, fit man who had made it clear he would do anything to protect her did make her feel safer. What neither of them admitted out loud was that they wouldn't be able to truly relax until V was identified and stopped. That didn't seem likely to happen anytime soon, so better for the two of them to stick together.

Chapter Seventeen

The next day, Tammy and Vince headed to the town park together. "How are you feeling?" he asked when they met, He
studied her face. "The swelling is almost all gone and the
bruises aren't as noticeable."

She resisted the urge to touch the worst of the bruises,
which she had attempted to cover with makeup. "I'm fine.
Really."

"Glad to hear it." He kept his arm around her on the walk
to the park, but once there, they parted ways. Tammy was
taking photographs of the parade while Vince helped set up
the search and rescue booth. Later, she would take pictures
of the Fun Fair while he fulfilled his duties at the SAR booth
and the first responders' part in the festivities. He was also
meeting his parents to spend time with them. The plan was
for her to join them as soon as she was free. Later that evening, they would enjoy the fireworks.

The Eagle Mountain Fourth of July Parade was everything
a small-town parade should be, from the high school marching band to dignitaries waving from fire trucks to clusters of
kids pedaling red, white and blue-bedecked bicycles. Members
of the historical society, dressed in turn-of-the-last-century
garb, threw candy from a float decorated with papier-mâché
rocks and old mining implements, while a trio of miniature

horses and one full-size camel from a local hobby ranch enchanted onlookers.

The mayor's six-year-old son brought up the rear of the parade, riding a donkey with a placard attached to its backside that read *Follow My Ass to the First Responders Fun Fair*.

After a detour to photograph the historical society members handing out lemonade and brownies in front of the town museum, Tammy headed for the park, where the Fun Fair was in full swing. At the search and rescue booth, which was festooned with colorful T-shirts for sale and photographs from past rescues, she learned that Vince had just completed his shift. She took a photo to possibly run with her article, then hurried across the park, where she found Gage Walker supervising a pillow fight between two boys who straddled a sawhorse and flailed at each other until one slid to the sawdust below.

"Have you seen Vince?" she asked Gage after he had helped the children to their feet and sent them on their way.

"I think he's over at the dunking booth." Gage grinned. "He's probably pretty wet by now."

She had to stop and ask two people for directions to the dunking booth, but she arrived in time to see Vince, in swim trunks and nothing else, climb onto the narrow perch over a tank of water. "Just remember, that water's really cold," Deputy Shane Ellis teased Vince, egging on the crowd. "Five dollars for three throws," he said, holding up a baseball. "All the money goes to local first responders. Who wants to throw out the first pitch?"

"Why don't you show us how it's done, Shane?" someone called from the crowd.

"That wouldn't be fair, would it?" Shane demurred. He was a former big-league pitcher. Though an injury had ended his career, he was still feared on the local softball field.

"I'll go first." Ryan Welch stepped forward and handed over a five-dollar bill. His first pitch went wild, banging hard against the wood to the left of the target.

"A little more finesse there," Shane advised.

The second throw came closer but still failed to hit the bull's-eye.

"Come on," Vince taunted. "I'm getting hot up here."

Ryan clenched his jaw and palmed the ball, then hurled it, striking the bull's-eye dead center and sending Vince plunging into the tank.

He came up sputtering and laughing as the crowd cheered. Tammy snapped a series of photos; then he returned to his perch and Shane called for someone else to take a turn.

"Hey, Tammy."

She turned to see Mitch and Elisabeth working their way to her through the crowd. "So, that's Vince!" Elisabeth waggled her eyebrows at Tammy.

Mitch looked toward the dunk tank. "Looks like he's all wet," he said.

"Even better, huh?" She nudged Tammy.

"Anyone else want to take a try?" Shane called.

"I'll do it." Mitch raised his hand and pushed forward.

Elisabeth moved in closer to Tammy. "I didn't know Mitch was an athlete," she said.

"He's not." Tammy winced as her brother's first ball sailed past the dunk tank altogether. A trio of children chased after it.

"Steady there, Rocket," Shane said, and handed him another ball. "Go a little easier."

Mitch nodded and launched the second ball, which bounced harmlessly off the side of the tank.

Elisabeth cupped her hands around her mouth. "Go, Mitch!" she shouted.

Mitch waved back at her, then turned and fired the third

ball toward the target. It glanced off the edge, but without enough force to trip the trigger. The crowd groaned.

"Let me have a try!" Elisabeth called, and waved her hand.

Applause greeted her arrival. To the delight of the crowd, she dusted off the ball with her shirt, then leaned forward like a pitcher waiting for a sign. Then she straightened and let the ball fly. It landed harmlessly in the grass, just shy of the target.

"Put a little more behind it this time," Shane advised, and handed her a second ball.

This one struck to the left of the target. Vince clapped his hands together. "You can do better than that!" he shouted.

Elisabeth glared at him and accepted the third ball. This time she stared not at the target, but at Vince, until he looked away. She wound up, then let the ball fly. It hit the center of the target, and Vince went down with a shout. The crowd roared its approval.

"Way to go, babe," Mitch said as Elisabeth rejoined him. He hugged her close. She accepted congratulations from those around her.

"That was fun," she said. "What should we do now?"

"I don't know," Mitch said. "Do you want—"

But before he could finish the sentence, Elisabeth was moving away. "I just saw someone I need to talk to," she called over her shoulder, and was gone.

"What was that about?" Tammy asked.

"I don't know." Mitch stared after her. She was weaving through the crowd, already a quarter of the way across the park. "I'd better go after her," he said, and left.

"It's Tammy, isn't it?" An older couple squeezed in beside her. The woman smiled. "I'm Vince's mom. I thought I recognized you from your picture in the paper."

"It's good to meet you." She nodded to Mr. Shepherd.

"Have you been here long?" Mrs. Shepherd asked.

"Long enough to see Vince get dunked twice," Tammy said.

"Us too." Mr. Shepherd smiled, fine lines deepening at the corners of his eyes. "He looks like he's having fun up there."

A loud creak and a cheer from the crowd signaled that Vince had once again been dunked. "Three strikes and you're out," Shane announced. "Give us a few minutes, folks, and we'll have your next victim—I mean, volunteer—up."

He handed Vince a towel as he emerged from the tank. "Let's go see if he's ready for lunch," Mrs. Shepherd said.

The three of them met Vince as he was pulling on a T-shirt. "Give me a second to change into dry pants, and we'll get some food," he said.

"It's good to see you," Mrs. Shepherd said to Tammy. "Are you working on anything interesting right now?"

"I'm doing another piece about the search and rescue team," she said.

"Vince has told us about some of the rescues he's been on," Mrs. Shepherd said. "We're so proud of him for volunteering, though I worry about the dangerous situations he gets into."

"One thing I've learned in researching my articles is that the search and rescue team trains a lot, and they always put safety first. They've never lost a rescuer."

"That's reassuring."

Vince joined them. He put one arm around Tammy. "Can you join us for lunch?" he asked. "Or do you have to work?"

"I might try to get a few shots of the fireworks tonight, but I'm free for the rest of the afternoon."

"Great. Let's hit the food booths. I'm starved."

They followed the scent of barbecue ribs and roasted corn to a parking lot filled with food trucks and refreshment booths. Tammy ordered shrimp tempura from one truck, while Vince and his dad opted for the ribs, and Mrs. Shepherd chose a hot dog. "That looks delicious," she said, nodding to Tammy's tempura. "But I guess I'm a traditionalist."

"We always grilled hot dogs and brats on the Fourth when the kids were little," Mr. Shepherd said.

Someone who wasn't watching closely would have missed the sadness that fleetingly shadowed Vince's mother's face. Though she had acted cheerful all morning, now that she was closer, Tammy could read the strain in the dark circles beneath her eyes and the slight tremor in her hand as she poked a straw into her drink. When she noticed Tammy watching her, she leaned closer. "You haven't heard anything more from V, have you?" she asked softly.

"No." Vince had told her he had decided not to tell his parents about the attack on her, the message on her car or the late-night phone call. "Hearing all that would just upset and worry them," he had said. She had agreed. As much as she hated the harassment V had aimed at her and Vince, at least she hadn't targeted these two older people, who had suffered so much.

They finished lunch and spent another hour walking around the park, visiting the various vendors and stopping to listen to a woman who played "America the Beautiful" on a hammered dulcimer.

"I'm walked out," Mrs. Shepherd said as they approached the food court again.

"Time for us to head home," Mr. Shepherd said.

"You're not staying for the fireworks?" Tammy asked.

"We can see great fireworks from our backyard in Junction," Mrs. Shepherd said. "Maybe not as spectacular as here in the mountains, but when they're done, we can go right to bed." She laughed. "I can see the idea is appalling to you, but when you get to be our age, it's a plus."

They each hugged Vince goodbye, then surprised Tammy

by embracing her too. "Your parents are such nice people," Tammy said when they were gone.

"They are." He slipped his arm around her shoulders. "But it's good to be alone with you too."

"Was the water in the dunk tank cold?" she asked.

"Icy." He grimaced.

"It was for a good cause." She patted his chest. "And you looked good up there."

"That was your brother who tried to take me down toward the end, wasn't it?"

"Yes, that was Mitch. And the woman who got you afterwards is his girlfriend, Elisabeth."

"Elisabeth who?"

She frowned. "I don't remember." She or Mitch must have said, but the name escaped her. "She's from Nebraska, I think. Though I guess she's decided to stay here."

"Where in Nebraska?"

"I don't remember. Why?"

"She looked familiar."

"You've probably seen her around town. She's the kind of woman men notice."

"Nah. Not my type." He grinned. "I prefer curly-haired blondes."

They spotted Gage and Travis Walker, and Vince waved. The two law enforcement officers joined them. "I saw you at the dunking booth," Gage said. "You got soaked."

"Next year, I'm going to lobby for them to fill the tank with warm water," Vince said.

"It wouldn't be nearly as fun then."

"You can both pick your vehicles up from our impound lot tomorrow," Travis said. "We weren't able to get a great deal of information off of them, unfortunately."

"I'll have to call a wrecker to haul mine away," Vince said.

"I wish you could find who did that and make them pay for the repairs."

"No more love letters from V?" Gage asked.

"None," Vince said. Which wasn't a lie, Tammy reminded herself. Gage hadn't asked about phone calls.

She waited until the lawmen were some distance away before she asked, "Have you had any more phone calls?"

"No. I'm hoping we're done with all that. Whoever it was has moved on to bothering someone else."

She slipped her hand in his and they walked on, their lighter mood from earlier subdued. But they had a whole afternoon to regain that lighter feeling. And fireworks tonight, which never failed to lift her spirits.

"I need to stop here for a minute," she said when she spotted the restrooms. She slipped away to the ladies' room, leaving him waiting outside. When she emerged a few minutes later, Vince was talking to a dark-haired woman—one of the other search and rescue volunteers, Tammy remembered.

At Tammy's approach, the woman looked up, then hurried away. Tammy stared after her. "Who was that?" she asked.

"Bethany Ames. She's with search and rescue."

"Why did she run away when she saw me?"

Vince made a face. "I think she was embarrassed. She asked if I wanted to watch the fireworks with her tonight. I told her I was going with you. She stammered an apology and left."

Amused, she slipped her hand in his. "I didn't realize I had competition."

"No competition. Bethany isn't my type."

"She's cute."

"Yeah, but…she's a little too intense, you know? Something about her puts me off."

"How long have you known her?" Tammy asked.

"Not long. She just moved to town and joined the group."

Was it a coincidence that this woman had moved to town and taken an interest in Vince at the same time someone had started harassing him?

"What is it?" Vince asked.

"Nothing?"

"Are you sure? You look worried."

"It's nothing." No sense worrying Vince. She would do a little digging on her own to see what she could find out about Bethany Ames before she said anything. "Let's go back to the music stage," she urged. "There's supposed to be a bluegrass band there at four. I've heard good things about them."

The band deserved the praise she had heard, and she and Vince were soon tapping their toes and nodding their heads in time to the lively music. She was so engrossed that she didn't realize Vince had received a phone call until he moved away. One look at his expression set her heart racing, and she hurried to his side.

His eyes met hers, stricken. "It's my dad," he told her, then spoke into the phone again. "Are you and Mom okay? All right. I'll be there as soon as I can."

He ended the call, then pulled Tammy away from the crowd that had gathered to listen to the music. "My parents got home, and there were fire trucks lining their street. The fire was at their house."

Chapter Eighteen

"I'm coming with you to your parents'," Tammy said. It wasn't a question.

"You don't have to do that." He dug his keys out from his jeans pocket. Was there anything else he needed to do before he left?

"I want to come," she said.

"What about the fireworks photos?"

"Russ can take them. I want to be with you. And your parents."

He grabbed her hand and squeezed it. "Thanks. That means a lot."

He thought she understood what he was saying. After Valerie had disappeared, Vince had been left alone, his parents distracted by grief. It became a point of pride to get through things alone. Not having to do that anymore was a special gift.

They started walking toward his car. "Dad said the fire is out and most of the damage is to one upstairs bedroom," he said. "The rest of the house is okay except for smoke damage. He and Mom are waiting for the fire department to give them the green light to go inside."

"Do they have any idea what started it?" Tammy asked.

"Dad didn't say. The house is at least as old as I am. Maybe there was a fault in the electrical wiring?"

They didn't say much on the drive to Junction. Vince gripped the steering wheel and forced himself to keep within ten miles of the speed limit, willing the time to pass more quickly. His dad had said there wasn't a lot of damage, but what did that mean? Would his parents be able to remain in the house, or did they need somewhere else to stay? Was the fire an accident or deliberate? And why was all this happening now?

A lone fire truck sat at the curb when they arrived. A firefighter and a Junction police officer met them at the end of the drive, where Vince's parents also waited. "We're confident the fire is out," the firefighter said. "But call if you see any more smoke or flames."

"I don't understand," Mr. Shepherd said. "How did the fire start?"

The police officer introduced himself as Sergeant Fisk. "Where were you today, Mr. Shepherd?" he asked.

"We were in Eagle Mountain, visiting our son and attending the Fourth of July celebration," Dad said.

"Does anyone else live in the house besides you and your wife?"

"No."

"Do you know of anyone who might want to harm you and your wife or your home?"

"No. What are you talking about? Are you saying the fire was deliberately set?"

"The blaze started in the upstairs back bedroom," Fisk said. "Whose bedroom is that?"

"No one's," Dad said.

"That was our daughter, Valerie's, room," Mom said, her voice strained.

"Where is your daughter now?" Sergeant Fisk asked.

Her face crumpled and tears slid down her cheeks. Dad

pulled her close. "Our daughter disappeared fifteen years ago," he said. "We don't know where she is."

Fisk looked back toward the house. From this angle, it appeared undamaged. "Did someone set the fire intentionally?" Vince asked.

"It looks that way," Fisk said. He turned back to Vince. "You're the son?"

"Yes. I'm Vince Shepherd."

The officer turned to Tammy. "And you are?"

"Tammy Patterson. I'm Vince's friend."

"You two were in Eagle Mountain this morning also?"

"Yes," Vince said. "Tammy was taking photographs for the paper, and I worked a fundraising booth for the local search and rescue group. How did the fire start?"

The firefighter spoke. "Someone piled a bunch of papers—pages torn from books, from the looks of things—and set the fire in the middle of the bed. The neighbor whose backyard adjoins this one saw the smoke and called 911." He turned to Mr. and Mrs. Shepherd. "You can return to the house, but don't go into that bedroom. You'll need to have a restoration company see about cleaning it up. There's a lot of smoke damage, and we can't be sure there isn't structural damage from the flames."

Mom moaned, and Dad tightened his arm around her. "Did anyone see somebody near the house this morning?" he asked.

"We spoke with the neighbors," Fisk said. "No one remembers anything unusual. Have any of you noticed anything out of the ordinary recently?"

"No," Dad said. Mom shook her head.

Vince felt Tammy tense beside him, but he said nothing.

They waited until the firefighter and Sergeant Fisk had left before they went into the house. Vince smelled smoke when they entered, but the scent wasn't as strong as he had expected.

He followed his mother and father up the stairs, Tammy behind him. The closer they walked to the bedroom, the more intense the odor of smoke.

They halted outside the bedroom. His dad pushed open the door to reveal the smoke and soot-blackened remains of a little girl's bedroom. Parts of the pink comforter on the bed were still intact, though the center was a black hole. Half a dozen books lay scattered at the foot of the bed, some splayed with spines showing, others with charred pages. Black outlines showed where flames had charred the walls, and everything was sodden.

Mom turned away, sobbing, and fled past them down the hall. Vince started to go after her, but his dad took hold of his arm. "Let her go," he said. "She needs a little time alone." He closed the door, and the three of them returned to the living room.

"Why didn't you tell the police about the notes Vince and I have received, and the messages left on Vince's and my vehicles?" Tammy asked.

"Those things happened in Eagle Mountain," Dad said. "We don't know that they have anything to do with us."

"Except the person who wrote the notes signed them with a V and implied they were Valerie." Tammy's voice was gentle but insistent.

Dad sat heavily on the sofa. "Why would Valerie destroy her own room?" he asked. "And those notes—why would she blame any of us for what happened to her?"

Vince sat in an armchair facing the sofa. Tammy perched on the arm of the chair. "Why didn't you and Mom ever have Valerie declared dead?" he asked. He had never voiced the question before, not wanting to cause his parents more pain. But he wondered if they knew something he didn't.

"We considered it," Dad said. "But we didn't want to give up hope."

"Did anything happen to give you hope?" Tammy asked.

He didn't answer. Vince cleared his throat. "You mentioned seeing a young woman in a casino who looked like Valerie."

Dad sighed, his gaze focused on the rug. "There were two phone calls, years apart. Once, the person—a female—just said, 'Help.' Another time all she said was 'Dad?' and then hung up before I could answer. I'm sure they were just people being cruel, but we always wondered, what if they really were Valerie?"

Vince's stomach rolled, and he feared he might be sick. Rescue work had schooled him to be strong when faced with others' pain, but broken limbs and gashed heads were nothing compared to seeing his father tortured this way.

"You must have tried to find her over the years," Tammy said.

"We did. We hired private detectives twice, but they never came up with anything. They tried to find the camper that was in the mountains the day we were but never found a trace of him either."

"I didn't know that," Vince said. "About the detectives, I mean."

Dad glanced at him. "You had your own life to lead," he said. "We didn't want to burden you with our concerns."

"What will you do now?" Tammy asked.

"We'll get someone in to fix the house." He looked at Vince again. "And before you ask, no, we won't move. Your mother, especially, would never leave this place."

"Because Valerie might come home." Tammy's voice was scarcely above a whisper, but it was loud in the still room.

"Yes. When you have children of your own one day, you'll

understand. We can never give up hope. No matter how much it hurts."

When would the hurting stop? Vince wondered. Sure, the pain of grief and the memory of a smiling little girl who had once been part of their lives would always be part of them. But this new pain, of a wound constantly reopened, when would that end? How could he make it end?

Fifteen years ago.

"WE'RE GOING TO need to give you a new name."

She looked up at the man who stood over her. The man with the friendly smile who had brought her to this place—a place she didn't know. The smile frightened her now, though she didn't know why. He hadn't done anything to hurt her. "Can you think of a name you would like to go by now?" he asked.

"Why do I have to have a new name?" she asked. "Why can't I go home?"

The man—he had told her his name was Paul—squatted down so he could look at her directly. He had dark eyes. They looked all black, like a cartoon character's. They had frightened her at first, but she was getting used to them. "I explained this already," he said. "Your mom and dad didn't want you anymore. They were going to leave you up there in the mountains to die, until I agreed to take you instead."

"Why didn't they want me?" Her heart beat so fast it hurt at the idea. "They said they loved me."

"They were liars." He shrugged. "People are, sometimes. You'll learn that as you get older. They thought they'd be happier with just one kid, and they decided to keep your brother because he's a boy. Some people feel that way. But I don't." He reached out and gently stroked her head. "I always wanted a little girl like you."

She began to cry. He let her. They sat like that for a long

time, him stroking her hair. "It's going to be all right," he said. "You can help me with my work."

She sniffed and tried to control her tears. She didn't like the way crying felt. If she helped him, maybe he would let her talk to her parents. If she talked to them, she could get them to take her back. Whatever she had done to upset them, she could make up for it. She just had to convince Paul to let her see them again. "What kind of work?" she asked.

"People give me money to invest," he said. "You'll be good at persuading them to give me the money. You're a pretty child, and people will like you. Sometimes I'll ask you to talk to people while I take things they don't need anymore. Things we can use. You're smart. I could tell that just by watching you there at the camp."

"I got all As on my last report card," she said.

"I knew you were smart," he said. "I'm good at reading people. I'll teach you how to read them too. The two of us will make a fine team." He stood at last. "We'll be good together. You'll see. After a while you won't even think about your old family anymore."

I'll never forget my family, she thought. And that had turned out to be true. But over the years, she saw them differently. She saw them the way Paul saw them. It was an ugly view, but then, much of life was ugly. Paul had taught her that. She had learned a great deal from him. She had learned that a smart, daring person could get whatever she wanted from people who weren't as smart—money, admiration, sex.

Revenge.

Chapter Nineteen

"Should we tell the sheriff we think the fire at your parents' home might have been started by V?" Tammy asked as she and Vince made the drive back to Eagle Mountain.

"We don't have any proof at all that V started the fire," he said.

"Except that the fire was in Valerie's room, and V has connected herself with Valerie."

"That isn't proof, though, is it? And Junction isn't in Travis's jurisdiction. Not even close. Plus, my dad refuses to say anything to the Junction police about our troubles with V. He doesn't want to believe they're connected."

"Then what are we going to do?"

"I don't think we can do anything but wait for her to make another move. Travis has already admitted whoever this is hasn't left much evidence for them to trace."

Goose bumps rose on Tammy's arms, and she hugged herself, trying to fend off the sudden chill. "It feels like she's getting more dangerous—that attack on me and now this fire."

"The attack on you was terrible," he said. "And the fire was frightening and destructive, but she didn't try to burn down the whole house."

"If that neighbor hadn't seen the smoke and called 911, the whole house might have burned."

"I'm worried she might hurt my parents," Vince said. "But they won't move out of the house, even temporarily."

"They can't believe Valerie would hurt them."

"But someone pretending to be Valerie might. I tried to tell Dad that, but he won't listen."

"My mom never listens to me either," she said. "We're still kids to them, and they're still our parents. The police in Junction are still investigating the arson. Maybe they'll get lucky and find a witness or something else that leads them to V. In the meantime, you and I will have to keep our eyes open."

"It's not like either of us have the skills or the time to investigate this full-time," he said. "And I don't have money to hire a private investigator." He pounded his fist against the steering wheel. "It's so frustrating."

"It is," she agreed. "But we'll get through this. I have an idea we can try. I'll have to talk to Russ and see if he will agree, but I think he will."

"What's that?"

"I'm thinking I could do another story for the paper, about Valerie. V's version of what happened that day is so different from what actually happened, a new story might draw her out again."

"'Draw her out,' how? What if she tries to kill someone? What if she tries to kill you?"

Her stomach knotted with fear. "I'll be careful," she said. "I won't go anywhere alone. And it will be worth it if we can draw her out."

"But how are we going to catch her? What if your article just results in another taunting letter or phone call, or a sneak attack?"

Tammy chewed on her thumbnail, thinking. "We'll have to set a trap," she said. She sat up straight. "I know! We can say there's going to be a memorial to honor Valerie and keep awareness of her alive. In the park. The public is invited. She'll be sure to come. We can alert the sheriff, and they can have a deputy there. We can watch for anyone behaving suspiciously."

"It might work," Vince said. "Do you think the sheriff will agree?"

"We can ask. And the memorial itself will be news enough that I won't have any trouble getting Russ to run a small piece."

"If it's a memorial, we'll need to tell my parents. They'll want to come."

"They can come. But don't tell them it's a trap for V. Just say it's something you wanted to do to honor your sister. Tell them it was my idea, if that helps."

"Are people going to think it's strange we're doing this now, when we haven't done anything for fifteen years?"

"I don't think there's any timeline for these things," she said. "It might even help your parents to have a public ceremony like this. There will be other people who attend who remember Valerie, teachers and others who knew her. They'll know they're not alone in their grief."

"Like the funeral we never had." He nodded. "I think it will be a good thing—and if it helps stop V from harassing us, even better."

"You can talk to your parents tomorrow. I'll check with the sheriff and find out if we need a permit to hold the memorial in the park."

"It feels right to be doing something," Vince said. "Instead of sitting back, waiting for the next bad thing to happen."

VINCE WAS SURE his parents would resist the idea of a memorial for Valerie. He would have to work to persuade them, or even go through with the plan without their blessing. But once again, they surprised him. Instead of bursting into tears, as he had expected, his mother had responded with enthusiasm. "I have some wonderful pictures we can display at the memorial," she said. "And there's a poem I came across, not long after she went missing, that I found meaningful. I don't think I could read it out loud in front of people, but perhaps you could. Or maybe Tammy?"

"That sounds great, Mom. Tammy's arranging things with the city for us to be allowed to hold the memorial in the park."

"I used to think about doing something like this in the mountains, at the place we saw her last," his mom said. "But I suppose the park is more practical. Much easier for people to get to. Thank you for doing this."

"It wasn't my idea. It was Tammy's."

"She's a lovely young woman." His mother fixed him with the look that made him feel like a boy being quizzed on whether or not he had completed his homework. "Are things serious between you two?" she asked.

"We don't want to rush things," he said. Though the truth was, they were as good as living together, with Tammy spending every night at his place and most of her belongings there. He thought soon he would formally ask her to move in fulltime, with a change of address and everything. The idea made his heart race a little, but not in a bad way.

After getting his parents on board, the next step was a meeting with the sheriff. He and Tammy went to Travis's office and laid out their proposal for catching V. "She associates so strongly with Valerie, I don't think she'll be able to stay away from the service," Tammy said. "Eagle Mountain is a small enough community we ought to able to spot someone new or out of place."

"I can't arrest someone for being a stranger," Travis said. "And grief can make people behave in odd ways. That's not a crime either."

"But you can watch them, and if they do cause trouble, you can have a deputy there to put a stop to it," she said.

"All right," Travis agreed. "But you have to promise to let us handle any incidents. You focus on the memorial."

"I promise," Tammy said, and Vince agreed.

Travis sat back in his chair. "I understand there was a fire at your parents' house," he said. "In your sister's old bedroom."

"How did you hear about that?" Vince asked, unable to hide his alarm.

"I have friends with the Junction police. They called to verify that you and your parents were in Eagle Mountain the day of the fire."

"They were checking our alibis?" Vince's voice rose.

"It's routine in an arson investigation. They don't have any leads as to who set the fire. Do you think it was V?"

"It could have been," Vince admitted. "It's one reason we planned this memorial. I don't like her getting close to my parents. She's already hurt Tammy. I don't want her to hurt anyone else."

Travis turned to Tammy. "What do you plan to say in your article for the paper?"

"I'm just going to announce the memorial, say anyone who remembers Valerie is invited and give a brief outline of the circumstances of her disappearance."

"Play up the loving family who never stopped searching for her," Travis said. "That contradicts V's story that Valerie's disappearance was somehow orchestrated by the family. She may feel she has to show up to refute that."

"I thought we could have a portion of the memorial service where people can stand up and offer their memories of Valerie," she said. "Maybe V will have something to say."

"We could get lucky." Travis stood. "I'll have a couple of deputies at the service," he said. "Let me know if you need anything else."

THE DAY OF Valerie's memorial was hot and sunny. Vince's parents had insisted on a large flower arrangement, and a couple of Valerie's former teachers and a family friend had also ordered arrangements, which Tammy grouped around a series of enlarged photos of the little girl. Though she and Vince were not identical twins, the resemblance was definitely there, and one photo Mrs. Shepherd had provided showed the children together, arms around each other, grinning for the camera with such happiness it made Tammy's heart hurt.

"There are more people here than I thought there would be," Mrs. Shepherd said as they watched people fill the folding chairs they had set out. Latecomers stood around the chairs, all facing the small platform with the flowers and photographs. Tammy scanned the gathering, hoping to spot anyone who seemed out of place or who was behaving strangely. But no one stood out.

At two o'clock sharp, Tammy moved to the microphone set up in front of the platform. "On behalf of the Shepherd family, I want to thank you all for coming this afternoon," she said. "We are gathered to honor a beloved daughter, sister and friend. Valerie Shepherd vanished from our lives fifteen years ago, but she has never been forgotten. And the family has never stopped looking for her."

She looked out over the crowd and faltered for a moment when she recognized Mitch and Elisabeth, seated on the back row of chairs. She had mentioned she was planning this event for the family, and this show of support touched her. It wasn't the kind of thing Mitch would ever have done on his own, so it must be Elisabeth's influence. She would be sure to thank her later.

She looked down at her notes. "To start, I want to read a poem at the request of Valerie's mother." She read the poem, a sentimental piece about the joy a little girl brings to the family. By the time she was done, Mrs. Shepherd was wiping away tears, as were many others in the crowd.

"Now we'll have an opportunity for anyone who would like to share their memories of Valerie. Her brother, Vince, will start."

Vince, dressed in dark slacks and a blue dress shirt, sleeves rolled up and collar open, moved to the microphone. Tammy spotted a number of his fellow search and rescue volunteers in the crowd, some of whom must have been involved in the original search for Valerie. Bethany Ames was there. Did that mean she was Valerie?

Vince glanced at a note card in his hand, then cleared his throat and spoke: "When I think of my sister, Valerie, I think of her courage. We were twins, but she got most of the bravery in the family. She truly wasn't afraid of anything—spiders, heights, deep water, going fast on a mountain bike—all the things that made me nervous never fazed her.

"I remember once, we were riding our bikes in the woods behind our house. Our usual route took us over a ditch, where someone had laid down a couple of boards to make it possible to ride over. But on this day, spring snowmelt had the water in the ditch raging, and had washed the boards downstream. I told Valerie we would have to turn around and go back home the long way, but she insisted we could jump our bikes over the water.

"I looked at that rushing water and my other big fear—of drowning—had me almost paralyzed. I told Valerie I couldn't do it, but she insisted I could. She backed her bike up a hill, then pedaled furiously down it, gaining speed. When she reached the edge of the ditch, she yanked up on the handlebars and sailed over the gap with room to spare. She wheeled around, shouting in triumph, and told me it was my turn.

"I could have turned around and ridden home alone, but

I would have had to live with the shame—and the constant taunts from her—that she had beat me. So I backed my bike up the hill, pedaled with everything I had and held my breath as my bike cleared that gap. Valerie was thrilled, congratulating me and telling me she had known all along that I could do it. I was just relieved that I had survived unscathed.

"After she was gone, I realized how much I had relied on her to lead the way. It was a hard lesson to learn, but I'm a better man for it. I learned that I needed to be brave enough for both of us."

Tammy watched the faces of those in the crowd as he spoke. Many people were smiling, some nodding their heads. But no one looked angry or upset by the story. Deputies Jamie Douglas and Dwight Prentice stood on either side of the crowd, assessing the attendees but not reacting as if they had spotted anything concerning.

Vince left the microphone and returned to his seat on the front row between his mother and Tammy. Others took turns speaking—two different teachers spoke about how smart Valerie was. Her former soccer coach spoke about her talent for the sport and cheerful attitude. Mr. and Mrs. Shepherd each shared memories of their little girl, their voices breaking as they painted a picture of a cheerful and loved child.

And then it was over. Members of the crowd moved forward to speak with the family while others drifted away. Tammy looked for Mitch and Elisabeth, but they had already left. It didn't matter. She could thank them later for being there.

Jamie came to stand beside her. "Did you see anyone out of place?" she asked.

"No," Tammy admitted. "Did you?"

"No. Everyone was quiet and respectful. I didn't see anything off."

Dwight Prentice walked up. "Everything seems okay," he said.

"I guess our plan didn't work," Vince said.

"It was still a beautiful memorial," Jamie said. "I didn't know your sister, but it sounds like she was a great kid."

"She was." Vince took a deep breath and blew it out. "I'm glad we did this, even if we didn't catch V. We should have done it years ago."

Tammy slipped her arm in his. "I'm glad we did it too. It helped me to know Valerie and your family better."

They helped his parents load the flowers and pictures to take back to their home in Junction, which Mr. Shepherd reported was already in the process of being repaired.

Tammy and Vince were walking across the park toward the lot where they had left the Escape when Vince's text alert sounded. He pulled out his phone. "It's a search and rescue call," he said, and scrolled through the message. "Hikers reported an injured man at the base of the cliffs north of Dixon Pass." He met her eyes. "I should go."

"Do you need to change clothes and grab your gear?" she asked.

"I keep a change of clothes and a gear bag in the car," he said.

"Then go."

"I can drop you off at the condo," he said.

"I want to walk over and visit my mother," she said. "I'll get her to drive me to your condo."

"You should start thinking of it as *our* condo," he said. "You're spending all your time there."

"I am, but I don't want to presume."

He took her by the shoulders. "I like having you live with me. I think you should go ahead and move in. Permanently."

She grinned, a little numb and a lot excited. "Yes. Let's do it."

"We'll iron out the details later." He kissed her on the lips.

"Right now, I need to go." He started to open the car, then stopped. "Be careful. V is still out there somewhere."

"It'll be fine," she said. "It's broad daylight, and there are tons of people around. When I get to the condo I'll lock myself in. I promise. And you be careful too. Don't fall off a cliff or anything."

"I won't."

She waved goodbye and walked the three blocks to her mother's house. But her mother wasn't home. Neither was Mitch. Disappointed but undeterred, Tammy pulled her bicycle from the garage and set off toward the condo by the river.

Chapter Twenty

"It's a miracle anyone spotted this guy down there," SAR volunteer Harper Stanick said as she and a dozen other volunteers stood on the narrow shoulder of the highway, staring down into the canyon below.

"If those two guys hadn't decided to climb the cliff today, no telling how long he would have lain down there," Tony Meissner said. He looked around. "Where are they, anyway?"

"I sent them on their way," Deputy Ryker Vernon said. "We've got their names and contact info. They're locals, so they shouldn't be hard to get hold of if we need to talk to them later."

"They were pretty shook up," Deputy Declan Owen said. "They said they have no idea who the guy is. I think they were being truthful."

Danny lowered the binoculars he had been using to study the figure of the man below. "I can't tell if he's breathing or not," he said. "And there's a lot of blood. We need to get down there, ASAP."

"The descent is straightforward enough," Tony said. "But bringing him out is going to be pretty technical."

"Sheri, you and Tony go down first," Danny said. "Hannah, you're the medical on scene. Caleb, you and Vince up for following them down?"

"Sure thing," Caleb said.

"Of course," Vince answered. He had trained half a dozen times on similar climbs. He had never had any trouble and was anxious to try his skills in a real rescue situation.

Danny assigned other volunteers to help with the ropes and provide backup as needed. Ryker and Declan had already closed the road to traffic. Now they set about establishing a landing zone for a medical helicopter, should one be needed.

"Any idea how he ended up down there?" Vince asked as he and Caleb gathered their equipment.

"Solo climbing?" Caleb suggested. "Not a good idea, but people do it."

"There aren't any ropes, or even anchors at the top," Ryan said.

"Maybe he set an anchor and it pulled out." Eldon made a face. "If that happened, he's done for."

"No sense speculating," Tony said. "We'll find out when we get there."

The quartet carried their gear to the edge of the canyon above where the body lay. Tony and Sheri decided on the best place to set anchors, then directed the others in laying out the ropes, carabiners, brake bars and other equipment they would use to lower themselves to the man in the canyon and eventually bring a litter up to the top again.

They were all aware of the need to reach the man as soon as possible, but no one rushed. Safety required precision and attention to detail. They wanted the man to live, but not at the expense of any one of them.

Sheri started down first; then Tony set out, ten feet to the left of her. Experienced climbers and competitors on the climbing circuit, they descended smoothly and swiftly. The canyon walls were jagged but stable, providing plenty of hand- and footholds when necessary, though the two were able to glide down long stretches of the wall. Tony landed first, followed seconds later by Sheri. The others watched from the top as they surrounded the crumpled figure on the ground.

"He's alive," Sheri radioed. "Nonresponsive. He's lost a lot of blood. There's a head wound, but I don't see any ropes or a harness or other gear."

There was a pause, the crackle of the radio; then Tony transmitted: "This was no climbing accident. This guy's been shot. Right shoulder. He's got probable broken bones and the head injury. Get that chopper over here. We need to bring this guy up ASAP."

"Hannah, you ready to go?" Danny asked.

"I'm there." Hannah was already at the edge of the canyon, poised to begin the descent.

"Caleb, you and Vince take the litter and the vacuum mattress, and a helmet for the injured man. Ryan and Eldon, you set the high-angle rigging to bring up the litter. I'm calling for the chopper."

As soon as Hannah reached the bottom, Caleb and Vince set out, the litter and other equipment distributed between them, along with extra lines that would eventually be used to haul the patient in the litter to the surface. Eldon and Ryan took the belay position at the top and lowered them down the cliff.

Vince focused on keeping untangled and steady, and the descent happened so quickly he scarcely had time to be nervous. When he had unclipped from the line, he hurried to the huddle around the injured man.

"Get that mattress down here, and we'll shift him onto it," Tony directed.

"I've got the IV in," Hannah said. "I'll start a bag of saline. Somebody unpack a few chemical heat packs to help keep him warm." She keyed the radio and rattled off numbers for the man's pulse, blood pressure and oxygen levels.

Vince leaned in to get a closer look at the man. Maroon bloodstains painted his slacks and dress shirt—not clothing for a climb or a hike in the mountains. "Do you think someone shot him and pushed him down here?" he asked.

Tony looked up. "Either they pushed him or he fell."

"Do we know who he is?" Caleb asked.

"His wallet has an ID for Mitchell Patterson," Sheri said. "Do either of you know him?"

Vince stared at the man's battered shape, stunned. He never would have recognized Tammy's brother, he was so bruised and swollen. "That's Tammy's brother," he said.

"Tammy Patterson?" Hannah looked over her shoulder at them. "Of course. Mitch Patterson, the real estate agent." She turned back to him. "How did he end up down here?"

"That's for the sheriff to find out." Tony stood. "Let's get him in the litter and up to that helicopter."

They worked together to slide Mitch's body—which was fitted with the IV, an oxygen mask, and various splints and bandages—onto the vacuum mattress, which was then inflated to fit tightly around him, acting as a full-body splint. This was then placed in the litter. He was strapped in, along with heat packs, blankets, the IV fluids and oxygen tank.

The litter was attached to lines that hung down from a tripod at the canyon rim that helped to keep the litter suspended away from the canyon walls. Then Sheri and Tony began the arduous process of ascending the canyon walls while guiding the litter up between them.

Vince stood with Hannah and Caleb and watched the ascent. While the lines from the tripod would support most of the weight of the litter, the two climbers needed to hold it steady while navigating their own journey to the top.

"There's the chopper," Hannah said.

Vince listened and heard the faint throb of helicopter rotors. "Do you think he'll make it?" he asked.

She pulled off her latex gloves and tucked them in the pocket of her jacket. "He has a chance. I don't think he had been down here long when we got to him. We were able to stabilize him and ward off shock. But he has a lot of injuries. Probably some internal ones I wasn't able to assess. I couldn't tell you what his chances are."

When Mitch was safely to the top of the canyon, along with Sheri and Tony, Caleb and Vince helped Hannah gather the medical equipment and other supplies. They packed everything away. Hannah and Caleb ascended first, leaving Vince for last. He took out his phone and stared at the screen, even though he knew he had no signal here. He would need to contact Tammy and let her know what had happened to her brother.

But what had happened? Who had shot him and left him to die in this remote spot? He and his girlfriend had attended Valerie's memorial service a few hours ago—though now it seemed like days. The shooting must have happened shortly after that.

Fear lanced through him as another thought registered. Elisabeth was probably with Mitch when he was shot. What had happened to her?

TAMMY COASTED THE bicycle up to the front door of the condo and dismounted. The ride had energized her. Maybe she would start riding her bike to work. She wondered what Russ would think of that.

She took out her keys and unlocked the door, then wheeled the bicycle in ahead of her and left it against the wall in the front hall. She would need to find a better place to park it, but they would figure out something.

"Hello, Tammy. I was wondering what took you so long."

She froze, then slowly turned around to face Elisabeth. Or rather, she registered that the voice was Elisabeth's, but her gaze fixed on the gun in the woman's hand and refused to look away.

"Where's Vince?" Elisabeth asked.

"He had a search and rescue call. A climber fell in a canyon, up on Dixon Pass."

Elisabeth's laughter was another shock. "Oh, that's rich," she crowed. "Not what I had planned at all, but this might be even better."

Tammy forced her gaze away from the gun, but the expression on Elisabeth's face did nothing to calm her. The other woman was as sleek and put together as ever, with her long hair swept back in a low ponytail and the nails that rested against the gun sporting a perfect French manicure. But her eyes were dilated, her mouth fixed in a rictus of a smile. "How did you get in here?" Tammy asked.

"The first time I visited the manager's apartment, when I rented my place, I swiped a master key. I knew it would come in handy one day."

"What are you doing here?" Tammy tried to sound strong and in control. "And put away that gun."

"Who do you think you are, that you can tell me what to do? Now, get over there on that couch and sit down." She gestured toward the sofa with her free hand.

Tammy did as she was told, moving sideways so that her back was never to the other woman. "Where's Mitch?" she asked. "I saw the two of you at the memorial service."

"You didn't think I'd miss my own memorial service, did you?"

Elisabeth was V. Tammy had figured that out when she saw the gun in her hand. But did that also mean she was Valerie? "Where's Mitch?" she asked again.

"I left him at the bottom of a canyon, up on Dixon Pass. But apparently, my brother is helping to get him out. Or more probably, he's retrieving his body." She sat in a chair facing the sofa, the gun aimed at the middle of Tammy's chest. "That's inconvenient, but it will give us time to talk."

The idea that Mitch might be dead hit Tammy like a blow to the stomach. She wanted to protest that that couldn't be true, but she recognized the fruitlessness of arguing. She pushed the idea away entirely. She wouldn't think about Mitch right now. She had to focus on Valerie, and on keeping her from pulling the trigger. "What happened to you?" she asked. "That day on the camping trip, when you were ten?"

"I knew you'd have questions. I guess that's the reporter in you. Too bad you weren't around when I went missing. You strike me as someone who might actually have ferreted out the truth."

"What is the truth?" Tammy asked.

"I've been trying to tell you for weeks. My family—my mother and father and Vince—decided they didn't want me anymore. They were going to leave me up on that mountain to die. Instead, a man who was camping nearby offered to take care of me."

"The man kidnapped you," Tammy said.

"He didn't kidnap me. He did me a favor. I would have died without him."

Her agitation—and the way the gun shook in her hand—made Tammy nervous. She had to resist the impulse to argue. "What was the man's name?" she asked.

"Paul. Paul Rollins."

"And you're Elisabeth Rollins."

"Paul chose the name for me. Much better than Valerie."

"Where is Paul now?" Should Tammy expect him to walk through the door at any moment?

"He's dead. With him gone, I didn't have anyone left. Then I remembered my other family. The one who abandoned me."

Tammy bit her lip to keep from arguing that the Shepherds had not abandoned their daughter. Time to change the subject again. She needed to keep Valerie off-balance. "What happened with Mitch?" she asked.

"I needed him out of the way so I could take care of Vince and my parents." She crossed her legs and propped the grip of the handgun on her knee, her finger within easy reach of the trigger. "I would have liked to keep him around longer, at least until I had drained off more of his money. I thought I would have time to access all of his accounts before anyone discovered his body, but that may not be the case now."

"He loved you," Tammy said.

"So have the others." Her smile brightened. "I guess I'm just a very lovable person."

"I don't understand how Paul was able to keep you a secret all these years," Tammy said. "People were looking for you. Your parents hired a private detective. There were appeals in the media."

"Lies, all of it. If they were looking as hard as they said, they would have found me. Paul changed my name, sure, and he took me to a fancy salon and got me a good haircut—my first one. But the rest of me was just the same. It's not like we were living in a cave in the middle of nowhere. We lived in a beautiful house. We took vacations."

"What about school?"

"I was homeschooled. Paul had been a teacher, once upon a time. He taught me what I needed to know to help him in his business."

"What kind of business was that?"

That overly bright grin again. "Paul liked to say we taught

people important financial lessons. We taught people to be more careful with their money."

"You conned people," Tammy guessed.

"*Con* sounds so crass. What we did required more finesse. We persuaded people to trust us. Most of them did."

"Is that why you're here now? Because you want money?"

"I have money, and I always know how to get more. No, I'm here for a different kind of payback."

Tammy swallowed hard. The gun, and the fact that Valerie had admitted to killing Mitch, indicated the payback could be a fatal one. "I'm not part of your family," she said. "Why waste your time with me?"

"Because Vince *looooves* you." She drew out the word. "The first time I saw you together, I knew it. He didn't care about me, his twin, but he's all gaga for you. Hurting you will hurt him. I thought at first that beating you up would be enough. You put up quite a fight, by the way. I can admire that, even if it made things inconvenient for me. But it also made me realize that a beating wasn't going to be enough. Vince can watch you die, then I'll kill him. It will be perfect."

Tammy choked back a moan. "What about your parents?" she asked. She didn't want more horrible details, but she needed to keep Valerie talking.

"I'll get them next, but no hurry. I won't have to sneak up on them like I did you and Vince. They'll be happy to open the door for their long-lost little girl. Then I can take my time deciding how to put an end to them and all their lies about truly loving me."

Tammy heard the hurt behind the hatred. What had Paul done to this young woman to damage her so much?

But she couldn't let sympathy blind her to the danger she was in. And Vince. Could she find a way to warn him before he came home and walked into his own death sentence?

Chapter Twenty-One

It was after seven when Vince unlocked the Escape parked at search and rescue headquarters. He had tried calling Tammy as soon as he picked up a phone signal, but the call had gone to voice mail after six rings. Maybe she was in the shower or busy with something else.

It was better if he gave her the message about her brother in person. Or maybe she already knew. That might explain why she hadn't answered the phone. She might be with her mother. Vince had told Declan and Ryker about Elisabeth as soon as he reached the top of the canyon, and they had radioed the information to the sheriff and started the search for her. They would have reached out to Mrs. Patterson and Tammy too.

"Vince, wait up!" He looked up and let out a groan when he saw Bethany jogging toward him.

"I don't have time to talk now," he said.

She stopped in front of him. "This won't take long. I just want to apologize for being so, well, awkward around you." She studied the ground between them. "I came to town to make a fresh start, right? I was trying to be all independent, going after what I wanted and that kind of thing? And I thought you were cute and nice and would be a fun date. But I should have realized you were already involved. I was so embarrassed when I found out you were already with someone. But I just wanted you to know I won't bother you anymore. And no hard feelings—I hope."

"Sure. No hard feelings." She looked so sad, standing there with her head down. Harmless, and probably lonely too. "Are you okay?"

She looked up, a forced smiled on her lips. "I'm fine." She shrugged. "Being alone in a new place is hard, but I'm starting to make friends."

"Count me as one of them," he said. "Me and Tammy."

The smile became more genuine. "Thanks." She took a step back. "I'll let you go now." She turned and hurried away, this time with her head up.

Vince drove to his condo and parked. Tammy had left the outside light on for him. Keys in hand, he moved toward the door. But it wasn't locked. Not good. Maybe she had forgotten in her distress over her brother, but with V still at large, it wasn't safe to leave the condo unsecured.

The hallway was dark. He left his jacket and pack on the hooks by the door, then almost fell over a bicycle. What was that doing there?

"Tammy?" he called.

"Vince, don't— *Ahhh!*"

He sprinted toward the living room but skidded to a stop when he saw Elisabeth standing by the sofa, one hand gripping Tammy's arm, the other holding a gun pressed to the side of Tammy's head. Blood trickled from Tammy's temple.

"Don't worry. I just tapped her with the gun barrel this time," Elisabeth said. "But if you don't cooperate, I'll shoot her."

"You shot Mitch," he said.

"Am I supposed to tell you you're a clever boy because you figured that out?" She sneered. "Vin, Vin, Vinnie, Vince."

He almost staggered under the weight of the knowledge

that hit him then. Elisabeth was from Omaha, Nebraska. The town where his father had seen a young woman who looked like Valerie. She had shown up in Eagle Mountain about the time the messages from V began arriving. Her hair was darker than Valerie's, but she had the same slightly upturned nose and the same dimple in her left cheek that he had. "Valerie, what are you doing?" he asked.

"It took you long enough to recognize me. I shouldn't have to tell you how insulting it is that you didn't even know who I was. Your long-lost twin. The one you had supposedly mourned all these years. Such hypocrisy."

"What do you want from us?" he asked.

Valerie looked at Tammy. "You see how he gets right to the point? He doesn't care what I've been up to for the past fifteen years. He just wants to know the bottom line. What will it take to make me go away again?"

"That's not what I meant," he said. "And I do care—"

"Shut up! Don't waste my time with more lies. As for what I want from you, that's easy. You and Mom and Dad—mostly Mom and Dad, but I blame you too, because you were their favorite and you didn't do anything to stop them—took away my life. The life I could have had, anyway. Now you get to pay with *your* life."

Vince glanced at Tammy. She was pale, but calm. Strong. "Let Tammy go and I'll do whatever you want," he said.

"Let her go right to the sheriff? I don't think so. No, you two are the buy-one-get-one special today." She shoved Tammy onto the sofa. "Sit down over here beside your girlfriend, and we'll talk about what happens next."

Vince sat. He wanted to keep her talking. As long as she was talking, she wasn't shooting. And every word bought a little more time for the sheriff and his deputies to figure out that

Elisabeth was V. She had shot her boyfriend and come after him and his family. "Why did you shoot Mitch?" he asked.

"I've already explained everything to your girlfriend. He was in the way of what I needed to do. Is he dead yet? I figured if the bullet didn't finish him off, the fall into the canyon would."

"He's alive," Vince said. "He'll tell the cops everything."

Tammy let out a whimper. Valerie glared at her, then turned her attention back to Vince. "By the time they find me, it will be too late," she said. "I know how to change my appearance and my name and melt into the background. Paul taught me all that."

"Who is Paul?"

Valerie sighed. "Again, I've already told Tammy. I don't like repeating myself. He's the man who saved me when my *family* threw me out."

"He was the camper you saw?" Vince guessed. "The one with the blue tent?"

"Again, you're smarter than I thought. And a hero to boot, climbing mountains and descending into canyons to save complete strangers. That surprised me when I found out. You were always such a coward. Too bad you didn't try harder to save me."

He started to reply, but Tammy squeezed his hand, hard. A warning not to upset Valerie by arguing with her? He squeezed back, letting her know he got the message. "That was you in the casino in Omaha, the time Dad saw you, wasn't it?" he asked.

"He told you about that, did he? I heard he came snooping around the next day, looking for me. But the manager had a thing for me, so he didn't mind saying he didn't know anything about me. I told him the guy asking questions was a creepy old man who was hassling me."

"Was it you who made those phone calls—the ones saying 'Help me' and asking for Daddy?"

She looked away. "I don't want to talk about that anymore. Stand up, both of you." She motioned with the gun. "Time to get this show on the road."

They stood.

"Oh, isn't that sweet? You're holding hands. But don't think the two of you are going to get the better of me. I've had lots of time to think about this. Now, get into the bedroom and take off all your clothes."

He and Tammy looked at each other with a mixture of shock and confusion. "Get going," Valerie ordered. "It's not like you two haven't seen each other naked before."

They went into the bedroom. "Clothes off!" Valerie barked. "Quit wasting my time."

Vince sat on the edge of the bed and began unlacing his boots. Slowly. Instead of sitting beside him, Tammy moved to the other side of the bed and took off her earrings. Good idea. The more space between them, the more difficult it would be for Valerie to watch them both at once.

Boots off, Vince turned his attention to removing his belt. He weighed it in his hand, wondering if he could use it as a weapon.

The gunshot was deafening in the small space. He jumped up and saw that Valerie had fired into the mattress. "The next one will be right in her chest if you don't get moving," she said, pointing the gun at Tammy.

He draped the belt over the headboard, then moved more quickly, shucking his jeans and socks, then peeling off his shirt, until he was standing in front of her in his boxers. "That's enough," she said. "I can always strip the body later." She turned once more to Tammy. "You lie down on the bed. Vince, you tie her up with those scarves." She indicated two scarves draped around the bedposts. "One hand to each bedpost. And do a good job."

Tammy remained standing, also in her underwear. "Why have him tie me up?"

"I'm setting the scene. Vince, depressed over the loss of his dear little sister, kills himself. But first, he kills you. After subjecting you to kinky sex."

Valerie's love of drama hadn't changed. But he didn't see any way out of doing what she wanted. He believed her when she said the next bullet would be for Tammy.

Tammy lay back on the bed. "Sorry about this," Vince said, as he knelt beside her and picked up one of the scarves.

I love you, she mouthed, and he nodded, unable to get out any words past the lump in his throat. He tied her wrist to the bedpost, not too tight but in what he hoped was a convincing knot. Then he moved to the other wrist.

"Comfortable?" Valerie asked. She moved to check the wrist Vince had just tied and made a tsking sound. "As I suspected, not tight enough. Just for that, you're going to get an extra bullet, Vince."

The teasing tone she used enraged him. He watched out of the corner of his eye as she bent over the knot, the pistol balanced awkwardly in her right hand as she used her ring and pinkie fingers to hold the scarf in place as she tightened the knot.

He left the other wrist untied and grabbed hold of the belt. The heavy buckle hit Valerie hard on the cheek, drawing blood. She juggled the gun and it went off, but the bullet hit the wall. Tammy yanked her hand away and rolled off the bed, landing hard on the floor. Meanwhile, Vince had lunged, both hands around the wrist that held the gun, until he succeeded in wrenching it from her. But she knocked it from his hand, and it fired again as it hit the floor.

He continued to wrestle with Valerie, struggling to subdue her. She fought with incredible strength, biting and kicking, scratching at his face and trying to knee him in the groin. Tammy raced from the room and returned a few seconds later with something in her hand. "Hold her still!" she pleaded.

But just then, Valerie bit Vince's hand, drawing blood. He drew back instinctively, and she lunged, over-balancing him. They both fell to the floor, her on top, both hands around his throat. His vision blurred, and he was sure he would black out.

Then he heard a horrible sound, like a knife cleaving a watermelon. Valerie's grip loosened, and she fell to one side.

Tammy stood over them, spattered with blood, the ice ax from Vince's search and rescue pack in her hand.

Pounding on the door reverberated through the house. "This is the sheriff!" Travis shouted. "Come out with your hands up!"

Tammy dropped the ax, and Vince staggered to his feet. He put his arm around her. "Come on," he said.

"I can't go out there like this," she whispered.

He reached back and grabbed the top sheet from the bed and wrapped it around her, then took the bottom sheet for himself. They walked into the living room just as the door burst open and Gage and Travis entered.

Gage took in the bedclothes and their state of undress and frowned. "We had a report of multiple gunshots at this address," he said. "And Mitch Patterson's car is outside in the lot. We believe his girlfriend, Elisabeth Rollins, tried to kill him."

"His girlfriend is in the bedroom," Vince said. "She shot Mitch, then tried to kill us. And her name isn't Elisabeth Rollins. It's Valerie Shepherd."

Jamie Douglas stepped in behind the Walker brothers. "You two can come with me," she said.

Tammy was shaking by the time they reached the parking

lot, though the temperature was mild. Her eyes were glazed, her skin cold and clammy. "Call an ambulance," Vince said. "I think she's going into shock."

"One is on the way," Jamie said. "I've got a sweatshirt and pants in my patrol vehicle you can put on, Tammy, and Gage will have something that will fit you, Vince." She retrieved the clothes from the back of her SUV and started to help Tammy unwind the sheet when she saw the blood spatters. "Are you hurt?" she asked.

"That isn't my blood," Tammy said. "It's Valerie's." Then she broke down sobbing.

Vince gathered her close while Jamie radioed this information to Travis. More deputies arrived, along with an ambulance and most of Vince's neighbors. Tammy's boss, camera in hand, showed up. Vince only vaguely registered their presence. He held on to Tammy, smoothing her hair and murmuring, "It's going to be all right," over and over. As if by repetition, he could make himself believe it.

TAMMY SPENT THE night in the hospital, with Vince on one side of her bed and her mother on the other. She hadn't wanted to stay here, but the doctor had insisted it was necessary, then given her a sedative that made her not care anymore.

When she finally woke, sun streamed through the one window in her room. Vince got up from the chair where he had been sitting and came to the side of the bed. "How are you feeling?" he asked.

"I'm okay." She reached up and touched the bruise on the side of her face. It was tender, but the doctors had reassured her there was no lasting damage. She trembled when she thought of how much worse it could have been. "How are you?"

"Shaken up. But I'm going to be okay."

She turned to look at the chair where her mother had sat. "She went down to see your brother," Vince said.

Her eyes widened as she remembered Mitch. He had been in surgery when they installed her in this room last night. "Is he going to be okay?"

"He's got a long recovery ahead of him. Another surgery to pin his leg together. But he's going to be okay."

"And Valerie?"

"She's alive. You didn't kill her. You merely gave her a concussion. And saved both our lives."

Tammy's eyes filled with tears. "Your poor parents."

A tap on the door frame interrupted their discussion. Sheriff Travis Walker entered. "I stopped by to see how you're doing," he said.

"I'm going to be fine," Tammy said.

"I was just down getting a statement from your brother."

"What did he say?" Vince asked.

"He says the woman he knew as Elisabeth asked him to stop the car by the side of the road because she was feeling sick. Earlier in the day, she had surprised him with the news that she was pregnant, so he thought that was the reason she was feeling ill. He helped her over to the edge of the road. She pulled out a gun, shot him and pushed him over the edge."

"Cold blooded," Vince said.

"Vince has already given me his statement," Travis said. "Can you tell me what happened before he arrived at the condo yesterday evening?"

Tammy smoothed her hands over the sheets and tried to gather her thoughts. "I'll try to remember everything," she said.

Travis took out a recorder, recited her name and his and the time and date. Then she proceeded to tell her story, reliving those horrible moments when Valerie told her about

Mitch and threatened her own life and that of Vince and the Shepherds. Vince held her hand while she spoke, keeping her strong. When she was finished, Travis shut off the recorder. "What will happen to Valerie?" she asked.

"She's in custody now but will be transferred to a mental health unit soon," Travis said. "The court will determine if she stands trial for the arson and three counts of attempted murder. Not to mention the thousands and thousands of dollars she and Paul Rollins have stolen over the years."

"Did you find out anything about Paul Rollins?" Vince asked.

"He was a former school teacher in Ogallala, Nebraska. He was fired after accusations of improper conduct with a student. A nine-year-old girl. He left town and fell off the radar for nine months, until he showed up with a girl he called Elisabeth. He introduced her as his daughter. They're suspected of being involved in various con games all over the country, in Mexico and the Caribbean. They targeted wealthy, older people with either investment or charity schemes. He apparently used Valerie to lull his targets into trusting him."

"Valerie said he was dead," Tammy said.

"He died two months ago of an asthma attack," Travis said. "He had a history of the disease, but when I contacted authorities in Omaha, I learned they are considering opening an investigation into his death."

"Do they think Valerie killed him?" Vince asked.

"I don't know," Travis said.

"She scares me," Tammy admitted.

"Whether she stands trial for the things she's done or is committed for treatment, she won't be free to live on her own for a long time, if ever," Travis said.

"I'm trying to remind myself that she was hurt by what happened too," Tammy said. "Whatever this Paul guy did to her, it damaged her mind. I don't know if someone can ever come back from that."

"My parents are determined to help her any way they can," Vince said. "She's still their daughter, and they're relieved to know what happened to her, even if it hasn't resulted in the happy ending they're hoping for."

"One day, maybe she'll realize how fortunate she is to have them on her side," Travis said. He pocketed the recorder. "You'll need to stop by the office in the next day or so to sign this statement. And we may have other questions for both of you."

"Of course."

"Your condo will be unavailable for a few days," Travis said. "I can give you the name of a company that will clean it for you before you move back in."

"Okay," Vince said. "Thanks."

Travis took something from his pocket. Tammy thought it would be a business card for the cleaning company. Instead, he handed Vince a key. "You'll need a place to stay for a few days," he said. "Someplace quiet, away from the press and nosy neighbors. I have a cabin you can use. Up on Spirit Ridge. It's nothing fancy, but it's comfortable."

Vince stared at the key. "Thanks."

Travis left and Vince pocketed the key. "That was nice of him," Tammy said.

"He's a good man," Vince said. "He'll do right by Valerie, whether she deserves it or not."

"That cabin sounds like exactly what we need," she said. "When can I leave?"

"Whenever you want, I think," he said.

She looked toward the door. "I'd like to see Mitch, and I should say goodbye to my mother. What if she wants me to stay with her?"

"The hospital has an arrangement with a nearby hotel," he said. "She'll stay there until your brother transfers to a rehab facility."

She lay back on the pillows once more. "What a nightmare," she said.

He sat on the side of the bed and took her hand. "It will be a while before I can forget the sight of my sister standing there with a gun to your head," he said. "I came so close to losing you."

"You didn't lose me." She sat up and pulled him close. "And as awful as the next few months or years might be at times, you don't have to go through all this alone now."

"I know," he said. "That's the best thing to come out of all of this. Whatever happens, we'll get through it together."

Nothing he could have said would have meant more to her. She had broken off her relationship with Darrell because he wouldn't make a commitment. She didn't need a marriage proposal to believe Vince would be there for her. She trusted the connection they had would grow. They both knew loss, but out of that shared knowledge, they had found so much.

* * * * *

COMING SOON!

We really hope you enjoyed reading this book.
If you're looking for more romance
be sure to head to the shops when
new books are available on

Thursday 16th January

To see which titles are coming soon, please visit

millsandboon.co.uk/nextmonth

MILLS & BOON

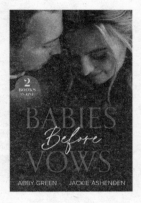
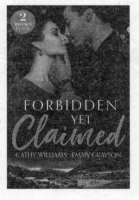

LET'S TALK

Romance

For exclusive extracts, competitions and special offers, find us online:

f MillsandBoon

X @MillsandBoon

⊙ @MillsandBoonUK

♪ @MillsandBoonUK

Get in touch on 01413 063 232

For all the latest titles coming soon, visit
millsandboon.co.uk/nextmonth